THE FINE COLOR
OF RUST

THE FINE COLOR OF RUST

a novel

P. A. O'Reilly

W

WASHINGTON SQUARE PRESS

NEW YORK   LONDON   TORONTO   SYDNEY   NEW DELHI

WASHINGTON SQUARE PRESS
A Division of Simon & Schuster, Inc.
1230 Avenue of the Americas
New York, NY 10020

First Washington Square Press trade paperback edition September 2012

WASHINGTON SQUARE PRESS and colophon are registered trademarks of Simon & Schuster, Inc.

For information about special discounts for bulk purchases, please contact Simon & Schuster Special Sales at 1-866-506-1949 or business@simonandschuster.com.

The Simon & Schuster Speakers Bureau can bring authors to your live event. For more information or to book an event contact the Simon & Schuster Speakers Bureau at 1-866-248-3049 or visit our website at www.simonspeakers.com.

Designed by Kyoko Watanabe

Manufactured in the United States of America

10 9 8 7 6 5 4 3 2 1

Library of Congress Cataloging-in-Publication Data

O'Reilly, P. A. (Paddy A.)
    The fine color of rust : a novel / by P. A. O'Reilly. — 1st Washington Square Press paperback ed.
        p. cm.
    1. Single mothers—Australia—Fiction. 2. Country life—Australia—Fiction. 3. School closings—Australia—Fiction. I. Title.
    PR9619.4.O74F56 2012
    823'.92—dc23
                                                                    2012021636

ISBN 978-1-4516-7816-1
ISBN 978-1-4516-7817-8 (ebook)

The Japanese have a word, *sabi*, which connotes the simple
beauty of worn and imperfect and impermanent things:
a weathered fence; an old cracking bough in a tree;
a silver bowl mottled with tarnish; the fine color of rust.

THE FINE COLOR OF RUST

1

NORM STEVENS SENIOR tells me I'll never get that truck off my land. He says it's too old, been there too long, the hoist will try to lift the thing and it will break apart into red stones of rust.

"Leave it," he says. "Let it rust away. One day you'll look and it won't be there anymore." He gives me a sideways glance. "Like husbands. You look away and when you look back they're gone, right?"

"Right."

"So have you heard from the bastard?"

"Nope."

"And you're getting by all right? For money?"

"I've got more money now than when he was here."

We both laugh.

"Now, Loretta, you know I can take the kids for a night if you need some time off."

"I might take you up on that. I've got a prospect. A biker, but a nice one, not a loser. On a Harley, no less."

"A Harley?" He raises his eyebrows. Whenever he does that, a pink scaly half-moon of skin above his left eyebrow wrinkles. He reaches up to touch it.

"You should have that looked at, Norm."

"Yeah, yeah, and I should give up the spare parts work and get out of the sun too."

He gestures around his junkyard. There are tractor parts, rolls of wire, tires, mowers, corrugated iron sheets all rusted and folded, bits of cars and engines, pots and pans, gas bottles, tools, toys, bed frames, oil drums, the chipped blades of threshers and harvesters. Some of the machinery is so bent and broken you can't even tell what it was meant for. In the center of the yard is a lemon tree, the only greenery in sight. It always has lemons. I'm sure I know what Norm does to help it along, but I don't ask. He's got four guard dogs too, tied up around the yard, vicious snarling things. As if anyone would want to steal any of this crap.

"Well, I'd better pick up the kids," I say. I don't want to pick up the kids. I want to send them to an orphanage and buy myself a nice dress and learn to live the way I used to, before I turned into the old scrag I am now.

"Don't you worry about that truck." Norm stretches out his long, skinny arm and pats me on the back. "It'll go back into the land."

I get into the car, pump the accelerator like I'm at the gym, and turn the key three times before the engine fires. I should have that looked at, I think. There's half a kilo of sausages on the seat beside me, and I realize they've been sitting in the sun for half an hour. When I unwrap the paper and have a sniff I get a funny sulfur smell. They'll cook up all right, I tell myself, and I gun the Holden and screech in a U-turn onto the road. I can't get used to this huge engine—every time I take off I sound like a pack of hoons at Bathurst.

It's three thirty already and Jake and Melissa will be waiting at the school gate, ready to jump in and whine about how everyone else's mum always gets there before I do. Maybe I will drop them off at the orphanage.

When I get to the school gate the kids are both standing with their hands on their hips. I wonder if they got that from me; old scrag standing with her hands on her hips, pursing her thin lips, squinting into the sun. You could make a statue of that. It would look like half the women in this town. Dust and a few plastic bags swirling around its feet, the taillights of the husband's car receding into the distance. They should cast it in bronze and put it in the foyer of Social Security.

"Mum, we have to have four sheets of colored cardboard for the project tomorrow."

"All right."

"And me too, Mum, I have to have a lead pencil and I don't want bananas in my lunch anymore because they stink."

"All right."

As I steer the great car down the highway toward home I have a little dream. I'll swing into the driveway and sitting next to the veranda will be a shiny maroon Harley-Davidson. I won't dare to look, but out of the corner of my eye I'll see a boot resting on the step, maybe with spurs on it. Then I'll slowly lift my head and he'll be staring at me the way George Clooney stared into J.Lo's eyes in *Out of Sight* and I'll take a deep breath and say to him, "Can you hang on five minutes while I drop the kids at the orphanage?"

What I actually find when we get home is a bag of lemons sitting on the veranda. Norm must have left them while we were at the newsagent.

"Who are these from?" Jake asks.

"Norm."

3

"How do you know?"

"Oil on the bag."

I bought Norm a cake of Solvol soap once. Delivered it to the junkyard wrapped in pretty pink paper with a bow. He rang to thank me. "I think you're insulting me."

"It's for your own good, Norm."

"You're a minx. If I was thirty years younger . . ."

"Fifty, more like," I told him, "before you'd get those paws on me."

That night, when the kids are finally settled in their rooms doing their homework, I get on the phone for the usual round of begging.

"Are you coming to the meeting tomorrow?"

"Oh, Loretta, I'm sorry, I completely forgot. I've made other plans."

I can imagine Helen's plans. They'll involve a cask of white and six changes of clothes before she collapses on the bed in tears and starts ringing her friends—me—asking why she can't find a man. Is she too old, has she lost her looks? It helps to leave the house occasionally, I have to remind her. She certainly hasn't lost her looks. Auburn hair without a single gray strand. Straight white teeth. A country tan. Unlike mousey-haired skinny scragwoman me, she even has a cleavage.

"The grade-three teacher's coming," I tell her, certain this will change her mind. "And Brianna's offered to mind all the kids at her place. She must have hired a bouncer."

"He's told you he's coming?"

"Yeah, he left a message on my machine," I lie.

So Helen's in. After I herd up seven others with more lies and false promises, I put the sausages on. Sure enough, the sulfur smell fades once they start to burn. I used to enjoy cooking quiche and fancy fried rice and mud cake. Gourmet, like on the telly, the boyfriend would boast to his mates. Then we get married and it's, "Listen, darl, I wouldn't mind a chop for a change." Now the kids think gourmet is pickles on your sandwich. They won't even look at a sun-dried tomato. Last time I tried that, Jake picked them out of the spaghetti sauce and left them lined up like red bits of chewed meat on the side of the plate. "Gross," he said, and I had to agree, seeing them like that.

The meeting's in the small room at the Neighbourhood House because the Church of Goodwill had already booked the large room by the time I got around to organizing to-night's meeting. We're sitting pretty much on top of each other, trying to balance cups of tea and Scotch Finger biscuits on our knees. Maxine is supposed to be taking the minutes.

I thought I'd made it up, but the grade-three teacher has come, and Helen's paralyzed with excitement and terror. She's wearing enough perfume to spontaneously combust, and the smell's so overwhelming that Maxine has to swing the door open. Two minutes later the noise from the meeting next door starts up.

"Yes!" they all shout. "Yes! I do, I do!"

"Well, I don't." Maxine swings the door half-shut so that we're dizzy with perfume but still having to shout over the frantic clapping of people being saved next door.

I give the list of apologies and welcome everyone who's come, introducing the grade-three teacher in case the others don't know him. Helen's gone as pink and glistening as a baby fresh out of the bath. She'll have a seizure if she's not careful. I can't see the attraction. The teacher's five foot four, stocky, and always says "At the end of the day."

"At the end of the day," he says when I introduce him, "I am totally committed to this cause. Our jobs are at risk too."

Just in case, I look down at his feet, but no spurs. I read out the list of agenda items. Brenda sighs loudly.

"Do we have to do all this agenda crap? And the motions? I motion, you motion. My Mark's doing motions you wouldn't believe and I have to be home by nine in case I need to take him to Emergency."

"Yes, we do. Because we're trying to be bloody official. And as you well know, an emergency department that closes at ten in a town half an hour away is one of the reasons we're here. Soon this town will have no services for a hundred kilometers."

"Oh, yes, ma'am."

I roll my eyes. Maxine rolls her eyes. For a moment I think of us all rolling our eyes like a bunch of lunatics in the asylum and I almost cheer up.

"Item one. I've written a letter to the member for our local constituency about the closure of the school." I pause for the inevitable joke about members, which, to my amazement, doesn't come. "We need everyone who has kids in the school to sign."

"It'll never work." Brenda is the optimist of the committee.

"Does anyone know how to drain the oil from a sump?" Kyleen pipes up.

Only another half an hour, I think, and I can pick up the kids from Brianna's, drop them at the orphanage, and drive straight down to Melbourne. With the experience I've got, I'll land a good job in a center for adults with attention deficit disorder.

• • •

When I pull up at Brianna's, the kids run to the front door, looking pleased to see me. They're way too quiet in the back-seat. They must have done something horrible.

"So did you have a good time?" I ask. I speed up to catch the amber light and the Holden roars with the might of a drunken trucker. I can't make out exactly what Melissa says, but I might have heard the word *fight*. I think back. Were they limping when they got into the car? Was there blood? I can't remember anything like that so I turn on the radio and keep driving along the dark highway, listening to the sooth-ing sound of a voice calling race seven of the trots, something I've learned to love since the radio got stuck on this station.

"Mum?" Melissa says as we pull into the unsurprisingly Harley-free driveway.

"Yes, sweetie?"

"I don't ever want to leave this house."

"I thought you wanted to live in a hundred-room man-sion with ten servants and a personal homework attendant."

"Nup."

"I know what it is—you love what I've done with the place." My children were so impressed when I fixed the damp patch beside the stove with a hair dryer, a bottle of glue paste, and three of Jake's artworks. I had been calling the agent about it for months, but my house is clearly outside the real estate zone of care and responsibility.

"Mum, I'm serious. If Dad sends a letter and we've moved we won't get it."

I want to believe he'll send a letter—to his children, at least.

"Well, that's settled. We're staying."

When we get inside, the kids brush their teeth without a single protest and climb into bed.

"You OK, Jakie?" I lean down to kiss him good night.

"Brianna and her boyfriend had a fight," he whispers. "I think he hit her."

I kiss him twice, then again.

"I'm sure she's all right. I'll call her tomorrow. You go to sleep now."

"I don't want bananas in my lunch."

"I wouldn't dream of it. Bananas stink," I say as I turn out the light.

Next morning, as I'm packing bananas into their lunch boxes, I realize I forgot to thank Norm for the lemons.

I drop into the yard on the way back from the shops. He's down the back of the block with three other blokes, all of them standing in a line with their arms folded, staring at the body of an old tractor. This would be the matching statue to mine: bloke standing, feet apart, arms folded, staring at a piece of broken machinery. No idea how to fix it. We could put Him and Her statues either side of the highway coming into Gunapan.

I wait beside the shed while the delicate sales negotiations go on. I've never understood exactly how the communication works. Perhaps the meaning is in the number of head nods, or the volume of the grunt as the customer shifts from one leg to the other. After they've stared at the tractor body in apparent silence for five minutes, Norm sees me and ambles up.

"Don't tell me you're going to sell something, Norm?"

"Not bloody likely. Every month these three clowns are here with some new scheme for making money."

"None of them happens to ride a Harley?"

He doesn't even bother answering, just nods his head at

their ute on the road. We step inside the shed for a cuppa. The radio's on the racing station.

"Harlequin Dancer made a good run from fourth in race seven last night," I remark.

"You need a new car. I'm working on it, love. Shouldn't be too much longer." Norm hands me a cup, covered in grease, and a paper towel to wipe it with.

There are enough parts in Norm's yard for him to put together ten perfectly good cars, and he has been trying to build me a new one for years. But his specialty is disassembly rather than assembly. As soon as the collection of engine parts and panels begins to bear a resemblance to an actual car, he decides it's not right and has to pull it apart and start again.

He takes a noisy slurp of his tea before he speaks. "Sorry I didn't get to the meeting."

"The school's not your problem."

"Course it's my problem. It's everybody's bloody problem."

We drink our tea. The three blokes wave as they pass the shed. There's a protest at Randwick in race two. The jockey on the second-place horse is alleging interference from the winner at the final turn.

"I've got money on that horse." Norm turns up the volume. "Which one?"

"The one that'll buy you a bottle of bubbly if it wins the protest. Long odds. Very long odds. Bring me luck, Loretta."

The day's starting to heat up and blowflies are banging against the tin roof of the shed. Norm picks up the trannie and holds it to his ear. I look out at the heat shimmering over the piles of junk. Norm's touching his crusty forehead as he listens for the outcome of the protest. He must win against the odds sometimes, I think—otherwise why bother betting?

2

*Thank you for your letter of 9 January. I fully
understand the concerns you have expressed and
would like to take this opportunity to explain
how these concerns are being addressed by your
government.*

WHEN I SHOW the committee members the letter at the next
meeting they hoot like owls. "Fully understand!" "Take this
opportunity!" It's as good as a party, they laugh so much.

"I told you it wouldn't work." Brenda nods sagely.

"It's a step." I'm not letting her get away with *I told you so.*
"The first step. It's a game. We make a bid, they try to negoti-
ate us down."

"Sure." She's still doing that nod. "Like we've got real negotiating power."

"Shut up, Brenda," Norm says.

Helen is here again but the grade-three teacher is missing,
so Helen is downcast. No, she's more than downcast. Her high
hair has flagged. Perhaps the heat in the air has melted the
gel. Whatever happened, the fluffy creation that brushed the
architrave when she walked in has flattened out to match her

spirit and she's slumped in the orange plastic chair beside me, motionless bar the occasional crackle as she winkles another Kool Mint from her open bag, pretending no one can hear the sighs and crunches of her working her way through the packet.

"I've written another letter," I tell them. "This time, I've copied it to our shire councillors, the local member, the prime minister, the headmaster, the school board, all the teachers, and all of the parents at the school."

Silence. Kyleen opens her mouth and closes it when Maxine jabs her in the ribs. Norm flips through the pages of minutes in his hands. The air is close and still, and next door at the Church of Goodwill meeting someone is talking loud and long in a deep voice.

"I spent our whole budget on photocopying and postage," I go on. "You'll get the letter in the mail tomorrow."

"Is that why we haven't got biscuits?" Trust Kyleen to ask. I've always wondered how many of them only came for the biscuits.

"I buy the biscuits," Maxine answers. "I didn't have time, that's all."

We fall back into silence.

Eventually I speak. "We could give up. Let them close the school—we can carpool to get the kids to Halstead Primary."

No one moves. Brenda's staring at the floor. I'm expecting her to jump in and agree with me. Her house is painted a dull army green and her clothes are beige and puce and brown, and her kids stay out on the streets till eight or nine at night as Brenda turns on light after light and stands silhouetted in the doorway with her cardigan pulled tight around her, waiting for them to come home. She turns up to my meetings as if she is only here to make sure nothing good happens from them. But tonight she reaches over to pat me on the knee.

"Loretta, I know it won't work, and you probably know deep down it won't work, but you can't give up now," she says.

Kyleen stands up and punches the air, as if she's at a footy match. "That's right! Don't give up, Loretta. Like they said in *Dead Poets Society*, '*Nil bastardum*—'" She pauses, then trails off, " '*Carburetorum*' . . ."

" 'Grindem down'?" Norm finishes.

Next day, Norm's cleaning motor parts with kerosene when I knock on the tin frame of his shed.

"Knew it was you. You should try braking a little earlier, Loretta." He doesn't even have to look up.

"Norm, what happened to your forehead?"

"Bloody doctor chopped off half my face."

"Oh, God, I knew it. I knew something was wrong with that patch of skin. Not skin cancer?" My heart is banging in my chest.

"Not anymore." He reaches up to touch the white bandage, which is already covered in oily fingerprints. "They think they got it all."

He dunks the engine part into the tin of kerosene and scrapes at it with a screwdriver. I want to hug him, but he and I don't do that sort of thing. I'm going to buy him sunscreen and make him wear it, especially on those sticking-out ears of his. I'll buy him a hat and long-sleeved shirts. I can't imagine life without him.

"Mum, I found some flat tin." Melissa is in the doorway, shading her eyes with her hand and watching Jake teetering on top of a beaten-up caravan, his arms whirling like propellers.

"Jake, don't move!" I scream.

My toe stubs a railway sleeper as I bolt toward the caravan.

He was probably fine until I panicked. His eyes widen when he looks down and realizes how high he is. His first howl sets off the guard dogs. His second howl sets off car alarms across town. By the time Norm and I coax him down we've both sustained permanent hearing loss. I hold him against me and his howls ease to sobbing.

"Come on, mate, it wasn't that bad." Norm lifts Jake from my grasp and swings him down to the ground. "I'll get you a can of lemonade."

Jake takes a long, hiccupping breath followed by a cat-in-heat kind of moan as he lets out the air.

"Mum! I told you, I found some." Melissa pulls me, limping, to the back of the yard.

My toe is throbbing and I'm sweating and cross. I wonder why I don't buy a couple of puce cardigans and sink back into the land myself, like Brenda or that truck.

We drag the bits of tin to the shed, where Jake is sitting on the counter listening to the golden oldies radio station while Norm scans *Best Bets*.

"Have you got any paint for this tin? I'm going to make signs for the school."

Norm shakes his head. "You're a battler, Loretta. And I suppose I'm expected to put them up?"

"On the fence."

One of my best dreams is Beemer Man. Beemer Man powers his BMW up to the front of the house and snaps off the engine. He swings open his door, jumps out, and strides up my path holding expensive wine in one hand and two tickets to Kiddieland in the other.

"We'll need the children out of the way for a week or so," he explains, "while I explore every inch of your gorgeous body."

"Taxi's here. Have a lovely week." I can feel his eyes on my effortlessly acquired size-ten torso as I give the kids a gentle push out the door.

They run happily to the taxi, clutching their all-you-can-eat-ride-and-destroy Kiddieland tickets, then Beemer Man closes the front door and presses me against the wall.

"Mum, you've painted 'Save Our Schol.' And you've got paint on your face," Melissa interrupts to tell me before I get to the good part.

Why did I decide to do this in the front yard? My arms are smeared to the elbows with marine paint, and I'm in the saggy old shorts I swore I'd never wear outside the house. Imagine if Harley Man or Beemer Man went by.

I have a terrible thought. Did Norm mean "battler" or "battleaxe"? The school had better be worth all this.

3

NORM'S COME BY to drop off more lemons and pick up a few of my lemon tarts. He leans in an old-man-at-the-pub kind of way on the mantelpiece and picks up a postcard I've propped against the candlestick.

"Who's this from?" he asks, turning it over without waiting for an answer.

"My sister Patsy, the one who works at the uni in Melbourne. She's on a research trip to Paris."

"She works at the uni?" He props the card back up after he's read it.

"Yep, she's a lecturer there."

"She must be pretty smart. What happened to you?" Norm winks at Jake, who giggles and scratches his face the way he's been doing since he got up. I know what's wrong but I'm trying to pretend it's not true. Even though the kids in his grade have all had the vaccine, some have still come down with a mild case of chickenpox.

"Dropped on my head as a baby. So did you get the windscreen?"

"Didn't get it, but tracked one down. A new bloke is doing car repairs out the end of the Bolton Road. Set up the

15

other week. Actually, he's about your age. Not bad looking either. Good business. Nice and polite."

"Beautiful wife, six well-behaved children," I add.

Norm leans back and frowns. "Really?"

"No, but probably."

"I don't think so. He smelled of bachelor to me. Divorced, maybe. Anyway, he quoted me a good price, said to bring the car and he'd put in the windscreen straightaway. So you can take it down whenever you like."

"What's his name?" I ask Norm.

"Merv Bull."

I shake my head. Only in Gunapan. Merv Bull sounds like an old farmer with black teeth and hay in his hair who scoops yellow gobs from his ear and stares at them for minutes on end like they'll forecast the weather. The image keeps replaying in my mind as I finish wrapping the lemon tarts in waxed paper.

"You can't judge people by their names, Loretta, or you'd be able to carry a tune."

"That's unkind, Norm. I may not have turned out to be the talented country-singing daughter my mother was hoping for, but then, neither did Patsy or Tammy. We haven't got the genes for it. I don't know why Mum keeps up these crazy fantasies."

A week and a half later, after having been held hostage in the house by a child even more itchy and irritable than normal, I set out to get the new windscreen.

It's years since I've driven down the Bolton Road. I remember when we first moved to Gunapan I got lost down here. I was heading for the Maternal Health Centre. My first pregnancy. My face was so puffed up with heat and water retention I looked like I had the mumps. I took a left turn at the ghost gum past the stock feed store as the nurse had advised on the phone, and suddenly I was in another world. Later, of course, after I'd found my way back into town, I realized I'd turned left at the wattle tree past the Pet Emporium, but anyway, it was as if I'd magically slipped out of Gunapan and into fairyland. The bush came right up to the roadside, and in the blazing heat of the day the shade from the eucalypts dropped the temperature at least five degrees. I got out of the car, waddled to a picnic bench in a clearing, and sat drinking water for twenty minutes. Hope bubbled up in me. The baby would be fine, my husband Tony would turn out not to be an idiot, we would definitely win the lottery that Saturday.

Only one of those things came true, but I've always loved that bit of bush. I'd come out here with the kids sometimes in the early days and walk the tracks, listening to the sound of the bush, when I could hear it above their endless chatter, and smelling the minty eucalypts.

We've just swung into the Bolton Road when Jake asks if he can have a Mooma Bar from the supermarket. His chickenpox has dwindled to a few annoying itchy spots, but they won't let him back into school yet, no matter how much I beg. He's bored and tailing me like a debt collector. Any excuse to get out is good.

"There's no supermarket out here." The moment I speak I see a shopping trolley on the side of the road. Someone must have walked that trolley five kilometers. Unless it was tossed in the back of a ute and driven here. Further along the road is one of those orange hats they use to steer drivers away from roadworks. A couple of minutes on we see a load of rubbish dumped a few meters off the road. A dozen beer bottles lie around the charcoal of an old fire with what looks like bits of an old picnic bench sticking out of it. A heap of lawn clippings molders beside a brown hoodie and a pair of torn-up jeans. I slow down, pull the Holden over to the side of the road. The trees still come right up to the roadside, but behind them is light, as if someone is shining a torch through the forest.

"We came here on my birthday," Jake reminds me.

He's right. We came out two years ago with green lemonade and presents and a birthday cake in the shape of a swimming pool. Kyleen and Maxine and their kids came, and we played hidey at the old shearers' hut. Three kangaroos burst out from behind the hut when we arrived and crashed off through the bush. We called them "shearing kangaroos" and Jake thought that was a real kind of 'roo till Norm put him right. But now I can't make sense of where that hut might be. The face of the forest is completely different. Ahead of us, a wide dusty dirt road leads in through the trees. I can't see the picnic area. And that light through the trees is wrong.

I drive along the bitumen to where the dirt road enters the bushland.

"I don't want to go in there," Jake says.

More rubbish litters the side of the track—plastic bags and bottles, juice containers, old clothes, building materials—as if this piece of bushland has become the local tip. I peer along the track. It seems to lead into a big clearing that wasn't there before. The bush used to stretch way back. I would never let the kids run too far in case they got lost. Now if they ran off they'd end up standing in a flat empty paddock the size of a footy field.

"Footy field," I mutter. "Maybe they're building a new footy field."

That can't be right, because even the old footy field is in trouble. The footy club has a sausage sizzle every Saturday morning outside the supermarket to raise money to buy in water. All the sports clubs around here are desperate for water. Some have had to close down because the ground is so hard it can crack the shins of anyone landing awkwardly on the surface.

"Let's go. I'm bored."

"Hey, Jake, open your mouth again and show me your teeth. I think it might be time for a trip to the dentist."

That always shuts him up. We climb back into the Holden and reverse into the Bolton Road to continue the journey to our new windscreen.

4

"LOOK AT ALL these cars, Jake." We pull in with a mighty shriek of brakes at Merv Bull's Motor and Machinery Maintenance and Repairs. "Why don't you hop out and have a look around while I talk to the man. Look at that one—a Monaro from the seventies! You don't see those much anymore. Especially in that dazzling aqua."

Jake purses his lips and rolls his eyes and waggles his head all at once. He keeps doing this lately. I wonder if he's seen a Bollywood film on the diet of daytime television that filled up chickenpox week.

"Are you trying to get rid of me, Mum?"

"Yes."

He sighs and swings open the car door. He slouches his way to the shade at the side of the shed while I quickly pat down my hair in the rearview mirror before I step out of the car. I can't see any sign of Merv Bull. A panting blue heeler stares at me from the doorway of the shed as if I'm a piece of meat.

"Hello?" I call. "Mr. Bull?"

The blue heeler slumps to the ground and lays its head on

its front paws, still staring at me. The sign on the side of the shed says *Nine to Five, Monday to Friday.* I look at my watch. Ten fifteen, Tuesday morning.

Jake scuffs his way over to my side. "There's no one here, Mum, let's go. Let's go to the milk bar. You promised that if I . . . you would . . . and then I . . . and then . . ."

As Jake goes on with his extended thesis on why I should buy him a Violet Crumble, I shout, "Mr. Bull!" one last time. A man emerges from the darkness of the shed. The first thing I notice is that he's hitching up his pants. He strides forward to greet me and stretches out his hand, but I'm not shaking anything I can't be sure was washed. When my hand fails to arrive he pulls back his arm and wipes both hands down the sides of his shirt. He's standing between me and the sun. I can't see his face let alone its expression.

Jake's jaw has dropped and he's staring at Merv Bull as if he's seen a vision. He's this way with any man who's around the age of his father when he left.

"Hi," Jake whispers.

"Hello." Merv Bull leans down to shake Jake's hand. "I'm Merv. Who are you, then?"

"Jake."

"Pardon me?"

Jake's awestruck voice has soared into a register that only the blue heeler and I can hear.

"This is Jake"—I step in—"and I'm Loretta. I think Norm Stevens told you I was coming?"

"Ah, you're the windscreen."

"That's me."

"Can't do it till this afternoon, sorry. But you could leave the car here and pick it up at five."

"Sure." I put on a bright fake smile. "Jake and I'll walk the five kilometers back into town in this shocking heat and have a pedicure while we wait."

"We could stay here and look at the cars," Jake whispers.

Merv Bull shades his eyes with his hand and looks down at me. I can see him better now. Norm was right, he's handsome in a parched, rural bloke kind of way. Blue eyes and dark eyelashes. Looks as if he squints a lot, but who doesn't around here. He's frowning at me like a schoolteacher frowns at the kid with the smart mouth.

"I do have a loan car you can use while yours is in the shop. To get you to your pedicure, that is."

"Ha, sorry, only joking." I'm turning into a bitter old hag. I'm reminding myself of Brenda. Soon I'll become strangely attracted to beige. "That would be great. Any old car will do. I mean, hey, we are used to the Rolls-Royce here."

"Mum! That's not a Rolls-Royce. It's a Holden!" Jake beams proudly at Merv.

"You certainly do know your cars, mate." Merv pats Jake on the shoulder.

Now I'll never get Jake out of here. Merv, to be addressed hereafter as God, goes back into the shed to get the keys for the exchange car, and Jake and the blue heeler trot faithfully after him. I watch his long lanky walk. My husband never walked that way, even though he was about the same size as Merv Bull. My husband, Tony—God love him wherever he may be and keep him there and never let him come back into my life—was a stomper. He stomped through the house as though he was trying to keep down unruly carpet; he stomped in and out of shops and pubs, letting doors slam around him; he stomped to work at the delivery company and stomped home stinking of his own fug after eight hours in the truck; and one day he stomped out to the good car and drove off and never stomped back.

We'd been married ten years. I never dreamed he'd leave me. After the second year of marriage, when I fell pregnant with Melissa, I settled down and stopped fretting that I'd married the wrong man. It was too late, so I decided to try to enjoy my life and not spend all my time thinking about what could have been. I thought he had decided that too.

A month after he'd gone a postcard arrived. By that time I'd already finished making a fool of myself telling the police he must have run his car off the road somewhere and insisting they find him. The postcard said he was sorry, he needed to get away. *I'll be in touch. Cheque coming soon.*

Still waiting for that cheque.

"It's the red Mazda with the sheepskin seat covers over by the fence." Merv Bull hands me a set of car keys on a key ring in the shape of a beer stubby. "She's a bit stiff in the clutch, but otherwise she drives pretty easy."

"Been getting a lot of business?" As I speak I take Jake's hand in mine and edge him quietly toward the Mazda before he realizes that we're about to leave his new hero.

"It's been good. They told me it'd take a while to get the ordinary car business going again, especially since no one's worked here for a few years, but I guess I've been lucky. I'll probably have to get an apprentice when the big machinery starts arriving."

"Big machinery?"

"For the development. Whenever it starts. I thought it was supposed to be in Phase One already. That's what they promised me when I bought the place."

"Right." I've lived in this town for years and I still haven't got a clue what's going on. "So that big hole in the bush on the Bolton Road is the development?"

"Yep. But for the moment what I've got is cars, and there seems to be no shortage."

I look at him again. I want to ask if it's been mainly women customers but I don't. I will have to tell Helen about Merv Bull. If Merv is single and if he doesn't hook up with anyone in a hurry, he'll be a rich man in this town. He'll be mystified at how many parts appear to have simply fallen off cars. I inch closer to our loan car, still not letting on to Jake what I'm doing.

I stop as my arm is yanked backward. Jake has caught on and he's trying to pull his hand out of mine.

"Can I stay here, Mum? Please!"

"No, Jakie. Mr. Bull has to do his work."

"I'll be quiet, I promise. I'll look at the cars. You go and I'll wait here."

Merv Bull looks at me.

"He can't bear to spend a minute without me," I say.

"I can see that," Merv answers.

Finally we maneuver Jake into the car with a promise of a workshop tour when we return.

"How much will it cost?" I remember to ask as I pump the accelerator and turn the key the way I would in the Holden. The tiny Mazda lets out a roar of protest. "Sorry, sorry!"

"Might drive a bit differently to your car." Merv calmly waves the exhaust smoke away from his face. "Should cost about a hundred dollars. Maybe a hundred and twenty, but no more."

While the magically vanishing husband was not good for

much, he did know how to change the oil in the car and do a few odd jobs. He probably could have managed fitting a secondhand windscreen. Now I have to pay for everything. And with Jake sick I'm taking time off work, and I have even less money than usual.

"Feeling better today? Ready to go back to school?" I ask Jake with a frisson of desperation as we drive along in the Mazda. The ride is so smooth we don't even have the sensation of movement.

"Can we have a car like this?" Jake asks. "When's Auntie Patsy coming to visit? How long will we be in town?"

"No. Soon. Until I've finished photocopying the Save Our School flyers and it's time to pick up Liss."

Helen's waiting to pick up her neighbor's boy at the school when Jake and I zip down the road to collect Melissa. I execute a neat U-turn, a feat impossible in the Holden, and pull up at the gate. Helen almost falls out of her car.

"Oh my God! A new car! Where'd you steal it?"

"It's a loaner from the mechanic."

"Oh." She screws up her face in sympathy. "Hey, a letter arrived for you at the school. Melissa's probably got it. Another one from the minister about the school."

I don't ask how she knows. I never ask how she knows what we watched on television the night before and what brand of hair dye I use and how Melissa's grades are going. But now I know something she doesn't. I decide I'll wait and see how long it takes her to find out about the new mechanic.

"Do you know what the letter says?"

"Loretta! As if we'd open your mail! But we've all guessed. It says, 'Thank you for your recent letter. I'd like to take this opportunity' . . . da de da de da."

Melissa appears at the car door, holding out the minister's

envelope as if it's a bad report card. I take it and fling it on the front seat, and Melissa leans through the passenger-side window and peers inside the car. "Is it ours?" she asks.

"Nope."

"Actually," Helen calls out on the way back to her car, "I've booked in to that new mechanic for a service, too. I've heard he's very good." She waggles her bottom and kicks up a heel. Of course she knew.

Poor Giorgio, I think. Giorgio is the old town mechanic, pushing eighty, bald and bowlegged. We've all used him for years to keep our cars running with bits of string and glue. I decide I'll keep going to him for my servicing, even if he is getting so absentminded that last time he forgot to put the oil back in the engine. Luckily Norm noticed the car hadn't leaked its normal drips onto his driveway.

When I get back to the garage I'm devastated at having to return the keys to the Mazda. We've been around town ten times playing the royal family, waving at everyone we know.

"That'll be eighty dollars. Didn't take as long as I thought."

Jake's rigid beside me as I hand over the cash. Melissa stands next to him chewing her thumb. I've had words with Jake in the car about not nagging Merv for a tour.

"Mr. Bull's a busy man," I said. "He doesn't want to be bothered by little boys. You don't want him to think you're a whining little boy, do you? So you wait and see if he offers again."

"Anyway, mate, bit of bad news." Merv crouches down in front of Jake. "I'm sorry, but I have to get away early tonight. Can we do our tour another time?"

"Yes, please," Jake whispers. Melissa puts her arm around

his shoulders, and they turn away and scramble onto the bench seat in the back of the Holden.

"I mean it," Merv says to me. "I'd love to give the little bloke a tour. Another day. Give me a call anytime." He reaches into his back pocket. "Here's my card."

Something's odd when I drive off: my vision. Through the new windscreen I can actually see the white line in the middle of the road. The Holden throbs and rattles down the Bolton Road, and I find myself humming to an old song that I can hear clearly in my head. I can hear it so clearly that I'm singing along with lyrics I didn't realize I knew. Even Jake seems happier. He and Melissa are bopping their heads along to the beat. Melissa leans over and turns up the volume on the radio and the tune bursts out of the speakers. We look at each other. Merv has fixed the radio. No more race calls, no more protests, no more ads for hemorrhoid cream.

"I love this car," I sing.

"Me too!" Jake shouts over the pumping beat. By the time we've reached the supermarket, we're all singing along at top volume, windows rolled down, faces pushed out of the car like excited Labradors. Brenda, who happens to be getting out of her car in the supermarket car park, hears us roar up, turns, frowns, and purses her lips. I'm convinced it's because we're exhibiting signs of happiness, until I pull into a parking spot and Brenda comes over to commiserate.

"I heard there was a letter from the minister. Never mind, Loretta. We knew it wouldn't work."

Once we're inside the supermarket, I tear open the envelope while the kids do their usual wistful lingering in the snack foods aisle. The letter doesn't say I've saved the school. No surprise there. But there is another big surprise. On the way home we drop into Norm's.

"Guess what?"

Norm's running his hand over my smooth windscreen.

"Nice. The old one had as many craters as the surface of the moon. It was a wonder you didn't run into a truck."

"I got a letter. The education minister's coming to Gunapan."

"Whoa. Here comes trouble." He reaches up and fingers the ridge of scar on his forehead. "I can feel it in my engine."

5

OVER THE NEXT week, the heat builds until at eight thirty on Monday morning it's already so hot that the birds are sitting on the fence with their beaks open. I walk out of the house with the children in tow and pull open the driver's door. It squeals as usual.

"Bush pig!" Jake shrieks. He opens the back passenger door, which also squeals.

"Bush pig!" Melissa's shriek is even louder. They fall about laughing, swinging their doors open and shut and imitating the squeals of metal against metal.

"Get in the car." No one should be laughing in this kind of heat.

The road to town is flat and empty. As we bump over the pitted tarmac, sprays of pink-and-gray galahs explode into the sky from the fields beside us. On a low hill to the north I can see Les on his tractor, motoring along in the leisurely fashion of a man on a Sunday drive. The sun picks out a shiny spot on one of his wheels and it flashes in a radiant signal each rotation.

"Mum, what's the collective noun for bush pigs?" Melissa asks, and Jake bursts into giggles that he tries to smother with his hand.

"I don't know. The same as domestic pigs, I suppose. What is that? Is that a herd?"

"A herd of bush pigs," Jake shouts.

"A pog of pigs!" Melissa says.

"A swog!"

"A swig! A swig of pigs!"

I wind down my window and push my arm out, leave it there for a moment so Les can see my wave.

"Is that Les?" Jake asks.

"Mr. Garrison to you."

"All the other kids call—"

"I don't care."

We pull up at the school gates. Melissa and Jake sit silently in the backseat as if they're hoping I'll turn around and announce a once-in-a-lifetime no-school day.

"What's all this about bush pigs anyway?" I look in the rearview mirror and see Melissa shaking her head vigorously at Jake.

"Nothing." She catches me watching her and blushes. She has her father's coloring, pale skin that stays freckly no matter how much sunscreen I slather on her, and sandy red hair. When she blushes her face blooms like a scarlet rose.

They jostle their way out of the car, mutter a goodbye, and run through the school gate, separating at the scraggly hedge and bolting away to their respective groups of friends.

Bush pigs, I think, and head off to work.

Gabrielle, the chair of the Management Committee at the Neighbourhood House where I work, can't answer when I ask her the collective noun for bush pigs. She has dropped in unexpectedly. The Management Committee consists of volunteers from the local community, most of them women from the larger, more wealthy properties outside Gunapan. Supposedly their role is to steer the direction of the Neighbourhood House, to use their skills and contacts in developing the profile of the house in the community, to oversee the efficient management of the house finances, and so on and so forth. In reality, they meet once a month to hear the report of the house managers and drink a glass of wine before they start talking about land values and the international wool and beef markets.

"Flock?" she guesses. *"Herd? Posse?"*

"Herd, that's what I said."

"Darling, I really haven't got time to chat about this. I'm on the trail of a wonderful opportunity. Very hush-hush, from my sources."

A thought occurs to me. "Are you talking about that development thing?"

"No, not the development. I'm talking about wool. The finest merino. I have access to a flock that these people need to sell immediately at a very nice price. Buy, shear, and sell in a month. A business proposition that could make someone a lot of money."

"I'll do it." A lot of money—exactly what I need.

"Oh, darling, if only you could. Except it will take about twenty thousand to get this thing off the ground."

"Ah." I am not surprised.

"So you carry on and I'll pop onto the computer for a moment. We have the contact details of the committee members here, don't we?"

"About that development—" I start to say, but Gabrielle waves me away.

"Sorry, darling, I must get on with this."

Gabrielle logs on to the computer and I go back to my work of sorting the donations for our book exchange. The covers are embossed in the silvers and royal blues with scarlet blood spatters that attract the average literary type here. Everyone in Gunapan obviously loves horror. Perhaps that's why they live in this fine town.

Norm has knocked us up a bookcase from the old floorboards of the Memorial Hall, and each time I slide a book onto the shelf a cream-colored puff of powder drifts from below the shelving. He said the insects are long gone. Powder post beetles, he called them. They sound exotic, like tiny rare insects making dust fine as talc, flitting away when they are grown. I told him I could imagine them with transparent iridescent wings, perhaps a glow like fireflies in the forest. "Nah, love," he said, "they're borers."

I shelve *Prey* and *The Dark Rider* and *Coma* and *Pet Sematary*, and soon I can't bear to see another cover promising supernatural thrills and chills. As I am about to check the spelling of *cemetery* in the dictionary—was all that schooling wasted?—I see a different kind of book in the pile. The cover has small writing and a picture of a woman in a dark red dress. She's lying on a couch. But when I look closer, because the picture is also small, I see she's not, in fact, lying on a couch. She's from a different world. Her world has divans, not couches. And she isn't lying on the divan. She's reclining on the divan. Her dress is draped in elegant folds across her slender thighs. Her high-heeled shoe dangles from her foot. I bet she never wears knickers with stretched elastic that slither down and end up in a smiley under each bum cheek.

After I've wiggled my hands down inside my jeans and hauled my undies back up to their rightful position, I open the cover. Inside is an inscription:

To my dear M, remember Paris. With love from Veronica.

I've never met a Veronica in Gunapan. I know a Vera, who makes the best ham sandwiches at the CWA but wants to sniff everyone's breath before they go into the hall because she's the last standing member of the Gunapan Temperance Union. But no Veronica. Maybe the "M" lives here. Could it be Merv Bull? He doesn't seem the type to recline on a divan in Paris. I flip the book over and read the reviews on the back.

An elegiac work that brilliantly explores the chiaroscuro of love. Hmm, I think. Elegiac. Exactly what I would have said. The dictionary is on the upper shelf of the bookcase and I pull it down.

"Gabrielle," I call into the office. "Have you read *The Paper Teacup*?"

"No, darling. Why?"

"Oh, well, it's absolutely marvelous, Gabrielle, you must read it. I found it rather elegiac."

Gabrielle doesn't answer. I wonder if I pronounced the word correctly. I tiptoe over and peer around the doorjamb to see if she's doubled over with laughter at this idiot who can't pronounce *elegiac*. Over her shoulder I see her typing *elliejayack* into the computer's search engine. I creep back to the bookshelf and start shelving more *Night of the Beast* and *Death Visitor* books.

Ten minutes later Gabrielle leans out through the doorway. "I don't like sad books. Give me a good thriller any day."

Once she's left with the information she needs, I finish up my work and make a phone call to the office of the Minister for Education, Elderly Care and Gaming. The night after I got the letter, I rang the SOS committee members to tell them that the minister was coming to Gunapan. It took a while to convince some of them.

"Is he coming for the BnS Ball?" Kyleen asked. She's been talking about the Lewisford Bachelors and Spinsters Ball for a while, usually bringing it up during completely irrelevant conversations. It's not the biggest BnS ball in the state, but it is known as the one with the lowest dress standard. A frock from the charity shop and a pair of boots is acceptable attire, which suits Kyleen well because that's what she wears a lot of the time anyway. I'm sure she mentioned the ball because she can't find anyone to drive her the hundred kilometers to Lewisford, but I doubt the minister would give her a lift, even if he was a bachelor on the lookout for a country spinster.

The letter had said to ring the minister's office to arrange a date for his visit. I organized an emergency SOS meeting, where we got through two packets of Jam Jamboree biscuits and four pots of tea and argued about the merits of an earlier visit or a later visit, as if we'd have any say in the matter anyway, and didn't decide anything except that there was less jam in a Jam Jamboree than there used to be.

Maxine had the answer. "Give him a call. Sort it out over the phone." As if calling government ministers is an everyday chore of mine.

The minister's assistant answers the phone.

"Gunapan," he repeats slowly, as if he is running his finger down a long list.

Surely not that many people write letters to the minister every second week?

"OK, here we are. Correspondence Item 6,752/11. Yes, action required. Schedule a ministerial visit. So, how many minutes do you want him to speak for?"

"I don't want him to speak. I want him to save our school."

"Ah, you're that lady."

"Yes, I am." It's good to take a firm stand, even though

I suspect "that lady" is ministerial office code for "raving lunatic."

"And he'll need a half-day to get there and back . . ."

I can hear him flipping through pages.

"All right. It could be either June 27th or July 19th."

"But you've threatened to close the school by the end of the second term in April. Not much point in visiting a school that's already closed."

I hope he's blushing. He reluctantly suggests a day in March, complaining all the while that he'll have to reschedule appointments to make it happen. I complain back that we all have commitments and it's not so easy for us in Gunapan to rearrange things either. I don't mention that he's proposed the visit for a pension day, when the whole town is aflurry with shopping and bill paying. It's very hard to get anyone to do anything else. But since there's no other possibility we agree to set the date.

By midafternoon even more birds are sitting stupidly in the trees with their beaks open. This is one of those days when they might fall stone dead to the ground, heatstruck. On the horizon a thin column of gray smoke rises and forms a wispy cloud in the pale sky. The start of a bushfire. Or some farmer trying to burn off on a day when leaving your specs lying on a newspaper could make it burst into flame. There's no way to be in a good mood on a day like this. No way, when the air-conditioning in the car is broken and the steering wheel leaves heat welts on your palms. Days like this it seems as if summer will never end. We'll go on sweltering and we'll cook from the inside out, like meat in the microwave. They'll cut us open at the morgue and find us filled with steak and kidney pudding. On the outside we'll be nicely pink.

Days like this I think about picking up Melissa and Jake

from school and I can see everything before it happens. They'll fall into the car and yelp at the heat on the vinyl seats. They'll ask for icy poles from the shop, or ice creams, or they'll want to go down to the waterhole for a swim. The council swimming pool's shut for renovations. All winter it was open, the heated pool empty except for five or six people who have moved here from the city and who put on their designer goggles and churn up and down the pool thirty or forty times every morning before they purr back to their farmlets in huge recreational vehicles.

One time I decided to get fit and I went along at six thirty in the dark with the kids. After they got tired of messing around in the free lane, the kids sat on the edge of the pool dangling their feet in the water and shouting, "Go, Mum!" as if I was in the Olympics. The other swimmers lapped me four times to my one and by lap five I was dangerously close to going under for the third time.

"Never mind, Mum," Melissa reassured me. "We love you even if you are fat."

Then during the third month of spring this year, the council announces the swimming pool will close for renovations. Right over summer. What renovations? we ask. What can you do to a swimming pool? It either holds the water or it doesn't. And in summer, after years of drought, when we save the water we use to wash vegetables and time our showers, the pool is our one indulgence in this town. No, they say, we're putting in a sauna and a spa and we're building a café. You'll be glad when it's done, they tell us. We've subcontracted the work. It will only take five months. Why? we ask again, but no one answers. Truly something stinks at that council.

"Don't say a word," I tell the kids when they stagger past the wilted gum trees of the schoolyard and into the car.

"We're going to buy icy poles and we're going to the water-hole."

If they had any energy left they'd cheer, I'm sure, but Jake has dark circles under his eyes from not sleeping in the heat and Melissa turns and looks out through the open window, lifting her face to catch the breeze.

"Mrs. Herbert said we don't have to do any homework tonight because it's too hot and I got a gold star for reading," Jake shouts above the hurricane of the wind rushing through the car.

I never bother locking the house in this kind of heat. If we shut the windows we'll never sleep. It's become a habit to walk through each room when I come home, counting off the valuables. While Jake and Melissa head off to their bedrooms I mentally mark off the computer, the DVD player, the change jar. The telly's not worth stealing. Melissa shuts her door while she changes. She's eleven now, but she reminds me of me when I was fifteen. One night not long ago she shaved her legs in the shower. I saw the blood from a cut seeping through her pajama leg.

"What on earth are you doing?" I sounded louder than I'd meant to. "Once you start you can't stop. The hair grows back all thick and black and soon you'll look like an orangutan. Then you'll have to shave all the time."

"You do it! Anyway, the other girls were laughing at me." She was looking down at her hands and sitting rigidly still, the way she does when she lies.

"They were not. I bet you saw it in a magazine. Or on TV."

Melissa arched her head in the kind of movie-star huff it took me years to master and stamped off to her room.

Now Jake and I wait ten minutes, fifteen, while she changes into her bathers.

"Come on, Liss," Jake calls, "we're boiling. Let's go."

Melissa's room is silent. I knock on the door.

"Sweetie, don't you want to cool down?"

"I'm not going." The door stays firmly shut.

Jake does an exaggerated sigh and collapses onto a chair. I can feel the sweat on my face, running down between my breasts, soaking into my bathers under my dress. Three flies are circling me, landing whenever I let my attention drift.

"You go." Her voice is muffled behind the door. "I'll have a shower."

"Please, let's go, Mum." Jake reaches out to take my hand and pull me toward the front door.

Melissa's a mature eleven-year-old, but I am convinced that if I leave her alone in the house for more than twenty minutes a spectacular disaster will happen and she'll die and I'll be tortured by guilt for the rest of my life. I've pictured the LP gas tanks exploding, the blue gum tree in the yard toppling onto the house, a brown snake slithering out of a kitchen cupboard. Of course, any of those things could happen while I'm at home too, but I would have no guilt factor. The guilt factor means I may never have sex again, because attractive men looking for a good time rarely drop in spontaneously at my house. On the other hand, it has saved me from many of Helen's girls' nights, involving outings to pubs that the same attractive men looking for a good time never visit. I was also lucky enough to miss Helen's ladies-only party where an enthusiastic twenty-year-old tried to sell dildos and crotchless panties to astonished Gunapan farm wives.

"Melissa, either you come or we don't go at all, you know that."

"Noooooo!" Jake's cry of anguish echoes on and on in a yodeling crow call.

Finally Melissa agrees to come and wait on the bank while we take a dip. I tell her that I'm going in even though I have thighs as thick as tree stumps.

"It doesn't worry me." My bright voice makes my lie obvious.

"That'd be right," Melissa mutters from the backseat.

"Young lady," I start, but it's too hot to argue, so I swing the car backward out of the driveway and set off.

It's been three years since Tony left us. Three years in real time, and more like thirty years in looking-after-children time. I'm sure mothering years go even faster than dog years. I can feel my back turning into a question mark. Sometimes I catch myself hunched over the steering wheel or sagging in a kitchen chair, and I can imagine myself after a few more mothering years, drooling into my porridge in the retirement home. Come on, luvvie, they'll say to me, sit up straight now; after all, you're only forty.

The road leading into the gully swings around the bend and we can see the whole town, or at least as many people as would normally be at the swimming pool, clustered around the small waterhole like ants at a droplet of sugar water. Bush pigs at a billabong, maybe. The waterhole's half the size it used to be because we get no rain, but it's still deep enough to swim.

"What were you two talking about this morning? Bush pigs, was it?"

"Yeah."

"No."

With the ground near the edge of the water trampled to mud, we find a spot farther back underneath a stringybark tree and lay down our towels and unpack the iced lemonade and biscuits. Melissa goes off to sit next to her friend Taylah.

Jake and I make our way down to the water, saying hello to everyone on the way. Some of the mothers who have caught sight of me pretend to be reading the messages on their children's T-shirts or searching for something in their bags. I know they're afraid I'm going to ask them to do something for the Save Our School Committee, but I don't have to now because the minister's coming to Gunapan.

"The minister's coming to Gunapan," I call out cheerily, making a fist of victory, and they nod and smile anxiously as you do when a lunatic has decided to talk to you.

Further up on the hill I can see a family sitting apart from everyone else. Four children and a woman. They lean in together, talking.

"Who's that up there?" I ask Jake.

"Dunno." He doesn't even glance up, as if he knows without looking who I'm talking about.

I keep squinting at them as I wade in, but I can't make out their faces. Then I feel an eddy of water around my knees and before I can move someone has grabbed my ankles and I'm under, flailing around in the murky water, trying not to swallow any. I make it to the surface for a breath before Jake sits on my head. Even underwater I can hear his shrieks and Kyleen's unmistakable snorting laugh. I finally manage to stand up straight, my feet anchoring themselves on the squelchy bottom where the silt oozes in silky bands between my toes.

"Very funny."

"Yep," she says between snorts.

Further out, the bottom of the waterhole falls away and the water is dark and deep. Even on a day like this when half the town has swum here, water from the depths still swirls in cold ribbons to the surface. I leave Jake playing with Kyleen and her little girl near the edge of the waterhole and I swim out and roll onto my back where the water is cooler. The sun seems to have less power here.

Up on the hill I can see the lonely family still huddled together. They're moving about now, gathering their things and putting them into plastic bags. They start making their way back to the road, but instead of walking down through the people bunched around the banks of the waterhole, they skirt the long way around the top of the hill until they reach the bus stop farther down the ridge. I close my eyes and float for a while, trying to block out the sounds of kids screaming and parents bellowing and the rustle and crackle of the grass and leaves in the heat.

Melissa is waiting when Jake and I clamber back up to dry ourselves with our hot, dusty towels. She's wearing jeans and a long-sleeved top and her face is scarlet with the heat. I wonder if she's nicked herself shaving again. It would be typical of a child of mine to decide that self-mutilation of the legs wasn't enough. Why not shave your arms as well? And your stomach and neck while you're at it?

"Where's Taylah?" Jake asks her.

"Gone home."

"Sweetie, I've got a spare T-shirt in the car boot, why don't you put that on."

"I want to go home. You said you were only going in for a dip."

I stretch out my hand to help her up. She ignores it and pulls herself up with the aid of a tree branch, then winces and brushes her dirty hand on her jeans. I can see that nothing will make her happy today. Melissa was always Tony's little girl. When he left I didn't know how to make it up to her. She's grown old in the time he's been gone. I offered her a puppy for her last birthday and she refused it.

41

"Why?" I asked her.

"Because it'll die. And you never know when."

At home Melissa goes off to her room and Jake hangs around the kitchen while I boil the water for frankfurters. I get him buttering the bread and I lean out of the kitchen window, trying to catch some air on my face. Across from our block is a small farm. Fancy clean white sheep appear in the paddock one day and are gone the next. The farm owners don't speak to us. A few times a week I see the wife driving past in her Range Rover with the windows closed. She wears sunglasses and dark red lipstick. I can't imagine her crutching a sheep, much as I try.

I've spent some of my great fantasy moments being that woman, usually on days like this when I'm hanging out of the window and moving my face around like a ping-pong clown to try to catch a breeze. In my imagination I've sat in her air-conditioned dining room, laughing gaily, my manicured hands and painted nails flitting about like colored birds as I discuss the latest in day spas. I've waved goodbye to my tiresome yet fabulously wealthy and doting husband, and changed into a negligee to welcome my lover, the Latin horse whisperer who lives above the stables and takes me bareback riding in the moonlight. In this dream, my boobs are so firm that even the thundering gallop of the stallion cannot shake them.

"Mum," Jake interrupts as I'm about to drift into my other world.

"Mmm?"

"Melissa's crying."

"Don't touch the saucepan," I say, turning off the gas. "And butter four more pieces of bread for your lunches tomorrow."

She doesn't want to open the door when I knock, but I can hear the phlegm in her voice, so I push the door open anyway. Melissa's sitting on the carpet beside her bed. I go and sit beside her, my bones creaking as I lower myself to the floor. It's a little cooler down here, but I'm still sweating. Melissa's face is all splotchy and snot is coming out her nose. I pull one of my endless supply of tissues out of my pocket and wipe her face. She tries to push my hand away.

"I'm not a baby," she sniffles.

"I know."

We sit quietly for a few minutes and eventually I slip my arm around her shoulders and kiss her forehead. She leans into me and sighs a big shuddering sigh.

"What's up, kiddo?"

"Nothing."

We sit for a while longer. Her breathing gets easier and slower. She's not going to tell me anything, that's obvious, so I decide to finish making tea. When I get to the kitchen, Jake's so hungry he's ripped open the packet of frankfurters and is gnawing on a cold one.

"Did you do girl talk?"

"Where did you hear that line?" I'm trying not to laugh.

"Norm told me that's what girls say they do, but really they're gossiping about how to get boys."

"Well, Norm's wrong. And I'll be letting him know that next time I see him."

"Why don't you marry Norm?"

"Because he's a hundred years old and smells of tractor. Why don't you marry Kimberley? You play with her at school every day."

"Yuk!"

"Yeah!"

43

At least that's sorted.

When she finally emerges from her room, Melissa eats two frankfurters in bread, dripping with butter and tomato sauce, and a few forks of salad. After we've washed up she drifts back to her room to do her homework. I've pulled all the flywire screens shut and I make the kids hold their breath while I go around the house spraying the mozzies. In Melissa's room I glance over her shoulder. She's on the internet, looking at a page about the United Nations.

"Mum, were you around when the United Nations started?"

"Possibly, if I'm as old as I feel. But no, I don't think so. Are you doing a project?"

She nods. She switches screens to show me her essay and I see that at the top of the page she has made a typing mistake and it says *The Untied Nations*. I like that title. It makes me think of Gunapan, a town lost in the scrubby bush, untied from the big cities and the important people and the TV stations and the government. Gunapan keeps struggling on the way it always has and no one takes any notice at all except to cut a few more services. There are probably thousands of towns like us around the country. The untied nations.

"Why don't you look up the collective noun for bush pigs?" I must learn to use the computer better myself.

"I did—it's a sounder," Melissa says.

"What a great word! Sounder. Sounder."

"It's not that good, Mum."

"Sounder, sounder, sounder. A sounder of bush pigs."

"Mum, I have to do my homework." She heaves an exasperated sigh that would do a shop assistant in a toffy dress emporium proud. "Please, I need some peace and quiet."

6

A GOOD MOTHER would be culturing organic yogurt or studying nutritional tables at this time of night, when the kids are asleep and the evening stretches out ahead, empty and lonely. I've checked every channel on the TV and tried to read a magazine, but it's all rubbish. I'm too hot to concentrate on a book. I should be planning spectacular entertainments for the visit from the education minister, but that seems too much like hard work. Now I'm bored. I sound like Jake. Bored, bored, bored. If I was a bloke, I'd wheel the computer out of Melissa's room and look at porn for a while.

The only trouble with the secondhand computer stand I bought is that it squeaks whenever you move it. Melissa half-wakes and moans, and I shush her and hurry the computer out of the room. I'm not interested in porn, but Helen's promised me a whole other world of fun on the internet and I think it's time I found out more about it, as research of course, to protect my children. Last time I played around on the computer, Melissa, through child technomagic, tracked what I'd been looking at the night before. "Are you going to buy a motorbike, Mum?" she asked. "What are spurs, anyway?" Now I've learned how to clear the history of what I've been browsing, so I'm feeling daring. I pull down the ancient bottle of Johnnie Walker from the top of the cupboard, pour a shot, add a splash of water, and realize the only ice I have is flavored. What the hell, I think, and drop the homemade icy pole upside down into the glass.

Outside the flywire screens, the night noise of the bush carries on. It's not the white noise of the city where I grew up—the drone of cars and the rattle of trams, the hum of streetlights and televisions muttering early into the morning. It is an uproar. When we first moved out here I was terrified by the racket. It sounded as if the bunyips and the banshees had gone to war: screaming, howling, grunting, crashing through the bush, tearing trees apart, and scraping their claws along the boards of the house. Soon enough I realized that the noises were frogs and cicadas and night birds. Kangaroos thumping along their tracks; rutting koalas sending out bellows you'd never imagine their cute little bodies could produce; the hissing throat rattle of territorial possums; and an occasional growling feral cat. Against all that the whirring of the computer is like the purr of a house pet.

Once I'm connected to the internet I do a search on myself, in case I've become famous while I wasn't paying attention. I'm not there, so I try my maiden name, Loretta O'Brien. Someone with my name is a judge in North Carolina, and another person called me died recently and her grandchildren have put up pictures of her. She has a touch of the old scrag about her. I wonder if it's the first name that does it to us. All that unfulfilled singing potential.

The lemon icy pole sure adds a distinctive tang to Johnnie Walker. I top up the glass with water and take another sip, shards of melting ice sticking to my lips as I type in *Gunapan*. We're part of a geological survey. The Department of Lands has posted a topographical map of the region. *Gunapan* is an Aboriginal place name. Well, duh, I think, tossing back more of the tasty lemon whisky and adding a touch more water. The next hit is an online diary of a backpacker from Llanfairfechan in Wales who stayed for a night in a room above the Gunapan pub. *One night is plenty enough in this place*, she writes. *I had very bad dreams.*

Jake calls out in his sleep. He does this—occasionally shrieks in the night—but it means nothing. Bush pig, I think, refilling my glass and pulling a strawberry icy pole from the freezer. It's weeks since I've been tempted to drop the kids at the orphanage and drive to Melbourne to take up my new life of glamour with a hairless, odorless body. The little bush pigs have been behaving quite well. Now I realize that was the calm. Something's coming, but I don't know what.

I lean back and sip my drink—Johnnie and a strawberry icy pole, it's a Gunapan cocktail—and click away until I'm looking at the guest login for online dating in Victoria. I hesitate on that page awhile.

"It's not only weirdos," Helen told me once. "Some blokes look quite handsome. Although that does seem to be mainly the shorter ones. Anyway, you don't have to do anything. It's soft-core girl porn."

I select *Rural southwest* and *Male* and *Over six feet* and *Doesn't matter* about children. Then *Go*. The screen comes up with five photos on the first page and a big list of other hits. One hundred and forty-two single men in rural southwest Victoria? This deserves a green icy pole and another shot of Johnnie.

I read about Jim, who likes long walks on the beach and romantic dinners. Jim lives in Shepparton in central Victoria, many hours' drive from the beach. Giuseppe has two grown children and likes working out. Mel loves movies and romantic dinners and golf, and would like to share his wonderful life with a special lady. Joe's looking for a happy busty lady with no issues. Good luck, Joe.

As I scroll down the list I start finding these people funnier and funnier. Matthew's spent a lot of time working on his spirituality and he'd like to meet a woman with the same interests so they can grow together. Like a fungus, I think. Shelby would like a petite Asian lady with large breasts who's open-minded and looking for a good time. Hey, Shelby, most of the men in this town pay good money for that. I open up my password-protected email and send Helen a message. *Looking for a handsome wealthy man with no issues and a Beemer. Must love slumming it and buying expensive presents for the lady in his life, and have no objections to feral children.*

I slump back into the kitchen chair, which is a few inches too short for the computer table. My neck hurts. The screen in front of me has ads all over it. Casinos, jobs, real estate. Maybe I should look for a new house to rent, one that doesn't heat up to 400 degrees. Thinking about real estate reminds me of the hole in the bush on the Bolton Road.

I type *Gunapan development* into the search bar. You get thousands and thousands of answers in these searches and none of them are what you want. The council minutes are online. That should send me off to sleep. The local supermarket's car park resurfacing process is described in glorious detail. I cannot understand why these things would be on the internet. I find the council's forms for applying for a building permit. I try another search, this time on *Gunapan bush.* Then I type in more place names from the local region combined with *development* and then I try *bush clearing* and then something else and by this time I'm pretty tired of it but I click through to one more page and that's where I find the article.

It doesn't have Gunapan in the title, or even in the article, which is from a newspaper in Western Australia, and which is talking about a resort development to take place on twelve hectares outside Halstead. Outside Halstead? The map in the article shows where the development will take place and I can see that it's the old bush reserve in Gunapan, but our town isn't mentioned. Only a few lines about how the development may help to *revive the depressed small community nearby.* Depressed! The only depressed person here is Brenda, and even she picks up during the Gunapan Fair.

The company building the resort is a Western Australian developer *with successful resorts in Queensland, WA and the Territory, as well as significant investment in plantation forestry and logging.* I want to print this page out but the printer's still in Melissa's room.

"Mum?"

The cry comes from down the hall. Jake's awake.

"Mummy."

He only calls me Mummy when he's frightened. I clean up the browser and close it down, then hurry to Jake's room, taking deep breaths to expel the smell of Johnnie from my mouth. Jake's nightlight is on, a rotating globe with fish painted on the outside and a static seascape behind. The mechanical rotation of the outer plastic globe makes a reassuring grinding sound once each cycle like the slow purr of a contented cat.

"What is it, Jakie?" I whisper from the doorway.

"I'm not a bush pig," he whispers.

"Of course you're not," I say firmly. I sit down beside him on the bed and rest my hand on his hot, sweaty chest. "Why would you think that?"

"They said so."

"Who said so?" Anger starts to rise inside me. I remember I started thinking about bush pigs after Melissa and Jake began joking about them. "Where did this come from, anyway?"

He doesn't answer. His steady breathing makes my hand rise and fall as he drifts back to sleep.

Next morning I'm waiting for them at the breakfast table with a pile of bacon on a plate and the spatula jutting from my hand. Melissa and Jake both sit down at the table without speaking, without looking at the bacon. I dish the crispy strips onto buttered toast, slop on scrambled eggs from the frying pan, and hand them a plate each.

"What's going on?" I ask. "What's this bush pig business?"

"Nothing." Melissa has her stubborn face on.

Jake's eyes begin to redden. The circles under his eyes are even darker today. The heat went on and on all night until even the bugs got exhausted and stopped making noise at about four in the morning. There was an occasional crack as the tin roof shucked off the heat of the day and the house settled and sighed. Not only did no one sleep properly, I'm also feeling the effects of my romantic night with Johnnie Walker, and I'm in no mood to be messed with.

"I don't want silence or sulking or tantrums. Tell me what it's about. Who called you a bush pig, Jake?"

Silence. My throbbing head. Jake and Melissa stare at their plates. The crispy bacon is wilting, the eggs are getting cold, the toast is going soggy. The urge to shout is rising in me and I want to smother it—I must not become a shrieking single mother.

"So . . ." I lighten my tone of voice. My back is still to the children. "I'm not cross. I want to know, that's all."

"I had a project on bush pigs," Melissa says.

"Then why would Jake be upset?" I turn around to face them, my expression a mask of control and calm.

"I called him a bush pig." Melissa shoves a blackened curl of bacon into her mouth as if that will stop me asking her questions.

"Is that it, Jake? Did your sister call you a bush pig?"

Melissa's staring so hard at Jake he'll start sending off smoke in a minute. He crosses his hands over his lap.

"I need to go to the toilet," he says. Little liar.

"It's true! It is, Mum. I did call him a bush pig. I'm sorry."

Something smells here. I'm sure she's lying. But she's as stubborn as her father. I turn to Jake.

"Lies come back to bite you on the bum. You know that, don't you, Jake?"

"I want to go to school now," he says for the first and probably last time in his life. "Did you put a banana in my lunch?"

The boy is obsessive. I take the banana out of his lunch box and open Melissa's.

"I'm not having it!" she yelps.

"What is it with bananas and this family?" I say. "They're good nutritious food and they're cheap."

"They stink!" Jake and Melissa say together.

By the time I've finished the washing-up, Melissa and Jake are ready to head off. I drop them at school and drive on to the Neighbourhood House, sweating in the hot morning sun.

At ten thirty my sister Tammy calls to let me know Mum's in hospital in Melbourne.

7

"**WHAT'S THAT NOISE?**" Jake has an unerring knack for asking awkward questions.

He leans down and peers under the seat between his legs, sits up and cranes his neck, looking around the corridor. I reach over and poke him to be quiet.

"Mum, your bra is creaking again," Melissa whispers crossly.

"Sshh," I tell her.

"It's creepy, Mum. You should throw it out."

"I'm sure you'd be very happy to have me arriving at school to pick you up with my breasts flopping around."

"Oh, disgusting." Melissa looks as if she's about to faint.

"You'll have these troubles soon enough, my girl."

"No, I won't, because I'm never buying underwear at the two-dollar shop."

I was sure I'd never told anyone about buying that bra at the two-dollar shop. It seemed such a bargain until the creaking started. Even with that, I thought it was a waste to throw it away.

"You can go in now, she's decent," the nurse calls from the doorway of Mum's room.

Jake runs in first, calling out, "Hi, Nanna!" Melissa and I follow more slowly. Jake stops as soon as he gets in the doorway and sees his nanna tiny and yellowish in the big hospital bed. He backs up and presses against me. Melissa stands rigid at our side. Their nanna's bed is one of four in the room. Two are empty. An ancient man with a liver-spotted head is snoring in the one diagonally opposite.

"Hi, Mum. How are you feeling?"

She turns her gaunt sallow face to me and frowns. "Did you bring me a Milk Tray?"

I produce the box of chocolates with a flourish from my handbag and pass it to Melissa. "Give these to your grandmother, sweetie."

"My name is Melissa," my gracious daughter answers.

"Give me the chocolates, girl," my even more gracious mother says. "I've been waiting for them since eleven o'clock."

"Are you sure you can eat those, with your liver?"

My mother reaches for the nurse alarm button.

"OK," I say, taking the box from Melissa and tossing it onto the bed. "So how are you feeling?"

I send Jake to the vending machine next to the ward for a packet of chips while Mum tells me about my sisters, Tammy and Patsy. Tammy visited yesterday with her three immaculate children. Tammy brought a hand-knitted bedjacket, five novels, a basket of fruit, and best wishes from her husband, Rob, who is smarter than Einstein and a better businessman than Bill Gates—apparently Bill could learn a thing or two from Rob about point-of-sale software. One of the children had written a poem for her nanna.

"Melissa, do you want to read your cousin's poem?" I ask sweetly.

Melissa smirks into the magazine she's picked up.

My other sister, Patsy, visited with her friend. Mum thinks that Patsy's friend would look so much nicer if she lost some weight and started wearing more feminine clothing. And took care of that facial hair, for God's sake. Then she might be able to get a man.

"Speaking of which, have you heard from thingo?" she asks.

"Nope," I say. "So when do you get out of here?"

"Where are you staying?"

"We're in a motel."

"It's horrible," Melissa says. "The bedspreads smell of cigarettes. And they're baby-shit yellow."

"Melissa!" I protest, but she gives me the as-if-you've-never-said-it-yourself look.

"You could always stay with Tammy. They have a six-bedroom house."

They do have plenty of room at the house and we did try staying once, but Tammy and I discovered that these days we can only tolerate two hours of each other's company before sisterly love turns sour. It became clear that she thinks her wealthy lifestyle exemplifies cultured good taste and mine has degenerated into hillbilly destitution, whereas I think Tammy is living a nouveau riche nightmare while I represent a dignified insufficiency.

Tammy's husband rarely comes home because he's so busy being successful. When he does arrive he's late, and Tammy's favorite nickname for him is "my late husband." "Allow me to introduce 'my late husband,'" she announces to startled guests. Her husband smiles distantly and gives her a shoulder squeeze like she's an athlete. Last time the kids and I came down we ate luncheon—not the meat but the meal—at their place on Sunday. Jake swallowed a mouthful of the smoked trout and dill pasta and before it even reached his stomach he had puked it back into the plate. It looked much the same as before he had chewed it, but the sight of the regurgitation had Tammy's delicate children heaving and shrieking. "Haven't they ever seen anyone chunder before?" Melissa remarked scornfully on the way home.

My mother turns her attention to Melissa. "And you, young lady, are you doing well at school?"

Melissa looks at her grandmother with an arched eyebrow. "Yes, Grandmother," she answers.

"I won't have any granddaughter of mine being a dunce."

Melissa turns her head and gives me a dead stare. I can't believe she's only eleven.

"All right," I intervene briskly, "let's talk about you, Mum. How are you feeling? When do you get out?"

"I'm yellow, in case you hadn't noticed."

"Can I get a packet of chips too?" Melissa says, so I give her some money and tell her to find Jake while she's at it.

"Good." My mother pushes herself upright in the bed as soon as Melissa has left the ward. "Now the children are gone we can talk. I'm going to sell up and move to Queensland, the Gold Coast. Albert's bought a house on the canals with a swimming pool and a sauna. My liver's packing up. I don't know how I got this hepatitis thing, but I can only guess it was from your father all those years ago. That lying cheat. Apparently it's contagious. You and the kids had the test like I told you?"

"Yes, we're fine. Who's Albert?" I am incredulous.

"He's from the bingo. He's no great catch, I admit that, but who else is offering me a house in the sunshine?"

"Not the one with the five Chihuahuas? The one you used to make jokes about?"

"Having those dogs doesn't actually mean he's homo-sexual. He's quite virile for an older gentleman."

"Oh, Mum, enough detail. And why can't you say this in front of the kids?"

"You need to tell them in your own time. I know they'll be upset I'm leaving, but when they get older they'll under-stand."

"I'll break it to them gently." I don't want to point out that we only come down to Melbourne at Christmas and her birthday anyway.

"Tammy and Patsy'll miss you," I say. "And the junior poets."

My mother almost smiles before she says, "I love Tammy's children dearly, you know that, Loretta."

"I know."

"Anyway, when I sell, I'm giving you a few thousand dol-lars. Don't tell Tammy or Patsy. You need it, they don't."

From down the corridor comes a long howl, followed by grievous sobbing.

"They torture people in here, you know," Mum says. "The nights are hell. The screaming and moaning, it's like being inside a horror film."

I have a bad feeling that I recognize that howl. But rather than spoil the moment, I think about the good things.

"A few thousand dollars?" I say.

"Depending on the price I get for the flat. You'll get some-thing, anyway. Five or six thousand, maybe."

A holiday for one—or two?—in Bali, I think. Or an air conditioner. Or both! A proper haircut and blond tips! A bra that doesn't creak! Champagne and sloppy French cheese and pâté! Silk knickers!

"I expect you'll want to spend it on the kids, but keep a

couple of dollars for yourself, won't you. You could use a bit of smartening up. Any men on the horizon?"

"Actually," I say, "there's a rather good-looking mechanic who definitely has eyes for me. He keeps himself quite clean, too."

"As opposed to that grubby old junk man you hang around with?"

"Yes, as opposed to Norm, who has his own special standard of hygiene."

"And has this bloke asked you out?"

"Not yet." Needless to say, he hasn't recognized yet that he has eyes for me. I wonder if I am talking about Merv Bull. Have I developed a crush? Am I becoming Helen?

From down the corridor, the howling and sobbing is growing louder. I can't avoid it now.

"You need to look for your mother," I can hear a woman telling Jake. "Open your eyes, dear."

"Loretta, you should give up that political hocus-pocus you've got yourself into. Put your energy into finding a partner and a father for those children."

"The Save Our School Committee is precisely for 'those children.' Anyway, we've had a win. The minister for education's coming to Gunapan in a few weeks. We've got a chance to change his mind about closing the school."

"Is he married?"

Jake's sobbing, very close now, startles awake the man in the bed across from Mum. He raises his spotty head and shouts, "You buggers! You buggers! Get out of it, you buggers!"

"Shut up," my mother calls over at him, and he stops immediately.

"Nutcase," she says to me. "Every time he wakes up he

thinks the Germans are coming for him." Mum lets her head drop back onto the pillow and stares at the ceiling. "The Gold Coast. I can't wait."

"So when do you go?"

"Mummeeeeeeee," Jake screams as he runs into the room and flings his round little body onto my lap. He buries his face in my shirt, covering me in snot and tears. Melissa strolls in behind him eating a chocolate bar.

"The lady says she's going to clean up Jake's chips."

With Jake in my arms I stagger out to the corridor and call out thanks to his rescuer, a woman in a blue cleaner's uniform who is hurrying back toward the lift.

"What were you doing on the second floor, Jakie?"

"Idroppedmychipsntheysaidicouldn'teatthemoffthefloor ndicouldn'tfindyoooooooo." His sobbing is slowing now. "So, so so Itriedtofindyouand, hic, Icouldn'tfindyouandIwent, hm, downthestairsand, ugh, theladysawmeand . . ."

"Ssh, ssh." I squeeze him tightly to me.

"I'm tired now," my mother says from the bed. "Thanks for visiting, darlings."

On the way back to the motel I ask the kids what they'd buy if they had a thousand dollars.

"A motel!" Jake screams.

"What would you buy, Liss?" I can see her in the rearview mirror. She looks out through the window for a while, down at her hands, back out through the window.

"I dunno."

"Go on, a thousand dollars. What would you get?"

She sighs a great heaving sigh and writes something on the car window with her fingertip.

"Some proper clothes. From a proper shop so I'm not the world's biggest dork."

"Don't be silly, you look beautiful. You could wear a sack and you'd look beautiful."

We pull into the motel car park to pick up our bags from reception and have a toilet break before the long drive back to Gunapan. Once we're on the highway I drive for an hour, and when it gets dark we stop at a roadhouse. We order the lamb stew with chips and milkshakes and sit down at a table beside a man who resembles a side of beef and who appears to be eating a side of beef. At the far end of the roadhouse café is another family. They seem to be trying to stay away from everyone else, like that family at the waterhole.

"Who are those people we saw up on the hill at the waterhole the other day?" I ask Melissa, who's leafing through an ancient women's magazine she found on the table. She shrugs. "I don't think I've seen them before," I go on, talking to myself.

"Can I watch TV when we get home tonight?" Jake asks.

"No."

"Miss Claffy had an engagement ring on yesterday," Melissa says. The magazine is open at the page of a starlet wearing an engagement ring that could sink the *Titanic*. The food arrives at the table. I can tell immediately that I've made a mistake ordering the stew. I thought it would be healthier than hamburgers.

"Is this lamb?" Jake asks.

"I think it was lamb a few years ago," I tell him through a mouthful of gristle. Grinding this meat down to a consistency I can swallow is a full-body workout.

"Can we have pizza tomorrow night?"

"The ring had a diamond on it. Miss Claffy said diamond can cut a hole in glass."

"You must have seen those kids at school. Isn't one of them in a class with you?"

"I don't want anchovies on my pizza tomorrow. I want double cheese."

"Someone should welcome them. You kids have no idea how hard it is for a new family in a small town."

"Why don't you have an engagement ring, Mum?"

"What?"

"Didn't Dad give you an engagement ring?"

"I don't want olives either. I hate olives."

"We didn't really have an engagement. We just got married."

"Miss Claffy said her fiancé asked her to marry him in a restaurant and everyone heard and they all clapped."

"We had a lovely wedding, though. I can show you the pictures."

"We've seen them," they both say quickly.

Melissa and Jake have pushed aside their stew. They dip their chips in the stew sauce and suck on their milkshakes. I wish I'd ordered myself a milkshake. The side of beef beside us finishes his meal, burps ferociously, and sways his bulk out to the car park, where his rig is waiting for him like a tame *T. rex*. Jake wants to go out and have a better look, but I hold him back.

"Is Nanna going to die?" Melissa asks.

"Oh, Lissie girl, of course she's not. It's worse. She's moving to the Gold Coast."

"Really?"

"Really. With her new boyfriend."

"She's an old lady! She can't have a boyfriend."

"And what about your poor mother? Am I too old to have a boyfriend?"

"You're married." Melissa's disapproving frown would qualify her instantly as a headmistress. "To Dad," she adds, in case I'd forgotten.

8

MY SISTER PATSY has only been in the house for five minutes and she is already enthusiastically embracing the joys of country life.

"When are you going to leave this dump and come back to Melbourne?" she says.

She's parked her brand-new Peugeot on the street in front of the house, and I think nervously of Les, the farmer farther down the road. On a hot day Les sometimes drives the tractor straight off the field and heads to the pub. His Kelpie sits beside him on the wheel hub, barking madly at cars overtaking them. Late at night, Les will steer the tractor back home down the road, singing and laughing and nattering to himself, the dog still barking. No one worries because the worst that can happen is him driving the tractor off the road somewhere and him and the dog sleeping in a field. But no one ever parks on this road at night.

"So, Patsy, let's move that beautiful car of yours into the driveway and swap with mine. Wouldn't want anyone to steal it!"

"You've got no reason to stay here," Patsy goes on. "That bastard's not coming back and the kids are young enough to move schools. Mum's gone to the Gold Coast, so she won't bother you. Come back to the real world."

I have thought about going back to Melbourne. A part of me believes that being in Melbourne would magically make me more sophisticated and capable. My hair, cut by a hairdresser to the stars, would curve flatteringly around my face and my kids' teeth would straighten out of their own accord.

"Can't take the kids away from the clean country air," I tell Patsy. When Tony and I first moved to the country for a better-paid driving job he'd been offered, we shifted from an outer western suburb, treeless, gray, and smelling of diesel, the only place we could afford a flat. Everyone there was miserable and angry and even our neighbors tried to rip us off. For the same money as that poky flat we rented a three-bedroom house with a yard in Gunapan, only forty minutes' drive from his work in Halstead, and still had enough money for dinner out once a week. Now I'm a single mother with two kids, I could never survive back in the city. I've developed a vision of a life where I, deserted mother scrag, can't get a job in the city, don't know anyone, spiral down the poverty gurgler until I become an over-the-counter pill junkie watching *Judge Judy* in my rented house in a suburb so far from the center of Melbourne it has its own moon. I can't feed the kids because I've spent all our money on an Abserciser off the telly and the chemist keeps asking me has my cold cleared up yet.

"Loretta!" Patsy shouts. "I said, are you a member of the golf club? George is getting into golf in a big way, so I thought we could play a round when she gets here. Apparently the local course isn't too bad."

"No," I mutter, still feeling queasy from my Melbourne vision. "I think you can buy a day pass. It's a bit yellow, though. They're using recycled water on the greens."

The next evening, when Norm drops in, George has arrived. She's sitting on the couch with her arm around Patsy. I've wondered how Norm will react when he finally meets Patsy and George. I haven't told him a lot about my sisters and their families.

"Unbloodybelievable," Norm announces from the doorway, before he's even put a foot in the room.

"What's that?"

He's got something under his arm. Something green, with wheels.

Norm looks down as if he's forgotten he was carrying anything. "Oh, a trike for Jake. Found it when I was rearranging the junk in the yard. It must have been hidden in that tractor rim for years. No, what's unbloodybelievable"—he puts the tricycle on the floor and waves a sheet of paper in my direction—"is this."

"You'd better meet my sister and her friend first."

I introduce them all and Norm stuffs the paper in his pocket before shaking Patsy's hand, then George's. He looks George in the eye and says, "Welcome to Gunapan."

"Thanks," George says, wiping her hand on her jeans. "Into cars?"

"Nah, love, I'm a recycler. Salvage and parts for all things man-made," Norm says. He splays his hands in front of him. They're spectacularly dirty today.

"Norm, didn't I buy you some soap?"

"Don't want to strip the natural oils from my sensitive skin," he says, turning his hands over to examine the palms, which are equally filthy.

In the old cars and house lots that turn up at Norm's junkyard, he finds women's magazines and house-and-garden magazines and reads them cover to cover. Then at unexpected moments he'll give you a beauty tip. "Your hair could do with a lift, Loretta," he'll say. "Have you tried lemon juice to bring out the blond highlights?" Sometimes he puts on a camp voice to do it. Other times, like today, he'll be completely deadpan. Most people don't know how to react, but George looks back at him, equally deadpan.

"Very wise. That must be how you've maintained that remarkable complexion."

Norm's fingers reach up and play gently across his stubble. "Exactly. And I'm very careful about my diet. Not too many colorful foods."

"Like vegetables?" George suggests.

"Exactly," Norm answers.

I'm thrilled that George and Norm are getting on so well. I've never seen Norm be rude to anyone who didn't deserve it, but I was wondering last night how well I actually know him. Sure, Norm's looked out for us like a grandfather since Tony left, but I hardly hear anything about his life before we met him. For all I know he might have been a member of the Ku Klux Klan or the anti-lesbian league of Gunapan.

Norm stays for tea and we cram around the kitchen table with our plates of wild-mushroom risotto. Having George, a two-star chef, in the house, I decided to have a go at something more adventurous than my usual Tuesday-night chops and salad, but the anxiety of cooking for a professional was too much for me. I'm shattered. Now I've drunk a glass of the wine Patsy brought and all my anxiety is gone. The light around the table is glowing golden and everyone is charming and attractive, even Norm. I look at my darling children, full of wonder at their beauty and intelligence.

"Mum, is the rice supposed to be crunchy?" Jake comes in once again with the wrong question at the wrong time.

Patsy leans over and whispers in Jake's ear. The wild mushrooms cost a fortune so I keep chewing, trying to ignore the gritty bits grinding against my teeth. George is telling Norm all about Paris.

"Patsy was writing notes for her book and I was shopping for meals and washing the clothes. Very Gertrude and Alice."

"Right, Gertrude and Alice," Norm says. He looks at me and I smile a knowing smile. George is obviously talking about a fashion label.

"Anyway, Paris has the most amazing charcuteries full of cured meat. I wish my French was better. I pointed at things in the display cabinet and took them home to try and figure out what they were. The most amazing flavors! I never realized you could get so much out of a pig."

Patsy groans. "Here we go. Now we've been to Paris she's obsessed. She's threatening to build a meat-curing shed in the backyard in Carlton. She'll be wanting a piggery next."

"I might have a few odds and ends at the yard to help out with a shed. You could even knock up a smokehouse," Norm remarks. He lifts Jake's books and pencils off the dresser and he and George start sketching smokehouse plans on the back page of an exercise book.

"What was unbloodybelievable?" I finally remember to ask Norm.

He colors a watermelon pink under his stubble. A pink of righteous outrage by the tone of his voice.

"That bloody council has sent me a bloody notice telling me that the yard is 'unsightly' and has to be tidied up." He pulls the crumpled letter from his pocket and hands it to me. "Unsightly? If you call Picasso unsightly! That yard is an abstract interpretation of the changing face of Gunapan,

I'll have you know. It's art. And they want me to clean it up before May."

"Why?" I scan the letter, but it has no explanation of why anyone would care about whether Norm's yard is unsightly or not.

"It's got to be the development."

At last, someone who knows about the development. I should have asked Norm in the first place. He knows everything about this town.

"What's going on, Norm? I saw a big hole in the forest."

"The development," Norm says again, as if he's talking to himself. He's like me—we spend far too much time talking to ourselves, even when people are in the room with us. "What else could it be but the development trying to smarten up the town for when the tourists drive through? That council has got a lot to answer for."

"Sorry." I turn to Patsy and George. "This must be boring for you, but I want to find out about this development thing. They've trashed the forest down on the Bolton Road and—"

"Mike from the council's waste department said he'd seen that councillor Samantha Patterson with a whole lot of blokes in suits, poking around the bushland, and next thing they've got a license to pump water from a spring underneath," Norm butts in.

"Pump water? But this town's desperate for water! If there's water, it should be coming into the town."

"I'll do the dishes," Patsy says, standing and stretching.

"You help Aunty Patsy with the dishes, Liss." I've already worded up Patsy on the bush-pig question, hoping Melissa might feel more inclined to talk to a more glamorous relative. I tow Norm off to the lounge room to interrogate him about what's going on while George takes Jake outside in the last of the evening light to teach him about riding a trike.

By the time Norm's told me everything he knows about the development, which is only that some big corporation bought the land and the council approved the building plans and the pumping of the spring, I'm spent. With Patsy here for two full days already and George for one, I've run out of words. Adult conversation takes so much more work than telling someone to brush their teeth. After Norm heads off to the pub to show his unsightly letter around, I decide to take a catnap before dessert.

9

THE NEXT MORNING at seven o'clock, mouth gluey, skirt rucked up around my waist, blouse twisted into an armlock, I struggle off the bed, calling out that the kids should be getting up now. Melissa pops her head around the door.

"Aunty George is making homemade crumpets for breakfast." She shakes her head reproachfully at me. "You slept in your clothes last night!"

Jake races into the room and throws himself on the bed. "Aunty Patsy says I'm probably the smartest boy she's met in her whole life!"

We're eating crumpets with butter and jam when the doorbell rings. It's too early for anyone I know to visit so I decide to ignore it. Everyone looks at me.

"It's seven thirty! Who could it be? The Queen? Someone's probably asking for money for charity."

The doorbell rings again. I keep chewing my crumpet. I had no idea homemade crumpets were so muscular.

A head passes the kitchen window and a minute later something clatters on the back veranda.

"Wait," I hear Norm say.

George opens the back door. Patsy screams. Jake jumps up from the table and starts running.

"Meet your lawn mower," Norm declares.

The goat stands as high as his waist. It's rubbing its stubby horns up and down the veranda post and pawing at the floorboards.

"Good God." George steps closer to inspect the goat. "Look at the size of that thing. Is it, is it . . . ?"

"It's a goat, George," Norm replies calmly. "Loretta keeps complaining about mowing the lawn. Here's a free lawn mower."

"No," I protest.

"She's a beautiful goat. A lovely nature. She'll be a good family pet as well."

"No."

To my amazement, while Jake is cowering behind the kitchen door—there, he does take after his father—Melissa gets up from her chair and goes over to the goat. She leans down and presses her face into the goat's neck and sniffs. Then she moves around in front of it and looks into its eyes.

"Hello, goat," she says.

The goat pushes its head forward and gently butts her shoulder. I feel Patsy's hand take mine and squeeze it under the table. Melissa has her arms around the goat's neck and she's leaning her face against its creamy curly coat.

"I hope that goat's clean," I say to Norm. Norm shrugs, picking something black and crumbly off his pants and flicking it into the yard before he speaks.

"Animals have their own kind of clean."

We're all mesmerized by Melissa, who seems to have turned into a goat whisperer. The goat's nuzzling her right hand, and with her other hand she's stroking its chest.

"Is it a male or a female?" I ask Norm.

"Female," he answers. "You don't want a buck. Very smelly, bucks."

"Can I give it some crumpet?" Melissa asks George, who graciously agrees that Melissa can feed her two-star crumpet to an animal of a species known to eat clothes and the clothesline they came on.

The goat nibbles the crumpet from Melissa's hand. Without my noticing, Norm, Melissa, and the goat seem to have edged further and further forward so that now they are in the kitchen. As if it can hear my thoughts the goat turns to me and burps loudly.

"No," I protest again.

Melissa swings around from goat adoration to give me her well-practiced "evil mother" look.

"No goats in the kitchen." I have to take a stand. Norm and Melissa and the goat start backing out the door. They jam up halfway and have to wriggle around. It's the goat that clatters out backward first.

"It has to have a wash."

"I'll help Melissa with that," Patsy the traitor says.

"Never in the house."

Everyone nods. I realize they're all against me.

"We don't know how to look after it."

"Nothing to it." His jolly tone says that Norm knows he's won. "Let it eat the lawn and give it some feed from the livestock feed shop. A bit of water, and you're right. My mate who owns goats'll drop by now and again to check it's OK."

"I'm not picking up its poo."

Strangely, no one jumps in to solve that problem.

"I said, I'm not picking up its poo. If you want to keep it, Liss, you have to clean up after it."

"I will," she calls out from the veranda, where she's still busy having a goat love-in.

Norm leans in and whispers to her. At least, he thinks he's whispering. Norm's slowly going deaf, but he hasn't realized yet.

"Don't worry about the poo," he whispers to Melissa so loudly that the light fittings rattle. "It'll just go back into the land."

Melissa rushes into the kitchen to give me five sloppy kisses on the cheek. "Thanks, Mum. Thanks for letting us have her." Then she's back outside. Who could have guessed my daughter would fall in love with a goat? Staying in the country was a mistake, I knew it.

"How about you, Jake?" George asks. "What do you think of the goat?"

Like a grown man, Jake is reluctant to admit to being afraid of anything. Instead, he'll wait till the final minute of terror when he can't take it any longer and he'll burst into tears and start blubbering for his mummy. I recognize that quivering-underlip-and-stiff-upper-lip look.

"Terror," I say to George, at exactly the same time as Patsy asks, "What are you going to call it, Liss?"

"Yeah, that's great." Melissa is only half-listening.

"Terror's an unusual name," Patsy says, looking at me with her eyes wide.

Terror the goat? This could be some kind of warning from the universe.

"What about Daisy?" I suggest. "Or Olive? Or Jodie or Julia or Kim?"

"I like Terror," Melissa says firmly.

"You mean Terra as in 'earth,' right?" My wonderful, wonderful sister.

"I guess so," Melissa answers, mumbling because she has her face mashed into the goat's coat.

That will do. Terra. Although I know from now on I'll always think of the goat as Terror.

"Take Terror down to the yard and introduce her to her new home while I have a word with Norm," I tell Melissa.

Norm turns hurriedly. He's halfway down the veranda steps before I can even point the finger of blame.

"See you tomorrow, Loretta," he calls over his shoulder. We head to the front of the house to watch him from the front door. He's made it to his truck in record time. That old gammy leg doesn't seem to be playing up this morning. "I'll bring some stuff for Terror. 'Bye, George, 'bye, Patsy. Let me know if you need any materials for that smokehouse!" His last words are drifting off into the distance because he's already backed out of the drive and turned into the road.

After I've dropped Jake and Melissa at school, I come back and sit on the veranda with Patsy and George. We sip cups of tea, watching Terror munching her way through every speck of green in the yard.

"It adds a nice pastoral touch, having the goat." Patsy must be warming to our rural paradise where children fall in love with goats. "Of course, it's you who'll be picking up the poo."

"I know. So did Melissa tell you anything about the bush-pig business?"

Patsy rubs her forehead. "She said school was no fun anymore, but she didn't mention a bush pig. She mentioned some new girl."

Terror clops up the veranda steps and looks menacingly at Patsy, who hands over her biscuit.

"Don't do that, darling," George says. "You'll encourage it."

"I'm not saying no to that brute." Patsy hands Terror the last biscuit off the plate. Terror swallows and burps, noses the plate, jumps off the veranda, and returns to stripping the trees in the yard.

"What about the new girl?"

"It was hard to make out what she was on about. You know how kids tell a story as if you already know half of it? She was talking about a war, how the girl had been in a war."

I knew there was something odd about the family I saw sitting away from everyone at the waterhole. They seemed so alone up on the ridge, five silhouettes against the white-blue sky of late afternoon. They probably never even made it to the water, what with the whole town watching them take every step down that hill. I remember when I first came here with Tony, how people stopped their conversations and turned and stared when I walked by. Mind you, that was probably because they were wondering what kind of bird-brain had hooked up with Tony. If only someone had said something . . .

"When are you going to send the kids down to stay with us?" George asks.

My neck cracks with the speed of my head turning.

"You want to look after Melissa and Jake?"

"For a few days," George answers quickly. "We wouldn't want them to get homesick."

Patsy's looking dubious. She's told me about the time they had Tammy's children to stay. James, twelve years old, suggested that George should have put a little more pesto in the lamb crust. Eliza, nine, tripped the power overload switch in the house one night by using a hair dryer, a hair straightener, electric tweezers, an electric footbath for softening feet before a pedicure, and a neck massager all at once. When the power

73

came back on, Eliza wanted to go home because her hair had gone frizzy and she needed the gel she'd left in her bathroom.

"*Her* bathroom?" I asked.

"The new house," Patsy said. "They each have a bathroom. They're using enough water to irrigate the Mallee."

"I suppose I could let the kids go for a couple of weeks," I say, giddy with excitement.

"Days, Loretta, a couple of days."

"Five days?" I offer. "Six?"

If I could have a holiday from the children I love so much I sometimes want to smother them, who knows how my life would improve. I might take up gardening and cake decorating. I might discover a talent for painting watercolors or writing poetry. Brilliant small-business ideas would pop into my head as I worked up a sweat jogging around the Wilson Dam, knocking one more centimeter off my tiny waist and toning my long slender thighs.

"Oops, hang on a tick," I tell Patsy and George, putting down my chipped mug. "Got to get the chicken fillets out of the freezer for tonight."

When I get back the tea party is over. Patsy and George are packing their things inside, and Terror is nosing around the plates, checking for crumbs.

"Shoo! Off the veranda, Terror," I say. Terror stares at me without budging. She has pale green eyes and black horizontal pupils. "People sacrifice your type to the devil," I tell her. "Shoo." I point down the stairs, but Terror bends her head toward my hand. Her top lip stretches out and, like a hand in a mitten, her lips probe all over my fingers and the back of my palm. "You are one spooky goat," I tell her, drawing my hand away and stroking her side. Her coat is softer than it looks. She pushes her head against my belly.

"Sucked in," George says from the doorway. "I guess I won't be making goat curry out of that one."

"It's not a pet, George. It's a lawn mower."

"Sure. Next time we come I bet the lawn mower has its own place set at the table."

Terror nudges me once more before she heads back down into the yard.

"How about Easter?" Patsy says from behind George. "The kids can come and stay for a few days. I'll take a break from uni. We can do the aquarium, things like that."

"Great." That's all I have to say. Otherwise, I'm speechless. This will be my first holiday from the children in eleven years. I can see myself transformed. The pudge has magically fallen from my hips and I'm wearing a long, slinky silk dress. I'm in the function room of the golf course, tossing my newly blond-streaked hair and full of ennui or some other French feeling at these boring rich men crowding around me. I'm certain something like this will happen when I'm child-free. All I need to do is to stop eating immediately.

In the meantime, it's only a week until the minister comes to Gunapan. We have to get organized.

10

AT TEN THIRTY-FOUR on the day chosen for his Gunapan tour, the minister arrives in the manner of royalty, chauffeured inside a big white car that glides soundlessly to a stop in front of us. He steps out of the car, unplugs the mobile earpiece from his ear and tucks it into his suit pocket, smooths back his hair with the heel of his palm, and clears his throat.

We're standing in a line along the school fence like a bunch of schoolkids. The headmaster steps out of the welcoming committee line to thrust a hand in the minister's direction.

"Welcome to Gunapan, Minister."

The minister gives a regal nod.

I remember the day I first heard they were going to close the primary school. My whole pathetic do-as-you're-told life reared up in front of me and I said, "No, I'm not going to be walked over again. I'm going to stop this."

Helen, always supportive, suggested, "Can you end world poverty and bring peace to the Middle East while you're at it?"

Norm asked how my four-year-old découpage project was going.

They were both right. I've never finished anything in my

life. The ghost of some radical from the sixties must have taken over my body. I started using words like *mobilize* and *comrade*. Norm nicknamed me the Gunna Panther. I wrote letters and painted signs and demonstrated in front of the school to a crowd of mothers picking up their children while Melissa hid, humiliated, on the floor of the car. Jake did a protest war dance—one of the mothers thought he was busking and threw him a dollar.

Now, finally, the Minister for Education, Elderly Care and Gaming is here to visit Gunapan Primary School on his way to open a new agricultural campus farther up the highway, and I'm struck dumb. The radical spirit has deserted me, and all I can think about is how to ruff up my blouse to hide the butter stain from Jake's greasy breakfast fingers.

In front of the school, the minister, the mayor, and the headmaster shake hands vigorously, nodding and looking around, frowning and smiling in turn, as if they're having a whole conversation without words. After a moment I realize the minister's flummoxed because no one's taking his picture. I pull my old Kodak from my handbag and aim it. The flash lights up the gathering and the minister, obviously relieved, lets go of the headmaster's hand. I meant to get film yesterday, but the chemist told me it's cheaper to buy a new digital camera than to process three rolls of film so I didn't bother.

We've planned a tight half-day's entertainment for the minister—primary school, Country Women's Association, local industry, and lunch at the pub, where he can see his portfolios of elderly care and gaming taken care of simultaneously in the gambling room.

Last week we had a meeting about the visit. The first thirty minutes was spent discussing what we're supposed to call the minister. The headmaster was convinced we should address him as "Minister." Norm wanted to call him "mate." I preferred "Mr. Deguilio," but in the vote I lost because half the people in the room couldn't pronounce it.

"And if we mess it up we'll sound like a bunch of hicks," Helen said, as if that would be a surprise.

First stop is morning tea at the Country Women's Association Hall. The minister tells his driver to wait because he'd like to walk and see a bit of the town so we follow the mayor and the minister in file down the street. Bowden, our very own local hooligan, drives past in his hotted-up Torana, leaning on the horn the whole way to the milk bar, where he screams to a stop with a flourish of smoking tires.

"Membership of the CWA is very strong in Gunapan," the mayor tells the minister on the way into the hall. We crowd inside and jostle for a place near the food. "We're a tight-knit community, working together, and the CWA has a proud history in this town. If we have an emergency such as a bushfire, the CWA ladies make tea and sandwiches for the volunteer firefighters and prepare bedding for anyone who's had to abandon their home."

"Homemade country scones." The minister breathes a sigh of pleasure as he sits in front of the mound of freshly baked scones Kyleen bought first thing this morning at the supermarket. "You don't get food like this in the city anymore. It's all focaccias and squid-ink pasta."

"We have focaccias too, Mr. Minister," Kyleen says, "but I've never heard of skidding pasta." She pulls out the chair beside the minister and the headmaster dances around behind them in a panic. I don't think Kyleen's his first choice for ambassador of Gunapan.

"I always thought black pasta looked odd anyway," the

minister replies. He takes the cup of tea Kyleen has poured for him and helps himself to a scone.

On that signal, the rest of us launch ourselves in rugby-team fashion at the two trestle tables, load up with the scones and jam and cream, and settle down on the seats around the walls for our free feed.

I'm stuffing the last scone into my mouth when the headmaster sidles up. He's gripping his saucer so tightly the cup is rattling.

"You've got to do something about Kyleen," he hisses.

I look over and Kyleen waves to me. She's sporting a cream moustache. So's the minister. Kyleen's laughing. She leans in and whispers in his ear, leans back and laughs again.

"What? They seem to be having a great time."

"Kyleen's telling him the story of last year's power blackout."

I scuttle over, still chewing my scone, and stand beside Kyleen, grinning like an idiot.

"That's so funny, Kyleen. Maybe . . ." I interrupt as she gets to the part where Norm's stripping the copper wire from the old electricity substation while farther down the road the newly privatized power company is preparing to run a test surge on the safety equipment they've installed.

"Norm's never had a lot of hair," Kyleen goes on, ignoring me. "Well, not that anyone can remember."

She explains to the minister how she happened to be driving backward past the old substation at the time because every other gear in her car had stopped working and it was the only way she could get to the mechanic.

"Jeez, I got a crick in my neck. And as I'm passing the substation—"

The minister's smile is so rigid it's as though someone

sprayed his face with quickset cement. I imagine this is one of the skills a politician needs.

"Minister!" I shout. "We're running behind schedule. It's time to visit Morelli's Meats."

"Oh, we'd better be off. Terribly sorry to miss the end of your story." The minister puts out his hand to shake with Kyleen, who offers to ride in the government car with him so she can finish. But the headmaster has placed his hands affectionately on her shoulders and when she tries to stand she finds herself clamped to the seat. The mayor waves at me to hurry the minister away.

So I'm stuck with him. I rush him outside and take another pretend photo in front of the CWA Hall before racing him back to the car. Kyleen's in the background of the shot, struggling to get away from the headmaster.

"Can you send copies of those photos to my office?" He's panting as we charge along the footpath.

"No problem, Mr. Deluglo."

The emails we got from his staff before this visit requested a tour of local industry. We thought hard. The Social Security office is the obvious center of industry in this town. Most of us spend at least half a day a week in there trying to sort out missed payments or overpayments or underpayments or having a chat because it's the one place you know you'll find certain people on a Thursday morning. But that portfolio belongs to another minister.

Gabrielle from the Neighbourhood House Committee was eager to entertain the minister at her property, but we voted against letting him go to the big farms because they're the ones with money and he'd never believe how the rest of us live.

It was Norm who thought of Morelli's Meats.

"He can take a side of beef home for the barbie. And you've got to admit, they have a mighty presence in the town."

It's true. The monthly tallow and glue melt on a day with a north wind is something visitors never forget.

Mario Morelli was thrilled to be selected to represent the town's industry.

"We'll give him the full tour! I'll make sure everyone's got clean smocks." He patted Heck on the back. "I hope he comes on a butchery day. Youse people don't understand the skills Hector's got with a cleaver. He's a bloody artist."

When the minister and I arrive back at his car the driver is sprawled in the passenger seat reading the newspaper.

"Do you know how to get to the next stop?" the minister asks him, and the driver puffs scorn out through his nose.

"My charioteer," the minister says. "Honestly, you are a marvel, Nick. I don't . . ."

He's talking to no one because Nick's already in the driver's seat, fondling the steering wheel and gently revving the engine. Gunapan hasn't seen a car this shiny since my husband, Tony, did a runner in Delilah, the CRX.

The mayor's waiting for us outside Morelli's Meats. The pens in the slaughter yard are empty, so we're lucky. After he lost his first driving job in Halstead Tony did a stint here, which is how I know that slaughter day's the one to avoid. The staff turnover is very high, and we don't want the minister chatting to a trainee with a bolt gun.

Mario hurries out, pulling off his plastic apron and flinging it back to his son, who is hurrying behind. He wipes his hands on his trousers and steps up, arm outstretched, to the minister, who takes the hand and pumps.

"Mario Morelli, Morelli's Meats, Minister."

"Looking forward to seeing your men at work, Mr. Morelli."

Not to be left out, the mayor steps up. I sigh and drag out the empty Kodak, but luckily the cadet reporter from the *Shire Herald* is pulling up at the curb. He lifts a camera with a paparazzi-sized lens from a bag over his shoulder, and the minister's smile widens.

"Minister, could we have you shaking hands with Mario again? And the mayor?" the reporter says.

After they've finished the handshaking fiesta, Mario escorts us on the tour. The abattoir is white and clean—and empty. Mario hurries us through the killing room, the freezer filled with carcasses on hooks, the penning yard, the loading dock, and the staff room. When we reach a door we've already passed three times as we zigzagged through the building, Mario pauses, his hand on the knob.

"Minister, you are about to see art in motion. It's unusual to be doing this work at an abattoir, but when we found out what Hector could do, we couldn't let him go. So we run our own butcher shop as well as the abattoir." He swings open the door, the minister steps inside, and applause breaks out.

Half the town is inside the room. They must have sneaked in the back during our tour. They're sitting in rows facing a stainless-steel cutting bench where Hector stands, cleaver in one hand, rib cage of the pink and white fatty carcass of an enormous cow being massaged by the other. I'd never realized how tiny Hector is. He gives off an air of being a big man, but now I see that two and a half Hectors would fit inside that cow.

Norm waves to me from the front row. Kyleen's sitting next to the headmaster at the back. The staff of the abattoir take up the middle row. They are wearing glaringly white smocks and hats that remind me of shower caps, and their arms are folded to show off their tattoos to best advantage.

"Oh God," the reporter moans with pleasure, "I've got a great headline for this: *Meat the Minister.*"

The minister and the mayor get the seats directly in front of the bench. I move to the side and stand beside Mario and the reporter, who's scribbling fast and giggling to himself.

"Heck, you ready?" Mario calls.

Hector cracks his knuckles and flexes his arms, reaches over, and flicks the switch to start the band saw at one end of the long bench. A selection of cleavers and knives hangs from hooks above him.

"We had this bench made up specially for Hector after he won the state championship," Mario tells the reporter.

Hector steps away from the cutting bench, rolls his neck, and touches his toes twice. He moves back up to the bench and wrangles the monstrous carcass into his arms.

"Ready."

Mario holds the stopwatch up for the audience to see. As he presses the button he shouts, "Go!"

In the next thirteen minutes and twenty-four seconds, Hector slices the carcass down the middle, leaps up on the bench and wrestles the legs off, hammers the meat with a mallet that he seems to have pulled out of his T-shirt, carves slabs of meat from every part of the carcass, zooms more sections through the band saw, and thrusts his arm up to the shoulder into parts of the cow that magically fall apart into cuts of meat. The air gets thick with minute particles of meat and bone and gristle, and all the while Hector's grunting and shouting.

"Round!" he calls as he flings a fan-shaped selection of rump cuts to the front of the bench. "Rib eye! Brisket!"

"Done!" he screams, dropping his knife on the bench and raising his hands into the air. We turn to Mario, who's staring at the stopwatch.

"Holy Jesus," Mario whispers. "He's broken his own record."

It takes ten minutes for the applause and cheering to die down. The abattoir blokes crowd around Hector, slapping him on the back and punching him and hugging him.

"It's not official because we didn't have an independent timekeeper," Mario's telling the reporter, "but it shows you—Heck hasn't even reached his peak. We're going to take out the Australia-wide. Youse people don't understand the talent we've got in this town."

"Mario, you've been hiding this bloke away!" the mayor says. "We could get him on TV."

"He's got a big future. He's only nineteen."

We all look at Heck. I would have picked him as thirty-five.

"Outdoor work," Mario says, shaking his head.

The mayor keeps brushing at his robe. It's an odd mottled color. I reach over to pick a bone chip from his gold chain.

"Don't worry, that'll clean up. It was worth it to see Heck perform. He's a champion."

"The minister?" I ask.

Out in the yard Norm's got hold of a wet cloth and he's wiping the minister down while Nick, the charioteer, leans against the car, watching.

"Bit of a dry clean and the suit'll be fine. There, that feels better, doesn't it?" Norm's talking all cheery, like he's pacifying a child. The minister stands with his arms out. He raises his face to Norm to have it wiped. I think he's regressed. We can't send him back to Melbourne like this.

"School's next!" I say. "Let's get cleaned up before the choir."

The driver holds open the door while Norm and I help the minister into the car. Halfway to the school he snaps back to his old self, plugs himself into the mobile, and talks gobbledegook to someone about outcomes and competencies. When he pulls out the earplug he's got the concrete smile back, festooned with a morsel of raw steak glued to his upper lip.

"Fascinating. What an experience," he says. "So next it's the school?"

This would be the denial stage.

"Maybe we'll freshen up first at the Neighbourhood House," I suggest. We don't want him to go frightening the children.

"Good idea," he replies cheerfully.

In the front of the car Nick swats a fly away from the windscreen.

11

THE HEADMASTER'S TAKEN my signs off the school fence. I was happy with the misspelled one. It looked like one of the kids had made it. Now the schoolyard's back to its usual self. Waist-high cyclone wire fence, a few bedraggled trees, adventure equipment that stopped having adventures years ago. The education department seems to have forgotten the school already. Heat rises from the asphalt in the yard, and cicadas make attempts at calls that peter out after a few strokes like a chain saw that won't catch. I wonder if everyone arrived here before us, or if they've gone to the pub to celebrate Heck's record.

The door of the school opens and the grade-three teacher bounds down the steps and pitter-patters toward us, his hands waving and his little belly bouncing. I must remember to tell Helen I think he's gay.

"Minister, welcome to Gunapan Primary. We've prepared a tour for you, nothing too boring or too long. I understand you must see the same thing over and over again so we won't keep you, but we want you to know that you won't find a more dedicated staff or a better-run school than this. At the end of the day, what you're getting here is value for money, Minister, value for money."

The minister nods. He's still a little dazed, but back at the Neighbourhood House a brisk rub with a washcloth brought him back to reality. After I'd twisted the washcloth corner into a bud and cleaned out his ears he'd asked if he could go to the toilet.

"Yes, but hurry up, we haven't got all day," I told him. "And don't forget to wash your hands."

The Basic Ed kids were coming out of the Neighbourhood House classroom and two Down syndrome boys rushed into the toilet after the minister. I knew they'd be staring at him in that unnerving intent way they have, but I could hardly follow them into the men's toilet. Sure enough, after a few seconds I heard one boy shriek and giggle. Damien ran out of the toilet, his big flat feet slapping on the tiles and his hands flapping.

"The man farted!" he screamed, and laughed until he began to snort.

Tina, the Basic Ed teacher, came and stood beside me. She draped her arm around her giggling son, for whom the funniest thing in the world always has been, and always will be, farting. "Shut up, Damien. Who's in the toilet?" she asked.

"The Minister for Education, Elderly Care and Gaming," I told her.

"Oh, ha ha. Come on, kids, let's go," she called, and the boys tumbled off after her. A few seconds later the minister walked out.

"Ready, Mr. Degugulo?" I asked.

"Yes, thank you," he answered in a high-pitched voice, and walked unsteadily to the car.

Now I'm following the grade-three teacher, who is ushering the minister up the steps of the school and gabbling as if he's snorted speed.

"One hundred and twenty-three children, four teachers, and three teachers' aides, you can't complain about that for efficiency, Minister. Productivity up eleven percent in the last two years. All local children. We have a need, oh yes, we have a real need in the community. Where would they go, you ask? They'd have to go to a school forty kilometers away, a one-hour bus ride with all the pickups along the way, that's two hours' travel a day, into a school that already has seven hundred children. We run a sports program, oh no, you won't find an obesity problem in this school population . . ." He pauses, looks down, and pats his paunch. "Well, maybe the teachers could use a little work, but the children are fit and healthy and the grades they're getting, Minister, we're in the top twenty in the state for that even though . . ."

I drop back discreetly as he leads the minister into the headmaster's office, where the headmaster has appeared in a clean suit and spectacles, sitting behind his desk and shuffling papers.

"Where are you?" I ask Helen on the mobile. "I'm alone here with a traumatized member of parliament and a grade-three teacher who's taken mind-altering drugs. Did I tell you I think he's gay?"

"Figures. I'm on my way. We had an emergency at the surgery and I had to stay an extra half-hour while the doc fixed the guy up. Some idiot from the abattoir with a bone splinter in his eye."

I'm standing on the school steps when she pulls up.

"What do you want me to do?" she asks.

"I don't know. We've had a couple of hiccups. Heck dismembered a cow and spattered the minister with gore."

"Oh."

"And Kyleen told him all about Norm stripping the copper wire from the old substation."

"Oh."

"That's probably OK. I think that's all wiped from his memory. But now what? I didn't think this through, Helen. A visit to the school isn't going to change his mind. Every school can trot out a choir."

"I'm not so sure they all have a fire-eating team."

"Oh, God. I thought that teacher ran off to learn the lute in Nimbin."

"He left the gift of the grade-four circus club. They can all swallow fire. But I think it's only a demo with three girls today."

I close my eyes. If I believed in a compassionate God I'd pray. *Please, Your Benevolence, don't let the minister catch fire.* I'm sure all that fat from the abattoir is flammable. I can see it now. We're on track to send the minister back emotionally shattered, smeared with blood and bone, and barbecued. Of course you can keep your school, they'll say. Gunapan's an example to us all.

"We have to do something to convince him," I say. "What? What?"

The strains of "I Still Call Australia Home" are drifting from the classroom window. Helen winces.

"I knew they'd never hit that high note. Well, look over there. Who might that be?" Helen nods at Nick, the driver, who is still reading the paper. He must be memorizing it.

"The charioteer. At least that's what the minister calls him. Ministerial driver."

"So maybe Ben-Hur will have an idea. He probably knows this minister fella better than anyone." Helen turns away from me and pokes around in her handbag for what seems like only a moment. When she turns back, her face is fully made up and she's dabbing at her fresh lipstick with a tissue.

Nick watches us warily as we approach the gleaming chariot. He pulls a chamois from his back pocket and erases a fingerprint smudge from the passenger door. The performance reminds me of the way dogs sniff around the grass with feigned nonchalance when another dog approaches. He's a big man with thick upper arms and a sumo-wrestler kind of sway to his body when he walks.

"The car looks beautiful," Helen says to him. "Must be hard work keeping it so—"

"Ladies, no need to beat about the bush. How can I help you?" Nick's voice is deep and throaty. He flicks a mote of dust off the windscreen with the corner of his chamois before he leans back against the driver's door and folds his arms across his chest. I can tell Helen has taken a fancy to him by the way she's clutching my arm so tightly gangrene is setting in. He's a good-looking bloke, all right, but I don't think she should get her hopes up—after all, he's leaving town in one hour and fourteen minutes. That's even faster than your average Gunapan husband.

"Well, it's just that . . . well, you know, the minister is here because my friend Loretta"—she gestures back at me, even though I have become nothing to her in the presence of this shining knight—"organized all these petitions and letters and everything and got the headmaster and the mayor to sign and all that to try and stop them closing Gunapan Primary School." She pauses to take a deep breath. "And now the minister's here and we want to get him to change his mind, but he's had some bad experiences and we don't know what to do." Another breath. "And we thought that since you drive him around you must know lots about him and stuff and maybe you could, you know, give us some hints on how to—"

Nick raises his hand, which I notice is muscular also.

"I'd love to help. Especially when I'm asked for assistance by a stunning lady like yourself . . ."

I'm sure I hear Helen simper. I never knew how a simper sounded before today. She's going to start fanning herself and talking in a *Gone with the Wind* accent next.

"What can you do?" I ask. "I've been on the case for seven months and all I've got is a visit."

"Leave it to me. I'll have a word with the big man."

Right. While Helen continues her flirting I sigh and turn to watch the minister being herded down the steps of the school by the headmaster and the grade-three teacher, who's still talking at an incredible speed. I want to cry. All those months writing letters and calling people and chairing meetings that hardly anyone came to. And for nothing except a chance to see Hector disassemble a cow in record time. Which actually was amazing but doesn't help my kids.

The minister folds back into his car and reappears at his final destination, the Criterion, which used to be all green tiles and ancient toothless farmers propping up the bar, but has been renovated and is now pink and lemon with a new menu that includes confit of duck as well as some old favorites like surf and turf. The ancient toothless farmers have moved to the gambling machine room out the back.

We're having a set lunch in the dining lounge, paid for by my fund-raising efforts with the chocolate drive back in November, but I don't have any appetite. Helen's in the bar with Nick. I can see her through the servery hatch, simpering and fanning herself with a beer coaster. Nick notices me watching and gives a thumbs-up. I wonder if he's indicating his chances with Helen. He'd better get a move on. The minister's schedule has him out of here in eleven minutes.

When the minister stands up to give a speech, which he promises will only take a few minutes, I keep poking at my chicken parma. I think about what will happen to the school grounds when the school closes. Maybe they'll build a housing estate on the site. Couples will move in. They'll grow vegetable gardens and paint their houses and have babies. The mothers will start a campaign. A school for Gunapan! They'll paint signs and write letters and one day the Education Department will send a portable classroom and a teacher. Meanwhile, because it's Gunapan, the husbands will have mysteriously disappeared.

I only notice the minister's gone when Helen claps me on the back and sighs.

"That chauffeur! What a man. I'm in love."

I sniff and poke a little harder at the parma sauce.

"Aren't you excited?" she asks.

The headmaster and the mayor come back inside and order beers. It's the middle of the day. I've never seen the headmaster drink, even at night.

"To Loretta!" they shout, and raise their glasses.

"And to Nick!" Helen calls out, and swigs from her wineglass.

"Who?" the headmaster says.

They're crowded around me, laughing and talking about Heck's show and making plans for the biggest fete in the history of the school.

"It's not closing?" I say.

"Didn't you hear the minister? Changing demographics,

supporting the country constituency, the last meeting of the education advisory committee, blah blah blah. You did it, Loretta!"

The grade-three teacher bounds into the pub's dining room, brandishing a letter.

"They're not closing us down! This arrived today!"

"Old news, mate," Mario Morelli says. "Have a beer."

"That must be why the minister kept staring at me with this meaningful look," the grade-three teacher says musingly. "I'd finish saying something and he'd stare as though I was supposed to add something else, and it made me prattle away as if I was on speed. He must have been expecting me to say thank you."

Helen looks longingly through the open door at the puff of dust left by Nick's chariot. Even though the decision must have been made weeks ago, she clearly believes Nick rode in to save us.

"What's the catch?" I look around. I've lived in Gunapan for thirteen years. I know things aren't this easy.

"Catch? What catch?" the headmaster says, stretching his mouth in an unconvincing smile. "Drink up, Loretta."

"You'll have to tell me sometime."

"Let's have a nice drink and enjoy your victory."

Usually the headmaster enjoys the job of predicting dire consequences. Usually you can't stop him spreading bad news like jam on toast.

Something else occurs to me. "What's this about the development and Samantha Patterson?" I turn and ask Vaughan, the mayor. "What's going on?"

"Samantha Patterson? She's not involved with the development. That portfolio belongs to Chris Dunn. By all accounts the development is going to be great for this town.

So don't start on that, Loretta. Look! Here's Hector, the other man of the moment."

The headmaster pours champagne into my glass, and it froths over the rim like the lacy dress of a Southern belle.

"To us," I say to Helen, raising my glass.

"To Gunapan," she answers, and we down our drinks.

Don't start on that, the mayor says. But I can't help myself. Something is wrong with that development. Someone has to act. I'm the Gunna Panther.

12

"**HE'S GOT A** bloody cheek." Tina's talking on the phone when I walk into the Neighbourhood House office. She glances over her shoulder at me and smiles, then says, "OK, gotta go, talk to you soon," and hangs up the phone.

"Getting cooler at last," I remark as I hang my jacket on the peg behind the door. "How come you're still here?"

"Have to get this stuff out to the parents."

With five teachers and three part-time staff in the tiny office of the Neighbourhood House you'd think we'd be falling over each other, but our schedules rarely cross. Apart from running into her when I was dragging the minister around town, I haven't spoken to Tina for a month. She comes in to teach the Basic Education students who arrive by bus once a week to learn cooking and housekeeping skills. They race up to the office counter and push their round grinning faces in through the window. They are always laughing and joking except when they throw a tantrum and Tina has to physically restrain them.

Her son, Damien, sits beside her now, stuffing envelopes and licking the flaps with his sloppy tongue.

"Hi, Loretta," he says, smiling with drool running down his chin.

"Damien, clean up your face for heaven's sake." Tina holds out a tissue to him.

"Do you ever go to shire meetings?" I ask Tina.

"God no, why?"

"Just wondering. I'm trying to find out about this development and no one knows anything but gossip."

"I heard there's some commercial secrecy thing."

"See? I bet you don't even know what it is."

"It's a resort with a golf course and a spa and accommodation. Everyone knows that."

"But we've got a golf course!"

"It's not for us, Loretta. It's a resort for rich people. From outside, you know, who come to the resort and stay a few days and get pampered and go home."

"That's crazy. Gunapan's an ordinary town in a dry country on a dry road that's been in drought for seven years. Why would anyone want to come here?"

"Loretta, stop being dense. I told you, they won't come to Gunapan. They'll probably come by helicopter or limousine or something. We'll never see them. Don't worry about it."

"But the water!" I'm almost shouting now. "They're taking the water!"

"No, they've got their own spring," Tina says, sounding as cross as me. "They're not touching our water."

"But . . ." There's no point shouting at Tina. Doesn't anyone understand that the water under the ground should be ours? For Gunapan people and the farmers around us, water is life: water is crops, it's native animals surviving drought, it's one swimming pool for a thousand people. It's community. Those wealthy people will pour the water into perfumed spa baths and carve it into ice sculptures for parties. They'll use it to wash their already pristine recreational vehicles and hose stray leaves off the driveways of the resort.

"They say it'll generate twenty jobs for locals." Tina nods. "That bush land was a tip anyway. People dumped their rubbish there. It stank."

"Not before, it didn't. It used to be beautiful. It was green and quiet and cool." Of course, I get it now. It was green and cool when everywhere else was dry and hot because it had water underneath—the spring. Smart developers.

"Oh my God, he's back," Damien says to me in a monotone, still with a goofy grin. He's obviously repeating what he's heard, and Tina flushes a deep red.

"Did I tell you to clean up your face?" she says sharply.

"Who's back?" I ask.

"I can't bear it, I'll have to do it myself." She stands up and grasps Damien's hand to pull him toward the bathroom.

The phone starts ringing as soon as I sit down at the desk.

"Do you have patchwork classes?"

"I can't pay my power bill and they say they're going to cut me off next Monday."

I wander out to the kitchen for a cup of tea and stand by the window while the kettle boils. Sometimes this job wears you down. Everyone wants something. Outside the window a horse is straining over the barbed-wire fence of the paddock next door trying to reach a clump of green grass. The fence is decorated with shredded plastic bags that have been caught there in the wind. The earth of the paddock is baked like the brown dry top of a burned pie.

Back in the office, the phone rings again.

"Is that you, Loretta?" Helen asks.

"Mmm," I answer, my mouth full of teddy bear biscuit.

"He's back."

"Mwah? Phoo?"

"Him! The bastard!"

"Phoo oo meem?" I don't want to believe her. Why would he come back?

"I saw him. He was driving down past the supermarket toward the bridge. He's cut his hair, but it was him. Same car, the CRX."

For a moment there is silence on the line.

"I'm coming to the House. Don't move." Helen hangs up.

I can't move. I can't even swallow the teddy bear biscuit that's turned to dry crumbs in my mouth. What will happen when Jake and Melissa see their father? Does he want to take them? Would they go with him? Does he want to come back to us?

By the time Helen arrives I'm molded to the orange plastic office chair. My husband's return has flipped me back into the old Loretta, the Loretta who fretted and chewed her fingernails and smoked a packet of Winfields a day and rang around people's houses trying to track down her husband to ask him to bring back some milk, but in reality to find out where he was. The Loretta who nagged her children and let her hair go lank and was too nervous to even try to find a job because she knew she was too stupid to keep one. Just like that, the old Loretta is back because her husband is.

"Whatever you're thinking, you're wrong." Helen plonks a second strong cup of tea on the desk in front of me.

The tea is too hot to drink, but I take a scalding sip anyway to loosen the biscuit clag welded to the roof of my mouth.

"I'm not thinking anything. I can't think," I tell her. My scalp is so tight I feel like a ballerina.

"Do you want me to follow him, find out what he's doing?"

I shake my head.

"Do you want me to kill him?"

I nod. Then laugh a little. "And trash the CRX. Have you got any idea how much money he spent on that car?"

"I kind of guessed when I saw him licking the trim one time."

I choke on my tea.

"Good to laugh in times of crisis," she says, thumping me on the back.

After Helen heads off, I work hard for the rest of the day, trying not to think of him. His name barely crosses my mind. After all this time and after hearing everyone else call him "that bastard" and "whatshisname" and "the ex" so often, he has become those things to me. Even though the children and I carry his surname, Boskovic. What a surname for someone called Loretta. He turned my name into a tongue-twister. I try not to think of him, and I spend half the day running to the toilet because I think I'm going to throw up and the other half having flashbacks of our life together, the stomping angry life made for us by that bastard.

In the evening, as I'm dishing up macaroni and cheese with bits of vegetable cunningly hidden inside, I tell the kids that their father has been seen around town.

"Is he coming to visit?" Jake asks, as if this is some distant friend of the family.

"Of course he is." Melissa is so excited she drops a spoonful of macaroni in her lap. "He's come back for us. I knew he'd come back."

I make another slice through the crusty bread-crumb top of the macaroni and cheese and serve myself a massive helping.

"I'm sure he'll call soon," I say finally.

But he doesn't. Three days pass. Every day I think this will be the day he calls. People ring to tell me what he's doing. He drank at the pub Wednesday and Thursday nights. He played pool. He visited this bloke and that bloke, he took his car to Merv Bull to have the injectors cleaned, he bought four hubcaps from Norm. He met a woman who got off the bus late on Friday night and kissed her, then went back to his pub room with her.

Melissa's mood is black by the end of the week.

"It's you," she accuses me. "He doesn't want to see you so he won't come around."

She's only eleven years old, I keep telling myself. "He's busy, that's all. He'll be around soon."

Meanwhile, all I can do is go on doing what I always do. At the Neighbourhood House I sit in on the creative-writing class. Ruth, the teacher, asks one of the students to read her list aloud to us.

"The List of Pleasing Things. Looking out from my window on a moonlit night and seeing the silhouette of a kangaroo and her joey beyond the trees in the yard. Getting a handmade card from my granddaughter with the *r* in *Christmas* written backward. The scent of the sea on the breeze of a cool change, even though the coast is hundreds of miles away. Finding my photograph in the local paper after an event. The sound of the door closing after the last guest has left the house."

Ruth has her hands pressed hard to her lips when we look up. Whenever someone reads aloud in the class, we stare at the floor or our feet or our pens and paper on the gray Laminex table. Ruth suggested we close our eyes to listen, but we all seem to prefer to keep some vision. I'm not sure why the others do it. I keep my eyes open but my face down so no one can read what I'm thinking. I'm a plant, a spy, an espio-

THE FINE COLOR OF RUST

nage agent for the committee. They sent me in undercover to find out why three women insist that Ruth's class in creative writing at the Neighbourhood House continue term after term while everyone else who joins the class drops out after a couple of weeks.

Today we're writing lists. Earlier Ruth read out some lists from *The Pillow Book* by Sei Shonagon, a lady-in-waiting at the Japanese court in the eleventh century. The members of the imperial court were supported by the taxes on the population and their only job was to be royal. Ruth told us that poetry flourished, and art and calligraphy. The days of the people at court were spent in the pursuit of beauty. Moon-viewing parties were common. The ladies caught fireflies in the sleeves of their kimonos.

"Did you hear the detail in what Shonagon writes?" Ruth had said. "And the honesty? How many of us will admit to being pleased when we're chosen above the rest, the way Shonagon does when the empress calls her to her side before any of the other ladies? And the wickedness! The one where she talks about finding a letter that is torn up but not so torn up that you can't piece it back together again—delicious."

Now Ruth takes her hands away from her mouth. She reaches out as if she is about to hug the woman who read out her list.

"Perfect, Eleanor," Ruth says. "You have found exactly the right tone, the right spirit."

Eleanor blushes and laughs. I can imagine members of our committee enjoying this class. After all, they are our own landed gentry.

"Can you see how the ordinary is also full of beauty?" Ruth asks us, and we nod.

Next it's my turn to read aloud. "I don't think I've done it right. Maybe someone else should read theirs."

"Now, Loretta," Ruth says, shaking her head. "In this class, we don't judge each other. We're learning together."

I shrug my shoulders and pick up my piece of paper. I take a deep breath. Reading out my work makes me feel like I'm in primary school.

"OK," I say, and I look around at the four nodding faces of the teacher and my classmates. "OK, I wrote a few things. The List of Pleasing Things. Wednesday night comedy on the TV. A Kmart undies sale. The smell of the Scouts' sausage sizzle outside the supermarket on a Saturday. Reading my daughter's diary and not finding anything horrible about me. The jingle of spurs."

Ruth wipes her forehead with her hand. It's warm in here, all right, but not that hot.

"That's lovely, Loretta," she says. "Now, who's next?"

Everyone who hasn't read yet shoots their hand in the air. I remember this moment from school. It's when someone gives a dumb answer to the teacher's question and the others all realize immediately that they can do better. My career as a writer is over in thirty minutes. The other class members read out their lists and not one of them has anything as ordinary as Kmart in it. Roses, moonlight, the smell of mangoes, the swish of silk against your skin. Is this why my life turned out the way it did? Perhaps I should work on developing refined taste and lofty thoughts.

While they're reading I try to imagine what Norm's list of pleasing things might be. Finding an abandoned car on the side of the road and the tires still have tread? Or Melissa's. I think and think but I can't imagine what my own daughter's list of pleasing things might be. What kind of mother am I?

That night at tea I ask Melissa, "If you had to write a list of things that pleased you, what would they be?"

"Things that please me?"

"Things that make you feel good."

"Why?"

"I wondered, that's all. I had to do it today in writing class."

"Are you learning to write?" Jake says, and giggles.

"Very funny, Mr. Top of the Class in Spelling."

"I got a hundred percent."

"And that's the hundredth time you've told us," Melissa says.

"So what would they be, Lissie?"

"Dad coming back to live with us."

"I guessed that might be one. What else?"

"A pair of Manolo Blahnik shoes."

I stare at her. "I thought I told you that show was off-limits. That's American rubbish for grown-ups, not for children."

Melissa looks up at the ceiling and sighs.

"Didn't I?"

"No."

"I think I did, young lady."

"You told me I could never watch that show in this house."

I hate children. One minute they don't know which shoe goes on which foot, the next they're using logic that would make Aristotle proud.

"Who let you watch it?"

"Helen. She says I'll learn how to deal with men."

"And Helen's the champion of dealing with men, of course. Well, I'm telling you now—you are not allowed to watch that rubbish. Life's not like that. And it's certainly not like that around here. You go ask for Blahniks at the shoe shop in Halstead and they'll send you to the delicatessen."

"I'm going to Melbourne the minute I leave school."

"Don't think Melbourne's some great center of sophistication. Remember, I'm from there."

That came out all wrong. Melissa's sniggering. I hate children.

13

THE NEXT DAY I'm on the phone first thing. "Helen, how could you let Melissa watch *Sex and the City*?"

"She loved it. And I didn't explain what fellatio is. I told her you'd talk to her about that kind of thing."

"Oh God."

"She did ask if it was the same as a blow job, but I said to talk to you."

"Oh double God. Where did she learn that? She's eleven!"

"It's a new world, Loretta. They know everything. Anyway, I found out. The girlfriend's only twenty-four."

"What?"

"Tony's new girlfriend. The one staying with him at the pub. She's a child bride. Secretary at the place where he was working up in Mildura."

"They're married? They can't do that. We're not even divorced yet."

"A figure of speech, Loretta. Gee, relax."

Now I'm angry. He's brought his new girlfriend to town, he's paraded her around, he's been spending money and hanging out with his mates, and he hasn't even said hello to his children. I get off the phone from Helen, who's urging me not to do anything silly, and I ring the House and tell them I can't come in today.

First I visit the police station.

"Have you applied to the Family Court for maintenance?" Bill says.

"It's a bit hard to get money from someone who's disappeared. I mean, I know you can apply, but it didn't seem worth the trouble."

Bill taps his report sheet with his pen. "Not a lot I can do here. I feel for you, love. It's a common problem in this town."

At the Social Security office in Halstead I run into Brenda. She offers me a squashed tomato sandwich from her handbag. She's brought a blow-up neck pillow.

"What number are you?" I ask. She shows me her ticket, which says forty-three, and I look at mine, which says sixty-eight. At the counter a man's getting all steamed up and piling papers on the desk in front of the receptionist.

"This isn't a rates notice," she says flatly. "It's a title. We need the rates notice." She leans forward and rubs her forehead. "I'm sorry, Mr. O'Hagan. It's the rules. We're stuck with them too. If we don't follow the rules the whole process goes back to scratch and it takes even longer."

"Fuck!" he shouts. He scrunches the papers in his fist and turns to the queue. "Fuck them. Fuck youse. All this for a measly two hundred bucks. Fuck youse all."

Back at the Gunapan pub, the barmaid says my husband's gone out. "With his lady friend. Sorry, Loretta," she adds.

For an hour I drive aimlessly around town, then it's time to pick up the kids from school.

Tony's waiting at the school gate with his child bride.

It's so hard to walk I feel as if my legs have pins in them.

THE FINE COLOR OF RUST

They won't bend. I swing them around in half circles so I can move forward.

"Hey, Loretta," the bastard says. "What have you done to yourself? Been playing footy?"

"Hello, Tony," I whisper.

The child bride thrusts a hand at me. "Nice to meet you, Loretta. I'm Talee." She's neat. Pressed jeans and checked shirt. Dinky short hairdo and clean fingernails. Unbitten. My hand slides unwillingly into hers and she grips it for a moment, then lets go. "I'm sorry to surprise you this way, but Tony says he's been flat out all week and hasn't called. He's unbelievable. You must be so cross. I hope you'll forgive us."

My eyes roll across to look at Tony. Everything's going slow, or else my brain is shutting down. I think I heard her insult Tony, but he's still smiling. He's shaved off his sparse ginger moustache and goatee and he seems to have spent money on his teeth. My money. My kids' money.

"Can't wait to see the kids," Tony says.

My mouth may be open. Drool may be dribbling from my lower lip.

"Teeth," I say.

He rubs his forefinger with a squeak across his new white front teeth and laughs.

"Cost me a packet. I clean my teeth every night now, like you used to tell me, Loretta." He nudges Talee. "She was always on at me to clean my damn teeth."

"No wonder—they were a disgrace," Talee answers smartly.

Tony laughs again and I think I'm going to faint. I close my eyes. Talee asks me if I'm all right. I hear shouts as kids come running out through the school doors.

"Well, look what washed up out of the drain." A voice

speaks behind me. "I thought you were going to buy some hubcaps and then piss off for another few years."

Norm's big hand lands on my shoulder.

"And you must be the new one," he says to Talee. "Obviously as stupid as Loretta."

"Yes, I'm the new one. I'm Talee. I guess we all have our foibles."

"Foibles?" Norm laughs a quick bark. "So he's a foible now. Not the word I'd use."

My knees bend a little. Perhaps movement will return to them before I have to go back to the car. Jake's hand slips into mine and next minute Melissa comes running and flings herself against her father.

"I knew you'd come back for us!"

"Hey, baby girl."

Norm's hand tightens on my shoulder. Jake tugs my arm and I lean down so he can whisper in my ear.

"Is that Dad?"

I nod.

"He looks different."

I nod again.

Melissa's clinging to Tony as if he's a life buoy. Tony reaches out a hand to Jake. "Hey, Jake, how's my boy?"

"Very well, thank you."

Talee crouches down beside Jake. "Aren't you a cutie. How old are you?"

"Seven," Jake whispers. "In four months."

Talee looks up at me. She's got the clear skin of a twenty-year-old. No makeup except for a swipe of pink lipstick. She's the opposite of scrag.

"Could we take them to buy an ice cream? We'll bring them back in time for tea," she says.

I'm speechless. This can't be happening. She's acting as if this is a regular visit. Norm's gasping like he's run the Stawell Gift. Tony detaches Melissa from his side and reaches for Jake, but Jake steps behind me.

"Let's go, Dad." Melissa grasps Tony's hand and pulls him in the direction of the shops. "Come on."

"You've got more nerve—" Norm's wheezing now. I take hold of his arm and try to shush him.

"Listen, mate. This is none of your fucking business," Tony says through tight lips.

"Tony!" Talee squeaks out a protest.

This is more like the Tony I know. For the first time in two years I'm desperate for a smoke. The old Loretta's taken over my body again. I want to go home and have a glass of wine and wash some dishes. I want to wash every dish in the house. I'll sit in the dark for a while, smoking Winnies. Then I'll take a few clean dishes out the back and smash them on the rusted old truck carcass that squats in my yard and reminds me every day that this bastard left me nothing but crap.

My hand's still on Norm's arm and I can feel his bicep tensing and relaxing, tensing and relaxing with each breath. With time creeping glacially through this moment I find myself drifting up and floating above the impossible happenings at the school gate. I'm dissociating, I think dreamily, the way psycho killers do in horror movies. It feels oddly pleasant. What will I do with the money Mum's going to send me? Mmm. A list of pleasing things to do when I have a few thousand dollars. Look at Melissa's hair, I admonish myself. Flyaway tangles and uneven lengths. That girl needs a professional haircut. And maybe I'll dye my hair. We could have a girls' day at the salon. Melissa's never been to a proper salon.

Come to think of it, I haven't had a haircut from anyone except Helen for years. And cricket lessons for Jake so he can stop smashing the laundry window. My heart's slowing down at last. They're talking around me, but I can't make out the words. I might buy Helen lunch at the golf course restaurant as thanks for all those haircuts. I'll check out the BMWs in the car park. See if . . .

"Loretta!"

"Huh?"

"We've got to head off. But we'll drop around to the house later, after tea, OK?"

"Drop around to the house?"

"Just like the old Loretta," Tony says. "Off with the pixies."

Damn, my heart's starting to ramp up again. I used to think I'd have a heart attack when we were together. He'd be shouting at me and my heart would be hammering so hard my teeth would start to chatter.

"Honey, maybe Loretta's busy tonight. You should ask what suits her." Talee smiles at me.

A single mother busy on a week night? Who is this woman? She makes Kyleen seem intelligent. Norm wrenches his arm out of my grip and stands clenching and unclenching his fist.

"Dad, I want to go with you and the lady," Melissa says firmly.

Tony harrumphs uncomfortably. "No, you go with your mum. I'll see you tonight, Liss. Be a good girl."

"OK, Daddy. What time?"

I haven't seen this kind of obedient acceptance since she was eight.

"Later, all right?"

My body feels like it's been slammed back to earth. My

knees are bending fine now. They're bending so well I think I'm going to sit down right here in the dust at the school gate. Norm grabs me as I buckle. We watch Tony and Talee stroll back to the CRX. Talee slips her hand into Tony's and leans her head on his shoulder, then turns and waves goodbye. Melissa waves back.

"She's pretty," Melissa says accusingly.

"What are you doing up there, mate?" Norm helps Jake down from the tree behind us.

I ask Norm to come for tea and we eat our scrambled eggs on toast and watch TV without saying much. At nine o'clock Jake's asleep in my lap and I put him to bed. Melissa's wide-eyed and keyed up. She can't stop talking. She makes a list of things she wants to tell her dad and she writes them down in an exercise book so she won't forget. How she won first prize in English last year. Getting the best and fairest in netball the year before last. How they got a pet sheep at the school and everyone voted for the name she suggested.

"What else, Mum?" she keeps nagging me.

When the phone rings at nine thirty I hold my nose, trying not to cry. Melissa picks up the receiver, but she's too anxious to say hello. She listens for a minute, then hands the phone to me.

"Hello, Loretta? It's Talee here, we met today? Tony's called. He's stuck out on the highway with a flat so we won't be able to make it tonight. I'm very sorry to inconvenience you. Tony says he'll call you tomorrow."

"Fine," I say, and hang up without a goodbye. Melissa looks at me and I shake my head.

"I'm so sorry, sweetie. Maybe tomorrow."

I follow her to her room.

"Leave me alone," she says from the darkness.

111

In the lounge room Norm turns off the TV. He pats me on the back as he leaves.

I pick up Melissa's exercise book from the couch and read her long list, printed and numbered with scratchings out and arrows moving things to more important positions and asterisks with notes like *The only girl!*

Melissa's list of pleasing things.

14

THE NEXT NIGHT, Norm arrives on my doorstep and tells me I'm going out.

"You're not going to mooch around here feeling sorry for yourself. I want to see the Gunna Panther in action tonight, because it's the shire meeting. No one's getting away with calling my yard unsightly."

I sigh. "I can't, Norm. I haven't got a babysitter." I want to sit at home mooching around and feeling sorry for myself. Tony's postponed his visit for another night and Melissa is so furious with me, convinced it's all my fault, that she's on the internet looking up how to divorce your mother.

"It's all arranged," Norm says. "They set up child care a while ago because some mothers who had a petition in front of council made a hoo-ha about equal opportunity. For the older kids they've got that computer whiz, Joey, you know, Al's kid, giving some demo in the computer room. Helen's coming. No excuses, Loretta."

I remember being taught in school that local government is the face of democracy. If that's the case, then our democracy is an angry little ferret face pushed up against the glass of the complaints department, telling people no. Normally the monthly meeting about town issues would have two people trying to get out of paying their parking fines, someone objecting to a neighbor's building permit, and the usual Hotel Association rep pushing for a bigger car park outside the pub's poker machine annex. Tonight is different. Norm wants his Unsightly Property Notice withdrawn. Plus there's special entertainment. A witch has come to Gunapan, and she's been entered as an item on the agenda.

When we arrive, the room is packed with the biggest crowd the shire meeting has ever seen. The councillors are seated around a table at the front of the hall. They have jugs of water and bowls of mints and huge piles of paper beside them. A couple of council staff are making notes at a table behind.

Kyleen's brought two packets of chips and a can of lemonade, as if she's at the pictures, and the cadet reporter from the *Shire Herald* is snapping candid shots of the gallery. The council gallery is rows of seats divided into two blocks by an aisle. On the right of the aisle, the entire congregation of the Church of Goodwill is squashed uncomfortably next to the ten remaining aged Catholics and a few pious types who don't go to church but who you often hear boasting about God the way you would a close friend who's won a quiz show on the TV. To the left sits everyone else. The kids are in the computer room learning how to hack into NASA. Melissa's probably already found herself an internet foster family.

Two rows behind, I see Brianna. She's wearing a lot of makeup. Not enough to cover the bruise. I wander back. When I touch her arm she jumps.

"Are you OK, Brianna?" Everyone knows her boyfriend loses it after a drink or two, but we can't persuade her to leave him.

She leans into me and murmurs at my shoulder, "I'm sorry the kids saw us arguing the other week, Loretta. It was nothing, honestly. He's a good man with a hot temper, that's all. He's getting so much better."

I don't know what to say.

"Honestly, Loretta. It's OK."

When I step into the aisle to go back to my seat I almost crash into a portly figure, resplendent in red and gold, sailing toward the front of the room. Our mayor, Vaughan, loves the robes. He doesn't have to wear them—after all, this is Gunapan. We think dressing up is for weddings, funerals, and visits from the pension assessor. But he slips on the big scarlet cloak and the gold chain whenever he gets the chance, and he makes sure the chain jingles a little when he walks, his stomach pushed out in front and his head thrown back with the pride of leading this great community.

Tonight he walks down between the forces of good on the right and the forces of nothing-better-to-do-on-a-Thursday-night on the left without glancing either way. I heard him discussing the witch issue with Sandra, the checkout girl, at the supermarket the other day. In the background, the supermarket sound system was vibrating with the rage of a radio talkback caller from Halstead who was working his way through a long list of grievances, from the laziness of young people today to that appalling pantsuit the foreign minister was wearing at the OPEC conference and did she think orange was a suitable color to represent hardworking Australians in front of other world leaders who wore perfectly dignified suits and never dyed their hair either except that French bloke who was a ponce anyway.

"This witch business is the biggest thing ever to hit this town," Vaughan started saying to Sandra, like he was narrating the plot of a blockbuster movie. "I have to be very careful, very careful indeed, to be bipartisan."

Sandra reeled back. "You're bipartisan?" she asked, her voice a whisper.

"I try," the mayor said. "It's not always easy. Sometimes one side looks a lot better than the other."

"Does everyone know?" Sandra said, hurrying to swipe his groceries and pack them. She glanced past him at me. I pretended not to be listening and kept flipping through the magazine from the rack next to me, which happened to have George Michael on the cover.

"Oh, I think it's pretty clear that I spend plenty of time with both sides. They all have different wants and needs. You have to satisfy everyone—I tell you, what with the shop in the daytime and my mayoral duties at night and weekends, it's exhausting. The wife's not happy. She wants me to give it up, spend more time at home."

"I bet she does," Sandra muttered. She thrust his change at him, holding the coins between the tips of her fingers and dropping them into his hand.

"I've been trying to get on top of this witch business. Haven't heard back from her yet, but I might get lucky before the meeting. Cheerio then, Sandra," he said.

"Hmmph," she said.

I pushed my carton of milk up to the register and put George Michael back on the stand.

"Did you hear that?" Sandra asked.

"Nope," I said.

She rang up my milk and handed me the bag. On the speakers above, the radio talkback caller was winding down to a shuddering finale on refugees taking our jobs and how apples don't taste the same anymore. He seemed to have been given an excessive amount of time to talk. The DJ must have been out making a cup of tea.

"This town's changing," she said, shaking her head. "First the witch, then a bipartisan mayor. What next?"

The witch moved to town a month ago and began advertising on a board outside her newly rented house. The hand-painted board, strung by chains from the lacework on her veranda, offered spells, charms, curses and the lifting of curses, amulets, and an invitation to a monthly new-moon coven. The Witchery would open for business in July, and would start taking appointments from early June.

Helen said she was heading down the day the Witchery opened. She was going to get the town curse lifted.

"What town curse?" I asked.

"The one where men suddenly get the urge to bugger off back to the city as soon as they've fathered enough children. I used to think it was something in the water, but maybe it's a curse."

None of us is sure who the witch is. She's been out of town during most of the month the house has been rented. No one's seen her enter or leave. A stranger was spotted around town, a tall woman with black hair who had her roots dyed at Hair Today Gone Tomorrow in the main street and bought Chinese takeaway three nights in a row. Brianna saw her driving up and down the streets looking at the houses and we wondered if she was casting some kind of spell on the town. Next, she turned up at Norm's junkyard.

"She walked straight up to the door of the shed and the dogs never barked once. I look up and there she is in the doorway with this big black hairdo and a wand in her left hand that she's pointing at me. I nearly shit myself thinking I'm about to be hexed. Turns out the wand's a bit of pipe from the yard and she's come to try to sell me KwikKerb. 'Darl,' I said to her, 'if you can find anywhere to put a curb in this yard, good luck to you.'"

So it wasn't her. Now we're all looking around to see the witch, but she doesn't seem to be here.

"Maybe she's made herself invisible," Helen whispers.

The mayor calls the meeting to order. As they go through the usual agenda items, Kyleen passes around the chips while the crowd on the left side chats and laughs. Melissa creeps in and asks if she can go down to the shop with Taylah and I tell her she's not going anywhere and she pouts and I sigh and it's just like being at home.

"We have an agenda item put forward by Norm Stevens," the mayor reads out. "'An application to lift the Unsightly Property Notice on the property of Mr. Norman Stevens Snr., Lot 19, Minyip Road, Gunapan.'"

Samantha Patterson is shuffling paper on the table in front of her. She takes a sip of water without looking up.

"Would you care to speak to your application, Norm?" the mayor asks.

Norm edges past me and Helen and walks to the front of the gallery.

"I don't want to speak to my application, I want to speak to youse councillors. I don't know what you think you're doing, slapping an Unsightly Property Notice on a property that's looked like this for fifteen years. How come suddenly I'm unsightly?"

"Norm, please don't take this personally. I've had a look at this and it's obviously about the resolution to beautify Gunapan. Working on our community pride. Last council meeting we voted on a resolution that said"—he lifts a piece of paper and adjusts his glasses for reading—"'Gunapan should improve its image and encourage pride in the community.'" He looks up, adjusts his glasses again, and pats his stomach. He often does that. He's a bit of a worrier. Probably has an ulcer.

"I've got plenty of community pride, mate. And anyway, I wasn't unsightly when you came to buy that corrugated iron for your shed last month. What's the problem this month?"

"I'll check with the staff about this." The mayor leans across to mutter to the bloke who's sitting behind him taking notes. He leans in the other direction and mutters to a councillor, then turns back to face the gallery and Norm. The council officer tugs the mayor's sleeve to get his attention before handing him an open ring binder.

"Norm, I'll read you the shire's definition of unsightly property. 'Unsightly property is land that contains unconstrained rubbish, excessive waste and/or vegetation, disused machinery or vehicles, partially completed or partially demolished buildings, or graffiti.' Now, Norm, you'll have to admit your yard fits most of those categories."

"Yeah, like it did a month ago and a year ago and fifteen years ago. I'll ask again, what's changed? I think Councillor Samantha Patterson should answer that question."

She looks up. She's married to the owner of a big farm out past Wilson Dam. Before she was elected unopposed to the shire council, she used to run the Ladies Auxiliary of the Halstead Lions Club. She's not only the sole woman on the council, she's the youngest councillor too. She looks the same age as me, but without the scrag factor. Her nails are polished. Her brown hair is as glossy and preened as bird feathers. I bet she paid a lot of money for that dress too. It's a soft green jersey with satin around the neckline and half-length sleeves. I hope she gives it to the charity shop when she's tired of it.

"I don't know much about this aspect of shire business," she answers calmly. "As most people here probably know"—she looks around the room, smiling and nodding at a few people—"I was elected to council on a platform of community development." She smiles again with the white even teeth of someone on TV. "But as I understand it, doesn't someone have to make a complaint before an Unsightly Property Notice is issued? Perhaps Mr. Stevens might like to consider that. It could well be his neighbors."

I can see Norm is heating up. He's scratching the back of his scarlet neck. The mayor leafs hurriedly through the folder and reads out loud. " 'If a complaint is received by the shire that a property is unsightly, the first step will be for a local laws officer to inspect the property. If the officer deems that it does constitute an unsightly property, a Notice to Comply will be issued.' Yep, it sounds as if that's what's happened, Norm. Not a lot we can do about it. It's a bylaw."

"And if I don't comply?" Norm's talking slowly now. You don't see Norm angry very often. He's a pretty relaxed kind of a bloke. This is twice in a week. First Tony, now the Unsightly Property Notice.

The mayor runs his finger down the page.

"Da de da de da. Here it is. 'The Notice to Comply will outline the circumstances causing the land to be deemed unsightly, and will state the works required to be completed by a specific date. If the works are not completed by that date or alternative arrangements have not been made with the officer, a contractor may be enlisted to complete the work on behalf of the shire. Once the work is completed to the satisfaction of the shire an invoice will be sent for payment of these works.'"

"I hope you don't think we're stupid, Vaughan," Norm says. "It's not about my yard, we all know that."

"Huh? What are you talking about? I hadn't even heard

about this notice until I saw the agenda. There's no conspiracy here, Norm. Keep your hat on."

"Suit yourself. If you want a fight, I'm happy to oblige." Norm swings around and strides back to his seat next to me, breathing through his nose.

I pat him on the arm, lean toward his ear, and whisper, "Go, Norm!" before I rear back in shock. I think he's growing spuds in that ear.

He expels a great snort of air, then half-turns to the crowd in the gallery.

"We've all been pretty bloody tolerant of the secrecy and shenanigans at this council. Well, maybe we won't be so tolerant anymore."

Around us, a few people clap. Mario leans over and mutters to Norm, "Vaughan is a good mayor, Norm. We don't want to put the boot into the good blokes."

"Don't worry, Mario. If he's done nothing wrong, he's got nothing to fear, right?"

It's a side of Norm I've never seen. It is true, though, that Norm knows most of what goes on around Gunapan, thanks to the steady stream of customers who never buy anything, but stand around gasbagging for hours. If he wants to cause some damage, I'm sure he has the weapons.

"What's Samantha Patterson's connection?" I whisper to Norm. "Has she got shares in the development?"

"She's too smart for that. But I'll find out, don't you worry."

The next item for discussion is the water tanks to be installed by the side of the footy clubhouse. The club president says he's been waiting for four months and buying water to keep the ground safe for play and the club is now broke and he'll organize a demonstration if the council doesn't pull its finger out and put in the tanks. The councillor whose brief is shire amenities tells the president that the tanks have been bought and are waiting for installation but Kev the council plumber broke his ankle and they've been waiting for him to recover, and the president says, "Stuff that, mate, twenty-five plumbers in Halstead could do the job," and the councillor says, "Leave it with me and I'll see what can be done," and the president says, "You've done bugger all till now, so why should I believe that?" and the mayor says, "Now now, everyone," and the president storms back to his seat and the footballers in the back row drum their feet on the wooden floor and the mayor wipes his forehead and pats his stomach again.

Finally we get to the last item, the one the crowd is here for.

"Um, yes. The final item for tonight's meeting. This is certainly the most unusual shire meeting we've had in some time," he says with a weak laugh. "Now Trudy Walker has put forward this item. She wants to discuss satanism in Gunapan."

Trudy gets up and walks to the front of the room. Everyone is silent, except for Kyleen, who's munching chips steadily. Once she's in front of the microphone, Trudy adjusts her hair. It's been permed into a frizzy halo and she uses both hands to pat it down.

"We are a Christian community," she begins.

"I'm not a Christian," Sammy Lee calls from the back of the left gallery. "And I think you'll find that the Dhaliwal family aren't either."

"He's got a point," Norm says to me. "I've got more faith in *Best Bets* than Jesus."

The left gallery is muttering. "Well, I don't go to church, but . . . ," "Sister Theresa cured me in grade four . . ."

"OK," Trudy says, raising her hands. "OK. But we are a God-fearing community, aren't we?"

The Church of Goodwill gallery claps. I can hear Sammy

Lee in the row behind me chatting with Mrs. Edwards. "Honestly, I speak and nobody listens. I'm the invisible ethnic minority in this place. Sammy Lee, token Chinaman, non-Christian . . ."

"Mate," Brian Mack says from the row behind Sammy. "You think you've got problems. You should try being Aboriginal here. My family's so far out of the town's bloody consciousness we might as well be white."

"Jeez, don't wish that on us, hon," Brian's wife, Merle, mutters.

"You may think we are old-fashioned fuddy-duddies, but this is no joke." Trudy sounds so serious that everyone quiets down. "Witchcraft is not some innocent game with wands and tall hats. It's not a kids' book or a TV show. Real witchcraft is the work of the devil, and it can't be played with. You might think it's funny having a witch in the town, but you won't think it's funny when it gets out of hand. We need to stop this right now, before the devil sneaks into Gunapan while you're still laughing."

"Yes!" the right gallery calls. "Amen!"

"I think we ought to hear the other side of the story before we make any hasty decisions," the mayor points out, "except I'm not sure that the person in question is actually here. I did ask the council secretary to send a letter, though."

We all look around like a bunch of turkeys craning their long necks.

It seems as if the show is over until a voice comes from the back of the left gallery. It's a high voice, nasal and thin, and it seems oddly familiar.

"I studied hard to get this diploma and I'm not giving up because you don't like it. Witches can work for good too," the voice says.

123

She stands up and we stare with our mouths open. It's Leanne. Leanne grew up in Gunapan. She left a couple of years ago to study in Melbourne and hasn't been back as far as I know. Until now.

"Leanne?" Kyleen shouts through a mouthful of chips. "You're the witch?"

"I'd like to be addressed as Leonora. And yes, I'm now a trained witch from the Wiccan School of Herbal and Magickal Therapy in Melbourne. And I think I deserve some respect."

A blinding flash floods the room. My heart skips a beat as I wonder if we have been smote, then I see the cadet reporter focussing his lens on Leanne.

"Oh my Lord," Trudy says from the front of the room. "Leanne Bivens, what does your mother think about this?"

Leanne's mother stands up beside her. "I'm proud of Leanne. I mean, Leonora. What she's got is as good as a diploma from a college. And also, she's got rid of my shingles and I won a fifth division in Tattslotto last week and you can see her acne's completely gone."

Everyone inclines toward the back of the room and peers at Leanne. She holds her head high, tilts it from side to side. Sure enough, that acne's cleared right up.

"This is wrong," Trudy calls out. "Spells. Incantations. Do you think things come for free? A price will be exacted, young lady, and it will be your soul! Don't go thinking you can seduce the women of Gunapan into a coven."

Norm guffaws beside me, then tries to cover the guffaw with a cough. I'm picturing the coven of hefty Gunapan women dancing naked in the moonlight beside the stinky Wilson Dam. I wonder whether we'd dance around the old car bodies or between them.

"I suppose you pray to demons," Trudy goes on. "I've read

about it. You have black candles and upside-down crucifixes and goats. You're playing with forces you don't understand!"

We'll have to lock up Terror.

Leanne steps out from the row and walks down the center aisle toward Trudy. She does seem a lot more confident than when she was serving behind the makeup counter at the chemist shop. When she was younger she used to babysit for us occasionally. We'd come home and find her curled up asleep on the couch like a baby herself. Now she's wearing a long purple velvet dress and heavy silver jewelry that clanks as she walks. Beside me, Helen is fingering her face.

"Do you think she can get rid of wrinkles?" Helen whispers to me.

"I've got a bit of heavy-duty Spakfilla could help with that," Norm answers, and she punches him in the arm.

As she walks toward Trudy, Leanne raises her arm and points. Trudy steps back behind the podium as if it will protect her.

"They told us in class people wouldn't understand. I want you to know that not all magick is black magick. I studied white magick. I did Herbs and Spells, Incantations and Potions, Freeing Your Inner Goddess, Small Business Bookkeeping, Marketing and Promotion. And I got the highest grade in the class for Women's Mysteries."

The whole room goes quiet. I think we're all wondering about Women's Mysteries.

"Can you fly?" Kyleen asks.

"No, but if I do five more units and upgrade to a degree it's possible I'll be able to move from one place to another by magick."

"Of course, in India some yogis can levitate through deep spiritual practice," Mrs. Edwards behind me comments.

"Yeah, well, that's the same thing, isn't it? See?" Leanne adds, turning to Trudy. "And anyway, I come from Gunapan and I went to the city, but at least I came back. Everyone says that the young people leave and never come back and that's why Gunapan is in trouble. Well, here I am! Just because I'm doing something different you shouldn't treat me this way. I'm bringing new industry to town."

She has a point. In the last year the only new businesses to start up in town have been her and Merv Bull. Before that, a member of the Neighbourhood House Committee opened an antiques shop in the main street. What she called antique was the same stuff most of us use at home—Laminex tables, Bakelite flour canisters, old bassinets. If we had a lot of through traffic it might have worked, but the highway only passes by close enough for us to have the four a.m. thunder of the road trains without a single visitor ever pulling off the highway and driving into town.

Thinking about that reminds me of the development. How did they even find Gunapan to put a resort here?

"Let us pray for guidance," someone from the right gallery calls. The Church of Goodwillers and the Catholics get down on their knees, slowly and with much grunting and bone-cracking, to begin the Lord's Prayer.

"And one more thing," Leanne says. "Religious freedom. You'd never do this to a Jewish person or a Muslim person."

From out of a pocket hidden in her flowing dress, she produces a stubby silver knife. Trudy gasps.

"Trudy, get a grip," Leanne says, waving to her mother to come to the front of the room, where Leanne begins drawing a circle on the floor with the knife.

"Actually," the mayor says, his chain tinkling as he steps toward Leanne, then back again. "This is shire property. It's probably best not to mark the floor? Not that I want to inter-fere with your religious freedom."

Leanne turns to him, still pointing the knife, and the mayor clutches at his chest as if she has pierced it.

"Oops, sorry," Leanne says, and pockets the knife. She takes her mother's hand and pulls her into the circle. Her mother is beaming proudly as if this is Leanne's wedding day. She lifts her feet as she steps over the imaginary circle line, then clasps her hands together and nods at several people in the front row of the Church of Goodwill crowd.

"Hi, Moira, lovely to see you," Leanne's mother says. She seems not to have noticed that Moira believes Leanne is the spawn of Satan. I can't get the picture of Leanne behind the Revlon counter out of my mind. The white smock she always wore, and the blue satin eyeshadow.

The door at the back of the room swings open with a creak. Five children are standing there, my two at the front. They've obviously heard the praying.

"I'm bored," Jake says to no one in particular.

"Hi, Leanne," Melissa says.

"Hi, Melissa. Hi, Jake. It's Leonora now," Leanne answers.

The praying fades away. Everyone's looking at my children as they wander down to stand beside me. Jake's dropped half his dinner on his T-shirt. And I hadn't noticed when we left the house that Melissa's got hold of my foundation again. She's caked it on and it ends in a dark line at her jaw. I won-der if I look like that when I wear it.

"Hey, Leanne, you look great. No more pimples," Melissa says.

"Melissa!" I say. I pull the two of them into the row beside me and wonder if anyone would notice me holding my hands over their mouths and noses. Just for a little while.

"Can we go home now?" Jake whispers.

"Have you heard from Dad?" Melissa asks, as she does every five minutes at home. No, I haven't heard from her father, even though he's staying in a hotel ten minutes from where we are now. I used to hate him. Now I despise him.

Trudy has moved to the side of the room where her congregation is still praying.

"What about love potions?" Maxine calls out. "Can you make them, Leanne—sorry, Leonora?"

"Oh yeah, no worries. And amulets and charms to attract a lover. That's easy."

Excitement hums in a surge of current through the left gallery, made up mainly of single mothers. The Christians don't stand a chance. Before the mayor has an opportunity to make a pronouncement on satanic practices in the town, people are crowding around Leanne, who blushes and hands out business cards.

"I declare the meeting closed," the mayor shouts above the hubbub.

Jake's got hold of my hand and he's trying to pull me out the door. I call goodbye over my shoulder to Norm. As I get dragged past I see the members of the right gallery look at each other.

"All we can do is pray," one of them says, shaking her head sadly.

Jake, stronger than a runaway lawn mower, propels me through the corridor toward the car park. In the alcove near the front door stands a knot of people. Perhaps they came late. Helen has spotted them too. It is as though all the unmarried men of Helen's dreams have come together to taunt her. The grade-three teacher is talking earnestly with Merv Bull. Beside them, the widowed farmer from beyond Riddley's Creek stands with his thumbs hooked through his belt loops, staring into space.

I smile at the group as we pass. Helen tries to nod at the men, but she's carrying her neighbor's two-year-old on her shoulders and the sudden shift in balance makes her stagger past like a drunk.

"At the end of the day," the grade-three teacher says to Merv Bull, "it's all about civil liberties, isn't it."

Merv nods. "And a little bit of magic in your life never hurts either," he says.

I glance back when I hear him say that. He's looking straight at me and I feel a heat in my face. He nods. My face starts to burn. Jake tugs at my hand and before I know it I'm out on the street.

15

THE SHIRE MEETING last night was a distraction, but the moment I put the kids to bed and tried to get some sleep myself, the night demons arrived to torment me. Perhaps Melissa is right: it *is* my fault that Tony hasn't visited the kids. I am horrible. I am an ogre. He is right to have left me. And so on and so on until I sobbed myself to sleep. This morning I drifted through my chores in a dreary haze. In the afternoon I arrive at the school to pick up the kids. Helen is at the gate too. Today my life is small and pinched and the sky seems vast and filled with a relentless glare.

"What's wrong with you?" she asks, prodding my forearm with a finger. "Have you heard anything I've said?"

"No," I answer.

"I said we've only a two-year extension for keeping the school."

"I know."

"So are you going to do something about it?"

"Not right now."

Helen stares at me. I stare back. My eyes are so tired that staring makes them water and I rub them with my fists.

"Don't do that—it'll make your wrinkles worse," Helen says.

We peel ourselves away from the side of Helen's car, where we have been leaning as we wait for the kids to get out of school. She's picking up her cousin's eight-year-old twins. Helen had her boy, Alex, when she was eighteen and now he's doing an apprenticeship in Melbourne, so she's one of the people we call on to help out with our kids. She says she'll get it all back when Alex comes home with his own children, which will be fairly soon if family history is any indication.

"It's Tony. He left a message on the machine last night about how he's going to have them visit him in Mildura. He hasn't even left Gunapan! He hasn't even visited the house! Why is he taunting them with these stupid promises?"

I've left a sweat print of my body on the faded red paintwork of the car that could be mistaken for the crime scene outline of a corpse. I pluck my T-shirt away from my sweaty back.

"What did he say anyway? You didn't tell me. How did he explain three years without a word?"

"He didn't. He acted as if nothing was special. And the girlfriend's behaving like we're all going to be great mates . . ." I trail off, suddenly realizing.

"What?"

"He hasn't told her."

"What?"

"That's so typical."

"Loretta!"

"She doesn't know he ran off. That explains the other day here at the school, why she was acting as though it was a regular visit."

Tony's method of dealing with difficult situations was always to wait and see if he could get away with it. He never did. Only smart people can do that. Rather than get into trouble by telling the truth, he'd hedge or lie outright, even when he was bound to be caught out. If I asked him whether he'd been at the pub, he'd say no, he was working. That was after he'd parked the car on the flower bed, vomited at the foot of the steps, and tripped on the torn lino in the kitchen before landing on his face and shouting abuse at the floor.

"She's still a dimwit," I mutter. "Got a flat on the highway. Sure."

As kids come belting out of the school I look up and down the road. No sign of Tony and Miss Happy.

"I'll call you tonight," Helen says. The twins zoom up and immediately start asking what's for tea. Helen takes one in each hand and heads off. "Come on, we've got baked beans. The best money can buy."

"We don't like baked beans," they whine simultaneously. I'm sure their mother was in a childbirth fog when she named them Timothy and Tamsyn. Everyone else calls them the Tim Tams.

Jake climbs straight into the car and starts kicking the back of the passenger seat. Melissa shades her eyes and gazes up and down the road.

"They're not here, sweetie."

No response.

"Let's go home. They might call."

"No, wait. I want to wait a bit."

"Ten minutes, then we're leaving." I open the four doors of the car to let the air circulate and drape a towel across the windscreen.

"Your back's all sweaty," Melissa says with distaste.

Jake roots around in his school bag and comes up with a piece of prechewed bubble gum he's stored for emergencies such as this. I wave at Brenda and Kyleen and Maxine and Brianna and the grade-three teacher and the headmaster and Liz and the grade-six teacher and some woman I don't know but who waves at me. Small towns. Soon only two kids and us are left waiting at the gate.

"Melissa, we're going home."

In ten minutes of full sun her face has burned. I find some cream in my bag and try to dab it on her face, but she pushes my hand away and gets into the backseat of the car. We slam the four doors and I roar away from the curb, putting my foot down even harder than usual. Just like when we were married, Tony makes me angry when he's around, and even angrier when he's not.

As we're passing Norm's junkyard I toot the horn. Norm's skinny brown arm reaches out of the door of the shed, gives a thumbs-up, and disappears back inside.

"Why do you always do that? And why's he always coming around? And why do we go there all the time? That junkyard's stupid. You never buy anything."

"Because he's our friend, Liss. He cares about us."

"He's old and ugly. And he smells of petrol."

At home she pulls out the phone book, looks up the number of the pub where Tony's staying, and calls. I leave the room. When she comes into the kitchen I ask if she got hold of him.

"It was her," she says. "She doesn't know anything."

I'm glad we feel the same way about that. After tea, with Melissa crying in her room, I ring the pub again. They put me through to the room and the idiot child bride gets Tony on the phone.

"Listen and only say yes or no." I speak quietly so the kids won't hear. "You've made up some crap about seeing us regularly and sending us money and your girlfriend believes it, right?"

He makes nothing but a *mumumum* sound in reply.

"I'm way past taking any bullshit from you, Tony. Am I right?"

"Yes."

"And she wanted to come here and meet the kids, but you can't let her near them because she'll find out you deserted us."

No reply.

"Then leave her at the pub and get in your precious car and get down here. Your daughter's almost slashing her wrists in the bedroom, you bastard."

Silence.

"I'm not going to dob on you unless you make things worse by not seeing Liss. Get down here and pretend to be a father. If you don't turn up tonight I'll tell your girlfriend everything." I slam down the phone and then pick it up and inspect it to make sure I haven't broken it. I definitely cannot afford a new phone.

I've finished chewing my fingernails and moved on to the skin around them by the time he arrives. He stomps past me at the doorway. It reminds me of when we were together. Because he stomped everywhere I could never tell from his footsteps whether he was in a good mood or a bad one. I had to wait and cop it.

He's smiling. Those expensive white teeth put me in

even more of a fury. He's carrying a bulky white plastic bag stamped with the logo of a department store in Halstead.

"Loretta." He grins even wider and bends down to kiss me on the cheek. "You're a bloody champ. I swear I'll make it up to you. Talee's a great girl. She's making me a better man, you'll see."

My breath is steaming in and out of my nostrils like cigarette smoke. I try to steady my respiration, in through the nose, out through the mouth, yoga-style. Helen did a yoga class once. She used to come over after the class and demonstrate the positions to me in the lounge room.

"The positions massage different inner organs. Apparently this pelvic floor one makes your sex life dynamite. If you have a sex life, that is."

One of the positions she tried to demonstrate, before she got the cramp, was called the Camel. She was on her knees, face scarlet from the exertion, rump thrust in the air. The problem happened when she realized she was bent over in the wrong direction and attempted a backflip. After she had finished screaming, she explained to me what she'd done wrong from the get-go.

"It's the breathing. The key is how you breathe. Once you're doing the good yoga breaths, everything flows from there. Good breathing will change your life, that's what the teacher said." We practiced our yoga breaths between sips of wine cooler.

I warn Tony to stay twenty minutes only, and to come and see me before he leaves, then I call Melissa and Jake out to the lounge room. Melissa runs mewing like a kitten to her father and wraps her arms around him as he drops the bag of expensive presents by the wall.

A better man, ha. While I'm waiting for him to come out I perfect my yoga breathing in the dark on the veranda— breathe in through the nose, gnash the teeth, breathe out through the mouth. I should visit Leanne and find out what she's got in her bag of spells.

16

"**WHAT THE HELL** am I supposed to do?" Norm says straight-away when I answer the phone.

"Pardon me, Norm?" I use my poshest voice, trying to indicate that elegant ladies like myself prefer a conversation to be opened with a courteous greeting and an inquiry after our health.

"Justin's out on parole. He's coming to stay."

"Who?"

"My son."

The shock is too much. I sit down. Norm's son? Somewhere deep down I knew Norm and Marg had a son. Somewhere deep down I knew their son had gone to prison for armed robbery. Somewhere deep down I had decided to forget that information.

"Oh." My heart is beating a little too fast. I can hear my own breath. "Norm, can I ask you something?"

"No."

"OK then," I say in a sprightly voice.

"He was a stupid kid when he did it."

"Norm, if you're Norm Senior, isn't your son called Norm Junior?"

"He never liked it. Justin's his second name. Made us start calling him Justin when he was in high school."

"Ah."

"It was his bloody high-school mates who got him into it. No one got hurt in that stunt they pulled. But he wouldn't dob on his mates so they gave him fifteen years. Then while he was inside he got caught up in some fight and they gave him another five."

"Twenty years. Hmm." I don't know what I'm supposed to say.

"He's out in fourteen, though. Good behavior."

"Well, that's got to be a good thing." Five years on top of your sentence? Doesn't sound like good behavior to me.

"He never wanted me to visit. I went when he was first in, but he wouldn't come out to the visitors' room. Ten times I turned up at visiting time. I sat on my own for an hour every time, hoping he'd at least come and say hello."

I've never heard Norm string this many sentences together. It's as if we're having a conversation in reverse. Usually I'm the one banging on and Norm's going "Hmm" and "Yep" and "Is that right?" while he tinkers with a piece of scrap.

"Is that right?" I say.

"Marg neither. He never let her see him. She goes every year at Christmas and waits, but he's never shown his face."

"Is it that he . . ."

"I thought he hated us. We both thought he hated us."

Jake's tugging on my sleeve and making faces. He's been told so many times not to talk at me while I'm on the phone that now he mimes messages at me. He wrinkles up his face into a bad-smell kind of expression, then makes a big face of surprise with an O mouth and points at the sky. It could mean anything. OK, I mouth back at him, pushing him away. He's not screaming, so it can't be that bad.

"So, Norm, your son is—"

"Loretta, you don't get it. He sent a letter. He wants to come here. He wants to stay with me."

"And that's . . . I mean, is he . . . Gee."

"Marg's pretty upset. But what does it mean? What am I going to do? After all this time he's a stranger."

"Gosh, Norm."

"Jeez, Loretta, let me get a word in here. I don't know what to do, all right? What am I supposed to say to him?"

"Hello?"

"Hello, are you there, Loretta?"

"No, I mean, say 'Hello.' Start with hello. Let him do the talking."

He heaves a big sigh at the other end of the line.

"When he's coming, Norm? You'll have to get stuff in. Set up a room for him. Buy some food. You can't expect him to eat takeaway hamburgers every meal the way you do."

"Three o'clock."

After I put down the phone I understand what Jake was trying to tell me. The tomato soup I was heating for lunch has thickened up, burned onto the bottom of the saucepan—that would have been the bad-smell face—then sent small semiliquid missiles flying around the kitchen, which have stained the walls and floor in a gory red spatter pattern like a TV massacre scene. And—here's the surprise O—one dark brown gob of it is stuck to the ceiling in the shape of a map of Tasmania. At least Jake managed to turn off the gas before the saucepan burst into flames.

Cleaning the kitchen can wait. I bundle Melissa and Jake into the car and we run around the supermarket loading up with the basics that people keep in their houses—bread, butter, milk, eggs, cheese, fruit, a few vegetables, lollies, chocolates, more lollies.

"Take them back to the shelves," I tell Jake. "And bring me a jar of peanut butter. And, Liss, you go to the deli section and get some bacon."

"What if he's vegetarian?" Melissa says.

"He can eat the eggs. Hurry up, Lissie. It's twelve o'clock and we've got to get to the yard and make up a bed and clean the house and be out by two."

"Why can't we meet him?"

"We will, later."

Norm's house is quite difficult to distinguish from the surrounding junk in the yard. He shifted here when Marg threw him out eight years ago, worn down by his irredeemable passion for scrap. He couldn't stop bringing stuff home. After Marg woke up one day to find half a boat in the dining room, she sold their brick-veneer house and moved to Warrnambool. Norm lived in the junkyard shed for a while, then the house began to assemble itself around the shed. He had to knock up another shed as an office. "What's the point in having a scrap yard if I can't make use of it?" he always says.

The *Closed* sign is hanging on the gate. This is the first time I've seen the yard closed in the daytime when Norm's here. Norm is sitting at the kitchen table with his head in his hands. Jake climbs onto his lap the way he used to when he was a toddler.

"Hey, mate," Norm says.

Jake leans his head against Norm's chest. I don't know how he knows something is wrong. Norm gives him a hug.

"My dad came to visit," Jake tells Norm.

"I heard. Did you enjoy that?"

"He brought me a car and a machine gun and a truck and a T-shirt."

"Oh, bloody hell. I didn't buy Justin a present! I should have bought him a present."

"Don't be silly, Norm. He's a grown man. You and Jake put the groceries away and start cleaning the kitchen," I say. "Liss and I'll get started on the rest of the house."

Melissa steps into the bathroom and steps right back out again quick smart.

"I'm not going in there," she says.

It's years since I've been into this bathroom. Norm gave me a tour when he first built it. I remember nodding politely and admiring the claw-foot bath with bricks instead of claw feet, and the real estate agent's sign as flooring. I did wonder about the lack of windows and fans, but Norm said he liked his bathroom steamy. He said Marg had always complained about his steaming up the house, and now he could do it to his heart's content.

Today Melissa has glimpsed the terrifying results of that steaming process. I send her off to make up the bed in the lean-to room off the lounge where Norm's mates sometimes stay if they've had a few and don't want to drive, while I arm myself with gloves, cleaners, scrapers, brushes, disinfectants, and a head scarf before venturing in to do battle with the green velvet wallpaper.

By two o'clock, I can't lift my arms above my head any-more. Crippled by mold. I don't know how I'll explain that to Beemer Man when he has to help me into a cardigan after our armless lovemaking session. Melissa runs gratefully to the car, dragging Jake behind her, and we leave Norm standing in his doorway, his tall stooped frame bent over a little more than usual. He's given me a letter to drop into the postbox on our way home. I'm very curious. It's addressed to the editor of the *Shire Herald*, the local rag.

"What's Norm scared of?" Melissa asks as we pull away from the yard and Norm gives us a halfhearted wave. It's a good question.

"That's a good question. What do you think he's scared of?"

Melissa tips her head back and stares at the roof of the car.

"Intimacy," she finally pronounces.

"When's your birthday?"

"You're my mother! You're supposed to know that."

"If you were really Melissa Boskovic, you'd be turning twelve in August, but I seem to have a forty-year-old sitting next to me in the car. Intimacy indeed. And what kind of intimacy do you think Norm might be afraid of?"

"He's afraid of having to connect with the son he hasn't seen for a long time and he's worried they won't have anything to say to each other."

Hmm, that's exactly what I was thinking. But I'm not letting an eleven-year-old outpsychologize me. Isn't this the child who still believes her father's promise that he's coming back to Gunapan to visit again any day now?

"Actually, I think Norm's got a number of issues." I sound like Dr. Phil, but that's OK because Melissa's at school when his show's on TV.

"You sound like Dr. Phil," Melissa says.

"What's an 'issue'?" Jake asks.

"Have you done your homework?"

They both groan. "That's what you always say when you don't want to answer questions," Melissa complains.

We're pulling into the driveway when Melissa asks the question I've been dreading. "Where has he been? How come Norm never talked about him?"

I try not to lie to the kids. I know that one day they'll find out stuff anyway. But this is a hard one.

"It was somewhere bad, wasn't it?" Melissa tilts her head as she asks.

"Why do you say that?"

"Duh. No one talking about him?"

"Sometimes people do things without thinking," I start.

"Was he in jail?" She seems calm about it. I glance in the rearview mirror. Jake's eyes are wide.

"Yes, he was. But he's not a bad person. He made a stupid mistake when he was a boy, and he got locked up."

Melissa looks out of the window. Jake's edged forward on the seat.

"Is he a murderer?" Jake whispers.

Melissa laughs. She leans over and tickles Jake under the arms. "And he's coming to get yoooooo," she says in a spooky voice. Jake squeals and wriggles away from her tickling fingers.

"Of course he's not," she says to him. "He's Norm's son."

Once we're home I send them off to do their Saturday chores, and I turn on the computer. Information about Justin is impossible to find. I'd imagined that I would type in his name and find out everything from his favorite color to a blow-by-blow description of the crime he committed. But all that comes up is a world of worthless information. Norman Justin Stevens is the name of a young gynecologist in Maine, a jazz musician, an athlete, and some maniac who set his hair on fire and filmed it for the internet. I watch that video a few times before I wheel the computer back into

Melissa's room. I'm starting to think the internet is completely useless.

I want to ring and find out how Norm's going, but that would probably make Justin anxious. He might think people are ringing to check up on whether he's gone mad with the sudden freedom and chopped up his dad. Instead, a more productive task would be to start organizing, one more time, the Gunapan Save Our School Committee.

When the minister visited Gunapan and gave a speech about the value of education and his government's commitment to our rural communities, what he meant was he'd give funding to the school for two more years under a one-off assistance program for disadvantaged country towns. And that was probably only to stop me writing more letters.

At first, hearing that the school would stay open, the headmaster and teachers and parents thought I was some kind of hero. Not as good as Joshua Porter, the local footy player who was selected for the Australian Football League and now tells people he comes from Halstead instead of Gunapan. More like Hector from the abattoir, who did go on to win the Australia-wide championship and had *Speed Butcher* stenciled in silver Gothic lettering on the side of his black Falcon. For weeks afterward, blokes around town would raise their fists in a victory salute when the Speed Butcher drove by, similar to the way parents I'd never met would nod at me when I picked up the kids after school.

Now our fame has faded. The Speed Butcher's *S* has been scraped off his car, probably by Bowden, who doesn't like anyone else's car getting attention. At school, when I pull up in a cloud of Holden exhaust, the other mothers have gone back to coughing and spluttering in the exaggerated way they used to before I was a hero.

As I pull the file of the last Save Our School campaign out of the dresser drawer, I wonder again whether the Gunapan school is worth fighting for. The town's not growing. We've only got a population of a thousand, including the outlying farms. We have some local industry: the abattoir, a couple of organic farms, the alpacas.

The alpaca people set up five years ago on an old property out past the Wilson Dam. Last year I took Melissa and Jake out to see the animals. We left the car on the road and started walking down the driveway, hoping to see some cute fluffy alpacas. When we finally reached the end of the long farm road, we found a woman standing with her hands on her hips watching two alpacas in a pen near the house.

"I hope you don't mind," I said, introducing myself and the kids. "We wanted to see the alpacas. My daughter loves animals."

"No worries," the woman said. "Just don't leave any gates open, OK?"

In the pen, the male was sitting on top of the female and groaning. Melissa blushed and Jake asked what they were doing.

"They're making babies," Melissa muttered.

Jake stepped up close to the fence and peered at the alpacas. The female, crushed under the male, was chewing cud, staring off into the distance. The male rolled its eyes and groaned again.

"He's been at it for an hour already," the owner remarked.

Another drawn-out groan.

"That's enough," the woman shouted. "You've finished, you moron. Get off it. G'awn, get off."

She stepped inside the pen and flicked a whippy tree branch at the male, who rolled his eyes at her and moaned again. The female angled her long neck around, yawned, stared for a moment, then went back to chewing. They clearly don't bother faking it in the alpaca world. One more flick of the branch and the male fell off, scrambled to his feet, and strutted through the gate and into the paddock. The female tucked her legs further under her and nodded off. Their behavior seemed familiar, but I decided not to think too hard about it.

On the way back down the driveway we were followed along the fence by five alpacas that stared at us without blinking.

I heard the alpaca family turned a profit for the first time last year. What a good reason to keep the town alive—developing industry! And the meatworks is going great guns, as the minister saw. We produce a lot of children. Everyone says we need more children in this country. Yes, Gunapan certainly needs a school and a new, improved committee. Maybe I'll spice it up by making it the Save Our School and Stop Our Development Committee. We can help Norm out with his Unsightly Property Notice.

Luckily I kept my list of anyone who had ever turned up to a Save Our School meeting, offered to turn up to a meeting, asked about the meetings, mentioned the word *meeting*, or had not definitely said they would never attend a meeting. But I'm not quite ready for the whole telephone thing, so I settle down to write a letter of irresistible charm that will have everyone wanting to join the Save Our School and Stop Our Development Committee Mark II.

> *Dear local parents and concerned citizens,*
> *The school term is now well under way and—*

No. I sound like the principal.

Dear local parents and concerned citizens,
   You may remember the visit to Gunapan of our
Minister for Education, Elderly Care and Gaming—

Oops, another problem. Not only has the minister who came to Gunapan lost his ministership, it's no longer the Ministry of Education, Elderly Care and Gaming. The new minister, a woman, is the Minister for Education, Social Inclusion and the Service Economy. If we have to give her a tour I don't know what we'll show her. The school, the pub, and the meals on wheels? I'll leave that problem for later. Now I need to write this letter.

Dear comrades, local parents, and concerned citizens,
   Our community is faced with a crisis of—

Although, is something that will happen in two years' time a crisis? Or is a crisis something that is about to happen right now?

"Mum, I've finished dusting the lounge room. Can we go to a movie?"

"Call it a film, Jake. *Movie* makes you sound like an American."

"But I want to be American. Americans have cookies and cream."

"Ice cream, that's what we should have bought for Justin." I can't imagine what Norm's doing right now. How do you talk to a son who's been in prison for fourteen years?

"Mum, can I have some ice cream?"

"OK," I tell Jake.

He stands still beside me, astounded that I've given in without a fight.

"Go on," I tell him. "It's in the freezer."

Jake narrows his eyes at me as if he thinks it's a trick.

"I can't reach the freezer," he says. He's testing me back.

"Why don't you get the chair I saw you using last week and climb on that?"

He sits down beside me to think about the implications of this and I turn back to my letter. I've lost my enthusiasm. Norm and Justin are playing on my mind. I can't compare them with Tony and Melissa, who have only been apart for a few years, but even in that relationship the cracks are starting to show. When Tony left us, Melissa was a little girl who doted on her daddy. She thought she still doted on her daddy until her daddy turned up in the flesh as his old unreliable, untrustworthy self. He only stayed in Gunapan another two days after his visit to us. He told Melissa a few tall tales about the magnificent house where he lives and how he's going to have her and Jake over to stay and buy them whatever they want and he'll come back here and visit regularly. He went to the toy shop in Halstead and bought Melissa and Jake another armful of toys. Then he shot through again with Miss Happy Talee and sent a postcard. *Will call soon. Love, Dad.*

It's been two weeks of silence already, and I can see Melissa hardening. It's too much for an eleven-year-old. Too much disappointment. At least she's got Terror. Terror gallops over to Melissa when she goes out in the yard and nearly knocks her over in her joy. Sometimes Melissa sits on the back steps for half an hour combing the tangles out of Terror's coat while Terror makes little moaning noises of ecstasy. There isn't a single shrub standing in the yard.

"OK, I'll use the chair," Jake says, watching me intently to see my reaction.

"Clever boy." Tomorrow I'm going to buy a freezer lock.

If I start up the letter writing and meetings again I might lose the few friends I have left in Gunapan. That's something worth thinking about. Will Helen ever answer my phone calls if she thinks I'm going to ask her to do the door-to-door petition thing again? Will Kyleen almost decapitate the headmaster a second time, carrying a sign? And Norm seems so tired lately, I'm not sure he'd even have the energy to turn up to meetings. He's got his Unsightly Property Notice and Justin to deal with as well.

Plus, I am aware of one particular difficulty with starting up again. Melissa. She's going to be turning twelve soon. That means her mother-mortification meter will be calibrated to a degree only matched by Swiss watch–style precision engineering. And the way she blushes means that everyone knows when Melissa's embarrassed.

It's all too hard.

"Jake, Melissa," I call. "We're going to the pictures. Tidy yourselves up and we'll head off."

It seems that no time has passed before Jake is standing in front of me all dressed up in his best T-shirt.

"Get that off and put on a clean one."

17

AS WE HEAD off to Halstead along the road where Norm's junkyard is the spectacular landmark, mounds of glowing red rust, the metal mountain of the south, I try to slow down the Holden enough to see properly, but not so much that anyone can tell I'm trying to stickybeak.

"Mum, you're making me carsick. Can you please drive at one speed?" Melissa pleads.

"Tell me if you can see anything at Norm's. I have to keep my eyes on the road."

"See what?"

"Anything."

"Well, I can see Norm and I suppose that's his son with him."

I resist the urge to veer across the road and stare. "What are they doing?"

"They're staring at some piece of machinery."

"That's good. Very good." Norm's back to behaving like Norm again.

It's a forty-minute drive to Halstead and the cinema. By the time we get there, Melissa and Jake have had three fights in the back of the car. Jake's sniveling and Melissa is humming a pop song that is driving me mad. She's told me five times already that her father's friend Talee was once an extra in a movie about a Melbourne rock and roll band. I wonder if I can sneak away during the film and leave these horrible children to be raised by vagrants in Halstead. Or perhaps I could have them put in jail and fast-forward to when they're adults. I'll bake a cake for their release.

Inside, the cinema is cool, verging on arctic. Across the aisle, in the garish flickering light of the previews, I can see a family of four children and one woman. Something about them makes me think it might be the Gunapan family I saw at the waterhole. On the other side of me, Jake and Melissa are in the trance state that overcomes them whenever they're put in front of a screen. They each have a box of popcorn and a fizzy drink.

This excursion has cost me a fortune. The kids have no idea, of course. Tony turned up with a bagful of expensive presents, and from now on they'll sneer at anything I buy them. "Why can't I have a console for the computer?" Jake asked yesterday.

"Because the computer's so old it's got arthritis and Alzheimer's. It would be like buying Nanna a skateboard."

"I don't mind if she gets a skateboard." He's always been a generous boy.

I wonder how the woman with four children can possibly afford to bring them out to the pictures. I lean forward. The kids aren't holding popcorn boxes, but they are eating something. Probably mixed sandwiches filled with sprouts and carrot or health bars she whips up in her free time and sells as a sideline in Halstead's trendy cafés. Other mothers seem to be able to do these things. I reach across and take a handful of Jake's popcorn. He whines something unintelligible, never taking his eyes off the screen.

At the end of the film, while the credits are rolling, Melissa yawns and asks if we can look in the Halstead mall clothes shops. Jake hands me his empty popcorn box as if it's a gift. The lights come on in the cinema and everyone starts talking and stretching. When the Gunapan family stands up I turn to ask Melissa who they are, but she's gone. She's already halfway up the aisle, pulling Jake behind her and leaving me to gather up the bags and empty drink containers before I stumble up the aisle after them like their baggage-handling lackey.

"Young lady, do you mind?" I shout after her.

When I get outside she's already halfway up the main street heading toward the mall. Jake has dropped back and he's looking past me with an expression I can't quite identify. Horror, perhaps? I don't want to look. If Jake's expression is any indication, I don't want to see what's coming. Anyway, I'm puffed out. Melissa has disappeared around the corner and I refuse to chase an eleven-year-old as if she's a toddler. We'll see how she enjoys walking home from Halstead.

I can see myself in the shop window. Jake's backpack is slung over my left shoulder and my handbag hangs from my right. I have two popcorn boxes and two soft-drink containers in my left hand. My right hand is clenched around the waist of my Target jeans, which slide down my hips like a pole dancer whenever I walk too fast. My hair has turned into a strange beehive shape from slumping in the cinema seat and, since that same action gave me a bit of a crick in my neck, my head is tilting sideways. We could call this the Gunapan shuffle.

I dump the containers in a rubbish bin and take a seat beside it. I'm not moving. One of my children has run away and the other is staring at something behind me which could possibly be the monster from under the bed. On a more positive note, unlike in my dream of two nights ago, I am fully clothed.

"Let's go, Mum." Jake's looking at the ground now. "Let's go, come on."

"No." I wiggle myself backward on the bench outside the shop and drop Jake's backpack on the ground. I know I've hidden a packet of Caramellos deep inside my handbag. I keep them to bribe the children, but since one of them has run away and the other won't even look at me, those Caramellos have my name on them. At last I find the roll at the bottom of the bag, peel away the paper, and pop two into my mouth at once. My worries disappear in a haze of chocolate and caramel. My eyes flutter shut.

It seems like a pleasant quarter of an hour, but when I open my eyes, only seconds have passed. Jake is now behind the bench and the family I saw in the cinema is coming toward us. The mother grasps the shoulders of the smallest child, who looks about five, and pulls her close. All four children are staring at Jake sniffling behind me. I'm starting to wonder—have these kids been bullying Melissa and Jake? Are they the ones calling Jake a bush pig? They don't look like bullies, but I suppose people usually don't. The mother isn't staring at Jake. She's keeping her eye on me as if I'm holding a machete and about to lunge. She gathers her children in a huddle around her as they pass us.

"What's going on, Jake?" I ask once they've rounded the corner. "Is one of those kids being mean to you?"

"No." He's still sniffling.

"You can tell me."

"I want to find Melissa."

"We'll find her in a minute," I say, perfectly aware that she's lurking around the corner inside the mall waiting for us.

I can see her reflection in the window opposite. She's standing in a small crowd watching Brian Mack and his friend Al, who are busking at their usual spot.

As Jake swings around and heads for the mall I heave myself off the bench, pick up his backpack, sling my handbag over my shoulder, and hitch up my pants. I feel about a hundred years old. When I round the corner Brian's finished his song and Al's blowing the last mournful note on the didgeridoo. The onlookers toss a few coins into the guitar case and wander off.

"Hey, Loretta, doing some shopping?" I can tell Brian's politely trying not to look at my baggy pants and worn-down heels.

"I wish. I've just spent a fortune on a family trip to the pictures. Making much today?"

"Nah, stingy bastards can barely even give us a clap."

"Probably wouldn't even give us *the* clap if we asked for it," Al says, wiping the mouth of his didg with a cloth.

"Already did that when they first got here," Brian says.

"Mum." Jake pats my thigh. I can tell he's about to ask what they mean, so I grip his hand and give Melissa a touch on the back to urge her forward. She moves on to the next shop and gazes at the tops in the window.

"Got to head off. Hope you do better."

"It won't pick up as long as that friggin' statue is down there. Makes a packet from standing still. Where's the talent in that?" Brian's glaring down toward the other end of the mall, where a small woman dressed in a ball gown and covered in gray paint stands on a rock-shaped pedestal in front of the chocolate shop.

She sees us watching and raises her hand in a slow-motion wave that takes a full five seconds to reach the top of its arc.

"Hmph," Brian says. He begins twisting the pegs on the neck of his guitar and tuning the strings. "What that statue needs is a good chisel."

For some reason, the thought of taking a chisel to the statue person makes me feel cheerful. "Hey, Brian, speaking of building, what do you know about the development down the Bolton Road?"

"Don't get me started, Loretta. That place is bad news."

"So what is it? What's going on? Is it true they've got a license to take water out of the ground?"

"They've got a license to do whatever they bloody want."

"Is that land a sacred site for you?"

"No, not for our mob. Our country's further out west. It's a beautiful piece of bush, though. Or it was until the council stopped maintaining it. Let it turn into a rubbish dump. I heard they sold it for a song."

"Mum, let's go." Jake is tugging at my sleeve.

"Can I call you about it, Brian? I'm trying to find out what's going on."

"No point calling me, love. I don't know anything."

18

THE BOLTON ROAD seems particularly long today. My foot lifts off the accelerator as I pass the gash in the bush and peer down the dirt road toward the development site. I think about stopping and walking in, but only because I'm feeling a little wobbly about today's plan, which is to visit Merv Bull and get my windscreen wiper blades replaced. But before I can make up my mind to take a stroll into the development, the Holden, which needs at least a kilometer's warning before it can stop, has coasted into Merv Bull's yard and is throbbing uncertainly outside his shed. I turn the key and the engine dies with a shudder.

The blue heeler is at the door of the shed, basking in the sun. It lifts its head and looks at me for a moment, then flops onto its side and thumps its tail in a stretch before snoozing off. Last time I came the yard held an aqua Monaro, a Combi van, and an old Escort, but now it's jammed with cars of all shapes and sizes. I have to edge my way between two sleek new cars to reach the door. Lined up along the new cyclone wire fence are three earth-moving machines.

"Mr. Bull?" I call from the doorway. The heeler opens its eyes and watches me without moving.

Shadows inside the shed sway and dip, and then he's in front of me, wiping his hands on a rag.

"Yes?" he asks. He tucks a corner of the rag into the back pocket of his overalls and lifts his hand to shade his eyes. "What can I do for you?"

"I brought my car in when you first came to Gunapan, I'm not sure if you remember." I point to the Holden.

"Of course. Windscreen. Secondhand," Merv says, nodding. "Is there a problem?"

"Boss," a voice comes from inside the shed, "can we have smoko now?"

"All right," Merv shouts back, then turns to me again. "Slackers, the lot of them."

Three boys file out of a small door further along the wall of the shed and sit on plastic chairs in the sun. They pass around a packet of biscuits.

"So . . ." Merv says.

"It's only the wiper blades. The windscreen is great, but it rained the other day for the first time in ages and I couldn't see a thing."

"No worries. It's an '85 Holden, right?" Merv says. He disappears inside the shed for a moment and comes back with plastic-wrapped wiper blades.

We weave our way back to the car, and while he fits the rubber blades, I try to make conversation. I remark on the heat. I remark on the fading paintwork of my car. I remark on the color of the wilted scarlet geranium by the fence. I can hear my voice starting to quaver. When I told Helen I was coming to Merv Bull's garage, she raced around to the house and made me wear a pair of her high heels and put on makeup. I tried to protest that I only wanted new wiper blades, but she insisted. "He's an attractive man, you can't deny it," she said. "So why knock yourself out of the race by turning up in your trackie-daks?" I was cross about that. I never wear my tracksuit pants out of the house unless I'm one hundred percent sure I won't have to leave the car. Then once I'd got dressed up, it seemed as if I was on a date, or a mission, and I started to feel sick. All this for a pair of wiper blades.

"Nice shoes," Merv says after he's dropped the plastic wrapping and bent to pick it up.

"Thanks," I say in a cheery voice. A twitch above my left eye flickers like a broken neon light and I thrust my hips forward in an attempt to balance on Helen's high heels. I'm pretty sure I could pass for Quasimodo. I remark on the earth-moving machines. "I suppose they're for the development. When's it going to open? I heard—"

"Um," he interrupts. "Geez, I'm sorry, but I can't remember your name."

"Loretta Boskovic."

"Of course, sorry. So, Loretta, they brought the machinery up the other day and I signed an agreement. Part of the deal, you know. Commercial-in-confidence stuff, they said. So I'm not supposed to talk about it."

"Sorry! I didn't want to know anything secret," I say hurriedly. The sun is quite hot, even though it's only ten in the morning. I think my face is melting.

"Like I said, I've signed that thing."

"Sure." I try to think fast and stand steady on high heels at the same time. Make conversation, make conversation. "No problem. I was just excited. About having the development here. It's going to be great for the community, isn't it!"

"Yeah," Merv says. "Hey, hang on, aren't you the lady who organized the Save Our School thing? With the chocolate drive?"

"Mmm," I answer. I'm not sure I want to be known as the chocolate-drive lady.

Merv glances to the side and I realize the three apprentices are staring at us. One nudges the other and they slump back in their chairs and pretend to talk casually.

"I'd better be off. How much do I owe you?"

"Don't worry about it. Complimentary service," Merv says, and I hear a low whistle from one of the boys.

As I totter around to the driver's side with Merv following, I apologize for having disturbed him, for parking in the driveway, for not having brought my car in for a full oil and grease change. He has to catch my elbow when I stumble in my heels on a rut in the driveway. His hand is warm and firm on my arm. He doesn't let go, but guides me to the door.

"I must get the car tuned soon," I say stupidly. The yard is so packed with cars he must need five more apprentices.

"Anytime," Merv says. "We can always find a spot."

The car door squeals as I pull it open, ease myself in, then slam it shut.

"Can't have that," Merv says. He tells me to hang on while he gets something from the shed. In a minute he's back, spraying the hinges of the door. "There we go," he says, swinging the door soundlessly open and shut. "The smell won't last long, don't worry."

"Thanks." I hesitate. He didn't have to do that. "Thanks a lot."

"Boss! Phone!" a shout comes from the shed.

Merv looks around. One of the boys is holding the phone handset up at the door of the shed.

"It's the Fiat guy!"

Merv leans down to my window.

"Whenever you want that tune," he says.

I nod. He nods. My heart starts to thump a little. The boy shouts again, and Merv shouts back that he's coming.

Once I start the engine of the Holden I can't hear a thing. Merv says something—who knows what?—as I give a wave while I back out of the driveway and into the road, completely forgetting to look behind me. The screaming horn of the car that follows me down the Bolton Road is quite melodic to my ears.

19

IT'S UNCANNY SEEING Norm and Justin together when I drive into the yard on the following Monday. They're sitting in the shed, side by side, as if they've been here forever. Norm's got his radio up full volume, listening to the races at Moonee Valley, while Justin is bent over the table, screwing a plate onto a bicycle frame. They both look up when I knock on the corrugated iron wall. Even their movements are in sync, like an old couple who've lived together for years.

"Made too much pasta last night, Norm." I plonk the pot on the table. "Thought you might be able to use the leftovers."

"Thanks, Loretta. Have you met Justin, my son?"

Yes, I should answer, I sneaked in and met him while you were listening to race three. Instead I put out my hand and we shake.

"Loretta Boskovic. Loretta can't sing, but her pasta's all right," Norm tells Justin.

Justin nods and smiles. So this is how Norm looked thirty years ago. I only met Justin's mum, Marg, a couple of times, but I can't see anything of her in Justin. Only Norm's long face, wide mouth, sticking-out ears. The son's a lot cleaner, though.

Justin brushes dust and wood shavings off a chair and uses a hand gesture to offer me a seat. He hasn't spoken a word yet. I was nervous coming here this morning. I'd never met an armed robber before. I expected Justin to have a mean snarl and tats up to his ears, but he seems to be an even gentler version of Norm.

"How are you enjoying Gunapan?" I ask him.

He presses his lips together in a half-smile and looks at the ceiling and nods a few times.

"He hasn't seen much of it yet," Norm says. "We might head out for a pub tea tonight, right, Justin?"

Justin nods again. I'm starting to wonder if he has a tongue.

"They've put Thai curry on the menu at the Criterion." I'm trying to keep up the conversation.

Justin raises his eyebrows as if to say "Really?"

"What do you think of curry, Justin?" Norm asks.

Justin shrugs and shakes his head. I think this means he's never tried it. I suppose if he lived in Gunapan until he was twenty, then moved to Geelong and promptly got fourteen years for armed robbery, he's probably never eaten anything more exotic than a banana fritter. Sammy Lee's father used to run the Chinese café here fourteen years ago, but his Chinese food had more to do with Rosella tomato sauce than Chinese herbs and spices. Now the Chinese café is run by an Indian family.

"Well, that's settled," Norm says. "An early pub tea, then home to watch the footy on telly, eh?"

Justin smiles gratefully at his dad. He looks tired. So does Norm. Justin goes back to screwing the plate on the bike frame.

"Justin's thinking of working at Morelli's Meats," Norm says.

I guess we're going to chat about Justin as if he's not here so that he can go on being shy without having to pretend to enjoy talking, so I join in the spirit of the conversation.

"Has he ever worked in an abattoir?" I ask Norm.

"No, but he's been living in one, by the sounds of it," Norm says, perfectly straight-faced.

A soft laugh comes from Justin's bent head. He has a crew cut, and under the bristly dark hair I can see a scar on the back of his skull, running from the crown right down to his neck. As I'm sneaking a look at him he rolls his shoulders and flexes his fingers. He's long and muscular, like a racing greyhound.

"I suppose if the work's there." If I'd just been released from prison, I don't think I'd want to work in an abattoir. But what would I know?

"I hear they're short-staffed because Heck's competing again. Justin can probably get casual work to fill in for a couple of weeks."

I can't see Justin's face, but his scar shifts a little, as though his face is moving. I wonder if he truly wants to work at the abattoir.

"I offered him a job in the yard, but he said no." Norm looks away at the wall of the shed, which he has plastered with colorful centerfolds of Massey-Ferguson tractors.

An awful silence drags on. Justin doesn't raise his head. He's finished attaching the plate to the frame, and now he's sanding rust off the wheel forks. He's a natural for the yard. I can't imagine how Norm would pay him, though. People come into the yard, spend two hours talking at Norm, and leave with a five-dollar purchase. He doesn't sell a lot, but he knows everything about everyone. He could set up a good sideline in blackmail. Norm Stevens Sr.: spare parts, scrap, and confidential information to order.

"Anyway, Norm, are you coming to the next Save Our School Committee meeting?"

"Sure. I can help make up the numbers."

"Great. I want to talk about the development as well. And I'll make orange cake." I have to create an incentive or no one will come. "Feel free to come along, Justin."

"Thanks, yep. Ta," Justin mutters without raising his head.

Having succeeded in getting Justin to speak, I feel as if I've already done a good morning's work. "Well, I guess I'll be off. Have to clock on at the Neighbourhood House soon."

Actually, I don't want to go. This morning was chilly with the crispness of new autumn, and now the fog has disappeared and Norm's rusty shed is bathed in morning sunlight. I wouldn't mind sitting in companionable silence in the sun with the two Stevens men. I could pick up a piece of machinery and try to take it apart.

"Meant to say, Loretta." Norm turns down the volume of the racing, which has been droning on in the background. Outside the kookaburras are going crazy laughing in the stand of messmate trees across from Norm's yard. "Meant to say, Loretta," Norm says again. "Have you met the people in the old MacInerny house?"

"Nope. Why?"

"The lady with the four kids?"

"I think I know who you mean. What about them?"

Norm reaches up and touches his forehead, the place where he had the cancer cut away. I haven't seen him do that for ages. When he goes outdoors these days he always wears a hat, a battered straw boater he found in a cupboard of a caravan someone dumped on the side of the road near Magabar.

"She's a nice lady. From that place in Europe, Bosnia Herzagobbler, where they had the war. A bit shy. Maybe she could join your committee, meet some people."

"You don't want to tell me anything else?"

He shakes his head. I hate it when Norm does this. He's got more agendas than a school committee but he'd never admit to it. At least now I know they're not bullies. That's not something Norm would keep to himself. He's more protective of my kids than a Rottweiler.

"OK, I'll drop a letter at the house. The old MacInerny house on Ross Road?"

Norm nods. I step out of the shed and wave at the darkness inside. Two moving shadows show me that Norm and Justin are waving back. As I turn to head for the car, the fine color of rust shimmers in the thin sunshine. It has a strange beauty I will always associate with Norm.

Next day I finish work at eleven, so I drive to Ross Road on the outskirts of town. The MacInerny family left their house a long time ago but everyone kept calling it the MacInerny house because no one else had moved in. I thought it was derelict.

The house has dingy lace curtains in the window and a tan-colored dog the size of a horse lying on the veranda. When I pull the car into the driveway the beast raises its head and woofs one deep bark, then drops its head back on the veranda with a thump that shakes the neighborhood.

I've been driving inside a twister thanks to the bits of paper flying around the car. I unfold one of the pieces wrapped around the gearstick. It's a committee begging letter dated months ago. I scratch out the date with a pen that doesn't work anymore and fold the letter so the crease covers where I deleted it.

The moment the Holden door slams behind me, the house comes alive. Curtains tweak open in the left-hand window, the dog tries to haul its massive frame off the veranda floor, the door opens, and the woman I recognize from the Halstead mall steps outside and puts her hands on her hips. I guess they don't get many visitors out here.

I'm starting to get a bit of a hillbilly feeling, what with the car on blocks beside the house and the oil drum in the middle of the front yard stuffed with pieces of an old paling fence. I hesitate beside the car, waiting for the banjos to start, until it occurs to me that my yard has an unhappy similarity to this one, thanks to having my own rusting truck on blocks and a goat tethered to the washing line.

"Hello," I call out. Damn, Norm forgot to tell me her name.

She steps back inside the shadow of the door. Norm wasn't kidding about "a bit shy." She looks like she's going to be absorbed into the wall.

"Hi. I wanted to drop in this invitation." I'm shouting, but only to make sure she hears me from wherever she's disappeared to.

Inside the house someone speaks curtly in a foreign language. It has the commanding tone of an order. The curtain in the left window falls back into place.

"Hello?" Maybe it's not a hillbilly movie I'm stumbling around in but a horror. They probably have bodies stacked five deep in the shed.

"What you want?" an accented voice calls from the darkness.

Hmm. I want to invite you to join a committee. Even

thinking those words puts me in a coma of boredom. Surely I can find a better way to describe it. I will be talking to the air and an empty doorway, but I suppose she'll be listening from inside.

"I'm worried about our kids' future," I call out, realizing as the words leave my mouth that I am using the same line as an insurance salesman.

She darts out of the doorway and into the light like a spider that feels a tug on its web, her finger pointing at me.

"Your kids, no!"

The monster dog starts to growl. I was right. It is a horror movie.

I hold out the folded letter. I'm beside the car, next to the front gate. I'm not moving while the monster dog is alive and making noise.

"No good!" She's still pointing as if a laser is beaming from her fingertip, and my hand reaches up involuntarily to touch my chest.

The curtain tweaks open again. I'm close enough to see an old creased face peering out. I smile. The face frowns and the ancient one makes a shaky fist at me.

I never knew I could make such a strong impression. I creep along the fence, tuck the letter into the rusted old letter box beside the gate, and hurry back to the car. I'll be thanking Norm later for this experience.

Driving back from the MacInerny house, I see her kids get off the school bus. The little boy is holding the hand of a smaller girl, and the two others, an older boy and girl, are walking behind them. The young boy seems to be crying.

I gun the Holden down the road. Maybe someone's sick,

I think. Maybe the young boy has leukemia and they're exhausted from looking after him. Or the mother's suffering from post-traumatic stress after the war and she locks them in the house and won't let them out except for school. Or maybe that old crone in the window is . . . is something. I don't know. A witch, maybe, but a real one, not a glorified aromatherapist like Leanne. I feel a little shaky after that reception. I hope the new Mrs. MacInerny doesn't join the committee.

At the school gate Melissa's standing with her hands on her hips, lips pursed, squinting into the sun. If she keeps maturing at this rate she'll soon be a fully fledged Gunapan woman. She'll have married, had kids, and been deserted by the time she's fifteen. She and Jake climb into the backseat and I head off in my usual role of chauffeur.

"How come you always sit in the back, Liss?" I ask. "It's not as if you need a booster seat anymore. You could sit up with me and chat while I drive." If she's going to be a Gunapan woman, she'll need to learn the art of the car nod. A half-nod for acquaintances, a nod for friends, and a knowing head toss for best friends. This can only be done from the front seat. And while driving at speed. Preferably with an arm hanging casually out the window.

"Because you drive like a psycho," my daughter says casually. "And I don't want to die."

The minute that girl gets her license I'm never letting her in my car again.

"Are any of the kids from that new family in your class?"

"What new family?"

I check the rearview mirror. Melissa's sitting with a back as straight as a ballerina's and staring at her hands. She's lying.

"The one from Bosnia Hergesobbler. The foreigners."

Another glance at the reflection. Jake's looking out the window.

"Well?"

"Yeah, a girl."

"What's her name?"

"I don't know."

"You must know. There are only sixteen kids in your class."

"Something. I can't pronounce it."

"Well, what do you call her when you want to speak to her?" I'm starting to channel a dull policeman.

"Nothing."

A modern mother never resorts to violence. That's why I don't screech to a halt, lean over the back of the seat, and give my daughter a good thwack over the head. Instead, because I am a reasonable modern woman and a caring mother, I screech to a halt, lean over the back of the seat, and warn Melissa that serious consequences will occur if she doesn't smarten up and stop avoiding my questions.

"What serious consequences?" she asks.

The serious consequence is that my head may explode, but that's not going to sway Melissa.

"No TV for a week." I try not to think about the fact that Melissa is only eleven. If she's this way now, what will happen when she turns into a teenager? I might have to leave home. Get a flat in the city. Join an exercise class and discover the body that's been waiting underneath my flab for all these years. I'll be tired of Beemer Man and Harley Man by then. I'll be ready for Merc Man. Merc Man has divorced his ungrateful wife and is looking for someone to pamper. "Loretta," he says to me after we've made love on the king-sized bed in his penthouse with views of the Sydney Harbour

Bridge, "you are one delectable hunk of woman. You know, looking at this taut body, I can't believe you have children." "Actually, I don't," I'll tell him. "I sold them."

Melissa's been checking the letter box every day since Tony left town, and this afternoon I see her pull a few bits of mail out of the box, flip through them, then slip one into her pocket as she looks furtively around at the house. I am not hiding. It is a fluke that I am standing behind the curtain, from where I can see her but she can't see me. Exactly where I have been while she checked the letter box every day since her father's visit.

"Bills, Mum," she says with pretend innocence, dropping a few envelopes on the dresser and heading off to her room.

"Thanks, Liss," I answer with a winning smile, like a character in an Enid Blyton book. Sometimes I am amazed at how we learn to play these roles, as if we are in a movie.

Tony is too lazy and selfish to try to take the kids away from me, but whenever I think of the possibility, my stomach rolls over and I can feel my insides being rearranged. What if Talee wants them? I wonder. What if Tony and Talee have Melissa over for a visit and Melissa doesn't want to come home? Or Jake? They'd only have to buy Jake a Lego set and he'd go anywhere with them. Later in the night, when Melissa's asleep, I sneak into her room and slide the card from under her pillow.

Hi, Liss and Jake,
    Hope school's good and everything is great. Can't wait to see you again. Say hello to your mum.
                                              Love, Dad and Talee

Which would be fine, except it's not his handwriting. Miss Happy must have written it. They won't be coming to take my children. Tony has probably, once again, forgotten he even has children.

Next morning I ring Helen and tell her about my experience with the new family at the MacInerny house. She's never met the woman.

"I mean, I kind of know her. I've seen her and the kids plenty of times. We nod hello. I just never had a chance to talk to her. She's a refugee, poor thing. Try the Church of Goodwill. They have that outreach program."

After work, on the way to the church I drop in at the shire office. Norm's asked me to get the official documents for the development to use in his next try at getting the Unsightly Property Notice lifted. He's convinced they're connected.

"Give me everything you've got on the development on the Bolton Road," I say to the receptionist in my best private detective voice.

She yawns and turns to her computer. "You mean the resort?" she asks.

"That's it. I'll have whatever you've got. Plans, permits, letters, objections." That's odd, I think. "Did anyone object? I don't remember seeing any notices about this. Aren't you supposed to be able to object to new buildings?"

"Don't know. You'd have to ask in Planning about that." She taps and clicks with her keyboard and mouse, stifling yawns. "Nothing here, sorry."

"It's a huge development. Isn't there anything?"

"Yeah, but I can't find anything for the public. All the

stuff's in files I can't access and the manager's not in today. You'll probably have to put in a written request."

Next I head for the church.

The Church of Goodwill shopfront is on the main road between the betting shop and the fish and chippery. Hand-drawn pictures of rainbows and doves are sticky-taped to the window, and Christian rock and roll music blares in distorted waves from a tinny speaker above the front door. Inside, Trudy sits at the desk staring at a computer screen.

"I hate these things," she says to me when I walk in. "I preferred it when we wrote letters to each other by hand, and added up the week's offerings in a hardbound book with two columns. I'm not entirely convinced that computers aren't the work of the devil."

"Is that right?" I try to look as if I talk about the devil every day.

"I'm joking, Loretta. What can I do for you?"

"Have you ever met the Bosnia Herzabobble people down the old MacInerny place?"

"Mersiha and her family? Yes, of course. They're part of the Gunapan Revitalization and Welcoming Committee Community Project."

I might be imagining it, but Trudy seems to be avoiding looking me in the eye. I've been getting that feeling a lot lately. As if people are afraid to tell me the revived Save Our School Committee is a waste of time. I don't know why they'd hold back. They didn't last time. I distinctly remember Trudy telling me, "That Save Our School Committee is a waste of time, Loretta. Why don't you do some real work in the community and help clean up Wilson Dam next Saturday?" I wanted to answer that I didn't feel like contracting tetanus, but I didn't because Trudy's a Christian and a good worker in the community and one day I might need her help for Save Our School.

"She's already on a committee. Oh, that's OK then. Norm thought she might be good for Save Our School. But if she's busy . . ."

"She's not on the committee, Loretta. She's a refugee, struggling to get herself and her family settled here. Her sponsor is Maxine. Anyway, you must have seen her at the school and the fair and around the place. Mersiha's lovely. She's making a real effort to join in. People are starting to welcome her very warmly."

"Oh. Well, maybe I could ask Maxine to contact—"

"Actually, Loretta"—Trudy looks at the ceiling as if she's getting instructions from above—"Maxine and I have been meaning to talk to you. So here you are, and I think I'd better say it."

"About Save Our School?"

"No." She takes a deep breath. "About the bullying. Something has to be done."

"I knew it. I knew it was bullying." My face is tight with rage. "I'll do something all right." I feel the breath blazing out of my nose, hotter and angrier than the snorts of a bull at a matador fight. "They'll find out no one messes with my kids. I'll call their father to come and sort it out if I have to. I'm going around to that woman's place right now." I want to paw at the ground. The whole room is red.

Trudy stands up and squeezes out from behind the desk. She edges her way between me and the front door.

"Step away from the door, Loretta."

I take a long, deep breath, swell to twice my size like an angry puffer fish. "I'm going now, Trudy. Get out of my way."

Trudy presses her back against the door. "I can't let you."

"This is not about you, Trudy. It's about my children. Get out of the way or I'll throw you through that door."

"Loretta, listen to yourself. Think about where your children have learned their bad behavior. I had no idea you were this kind of person."

"My children's bad behavior? What about that woman's children? Oh, it's a lovely welcome for them, even though they're making my children's life hell. I know, they're traumatized by war and everything, but that's no excuse for bringing their problems here and bullying my kids. I won't take it, Trudy. Out of the way, please."

"Oh, dear," Trudy says. She has slumped against the glass of the door. She reaches out and takes my hand. "Oh, Loretta. We'd better have a cup of tea."

20

WHEN I ARRIVE, bawling, at Norm's yard, Justin is by himself.

"Dad's gone out," he says. He's sitting at the table in the shed, listening to the races and using an artist's paintbrush to paint fire-engine red enamel on an old toy car the size of a shoebox. "Thought your Jake might like this."

I hiccup in reply. Justin gestures to the seat on the other side of the table, but I shake my head. It's two o'clock. I have one and a half hours till the kids get out of school and I need to do something, but I don't know what.

"Cup of tea?"

I shake my head, then nod, then sob, then sniff a long wet snotty sniff.

"When's Norm back?" I manage to ask.

"Not till later tonight. He's gone down to the city."

I wonder what Norm would be doing in the city, but I can't allow myself to get off track. I have an urgent problem and I have to find a way to fix it.

"My daughter's a bully," I blurt out to Justin. "My son's a follower. They've been tormenting the new kids in town."

Justin nods slowly. I'm still standing in the doorway of

the shed, the sun burning the back of my neck in stinging fingers.

"I don't know what to do."

Justin nods again. "Seen a few bullies in my time."

"I'm going home." I start to sob and hiccup again. "Can you tell Norm I came by?"

"I might follow to see you get home all right. You probably can't see too well right now. Drive slowly, OK?"

He's right. My eyes are stinging and smarting, my whole face is swollen. I must look like I'm the one who's being bullied.

I only bump the veranda lightly when I steer the Holden into the driveway. Justin pulls up in the truck and waves to me, but I don't want to go into my empty house and cry, so I call him in. He sits patiently at the kitchen table as I start the kettle, lay out the cups and a plate of biscuits, work my way through five tissues, then finally stop crying. I pour the tea and slump into a kitchen chair.

"I'm a terrible mother," I tell him before I bite into a Chocolate Royal and suck the marshmallow. I've lined up the ten Chocolate Royals from the packet in two rows on the plate. Number one is still on its way down my throat when I pick up number two and start to peel the chocolate covering away from the marshmallow with my teeth. It's not easy to speak with my mouth full of chocolate, marshmallow, and biscuit base, but I do have experience.

"Melissa has been calling the Bosnian kids 'bush pigs.' She passes the little girl notes during class with curly pigs' tails drawn on them. She whispers to them that they should go home to the stinky country they came from. She—" My voice cracks here. I can't believe this is my daughter. "She tells them they smell bad and that they're dirty foreigners."

Justin blows on his cup of tea to cool it down before he takes a sip. "Does she hit them?"

"I don't think so. You'd better have one of these." There are only four Chocolate Royals left on the plate. I'm starting to feel nauseated as I suck the marshmallow off the biscuit base of number six.

"That's got to be a good thing. She doesn't hit them."

"Jake follows the younger ones around the schoolyard at recess making squealing noises. They escaped from a war, only to come out here and be bullied by my children! Is it because they're growing up without a father?"

"Dad said your kids have missed their dad."

I want to blame Tony. When he was here he was a bad father and now he's gone he's still being a bad father. I wonder if I should try to contact him. He neglected to leave his new address. I suppose I could ring around the country towns near Mildura and ask about a man with unnaturally white front teeth and a child bride.

"He never taught them how to behave. He was always stomping around in a permanent rage."

Justin nods, looks at his tea.

"How can I teach a little boy to be a good person? That's a man's job. Sure, it was fine to leave me, but did he have to abandon his kids?"

Justin keeps nodding, a quiet, calm motion.

"I thought everything got better after he left. We were happier. I thought I could bring them up on my own . . . I always joke about giving away the kids, but they're my life."

For a moment we sit in silence as I come around to the truth.

"I've done a bad job. I'm the worst kind of mother. I've raised monsters."

"So what do you reckon you'll do about it?" Justin asks.

"Here, you take this one," I say, pushing the last Chocolate Royal toward Justin. He shakes his head. As I swallow the last gluey crumbs, I wonder whether I still have that old block of rum-and-raisin chocolate from Christmas in the back of the freezer.

"I think. I think, I think . . . I think I'll wait till Norm gets back. Yes, that's what I'll do."

"Good idea."

"They probably hate me. That's why they're doing this. They hate me and they want to punish me. Unconsciously. You hated your parents, didn't you? Norm said that."

Justin sits back in his chair and stares at me. "Of course I didn't hate them. Did he mean because I wouldn't see them while I was inside?" He presses his lips tightly together for a moment, breathes in through his nose. "I was ashamed. I was a shitty, ungrateful kid who got caught, and then when they sent me to jail I realized what a fucking idiot I'd been. Sorry about the language."

I shake my head. That kind of language slides off me after ten years with Tony, who thought "fucking" was the most descriptive word in the English language. For Tony, "fucking" meant good and it meant bad. It meant funny and it meant someone who needed a good kicking. It meant hello or good-bye. Thank you or I never want to see you again. Delicious, or red, or belonging to the human race, or not.

"I told Mum," Justin mutters. "When I went up to Warrnambool. I explained why I couldn't come out when she visited."

"Because you were ashamed?"

He shrugs and picks up his mug, peers into it, then holds

it up high so he can look at the base. "Cracked," he says. "I'll get a new one for you."

"Don't worry, it's been like that for years."

Watching him at the table, I can't get over the resemblance. Justin hasn't seen his dad for fourteen years, and yet even the way he holds a cup is identical to Norm. His hands are the same plate shape. He looks off to the side when he's asking a question and he snorts softly when he doesn't believe something. And the ears. If he and Norm could learn to move those ears at will they could form a circus act—the Flying Stevenses.

"My friend Helen was going to come around tonight to watch a film after the kids have gone to bed. Maybe Norm and you could come too? To have a talk about this . . ."

He does his look-over-and-out-through-the-window thing while I gather the cups and switch the kettle on for another cup. He is so quiet and still that I feel like a punchy drunk, flailing around and rattling the whole kitchen with every move. I'm not helped by the wonky floor that bounces up and down every time I take a step and sets the kitchen dresser juddering and the plates chattering across the shelves.

So far poor quiet Justin has seen me blubbering, self-flagellating, moaning, complaining, and eating an entire packet of Chocolate Royals in eleven minutes. Prison and its standards of etiquette are probably looking pretty fancy right now.

"I'm not sure Dad'll be up for it tonight, but I'll ask him."

The kettle boils and I pour water onto two more tea bags and settle back at the kitchen table.

"I shouldn't keep you," Justin says into his teacup.

The trouble with gentle, calm, quiet people I don't know

well is that I find myself babbling to fill the spaces between bits of conversation. Useless information wells up out of me and dribbles all over the silence.

"I'm starting up the Save Our School Committee Mark II. I want to make it about the development too, because of what they've done to Norm."

"Dad said."

"No one will join now. I'm the mother with the bully children. Everyone else is probably hoping the school will close so they can get their kids away from mine."

Justin laughs. "Where I was, real bullies made a career out of it. Some other people did stupid bullying things because they were afraid. They thought it made them look strong. Once they found their place in the hierarchy, they settled down."

I suppose I'm in shock. I think about Melissa passing nasty notes to the girl in her class and Melissa seems to have become someone new, not my smart-arse daughter who's full of bravado but loves to cuddle up on the couch with me and hug me from behind when I'm at the sink. How could she be doing this?

Half an hour later, as I wait in the car outside the school, Melissa walks out of the school gate with Jake in tow. She has her father's narrow pointy features, I can see now. She looks behind her. The children she's been bullying are coming down the steps of the school in a tight group, not looking sideways or forward, only staring at their feet. Melissa pulls Jake aside and they stand hidden outside the gate.

Melissa could see me in the car if she turned around, but she doesn't. She's concentrating too hard on what's happening at the gate. Her arm, stretched behind her, holds Jake protectively against the fence as if she's afraid someone is going to snatch him away. The other children step out through the gate in one movement, then hurry off down the street in the opposite direction to where Melissa is standing. I see her call something after them. The oldest one turns around and for a moment she and Melissa stare at each other like animals, each waiting for the other to make the first move. The girl, hissing something so loudly I can hear the hiss but not the words, turns, gathers her siblings around her, and starts off for home. Melissa's body goes limp and her head nods toward her chest as if she is exhausted. Jake steps around her and takes her hand. She might be crying.

I have no idea what's going on, but I want to take her in my arms and hug her. They say she's a bully. All I see is my little girl, frightened and alone.

21

NORM TURNS UP at nine in the evening with a couple of stubbies of beer and a packet of beer nuts. He's got a Band-Aid on the inside of his arm.

"What happened?" I nod at the Band-Aid.

"Oh." He seems startled. Puts down the beer and nuts and rolls down his sleeve to cover the Band-Aid. "Scratch. Piece of metal."

"Make sure you get a tetanus shot," I warn him. Norm snickers.

Helen greets Norm when he comes into the kitchen. The kids are in bed, but I've left the TV blaring in the lounge room so they can't hear what we're saying if they wake up.

"Come to help sort out the Children of the Corn?" Helen says to Norm.

"Bloody menaces to society." He thumps into the same kitchen chair that Justin sat in this afternoon.

"Norm, tell Justin thanks for me, will you? I cried at him for a while, then forced him to drink about ten cups of tea and wouldn't let him have a single Chocolate Royal out of the whole packet."

"So what's new?"

"It's not funny, Norm. My children are bullies. I raised two bullies!"

"Sometimes these things fade away," Helen remarks. "Aren't the kids going to your sister's place next week? Maybe it'll blow over while they're gone."

"It might blow over, but I don't think I'll ever get over it."

"So they're calling kids names. So what? You didn't raise real bullies. Brenda Giles's boys, now they're real bullies," Helen says.

"Yeah, settle down, Loretta," Norm adds. "It's not like you're drunk every night or your kids are hacking babies into little pieces."

"Norm, you've got to stop reading the newspapers."

They may not have been hacking up babies, but last summer the Giles boys, Glenn and Gary, spent nights terrorizing anyone who dared to venture out on the streets. Brenda was having a bit of a bad patch with the stress of having all those children to feed, and she was passed out on the couch by nine every night. The younger kids stayed home eating rubbish and watching TV shopping shows till dawn, but the two older boys started to roam.

Any kid walking around after ten o'clock was in trouble if Glenn and Gary caught them. They were the angriest boys anyone had seen in this town for a long time. Bill, the local policeman, drove around the streets in his patrol car, trying to keep an eye out, but they were fast and on foot, and they always got away over fences and down lanes and through the paddocks on the outskirts of town.

The local lads who'd thought they were tough until Glenn and Gary were let loose came home with black eyes and bruises and a sudden desire to spend more time with their families. Bill once joked to me that the Giles boys had done a better job of cleaning up the streets than he ever could. But they got more and more violent. The black eyes turned into cuts. The bruises became broken bones. They started carrying chains and bats.

One night, after most of the local kids had learned their lesson about staying indoors after dark, a couple of boys visiting their cousins down the end of Ables Court ran into the Giles boys out in the scrub behind the abattoir. The visitors were from a tough part of Melbourne where proper gangs identified themselves with tattoos and pledges and special haircuts. No one knows exactly what happened, but the Giles boys disappeared for two days. Then, on the third day, they turned up at the emergency ward in Halstead Hospital. Glenn slipped into a coma and only woke up after five days. That's what got Brenda out of her bad patch. She had to farm out the other kids for a week and stay in the hospital while Glenn was in danger of not pulling through. When she got home the kids made her swear she'd never drink again. They told her that the people they'd stayed with had made them do their homework and no way were they going back to that.

I wonder if I've been neglecting my children. Is that why they've turned into monsters? A stinging tear forms in the corner of my left eye. Perhaps I should give up the campaigning.

"Have I been neglecting them?" I say out loud. "All the Save Our School stuff and the rest, don't they realize I'm doing it for them? So they have a good place to live? No one else is going to do it. No one cares about us in the small towns. We have to fight or we'll go under. But maybe they're asking why me? Why have I decided to do it? Maybe that's what's happened. I should be doing more things with them.

Nature walks. Art projects. I'll start sewing lessons, learn to make them clothes. I'll—"

"For God's sake, Loretta, snap out of it. Where's your sense of humor gone? It's not the end of the world." Norm sounds impatient.

I sniff. Pull another tissue from my pocket. Helen's tapping her foot and leafing through the TV guide.

"Sorry, love," Norm says. "I didn't mean to jump down your throat. I'm a bit tired. But will you leave it for a few days? Let the kids go to your sister's place and we can talk about it when they get back."

"You don't have to deal with it, Norm. I have to deal with it. Let me ask you something important. Should I try to get in contact with Tony? Is it because they haven't got a father?"

After they've finished laughing so much that Helen has a coughing fit and Norm spills his beer, Norm leans back in his chair and sighs.

"Norm's right. Give it a rest, Loretta," Helen says. "Let things settle. There's such a thing as being too proactive."

Too proactive? Helen's been reading the back of my breakfast cereal box. The other morning I was gazing dreamily at the box and the word caught my eye. Proactive. Or was it a margarine container? Whichever. I read it and realized I'd been in a non-proactive slump. That's what decided me to start up the SOS Committee Mark II. But how did Helen know? How does she know these things about me? It's unnerving. It makes me cross.

"I have no idea what you mean by 'proactive,' Helen. You must be picking up jargon from that therapist of yours."

Helen blinks slowly. "Actually, Loretta, therapy helps people with anger issues. You should try it. You and your bullying children."

So this is how a friend behaves when you're in trouble. Puts the boot in.

"Yes, Helen, you're right. My bullying children might need to see a therapist. At least they have a real problem. They're not middle-aged women so desperate for attention they'll pay for it."

Norm pushes his chair back from the table. "Right. I'm out of here."

From the bedroom comes one of Jake's shrieks. I ignore it like I usually do, knowing it's not a desperate shriek, only one of his night shrieks.

"Aren't you going to see what that's about?" Helen asks.

"It's nothing," I answer impatiently. "They both scream at night."

Helen raises one eyebrow. I've sat with her and laughed when she used that look on someone else. Now I know how it feels to be the victim of the single superior arched eyebrow.

"Not real screaming. Night cries."

"Everyday screaming, then," Helen says. If anything, the arched eyebrow goes even higher. She'll lose it in her hair if she's not careful.

Norm heaves himself up off the wooden kitchen chair and picks up his old straw hat.

"I'll drop by Sunday, once the kids are gone. Leave it a bit, OK, Loretta?"

They obviously don't care. I can't leave it. I'll have to do something before the kids go to Patsy's.

Helen, still looking miffed, is stuffing her phone into her handbag and rummaging around for her keys. Norm ducks on his way out the back door, but I notice he's shorter, or stooping lower, or something, because the top of his head is nowhere near touching the architrave anymore. He must be getting old. I hear him talking to Terror as he heads down the back stairs and the thudding of her hooves following him down. She likes to escort visitors to the gate.

"Do you want a coffee tomorrow?" I ask Helen as we walk down the hallway to the front door. I talk softly so I don't wake the kids.

"I'll be busy attention seeking tomorrow," she says, looking at me in the dim light of the moon that comes through the glass panel in the front door.

"Oh, Helen, don't. I didn't mean it. I'm sorry."

"You never mean it, Loretta."

She steps out through the front door and pulls it shut quietly behind her. I stand in the half-light, shocked, suddenly shivering.

22

THE NEXT DAY is the last day of term, and the parents are at
the school gate early. Helen's here to pick up the Tim Tams.
She's making a big show of chatting and laughing with everyone but me. I stay sitting in the driver's seat of the Holden,
my left bum cheek almost impaled on the broken spring that
poked its way through the vinyl last week.

Melissa and Jake are so excited about their visit to Patsy's
house that when they get into the car their shrill voices sound
like squeaking bats. Melissa is talking about the shops she's
going to visit in Melbourne and Jake keeps interrupting with
descriptions of the food George cooked both times she came
to visit us. He seems to expect she'll spend his whole visit in
the kitchen, whipping up culinary masterpieces to thrill a
six-year-old—chocolate crackles, hot dogs, toffee, pancakes.

"Auntie George is a chef!" he screams at no one from the
backseat.

I can't understand how I made these children.

It takes them a while to realize we're not going home.

"I have to pack!" Melissa shrieks. "Mum, we have to go
home now!"

Who knows what she thinks she's going to pack. It's as if

the promise of a trip to Melbourne has addled her mind and she thinks she has more than four outfits.

"Sit tight," I tell them. "We're going on a little trip."

In the rearview mirror I see Melissa fall back against the seat. How on earth will she have time to choose between her three good shirts if we waste our time driving around the countryside?

I take a full tour of Gunapan, starting at the CWA Hall, following the route of the annual Rhododendron Parade, which passes the eleven Gunapan houses with rhododendron bushes and ends at the local park, then I ease the car off north to the footy ground and travel the dirt road out to Wilson Dam and then further north. Melissa and Jake quiet down and sit staring out through the windows.

This is all a ploy to buy time while I plan what to say to them. I considered leaving "the talk" till they got back from their holiday, as Norm suggested, but I know I'll fret the whole time anyway so I might as well have a crack at this problem now.

When we reach the lookout on Bald Hill, I climb out of the car. Melissa and Jake stay sitting in the back. They won't look at me.

The wind is barely blowing down in town, but up here it's brisk and biting. We're the only people here. The view looks over Gunapan, the abattoir, the farms. The first autumn rain came last week, but the land is still dry and the grass and trees are like children's models made of straw and sticks. I can see our little house over to the south with the neatly paddocked hobby farm opposite. It's incredible to think I've been in Gunapan for thirteen years. Shouldn't I get some kind of award?

A long way away, to my left, the Bolton Road winds through the forest. The gash of the development is even bigger than I'd realized. In the center of the cleared land is a deep rectangular hole with large yellow machinery parked around it. Maxine told me she drove past last week on the way to Merv Bull's garage and they've put *Do Not Enter* signs all along the road. That used to be public land. I'm mad about this. Right now I'm mad about everything.

When I'm completely chilled through and the kids still haven't got out of the car, I go back and get into the driver's seat. At first I turn around to look at them, but twisting my neck is painful, so I turn to face the front and adjust the rear-view mirror to see their reactions. They're both looking down as if something very important is curled up in their laps.

"You're bullying those new children."

They don't reply. I thought Melissa would jump in to defend herself. I thought Jake might cry. Nothing. They sit still and stare at their hands.

"I'm ashamed." It's me who starts to cry. I press my lips tightly together and hold my breath, but tears gather at the corners of my eyes and run down my face. My nose fills with snot and I have to breathe through my mouth. I'm afraid to say anything else because my voice will give away that I'm crying, and I don't think they can see that I am because I'm facing the windscreen. I want them to know I'm angry, not think I'm a pathetic, crying mother.

The wind is buffeting the car, whistling through the perished rubber seals around the windows. A single splat of autumn rain hits the windscreen. Inside, we're saying nothing. The tears stop dribbling. I pull a hankie from my pocket and dab away the wetness, then blow my nose as quietly as I can, but the wet snot sound is a dead giveaway that I've been crying.

"Why? Are you unhappy?" I decided on the drive here not

to mention Tony. If it's about Tony, I'm sure Melissa will let me know.

Bald Hill isn't bald anymore. The Gunapan Beautification Committee built a park up here, with benches and a lookout tower and shrubs and trees and a toilet block. The vegetation is stunted from the hot wind in summer and the sudden frosts of winter. When we first moved to Gunapan, Tony and I came up here for a picnic. I dropped the sandwiches in the dirt, Tony drank too much beer and got a headache in the hot sun, his car battery went flat for no obvious reason, and we had to wait two hours for a tow truck. "Welcome to Gunapan," I said to Tony, laughing, as we sat waiting on the picnic bench and watching nothing move in the town below. He didn't laugh. That would be lesson number twenty-three no one taught me: don't marry a man who has no sense of humor.

"We're not leaving till I get some answers."

The only time they're this quiet is when they're asleep. I can outwait them. I know Jake simply cannot say silent for much longer. I'm fairly certain that Melissa is building a case in her mind and will soon present the argument for the defense. I reach for my bag and my trusty Caramellos. Chocolate and caramel can soothe any situation, if administered early enough. Naturally, my evil, bullying children will have to do without. They watch me cram three into my mouth. I consider a fourth, but decide that only a death in the family is a four-Caramello crisis.

I like to close my eyes when I'm sucking on a Caramello. It makes the taste stronger and the bad things of the outside world disappear for a few minutes. However, having my eyes closed doesn't mean that I lose my other faculties. I hear the click and creak as Melissa opens her door.

"Montchu dare nget outf dis kaa," I say, mouth glued up with Caramello.

The door groans and clunks as Melissa pulls it shut. In the rearview mirror I see her look at Jake. Jake looks back at her. I can't read their expressions. The silence continues, punctuated by the whistling of the wind. The Caramellos melt to nothing but a sweet aftertaste. As I'm wondering what to do next, a thick foul miasma creeps over the seat and encloses me.

"Jake!" Melissa screams. She flings open her door and falls out of the car. So do I. It's incredible that a six-year-old can produce so much stink. Jake sits with his legs clenched together.

"I need to do poo," he says firmly. "I need to do poo very soon."

The gray concrete public toilet block squats on the very peak of Bald Hill. I point Jake in that direction and stuff a wad of tissues in his hand.

"No more than five minutes!" I shout after him as he hurries off in a tight waddle. He's inherited his father's habit of spending fifteen to twenty minutes on the toilet, pondering whatever they ponder.

Over at the picnic area Melissa perches on a table with her feet resting on the bench below. She's having a growth spurt and her school dress is too short. I can see the faint outline of her budding breasts pressing against the cotton of the dress. I have to take a deep breath and remember how hard it is to be a girl going through puberty. Of course, my puberty only arrived when I was fourteen. A late developer in so many ways.

"What happened?" I ask when I'm sitting on the bench next to her feet.

"Nothing."

"What did you do to them?"

"Nothing."

"If you didn't do anything, how come I'm being told you're a bully?"

"I'm not a bully! They started it."

I reach up and hug myself against the cold. "Did you call them bush pigs?"

"No! Well, not before she called Jake a bush pig after our lesson about feral animals. He got upset so I joked about it to make him feel better."

"And what did you do to that girl to make her call Jake a bush pig?"

"She can't even speak English properly! She said the essay I read out in class was a lie and her sister said I was big and fat. She smells and she's always got those brothers tagging along."

I'm having trouble finding anything to hang on to here. "I think we'll have to cancel your trip to Melbourne. If you won't be honest, I can't trust you to be in charge of Jake. Maybe when you've grown up a bit."

Oh, hell. I believe I heard my mother speak through my mouth. I accused my child of being immature and threatened to punish her unless she grows up. My hands reach up and tug at my turkey neck. I look down and see, with despair in my heart, that I am wearing squarish sensible shoes.

"Melissa?" I heave myself up backward to sit beside her on the table. It's time to be straightforward. "Don't do it anymore. I don't understand what's going on and I don't care. Don't be mean. That's all. Don't be mean. If someone's mean to you, come and tell me. Don't be mean back. Don't call people names, don't tease them, don't try to scare them."

"Mmm."

"No nasty notes. Don't encourage Jake."

She stares down at her shoes.

"I mean it, Melissa Boskovic. I am so ashamed that my child is a bully. Those kids have come from a war zone! You should be helping them."

Tony told me once that his great-grandfather migrated to Australia during the gold rush. It's only dawning on me now that the name Boskovic might actually come from the region of that war zone. My kids could carry the same kind of blood as the children they are tormenting. When Helen and I were watching TV reports of the war and the ethnic cleansing, we talked about how we might behave if we were in a war. Would we be cowards? Would we be able to kill someone? War must make you do things you never imagined. Now that thought only makes me feel worse about my children, brought up in a safe, quiet country town and still behaving like bullies. What is their excuse? What is mine for raising them to be like this?

Melissa's voice has risen an octave. "They started it! It's not fair. I get the blame and she's the one that said I'm a liar and everyone believed her and not me!"

"What did you say that she would call you a liar?"

Melissa flushes. "Nothing."

"I'm warning you, young lady. I want the truth, or no trip to Melbourne."

"I said my dad was a spy who was undercover."

Tony an undercover spy? In the middle of these terrible negotiations, that nearly makes me laugh. "I see," I say in my most serious voice. "And is that because he's not around?"

"Yes," Melissa mumbles miserably.

"But most of the children in the school don't have a father around."

"Yeah, but they're losers."

"So are we losers too?"

"No!" she shouts indignantly. "That's the point!"

"Don't you realize that bullies are losers? They're the real losers because everyone's scared of them. No one respects them and absolutely no one likes them."

She turns her head and looks off into the distance.

"I won't have it, Liss. You stop this rubbish, or I'll come to the school myself and make you apologize to those children." I can see the tremor of horror that goes through her at the idea of me turning up in her classroom. "Will you promise to stop? To stay away from that girl and those children and not say nasty things to them?"

"What if they say something to me? Or Jake? What am I supposed to do then?"

Biff them, is what I want to say, because I hate the idea of anyone being nasty to my children. But that is exactly what a bully might do. And I am supposed to be the adult here. "You ignore them, and you walk away. And if it goes on, you tell me or your teacher. Clear?"

Melissa nods, still looking off to the horizon.

Maybe it's one of those situations you get into where you can't see a way out until someone tells you to stop. Two weeks of holiday are coming up. Even that might be enough. Kids move on, forget their enemies, and turn them into best friends.

"And, sweetie, you do know you're not fat, don't you?" The girl's comment is obviously why Melissa wouldn't change into her bathers and swim at the waterhole that day, and why she's been wearing winter clothes in the hot weather. I'd thought it was some weird fashion thing. It had crossed my mind that she might be anorexic, but her continuing enthusiastic appreciation of food of any kind eased my mind on that issue. "That girl only said you were fat to make you feel bad. She was retaliating, that's all. You're not fat at all."

"Really?" she says, hesitantly.

"Your grandmother told me she thought you were a skinny thing, and she never lets tact or flattery get in the way of her opinion." I put my arm around Melissa and pull her close. "Remember when she told us that we looked like escapees from Outer Woop Woop?"

She nods.

"And the time she thought Jake might be retarded because he couldn't tie his shoelaces? He was only three."

She nods again, and giggles. "And when she said you looked like an English sheepdog after you spent all that money on a haircut in Melbourne."

That smarts. I'd forgotten that particular remark. I'd thought my new cut was rather stylish, and I'd been practicing a sultry look from beneath my feathery fringe until we went to visit Mum.

"OK then. Now come with me while I get Jake out of that damn toilet."

She jumps off the table, no doubt relieved that our little chat is over.

When we reach the toilet block, Melissa calls from outside.

"Jake, let's go! We're ready to go home."

"Am I in trouble?" His high voice echoes around the concrete walls.

"Only if you don't come out immediately," I answer. A boy-toilet stink of ammonia clings to the block. I hope he doesn't smell like that when he gets into the car.

"Liss, I want Jake to understand what I've told you. You have to be an example to him. All right?"

Melissa nods. Her sandy hair is whipping against her cheeks. Her eyes are red.

I remember how hard school is, especially when you are growing breasts and having hormone storms. In Patsy's class one girl tried to bleach her moustache because the other girls were laughing at her and she ended up in hospital with a blistered lip. Every day for a month in grade seven someone put a note in my desk with a description of another of my horrible features. "Your nose is so bent they named a hairpin after it." "Your hands are so ugly they won't serve you in shops." I kept up a brave face at school and went home and sobbed every night.

23

YESTERDAY I DROVE down to Melbourne, dropped the kids at Patsy's house, visited Tammy, and did a wee in her toilet that blows air up your bottom to dry it, then drove back in the dark. This morning I set to cleaning the house thoroughly, giving it a scrub like it hasn't seen in years. Twenty minutes later, I am exhausted. I need to ring Helen. I've been a cow and I have to make it up to her.

"Please forgive me. I was worried about the kids and I was being a bitch. No wonder they're bullies." I take a breath. "Let's go to Halstead tonight and have dinner and a bottle of wine. My shout."

"I don't know. I'd have to check with my therapist first."

"Helen, please. I'm so sorry."

Silence. I wait. The house pulsates with the germs I've failed to destroy, the dust lurking in every crevice, the piles of dirty washing.

"Don't ever say that kind of thing to me again, Loretta."

"I won't. I won't, Helen, because it's not true and I didn't even mean it. I'm really sorry."

If she could see me now, flooded with shame, she wouldn't need to tell me not to do it again. After Tony left, it was my friends who pulled me and the kids through. Friends like Helen and Norm. And without them, I'd have to play bingo or join the CWA to pass the time. I'll do anything to keep them on my side.

After a rattling bus ride from Gunapan through the slums of outer Halstead, Helen and I end up at the Taste of India. We order lamb korma and butter chicken, which are suspiciously alike except in color, leaving us with the impression that there is only one taste in India, before walking to the pizza and pasta place in the mall for dessert. Helen pops the champagne cork and we toast each other, finding our lame jokes hilarious and laughing like we've had too much to drink. We toast again.

"Good evening, ladies. Your menus."

The last time I saw Bowden he was chatting up girls at the Gunapan waterhole, wearing jeans that were way too big for him and a grubby singlet that showed off his skinny white arms. His nose was scarlet with sunburn, and when he stopped squinting to glance around at me he had white lines around his eyes where the sun hadn't reached.

"Hi, Loretta," he said as I walked by on my way to deliver a tube of sunscreen to Helen.

"Mrs. Boskovic to you, Bowden," I replied.

"Bowie to you, Mrs. Boskovic," he muttered.

I was tempted to give him a clip over the head until I noticed his family a little way up the hill.

"Hi," I called up, smiling and waving. Not that I thought Bowden's father would ever hurt me, but even an accidental bump from someone with shoulders that wide could break your collarbone.

"Thank God you're here," Helen said, grabbing the cream from my outstretched hand. "I've completely destroyed the effect of the facial I had yesterday and gained ten more years."

"I don't think smearing your face with yogurt and laying slices of potato over the top can be called a facial."

"It's the poor woman's facial, Loretta. And I had no cucumber."

That was last summer. Now here is a brand-new Bowden, standing beside our table in ironed black pants and a white shirt, with a snowy napkin draped over his forearm and a pencil moustache so narrow and perfectly shaped that I think he might have drawn it on.

"Could we have the dessert menu please, Bowden."

"Ladies, please call me Bowie." He's using a voice much deeper than the one he uses to order a hot pie and sauce at the milk bar. He saunters away and pushes through the swing door to the kitchen.

"So. Have you heard about the mechanic?" Helen leans in conspiratorially.

"Merv Bull?"

"Yes, Merv Bull," she answers impatiently. "He had a date with Maxine."

"Maxine?" I keep smiling, trying to hide the glum face underneath. When I went to see Merv Bull for my wiper blades I thought I felt something. A flutter. A hint in the way he looked at me, the way he said I was welcome to a tune anytime. I read all kinds of innuendo into that line. So I was going to get tuned, I mean get the car tuned, except that Terror learned to open the gate latch and ruined everything. She somehow found her way to the alpaca farm and started cozying up to the alpaca herd. I thought it must be some kind of identity problem. And who would blame her, living with us? But apparently goats need constant company. Norm never mentioned that when he delivered our lawn mower. I ended up taking in another goat, Terror's sister, whom Melissa immediately named Panic. So the money I had set aside for some well-earned tuning went on extra feed costs. Now it looks like I've lost my chance at a thorough tune-up.

In the Merv Bull stakes, Helen had positioned herself at tight odds, thanks to a split radiator hose, a dud alternator, and a full service, including cleaning the fuel injectors and adjusting the computer.

"It's cost me a fortune, but I think he's about to ask me on a date," she told me a couple of weeks ago. "Kyleen was the odds-on favorite because she's so pretty, until she accidentally ran over his dog when she was backing her car out of the yard."

"Oh!"

"Don't worry, the dog's OK. Those heelers are built of steel. The car bounced off the dog, only gave it a fright. Merv had been shouting and waving at Kyleen to stop and she'd thought he was waving goodbye so she took her hands off the wheel to wave back. That's when they heard the yelp. Kyleen said Merv wasn't so friendly after that. So I think I'm closing in. Probably four to one now."

Things have obviously changed since then.

"Maxine. Who'd have thought." I can't deny I'm disappointed. A whisper of hope was thrilling me for a moment back there.

Bowden appears and produces the dessert menus with a flourish, before backing away to stand against the wall with his hands demurely locked in front of him as if he's the maître d' in a five-star restaurant.

"Is he making fun of us?" Helen whispers.

"I believe so. No tip for him."

"He'll really miss that two dollars."

We call him over and order the tiramisu to share and, when Bowden is gone, Helen pours us a sobering glass of water. The only other people in the restaurant are an older couple sitting near the wood-fired oven that's shaped like a clay igloo. The man is red and sweating. Outside the windows of the restaurant, the Halstead mall is lit by thin light. Neon brand names flicker feebly in shop windows, and every now and then kids in groups push each other past the window.

"So do you think Melissa will stop what she's been doing to the foreign kids? What about the girl? She might want to complain."

I tell Helen about getting the cruel notes when I was at school. "I didn't want revenge. I wanted to pretend no one had ever called me ugly."

It must be the champagne. My throat is tightening at the memory of the notes. I would sit at my desk wondering all day who had written them and why they hated me so much.

"Are you going all soppy on me, Loretta?"

I shake my head. Take another sip of champagne with a water chaser. The tiramisu arrives and we both scoop our spoons into the soft creamy center. That school episode never had a proper end. One day there was no note. After that I never had another one. Once I realized it was over I cried with relief.

"This tiramisu is almost as good as Caramellos."

"Hey, look." Helen points with her spoon.

Vaughan, the mayor, is walking arm in arm with his wife past the window of the restaurant.

"Back in a sec." I drop my spoon on the table and fling my napkin on the chair as I get up. Even as I stand I can see the mayor glimpse the movement from the corner of his eye. His eyes widen when I wave at him, and he waves back quickly, then grips his wife's arm and starts walking fast, away from the restaurant. He can't beat me, though. I've been chasing goats around the backyard and I have legs like pistons.

"Vaughan!" My voice echoes against the shop windows in the empty mall.

"Hi, Loretta. Great job on the school. We must have a meeting about what to do next," he calls back over his shoulder, still scurrying along at a surprisingly speedy pace and dragging his wife behind him.

"I need a signature from you for the next letter to the minister," I shout, even though I've nearly caught up. They stop, panting, and I lean over to catch my breath.

"How dare you," the mayor's wife, whose name I have forgotten, says to me. In the neon light of the mall, the fine spray from her mouth looks like a tiny rainbow-sheened fountain. She is dressed in black trousers and an orange silky top as if she's been out to a fancy dinner. Rings glint on her fingers. She has a gravelly voice like a transvestite, but I'm fairly sure she's not.

"Pardon?"

"Why are you making trouble like this? You should be looking after your children, not running around like a nutcase. Everyone knows you're only trying to get attention. You're probably trying to get onto council yourself, is that it? You're going to stand for election?"

"What?" I'm gobsmacked.

"Leave us alone. Don't you think you've done enough this week?"

"Vaughan? What's this about?"

The mayor looks at his feet. Or, if he could see his feet he would be looking at them. "Loretta, I think you went a bit far with the newspaper."

"What?" My vocabulary has shrunk to one word thanks to all the champagne.

When the wife leans in close to me I stumble backward. I don't want to be standing in the shower when she speaks.

She points at my chest. Her finger isn't exactly poking me, but I can almost feel the pressure on my breastbone. "Who do you think you are?"

"Darling, don't get upset." Vaughan takes his wife's arm, the one not pointing at me, and tugs her away. "We don't know for sure it was Loretta."

"What?" I say one more time.

"Of course it was her. She's the one who keeps sending out those endless letters about the school. She's the one who's always putting up signs and calling meetings. And she hangs around with that old junk man. I told you, Vaughan, she did it for him, to get that Unsightly Property Notice lifted."

"Stop calling me HER!" I shout.

"What?" Vaughan and his wife say together.

"I don't know what you're talking about. Why can't we discuss this like . . ." My words peter out as I wonder what I'm trying to say. "What *are* you talking about?"

"Don't get me started." The wife's lips are all tight and wrinkly. "Vaughan, let's go." She swings around, her shiny silk top rippling in shades of orange and ochre in the mall light.

"I'll call you, Loretta," he mutters as he turns to follow her, but she finishes the conversation for him. "You certainly will not. Goodbye."

"Whoa." I flop back in my seat at the table. "Have you read the newspaper lately?"

"The *Shire Herald*? Of course not. That's five minutes of my day I don't want to waste."

"I'll have to go to the library."

Helen pours more champers into my glass while I spoon up another velvety mouthful of the tiramisu.

"I've got news. I had a date too," Helen says.

I stare, open-mouthed, which must be disgusting considering what I'm eating.

"Last week. At the Thai restaurant down the road. I had green curry. We drank two bottles of wine. Then we had another date on Saturday. And spent a day together."

"Don't make me ask."

"Peter Rudnik." She grins at me.

I think that, in my thirteen years here, I have met every living person within twenty minutes' drive of Gunapan. Who is Peter Rudnik? It's obvious Helen expects me to know. "And . . . it was good?"

"It was fun. He relaxes when he's out of that environment. He's got a good sense of humor. And we're exactly the same height."

I'm starting to suspect. "So he's not gay, then?"

"Definitely not. And he's some kisser. Found that out at the end of the night on the first date."

"At the end of the day, you mean."

"Oh, ha ha. Everyone has things they say all the time. It's a habit."

"You sly dog. You kissed the grade-three teacher!"

"Oh yeah."

"I'm jealous."

"I know," she says triumphantly.

"Actually, I have a prospect of my own."

"A biker?"

"No, this one drives an Audi. He's widowed, a tragic light plane crash that only he survived. His grown-up children put in together to console him with a beach house at Sorrento and an annual trip to Tuscany."

Helen is still grinning.

"Are you going out again?"

"Wednesday on a picnic. It's school holidays, so he's free for two weeks."

"I'm very, very jealous."

"I know." If she was grinning any wider her face would split.

"If you get together with him, seriously, he has to join the Save Our School Committee Mark II."

"I'll keep that in mind."

"In fact, he has to be an office-bearer."

"I like him." She shakes her head at me and I laugh before plunging my spoon deep into the tiramisu.

"Eat up," I tell her. "You're going to need your strength."

"For what?"

"For when you start the horizontal foxtrotting."

Helen belts out a laugh and has to catch bits of tiramisu in her napkin. "Too late. We've already practiced the foxtrot, the waltz, and the barn dance."

24

"**LOOKING A BIT** the worse for wear," Norm says when I lean in the doorway of the shed.

"Tired," I mutter. Last night with Helen was fun, but I got home and cried about the kids and their bullying and how the mayor's wife told me I should be looking after them better and woke up ten times during the night and thought I heard a murderer coming in the back door and lay rigid for five minutes with my heart hammering until I realized it was Terror and Panic burping and butting each other on the outside stairs. Now that I'm up and about, the sparkly morning light has penetrated my exhausted hungover head and is making my brain wrinkle.

Norm stands up and pulls a seat from underneath a pile of newspapers, which cascade gracefully down to form a new pile on the ground. He empties the dregs of a cold cup of tea outside the shed door, wipes the rim of the cup on his shirt hem, and switches on the kettle.

"Hey, are any of those newspapers current?" I ask, remembering what the mayor's wife said last night.

"You saw it, then?" Norm's smiling.

"What?" I'm starting to hate myself for this word.

He points to a sheet of newspaper tacked to the cupboard door at the back of the shed. I get up and walk closer so I can read it. It's the front page of Saturday's edition of the *Shire Herald*. A perfect specimen of Norm's thumbprint in oil adorns the margin.

"'Councillors Need Probe,'" I read aloud and laugh. "They shouldn't let that cadet write the headlines. Last night the mayor's wife nearly punched me out, I guess because of this."

"Apparently," Norm says with a feigned look of horror, "not all our councillors are as honest as they should be."

It's hard to be shocked. Everyone knows local councils are about people making sure their friends' building projects are approved and traveling overseas on "research" missions and getting their names in the paper.

"But Vaughan? I can't believe Vaughan is corrupt."

"It's not Vaughan. He's all right. But he's been letting the others get away with things. We all have. I'm not putting up with it anymore, Loretta. They've gone too far."

"There's oil all over the newsprint on this, Norm. I'll read the article at the library. Where's Justin?"

"He's at work. Got two weeks at the abattoir. Hates it." Norm glances at the dashboard clock attached to a car battery on the bench. "His shift will be over soon."

An odd smell is permeating the shed. Usually it smells of metal and oil with a hint of old hamburger. I sniff and try to figure it out, but my senses are out of whack today. It seems to be a clean smell. In this shed where every surface is marked with the liquid tools of Norm's trade—oil, petrol, grease, beer, and tea—it is a very odd smell indeed.

"Has he been cleaning up in here?"

"Justin? Not in here. He knows better than to mess with

my filing system. Mind you, he keeps that room of his tidy. Must be all those years in a cell."

Norm turns off the whistling kettle and pours hot water into my cup, then drops a tea bag into it. He offers me milk, but I always think it's wise to stay away from dairy goods that have been sitting opened in Norm's shed for any length of time.

"It's quiet at my place, Norm. Terror's missing Melissa. She stands at the back door burping, then she chases Panic around the yard."

"She's a goat. Goats burp and play. And the kids have only been away two days."

We sit in the warm shed blowing on our tea and sipping it slowly. I move my feet closer to Norm's two-bar radiator under the table.

"Have you—"

Norm raises his hand for me to stop speaking. He nods toward the transistor, where the race caller is screaming like an assault victim. We wait until the caller has reached his highest pitch and sobbed out the result. Norm sighs.

"Bloody old nag. Knew it wouldn't win."

"So why did you bet on it?"

"Justin did. He's done his tenner. I told him he should put five each way on that old crock, but he likes to put his money on the nose. So, Loretta, heard you had a word with the kids."

How is it, I ask myself, that everyone knows these things about me? I talked to my children on Bald Hill out of sight and hearing of everyone except the fat black crow hopping around the rubbish bin, and somehow Norm has heard about it.

"I see," I answer huffily. "And what did I tell them?"

"They'll be all right now. Things get out of hand, that's all. Kids don't know how to stop. Yep, I think it's going to be fine."

He reaches under the table and pulls out an old tin.

"You deserve a biscuit." It takes him a while to pry the lid off the tin, but when he does, a delicious aroma of orange-cream biscuits drifts out.

"How old are these?" I turn my biscuit over and examine it for signs of mold. It's worth asking, because I'm fairly sure that lid was rusted on.

"Those use-by dates are a con so we'll throw things out. Don't take any notice of them, Loretta."

While Norm talks I can feel something happening in my head. Like a depth charge. A thought begins deep in my tired and fuzzy brain stem, working its way through the left and right hemispheres and out to the surface. I become convinced that the smell I caught before was antiseptic. Antiseptic is a smell I have never experienced in Norm's vicinity. And it smells like my mother. The connection sparks. Or it would do if I had any spark left in my brain. What happens is more like an underwater explosion. The smell is what I smelled back when we visited Mum in hospital.

"Heard you went into town last week," I say casually before slurping some hot tea. It tastes good and bitter. I take another sip. The caffeine is definitely helping to wake me up.

"I think that's Justin now." Norm inclines his head.

All I can hear is a faint whine somewhere down the road. Out in the yard the dogs start barking as if they know Justin's coming too. He's lengthened their chains and started feeding them more regularly. Norm told me he even walks them sometimes.

"By the way, has that dog near the gate changed color?"

"He washed them. He's turning them into bloody lap-dogs."

"Right. He's probably booked them in for a spa and massage too."

The whine is becoming a throb. A rhythmic pulsing throb powering down the road toward us.

"What is that noise?" The throb sounds a little like what was happening in my head all night as I lay awake fretting.

"The boy bought himself a Honda 500cc on the never-never."

Justin pulls up outside the shed with a spurt of gravel, swings his leg over the bike, and eases off his helmet. Norm's already poured him a cup of tea by the time he gets inside the shed. Justin nods at me as he pulls out a chair from behind a cupboard. Norm's shed is like a magician's trunk. Whenever you want something you reach under the table or behind a cupboard, and presto, there it is.

"Have you told her?" he says to Norm.

Norm shrugs and turns up the radio. Justin reaches over and turns it back down again.

"Tell her."

"What am I, a child?" Norm's using his long-suffering voice, the one he puts on whenever he complains about the poor return on scrap metal.

I'll sit quietly and mind my own business while they bicker. I wonder how Norm's enjoying being a parent again. At least he's past the stage of cleaning up vomit. And he doesn't have to drive Justin to school and back every day. If we moved closer to the school Melissa and Jake could walk. I'd save a good forty minutes each day, which I could then use sewing chic evening wear and looking after my skin. My scrag-woman image would slowly fade. I'd learn to walk with my head up and my shoulders back, instead of hurrying around like the hunchback of Gunapan. But we could never afford a proper yard that close to the school. What would we do with Terror and Panic? I've grown rather fond of the goats. They're excellent listeners. Of course, they're not the perfect pets. They do burp a lot. Sometimes it's alarmingly loud. And they shed. Not to mention the poo problem. But they seem so smart. I wonder if they can be house-trained?

"Loretta?"

I pick up my cup of cold tea and smile at Justin. "Sorry, off in a dream."

Justin looks down at the table. Norm clears his throat.

"I'm going to lose my hair," Norm mutters.

"It's a bit late to be realizing that." I look at his fast-receding hairline.

"From the chemo," Justin adds.

The whole shed seems to slide sideways. I feel the cup wobble in my hand and I reach up with my other hand to grip it and lower it carefully to the table.

"Chemo?" I repeat.

"The big C. In the liver." Norm sounds tired.

"Liver?" My voice sounds like an old record.

Justin lays his hand on mine. He closes the palm and fingers tightly over the top of my hand and nods at me. One of the dogs in the yard barks and the rest follow, growing louder and crazier until one starts howling.

"Customer." Norm pushes himself up off the seat.

"I'll get it, Dad." Justin waves Norm down.

My hand is instantly cold when Justin takes his away. He swings the door open and a gust of chilly air swirls around my ankles.

"Liver cancer? But you're not a drinker." I should have noticed how thin Norm's got.

"There's only a sixty percent chance the chemo'll work. I don't want to do it, Loretta. Remember when Jim from the railways had the stomach cancer and they gave him chemo? And he looked like shit and he said he felt like shit and all his hair fell out and he couldn't eat and then he bloody died anyway. What's the point?"

"Sixty percent, that's the point!" I answer hysterically. "Norm, what are you talking about? Of course you'll have it. Don't be stupid."

"If it wasn't for Justin making me swear, I don't think I would."

"Not for me? Not for Melissa and Jake?"

"Exactly. I don't want your kids to see me looking half-dead. I'd rather they remember me like I am now."

"Stupid, you mean? You want them to remember you as the stupid man who wouldn't get treatment?"

"Settle down, Loretta. I said I was getting it, didn't I? Justin's made me promise."

Even in my state of fury, I can see how odd it is that my best friend, the man who is like a grandfather to my children, has told me he's very ill and my reaction is to want to cut his throat. We both look out through the window at Justin, who's listening, head bowed, to a bloke talking as he pulls bits off some kind of engine. We can't hear their conversation from inside because the dogs are still going at full throttle and someone else is driving a pounding ute right up to the door of the shed. Norm heaves himself up off the chair and opens the door.

I don't know what's wrong with me. I look at Norm standing at the door and gesturing the driver to come into the shed, and I want to punch him. I want to slap him. I want to stamp my feet in front of him and scream like a two-year-old having a tantrum. I am furious. I feel as if my heart is about to explode. How dare he be sick? How dare he have cancer?

He comes back into the shed followed by Merv Bull.

"Merv, you remember Loretta, don't you?"

"Of course." He lowers his voice and turns away from Norm to speak. "Actually, I was hoping to have a quick word with you if you've got a moment."

"Sorry, have to rush," I say. Right now, I need to go home and scream. "Nice to see you, Merv."

I set off smiling and waving goodbye and get into the car and rev the engine so hard it almost has a prolapse. Then I scream backward onto the road before powering off, leaving two smoking streaks of rubber on the tarmac.

25

NORM'S NEWS HAS given me the strength of seven Lorettas. In six days I've stormed the post office with letters asking for old and potential new SOS committee members to come to the first meeting. I've coaxed sponsorship from the abattoir, the supermarket, the CWA, and the winery outside Halstead for a fund-raising dinner. I'm organizing an auction of donated goods on the night of the dinner. So far Leanne's put up a voucher for a spell or hex of the winner's choice, Morelli's Meats has offered a side of beef, Norm's repairing a vintage stationary engine that should be ready for the night, the Church of Goodwill is donating a month's housecleaning, and the local pub is giving a dinner for two.

My children's absence has also helped to inspire my burst of activity. Terror and Panic have put on so much weight they look like they're about to have kids of their own. Yesterday I found myself thinking how attractive Terror would look with a ribbon in her beard.

I had dreamed that while Melissa and Jake were away I'd be out at romantic dinners, tossing my newly styled and tipped hair as I laughed and making witty repartee with Merc Man or some other suitably loaded and charming suitor.

But I couldn't even get an appointment at the hairdressers until next Tuesday, and once that part of the plan collapsed, it seemed like I'd have to go on with my old life. I'm not allowed to tell Norm's news to anyone, even Helen, but I can't stop thinking about what might happen to him, and I can't stop trying not to think about it, and I can't sleep. That adds five more hours in the day to fill.

And on top of all that, I can't find out anything about the development. I've failed Norm completely. I've heard plenty of rumors, but no facts.

"Are you sure there's going to be a pool and spa and sauna?" I asked Kyleen.

"Of course," she scoffed. "How could you have a top-quality luxury resort without them?"

The whole population of Gunapan, one of the region's most disadvantaged small towns, has become an authority on what makes a top-quality luxury resort.

"I hope they don't get Sleepover linen," Brianna remarked. "It doesn't last. They'll have to go better quality than that. And I can't wait to see what kind of TVs they have."

"What are you talking about? They won't let us within shouting distance of the place. Why is everyone being so nice about it?"

"More to the question, Loretta, why are you so mad about it?"

"Because they're taking our water! Because Norm's been landed with an Unsightly Property Notice!"

"It's not our water. Our water comes from the Goonah Reservoir."

"Which is at fourteen percent capacity. And we go selling off water that bubbles up out of the ground!" I can hear my voice rising in frustration. Soon I'll be reaching the high notes of opera, only with a kind of whining sound. A lot of complaining goes on around here. We could set up the Gunapan opera company. Performing live every weeknight, the Gunapan Whingers. You pick a topic, we'll complain about it.

Brianna shrugged. "Anyway, I'm going to get my Responsible Service of Alcohol certificate. Maybe get a job in the bar. I bet those guests will leave good tips."

"Sure, why don't you help them suck the water out of our town? Well, I'm not going to put up with it. If I'm going to keep campaigning about the school, I might as well campaign about the development too."

My friends have been as encouraging as usual.

"Give it up, Loretta," Helen said this morning. She looked down at the latest letter to the education minister.

"I can't. It's turned into an addiction. I can't stop writing letters to ministers."

"Like heroin." She nodded sympathetically.

"Or beer, but not as pleasant. Actually, it's more like an addiction to ground glass, or whipping yourself with wet rope every morning at dawn."

"Great. My best friend has turned into a pain junkie."

"Helen, do you remember what I said when I first started the Save Our School business?"

She shook her head.

"I said that you should tell me if the whole town started to hate me. It's happened, hasn't it?"

"What makes you say that?" Helen inclined her head doll fashion, smiling a fake smile showing no teeth, only tight lips with upturned corners.

"I saw Maxine in the grocery store yesterday. She didn't have time to say hello. You know why? Because she was running. Yes, people are running away from me now."

"Maybe she was busy?"

"She hadn't bought anything. She dropped a tin of tomatoes as she ran out the front door."

"I think you're exaggerating, Loretta."

"I didn't ask her to pay for the biscuits in the meetings."

Helen rolled her eyes. "Don't blame me when this obsessive-compulsive thing puts you in a straitjacket," she said on her way out the door.

Underneath every conversation, like having an electric current buzzing through my brain, is the fretting about Norm. Each day I ring or drop in and try not to ask him about his health.

"Don't start asking about my health all the time," he warned me on Monday. "I know what a terrier you are. I'll tell you if there's anything you need to know."

So I don't. I've been pestering Justin instead. Yesterday Justin asked me if I wanted to know about Norm's bowel movements.

"Well," I said dubiously, "I suppose. If it's important."

Justin looked away, smiling.

"Oh, you were joking." I thought I should probably go home. Norm's illness seemed to have stripped me of my sense of humor.

"He's doing OK. Really." Justin was still smiling. Thought he was a pretty funny bloke.

"Hey, forgot to mention you're signed up for the Save Our School and Stop Our Development Committee. Norm said you're good at math, so you're the treasurer."

No more smiling for Mr. Funny Man. I pulled a meeting

flyer from my handbag and dropped it on the table. He's not really the treasurer, but neither is anyone else, and since he didn't say an immediate no, I think I might have done something smart for a change.

"See you tomorrow night!" I called back gaily over my shoulder on my way out of the shed.

This afternoon I remembered to drop into the library and read the article in the *Shire Herald* about the council.

COUNCILLORS NEED PROBE

It has been leaked to the *Shire Herald* that last year certain shire councillors and council staff took trips, sometimes with spouses and children, which our source claims were paid for by a corporation involved in land acquisition in the shire. Three of these trips were to Western Australia, ostensibly to investigate small-scale agriculture, and included winery tours and boat cruises. The cost of the trips is estimated by the *Herald* at approximately forty thousand dollars.

And I was worried about the amount of petrol it took to drive the kids to Melbourne.

It has been suggested by the source close to the council that there are inappropriate links between council and local builders, as well as larger development companies based out of the shire. The source suggested that there may have been intervention in planning processes for building applications that violate the local building codes.

The *Shire Herald* is also investigating allegations that a major development company made large campaign donations before the election, but that these donations were not declared.

Hot stuff! No wonder Mrs. Mayor almost went at me with her handbag the other night. Even if Vaughan isn't one of the people the article is talking about, he looks like an idiot for letting this go on.

I made twenty copies of the article to bring to the meeting tonight. I had already changed the night of the meeting so we wouldn't be competing with the Church of Goodwill, so this time we're in the big room. Brianna has offered to mind the kids again—she really has no fear.

When I arrive, Helen's sitting alone in a circle of orange plastic chairs at the front of the room, reading. Behind her is the stage where every year the Halstead Players do a performance of a musical, which has been *The Sound of Music* five years out of eight. We Gunapanians feel obliged to pay good money to hear them yowling and yodeling, then tell them over a cup of tea afterward how much we loved it.

Helen looks up as I head for the board to write up the agenda. "Peter sent his apologies. He's had to stay back for a school staff meeting tonight."

"OK. Good book?"

She turns it over and reads the blurb aloud. " 'Heather thinks this holiday in her hometown of Darwin will be just the thing to cheer her up after the breakdown of her marriage. But when she meets a mysterious man claiming to be her long-lost uncle, family secrets emerge that will rock her world and set her on a surprising course to new love.' How come thrilling secrets never emerge from my family?"

"I've discovered some dark secrets in mine."

"Yeah, right."

"It's true," I tell her. "A mysterious man. Five Chihuahuas. A sudden trip to a tropical destination."

"Your mother marrying a geriatric and retiring to the Gold Coast is not thrilling or mysterious."

"Here's a real secret. I got the check from Mum from the sale of her flat. Five thousand dollars!"

Helen whoops as Justin walks in the door. He's alone.

"Norm not coming?"

Justin shakes his head. "Next meeting, he says. He's sent me to represent the Stevenses."

"And don't forget you're the treasurer."

For the next ten minutes I sit on the edge of my vinyl chair, biting my nails, while Helen reads and Justin wanders around the room, hands clasped behind his back, looking at *Vaccination Works!* and *Literacy Week* posters. The hall is the original building that the community center has been constructed around. It's paneled in oak and the ceiling is painted the original toilet-block green. On one wall is a portrait of Queen Elizabeth, who never made it to Gunapan on her coronation tour but sent a framed picture instead. The back wall has the names of all the mayors listed in gold lettering.

I can't wait any longer so I pass them copies of the *Shire Herald* article. "Did you read this?"

"Typical." Helen goes back to reading her book.

"I saw a copy on Dad's door," Justin says. "And I don't think he's finished with them yet."

Now Helen looks up. "Norm's the source? He is full of surprises, that man."

At seven fifteen, Leanne appears at the door. She looks around the empty room.

"Is this . . . ?"

"The Save Our School and Sod Off Development Committee." I gesture around the empty room. "Maybe someone's meeting in the room next door, but I haven't heard anything."

"That's right, I'm here to save the school." Leanne sweeps into the room. Ever since she reappeared as Leonora, she's been wearing clothes that sweep and swish and pretty much walk around with a life of their own, while little Leanne gets carried inside. And she loves the heavy jewelry. Tonight she's wearing a necklace and bracelet of ruby-red glass baubles the size of knucklebones.

"Did your mum send you?" I ask.

"I'm not your babysitter anymore, Mrs. Boskovic. I'm a grown woman and a practicing Wiccan."

"Sorry, Lea—Leonora. And you'd better call me Loretta."

"So why are you here?" Helen asks Leanne. "No offense."

Justin meanders back to the chair circle and sits beside Leanne.

"That's OK. I want to have kids one day. And I want a proper town for them to grow up in. Everyone thinks I'm weird coming back here, but I like Gunapan."

Justin and Helen and I nod as we ponder this.

"Why?" I ask finally.

"That's what everyone says! I dunno. It's home."

"The vision splendid," Justin murmurs.

"Pardon me?"

"I mean, is it the countryside? Fresh air, all that. You 'see the vision splendid of the sunlit plains extended and at night the wond'rous glory of the everlasting stars.'"

"I'm guessing you didn't make that up," Helen says. At least she's showing enough interest now to drop her book into her bag.

"Can you do the whole thing?" Even as the words come

out of my mouth I wonder if I've gone too far by asking shy Justin to recite a poem to three women. But he leans back and closes his eyes and starts to intone.

"'I had written him a letter which I had, for want of better knowledge, sent to where I met him down the Lachlan years ago.

"'He was shearing when I knew him so I sent the letter to him just on spec, addressed as follows, Clancy of the Overflow.'"

He continues with the poem. I'm stunned at his memory. I'm lucky if I can remember the three things I went to the supermarket to buy. Quite often I arrive home with seven completely different items, none of which we need. That is why we have a whole cupboard for toilet paper storage. If there is ever a major oil spill in Gunapan, my household will have enough absorbent paper to effect a full cleanup.

"'But I doubt he'd suit the office, Clancy, of the Overflow,'" Justin finishes, and opens his eyes. Which are blue, washed-denim blue.

Leanne and Helen clap wildly.

I can take a joke. "I see, Justin. You're telling us that Gunapan is 'the vision splendid.' Obviously it would be from the west with the glowing mountain of Norm's junkyard on the horizon. Or at night, the wondrous glory of the abattoir's all-night shift lighting up the sky. And that must be why you came back, Leanne—sorry, Leonora."

"Don't worry, everyone still calls me Leanne. I'm not sure about a vision splendid, but it is nice here. And I can rent a house for a quarter of what I'd pay in the city."

"Yes, Norm's yard." I'm on a roll. "The vision splendid. You can see it from the moon—all those bits and pieces of broken machinery glinting in the sunshine. Well, the parts of them that aren't half rusted away. And it is smack bang in the middle of the, what did you call it, 'sunny plains extended'?"

"Settle down, Loretta," Helen says. "Norm's yard is so far from splendid it needs a new word. It's a blight on the landscape. So, Justin, do you know any other poems?"

"A few. Had a bit of time for reading. I read a book of poems and they kind of went in without me even trying. I can recite them all."

"What were you doing?" Leanne leans forward in her chair.

"Time."

Leanne opens her mouth to ask the next question, but I jump in. "Do another one."

"What kind?" He doesn't look very enthusiastic.

"Anything, honestly, anything. Love poem, hate poem. Whatever." I'm stalling. If we sit through the time it takes Justin to recite another poem, fifty excited Gunapan citizens might storm the room, pitchforks raised, ready to make kebabs out of the Minister for Education, Social Inclusion and the Service Economy if she won't save our school. Because if someone doesn't arrive soon, I'll break into the wailing country music song of self-pity my mother always hoped would issue in glorious twang from at least one of her daughters. Except without any kind of tune because we've all inherited her tone deafness.

"Another day, maybe." Justin keeps his head lowered.

We sit in silence for a few more moments.

"All right then, we might as well go home. The Save Our School and Stupid Obnoxious Development Committee is obviously finished."

No one charges in to protest. At least if Kyleen was here she'd be telling me not to let the carburetors grind me down, but she's in Halstead working her new job at the cinema's candy bar.

I turn to Leanne. "I'm sorry you came along for nothing."

"No, it was good." She's still staring at Justin.

I think she's in love. A strange bubble forms in my gut. "I'm sorry, everyone. You go, I'll pack up the chairs."

Against their protests and offers to help tidy up, I herd the three of them out the door and shut it behind them. After I've dragged the chairs back to their spots lining the walls and rubbed the agenda off the whiteboard, I lock the door and head for the car, thinking about the Freedom of Information application I put into the council yesterday to find out about the development. It took me two hours to fill in the forms and, what's worse, it cost twenty-six dollars. I wonder if I can get that money back.

26

IT'S DARK IN the Community Centre car park. We've asked the shire a million times to put some lighting in here. It would serve them right if I got raped and murdered right here on the concrete. Then they'd be sorry. Or I could trip on this poorly maintained surface and crack my head open. I find tears springing to my eyes at the satisfying image of how right I'd be and how sorry they'd feel when they visited me in hospital and found me hovering at the edge of death, pale and delicate, the trauma surgeon—who has fallen in love with my quiet courage—at my bedside wringing his hands and praying for steady nerves to perform the surgery that could save my life.

A rap on the driver's-side window makes me jump so high I nearly do end up with head trauma. My heart is still battering the wall of my chest as I wind down the window.

"Didn't mean to startle you. Are you OK?" Justin leans in close.

"Apart from this heart attack?"

"Wondered if you were all right. You sounded a bit wobbly before."

"Thanks, but I'm fine." I wait until he's ambled off and the rumble of his motorcycle engine has faded into the distance before I slump into the seat.

This is the freedom I used to dream about. The kids off at their auntie's house and me with a tank full of petrol and an empty evening ahead. I only wish I could think of something to do. Now that mine is the only car left, the gloom in the car park seems to be even darker. In fact, over near the community hall, a patch of darkness is moving as though it's caught on a breeze. Must be the shadow of a tree, I think, until it emerges from the bushes and starts moving toward me.

I know I'm screaming because my ears are hurting, but I don't have any control over it. The darkness slips closer to me as I suck in another lungful of breath and scream again so loudly that the steering wheel thrums. My keys, which were in my lap, have jiggled loose and I know they're on the floor, but I can't lean down in case the black specter flows into the car and smothers me while I've got my head between my knees. The darkness is pressing in on me and I can't help turning my head and seeing . . . a smiling woman in dark clothes standing outside the car door. I wind down the driver's-side window. That's two terrifying moments I've had tonight. I don't think my heart can take it. I must stop reading those books from the Neighbourhood House donations shelf.

"I come to meeting," says the mother of the children my kids were bullying. "Your friend Mr. Stevens, he tell me to come."

I explain to her that the meeting is over without mentioning that it's because no one came. The night is chilling down. She is shivering and holding her arms close around her.

"Hop in, please."

"Thank you. Mr. Stevens say you bring me home."

Trust Norm to have worked it out so that we end up

together in a confined space. Heroic war widow and mother of four, beautifully dressed on a shoestring budget, well mannered, helpful, and toast of the town, clutching the dashboard and sliding around on the vinyl seat of the Holden beside me, the old scrag, deserted mother of two Gunapan-bred bush pig bullying children. I'm certain Norm only does these things to humiliate me. On the drive back to her house, I find out her name and the correct name of her country and repeat the names to myself twenty times so I won't get them wrong. Mersiha, Bosnia Herzegovina. Mersiha, Bosnia Herzegovina. Mersiha, Bosnia Herzebogova. Mersiha, Bosnia Herzeboggler . . . In between gear changes and mental exertions, I attempt chitchat about the weather, about the school, about the annual Kmart underwear sale in Halstead next week.

"It's a highlight of the Gunapan calendar. I'm heading over with Helen and Kyleen first thing Monday. Feel free to come along if you need undies." The moment I've spoken, it dawns on me that I don't often have the opportunity to converse with people outside my normal circle. Perhaps underwear isn't the most appropriate conversation topic for a first meeting. It will have to do though, because I'm desperate to avoid the other topic, the real topic—my bullying children.

"I find that the elastic only lasts ten to eleven months, which makes these last few weeks before the sale pretty dicey. I try not to run or make too many vigorous movements and that usually—"

"I'm sorry," Mersiha interrupts.

"Pardon?"

"My children. They say rude things to your children. I am very sorry. They had a hard time. Their father, the war, the camp. I speak to them. I tell them to be kind, to be good—"

I burst in and apologize to her for *my* horrible children.

They should have known better. It's my fault, I say. I'm a delinquent mother. I tell her that I'm sending them to the revenge camp for bullies and their bullied where they'll find out what it's like, and she gasps and I have to stop the car and explain that it was only a joke. How stupid am I to make a joke about revenge camp to a woman who has come from a war? Stopping the car also allows her a moment to unclamp her fingers from the edge of the dashboard. Perhaps Melissa is onto something about that refresher driving course.

While we're stopped on the side of the road near the turnoff to the old MacInerny place, the headlights of the car catching flitting night bugs and a few seedy grass heads in their beams, I make Mersiha promise she will tell me if my children ever bully her children again.

"My children too, please tell me if they say the bad things again. What is the word they say to your children? Bogan? I think it means bad thing."

That's depressing. My children are being called bogans. I admit, I have occasionally called myself a bogan in jest, mainly when I was wearing sheepskin slippers or enjoying an AC/DC song on the radio. But I'm not a bogan. Bogans are proud wearers of checked flannelette shirts and trackie-daks as their costume of choice. Women bogans color their hair auburn and swear loudly, all the time, while swigging beer from long-necked bottles. Or there are the new bogans, the over-the-hill footballers who end up living in ridiculous houses and appearing on TV shows being rude to their fans, or the multimillionaire children of successful businessmen who swan about the world in tasteless expensive fashion and cockatoo hairstyles trying to be photographed. No, neither of those types are me, I'm certain. If my children are bogans, they must have got it from their father.

"Mrs. Loretta?" Mersiha presses her warm hand on my arm. "Are you all right?"

I nod glumly and put the car into gear. The tires spin on the gravel on the side of the road as we take off, sounding suitably boganish. As we turn into her road I start on the polite questions she must have heard a hundred times. How long she's been in Australia. Where she lived before. Her family.

"My husband was killed in war." She shakes her head in the dark car beside me, as if she wants to shake out what she has just said.

"I'm sorry. It must be so hard for you."

"No!" she says so loudly I almost slam my foot on the brake before I realize she's not angry. "No, please do not be sorry for me. For us. Everyone always staring at us, always sorry." She thumps her hand against the dashboard. The radio turns on, but she doesn't seem to notice. "I do not want sorry."

"I see." I hesitate. Should I stop asking her questions?

"No one ask me about my husband because they are so sorry. When they introduce me, they say this is Mersiha, the refugee."

"Right." I'm treading carefully because this is exactly the kind of moment where I'm likely to say the wrong thing.

"I am more than refugee. I am normal person. My kids, they are normal kids. We want to be normal, not always everyone so sorry, so sorry."

"Got it."

Driving down the road to her house, I think about what she said. One day I will ask about her husband. When we reach the house, the veranda light is on and the monster dog is lying in its usual spot.

"That is an enormous dog," I remark.

"You know this dog?" Her eyes are wide. "You know who belong to this dog? Please take this dog!"

"You mean it's not yours? Who feeds it?" I wonder if she used to have more children.

"I do not know. In the morning it goes away. In the afternoon it comes back and stays all the time until the next morning."

While we sit in the car talking, the ancient evil woman I saw the day I came here twitches open the curtain to the left of the front door and spears me with a death ray.

"My grandmother," Mersiha says. "She is very old."

No kidding. I think she might be a first cousin of Methuselah. "I'll get Norm to take the dog to the pound. And thanks for coming to the meeting. The committee is finished, though. No more Save Our School." I have to admit it. I've failed.

Mersiha shrugs. "That is too bad."

"But if you'd like to join a committee, the Neighbourhood House Management Committee has a vacancy coming up." At last, we might have a committee member who doesn't own a four-wheel drive and property. They won't be happy about that. I feel an uncharitable glee. We could stack the committee with migrants, refugees, and bogans. Of course, we'd never get another grant. We're supposed to help the disadvantaged, not be the disadvantaged.

"Please, come inside. A cup of tea."

I tell her I'd better head off. It's only eight o'clock, so I'll drop by and ask Norm to take care of the monster dog. Another excellent excuse to see how he's doing.

. . .

The screech of my car tires must have alerted Justin. He's standing in the doorway of Norm's place, framed by light, when I walk up the drive.

"Loretta?"

"That's me," I reply, still pleased at the thought of our new Neighbourhood House committee member.

"How did you know?"

The thumping of my heart begins as a slow erratic stutter and quickly rises to a fast drum roll.

"Know what?"

"He's gone in the ambulance to Halstead. I'm about to follow."

27

"STOP IT," I tell Norm.

He breathes quietly. His chest lifts the bedsheet in a small, quick billow, like a puff of air under a silk dress. He is sunburned dark brown against the whiteness of this hospital ward, with the scar on his forehead a lighter color, as though he has missed with the fake tan.

"Stop this rubbish and wake up, Norm."

I take his hand and rub it briskly in mine. Justin sits on the other side of the bed watching as I fuss around. Norm's hand feels strange. The skin slides over the flesh and bones like a soft glove when I rub, as if his body has separated into different parts.

The doctor told us earlier that Norm might not wake up.

"Don't be stupid. Of course he'll wake up," I replied.

The doctor nodded sympathetically at me as if I was the sick one.

"He's repairing a stationary engine for my auction," I explained. "It's one of the big-ticket items."

He nodded again and patted me on the arm before moving to a bed further down the unit.

I'm tucking the bedsheet more neatly under the bed when I

think Norm has stopped breathing. With my heart banging so loudly I can't hear anything anyway, I lean down and place my ear against his chest. The sparse gray hairs tickle my ear. His chest rises to meet my ear and Norm's warmth presses against my cheek. I stand up and take a deep shuddering breath. No matter how much air I suck in, I can't get enough into my lungs, as if I'm leaking from a thousand tiny pinpricks.

"Loretta, sit down," Justin says.

"Did he knock back treatment? I'll kill him if he refused the chemo."

I move Norm's hand gently along the heavy cotton sheet. His other hand is wired up. So is his nose, and there's another line snaking up under the bedclothes from a machine on a wheelie stand beside the bed.

"What's wrong with him?" I hear my voice becoming increasingly shrill. "He said he'd be fine. He said even if he didn't have treatment he'd be alive for years."

"He has been having treatment. It's an infection. The doctor just told us that, Loretta."

Justin stands up. He pats his own cheeks as if he's trying to wake himself up.

"You go home. I'll call you if there's a change," he says.

"No, I'm here till he wakes up."

"Mum's coming soon. We're only allowed two visitors at a time."

So that's it. I'm being thrown out. My life with Norm tossed aside by a son who hasn't seen him for fourteen years and a wife who dumped him. I never did understand the story of the prodigal son. The one who has been good and faithful and devoted all those years is taken for granted while the one who abandoned his family gets a party and a pig on a spit. What's right about that?

My feeling of airlessness grows even stronger in this stuffy hospital room. I'd better get home and clean up for the kids. They'll be home the day after tomorrow. I have to make a good home for them so they don't go out and rob a bank and go to jail and abandon me, then waltz back in after fourteen years and turf out the poor sods who've been my good friends while they were gone.

I can't even squeeze out a goodbye. I swing around and charge out through the open door of the ward, wheel past the nurses' station, and thunder down the hallway, tears blurring my vision and a trail of runny snot winding its way around my top lip.

At home, Terror edges her way hesitantly into the kitchen and begins nosing around the kitchen table.

"Help yourself," I tell her as I take the kettle to the sink to fill it.

Panic clatters into the room and butts her way past Terror to join in.

A bar of soap sits on the kitchen windowsill for Norm to wash his hands when he comes to tea. He is everywhere in this house. Lemons from the tree in his yard fill the fruit bowl. Terror, his lawn-mowing gift to us, stands in front of me with her spooky green eyes. I pull her close and she burrows her head into my armpit. Her coat smells of hay and eucalyptus. She's wearing a bell that Norm welded together from a Toyota cylinder housing and the key to an old tractor.

At eight in the evening I drive back to the hospital. The nurse making notes at the nurses' station tells me that Norm has two relatives with him, so I'll have to wait in the visitors' room at the end of the floor. A man and a child are waiting in there too. The little girl sits astride her father's knee, playing an electronic game, while he stares, with the same hollowed expression as mine, at the gaudy figures on the television screen flickering silently on its bracket above us. As the minutes tick on, I wish my children were here for me to hold, to hug tight, even though I know it is better that they don't have to experience this descent, this excavation of hope. The longer I wait, the more I sense the dreadful impending absence of my closest friend.

At nine twenty, Justin and Marg walk slowly past the visitors' room toward the lifts. Marg is weeping. Neither of them sees me.

At nine twenty-four I stand beside Norm's bed. An orderly waits at the entrance to the intensive care unit. Around us the hospital is alive with the sounds of coughs and televisions and muttering and squeaky trolley wheels and the hum of machinery. The activity makes the silence and stillness at this bed seem like a hollow core.

Norm's face is stubbled with gray as usual. His head is turned to the side, as if he was looking off to the horizon before he closed his eyes. I lean my face down to his, dripping tears onto his creased skin. No breath comes from his mouth. No smart-aleck comments, no bad jokes, no deadpan asides. He isn't telling me off anymore, or shaking his head in disbelief.

"Take your time," the orderly says before he draws the curtain around me and Norm.

I sit down on the bed beside his long skinny body. I take his cool hand in mine, examine the fingernails, their black rinds of grease from broken machines and rusty spare parts. I press his cobbled fingertips against my cheek. I imagine I can feel his body turning into something other than Norm, powering down to a cold hard object like a machine that has been turned off.

He has no last words for me. I turned my back and he slipped away.

"Damn you. Damn you, Norm Stevens."

28

WHEN I WAKE up the next day, the house is roaring with emptiness. I lie in bed most of the day waiting. Waiting, like the house, for Norm to appear, his narrow frame leaning against the doorjamb. Waiting for the phone to ring so he can ask me to drop by and help him get the lid off a jam jar. He could fix any machine, could build anything given enough time, but he could never get the lids off jam jars. Or maybe that was an excuse to ask me to come around. The house creaks with faint echoes of his voice. It is so unbelievable that he is gone that I doze and wake up with a shout of shock. He's not coming around. How will I tell the kids? My breath is all caught up in my chest like a wound-up scarf. How will I tell the kids?

When I wake up the next morning I know I have to drive. I stop at the hole in the wall in Halstead and take out money for petrol. I fill the tank of the Holden, and I head out to the highway. An emptiness seems to follow me, so I put down my foot and speed along the bitumen past the Myrnabool junction until I reach a road I've never heard of, and I turn off. Thoughts about how to tell the kids, whether to call them at Patsy's or wait, drift into my mind but I push them out.

I don't want to think, only cover distance, feel the tarmac grumbling against my tires, the engine throbbing and choking and roaring as I swing around curves, accelerate through level crossings, fly up and down the hills of the countryside. Always the emptiness looming up behind me like a darkness in the rearview mirror.

I drive past houses with neat trim gardens and colorful flower beds, past broken-down shacks whose roofs are rusted and patched with tin. Past farms of fluorescent green canola and past dry, dusty paddocks where sheep scratch around for a few stalks of yellowed grass. Through single-road towns with one general store and one pub, a park bench outside for the smokers, an antiques shop, and someone selling free-range eggs from a self-service stand on the side of the road. Through bigger towns with a bakery sending out the stink of confectionery sugar and a fish and chip shop with a Friday family special painted on the window. I gun the Holden up hills to local lookouts from where the vast flat plains of the country stretch out and a tired old sign declares this to be a place where the explorers Burke and Wills stopped on their ill-fated trip.

On a road outside a grain town I see a small half-starved brindle dog trotting along the verge of the road and I cry. The reptile tourist park near the Goonah Reservoir has a hand-painted tin sign attached to the gate saying *Closed for Business*. I cry. A magpie swoops across the road so close to the car I am afraid I've killed it, and even when I see it soar into the air behind me, I cry.

After two hours, the car's temperature is heading toward the red zone, so I pull over into a truck rest stop and turn off the engine.

I don't know how I can live in Gunapan without Norm.

29

I REMEMBER NORM saying to me once that he wished he was Irish because they knew how to send people off.

"A slab of beer, a barbie, and a good laugh," he said. "That's how I like to say goodbye to a mate."

But no one laughed at Norm's send-off. It was too sudden. We weren't prepared.

In the days after he died, the *Shire Herald* was full of notices from people everywhere. Melissa and Jake and I cut them out of the newspaper and pasted them into a book. We put in photos of Norm that I'd taken over the years, and some of the notes from him—often written on the backs of betting slips—that I'd stuck to the fridge because of their Normness.

The service passed by in a flash with women crying and sobbing and blokes consoling each other with handshakes, arm jabs, and nods. Marg said a few words and so did Justin. I hardly heard a thing because I was blowing my nose most of the time, or trying to cuddle Melissa, who wanted a cuddle but was trying to pretend she didn't, or grabbing hold of Jake every time he started inching toward the door of the church where men had gathered in the back pews to slap each other's backs and nod and grunt meaningfully before they headed off to the pub for a few beers. I heard there was some unrestrained male sobbing in the pub car park later that night.

Now that a week has passed, the number of people dropping off casseroles and cakes and frozen meals has slowed down. I'd been delivering most of them on to Justin anyway. I'm sure they would have taken stuff directly to him, but barely anyone in town has officially met him yet, although a few blokes have started turning up to the yard again, probably missing their long consultations. When I delivered the last batch of food, I found Justin standing in the middle of the yard, staring at the horizon. He looked so lonely I wanted to hug him.

"Are you OK?" I asked after I had dropped off the three frozen soups at the door of the shed. We turned toward the warming sun and both crossed our arms as we squinted out over the yard.

Justin nodded. "Thanks, Loretta," he said.

"Marg's gone home?"

He nodded again.

I hesitated before I said, "You know, Justin, I'd never seen Norm as happy as when you came to live here." I wasn't sure whether that would please Justin or make him even sadder, but it was worth saying.

At home, we are in shock, unable to believe Norm isn't going to appear at the back door with a bag of lemons and all the news of the town. It's as if no one has any news to tell anyway. Gunapan has gone quiet. We're all in mourning.

It seems important to go back to routines. For a week Melissa and Jake, distraught as they were, got away with doing no chores, eating whatever they wanted whenever they wanted, and watching endless hours of television. Today we stop that. Today we go back to life and try to find a way back in without Norm.

"I don't want to go to school," Jake says in the car. "The holidays were good. Let's put more pictures of Norm in the book."

When I pull up at the gate, Melissa and Jake stay sitting in the car.

"What's up?" I ask.

"What if they ask us about Norm?" Melissa puts her hand up to her mouth and begins to nibble at a nail. Another bad habit she's got from me.

"Sweetie, everyone knows Norm died. Don't worry, they'll try to make you comfortable."

They climb reluctantly out of the car and shuffle toward the school steps. Around them, kids stare silently. I was wrong. No one knows how to behave when someone close to you has died. My poor kids will probably sit alone all day while the other children gawk at them as if they're zoo animals.

At the Neighbourhood House, the reaction is quite different.

"Welcome back," Gabrielle says at the front door. She holds the wire screen open while I unlock the front door, then follows me into the office.

"How come you're here today? The committee meeting's not for another two weeks."

"Oh, darling, I wanted to see that you were OK. I heard your friend Mr. Stevens died. That's so awful. I am sorry, Loretta."

"Thanks, Gabrielle." I am more than surprised. I was certain she didn't know my name.

Gabrielle sits in the office armchair with the foam spilling out of the holes in the fabric and leafs through some old committee minutes while I walk around turning off the alarm, unlocking the rooms of the House, switching on lights. The House seems even shabbier than usual today. We can't get money to paint the rooms, so the walls are scuffed and the paint on the woodwork is chipped. The colors they chose originally were jolly lemons and greens, supposed to cheer people up. Now they look like prison colors. The furniture is all mismatched. The polished floorboards have lost their polish where everyone walks and dirt is being ground into the boards. I trudge back to the office, making a note to apply for funding to repair the floors.

"So how are you coping, darling?" Gabrielle asks once I've dropped into the office chair.

My email opens as she speaks. I have three hundred and forty-four unread messages after two weeks of being away. I don't want to talk about how I'm coping. For the first time in my life I want to work slowly through a huge number of outstanding emails and think about nothing else.

"We're OK. Thanks for asking, Gabrielle," I answer in a crisp, businesslike voice. I move a pile of papers from the left side of the desk to the right. "Look at all this. I'd better get on with it."

Gabrielle doesn't look as if she's about to move, so I open my emails one by one. The first twenty or so are course and child-care inquiries. Why these people can write an email but not look at a web page is beyond me. I reply with a link to the web page. At least thirty emails are from the funding bodies who think the main purpose of the Neighborhood House is to fill in forms about funding. If you fill in enough forms and are lucky enough to get some funding, you'll spend the rest of the year filling in forms about how you intend to spend the funding, how you are spending the funding, and then how you did spend the funding. And then they'll want a report on the success of the funded project. Which you haven't had time to do because you've been flat out filling out forms about funding and they only gave you a quarter of what you needed to do the project anyway.

Helen's sent me a joke. I'm scared to open it because it might have sound, and Gabrielle is still sitting beside me in the House's most uncomfortable chair, the one we put in the office to discourage people from sitting and complaining for hours. The last joke I opened from Helen was a jaunty song about penises that rang out across the office of the Neighbourhood House for what seemed like an hour while I withered at the desk, apologizing, because I didn't know how to turn it off. Helen doesn't realize that I'm a professional woman doing a professional job and I have an image to uphold. Plus we have a large sign over the office window saying *Offensive language will not be tolerated in this House*, which Tina put up after her son Damien heard one of the visitors shouting abuse at someone on the phone. I was the first to be graced with his new vocabulary when I arrived on a Tuesday morning and said, "Hi, Damien," only to be answered with, "Hi, you fucking slag." Tina was mortified.

"What's going to happen to Mr. Stevens's yard?" Gabrielle asks out of the blue.

"I don't know." I keep clicking through my emails as we speak, hoping she'll get the hint.

"It is an eyesore. I don't think many people will be sorry to see it go."

"An eyesore?" I repeat. I remember Norm's description of it—an abstract interpretation of the changing face of Gunapan—and smile. "I find it rather attractive. An unusual work of art."

"But most people won't think that way, will they, darling. Most people will be glad when it's gone."

"I'm not sure why we're talking about this, Gabrielle. The yard is none of my business. And I don't feel up to talking about Norm, I'm sorry." I turn reluctantly away from the computer to face Gabrielle and find to my astonishment that she has tears on her cheeks. "What is it? What's wrong?"

"I didn't know he was ill," she says, breathing in with a stutter between words.

"Nobody knew. It's OK."

"It's just that we were at supper and talking about the yard and how ugly it made that road and how it wouldn't look good for people driving to the resort, and I don't know, suddenly I was the one who was going to make the complaint. I didn't want to. And if I'd known he wasn't well . . ."

"You mean to the council?"

"I only said to them that they should ask him to put up a fence! And then they sent him that notice and everything blew up." She takes in a long, shaky breath. "And then he died." She pulls a tissue from her bag and honks into it.

"Who was at supper?"

"No one special. Just our book group." She does another honk and brings out her makeup mirror. "Oh, look at me. I'm a mess."

"Who's in the book group?"

"It's no one you'd know, darling. A couple of ladies from Halstead, a councillor, members of the Lions Ladies Auxiliary. We have a glass of wine and a nibble once a month and sometimes we even talk about the book." Gabrielle's perking up now. She smiles as she mentions the glass of wine.

"Samantha Patterson?"

"Yes, Samantha. And Ann-Maree, who makes the most

delicious tiny party pies. Or maybe she buys them from that Halstead patisserie. I try to put on a lovely supper too, but some of those Lions ladies can cook like chefs. It's rather intimidating, I have to say. I've been tempted to cater, but that wouldn't be in the spirit of things, would it."

"Samantha Patterson," I mutter again. "Samantha Patterson suggested you complain."

"No. No, it wasn't Samantha. I can't remember who it was. It was everyone. We were all talking about it. It just came up."

"He was a sick man."

Gabrielle's eyes fill with tears again. "I didn't know."

"It *was* Samantha Patterson, wasn't it?"

"I can't remember. We were chatting. It was only a harmless little message to get him to clean up."

"But it wasn't harmless, was it? He was ill. It caused him terrible stress." I feel a little ill myself, hearing these words coming out of my mouth. But I'm furious. Norm knew Samantha Patterson had something to do with it. How dare they do this to Norm, my Norm.

Gabrielle dabs at her eyes with a new tissue. "I'm sorry. I'm so sorry."

"I have to get to work now, Gabrielle." I feel unkind, but not as unkind as I'm going to feel when I get hold of Samantha Patterson.

The day flies past as I answer emails and fend off sympathetic calls, and when I knock off I only have two hours until I have to pick up the kids. Luckily, I know exactly where Samantha Patterson will be. She'll be where all the wealthy women of this area appear on the first Monday of the month. The mobile day spa.

30

THE WOMEN WHO go to the day spa would never have a haircut at Hair Today Gone Tomorrow in the main street of Gunapan. They have their hair done in Melbourne. But once a month a van arrives in Gunapan and spills young Asian women carrying manicure and pedicure kits and boxes of creams and lotions into Hair Today. The blinds go down in the windows. The pub delivers bottles of champagne. Four-wheel drives pull up and park along the street like some beauty-hunting club and the women disappear into Hair Today, which is closed to normal business for four hours in the afternoon. Helen tried to book in last year, but they told her it was full up. "Full up, my arse," she said to me.

When I push open the door of the salon, the first person I see is Gabrielle in a bathrobe. She's sitting with her hands spread flat on a table. The girl on the other side of the table is shaking a bottle of nail polish. Farther inside are two women, lounging in reclining chairs with their feet in footbaths, chatting and laughing. Several more toward the back of the room are lying on massage tables, their faces covered in goop. Jazz music and a delicious smell of orange and cardamom fill the room. Candles are burning. A young woman comes toward me carrying a tray of hors d'oeuvres. Am I still in Gunapan?

"Do you have a booking?" the young woman asks, surprised, looking me up and down.

"No, I'm here to see someone."

At the sound of my voice Gabrielle looks up. When I shake my head at her she looks away again, her face pink. I don't want to cause Gabrielle any harm. I have never wanted to cause anyone harm—until today.

"Sorry," the young woman says quietly, "this is a private club." She puts the tray on the shop counter and moves behind me to open the door and usher me out, but I'm headed for the back of the salon.

The elegant figure lying with its eyes closed and cream all over its face on the table near the basins is unmistakably Samantha Patterson. Her sleek hair is fanned across the pillow. Like the other women she's wearing a fluffy white robe and pink toweling scuffs. Her fine-boned hands, which have obviously never encountered a scourer, are crossed daintily over her flat stomach.

At this moment, the full extent of my scragness is very clear to me. My rage deserts me. I have a terrible feeling I'm going to open my mouth and a screech will come out.

Samantha opens her eyes, frowns at me for a moment, and closes them again.

"Tran, somebody's here," she says, her eyes still closed. "Can you look after them, please."

So much for my rage deserting me. It was only on a brief holiday. "I'm here to speak to you, Samantha." I can hear a shade of screech in my voice, but there's nothing I can do about that.

She opens her eyes again and gives me the once-over. "I'm sorry. I don't think I know you."

"I'm a friend of Norm Stevens. You know Norm, the one with the unsightly property. I'm also interested in the development on the Bolton Road. I think you might be the person to talk to about that."

Samantha doesn't even blink. She lies on the massage table like Cleopatra waiting for her slaves and turns her face away from me before she says, "I am in the middle of a facial. Do you mind?"

"Yes, I do mind. I want to know what's going on."

"I'm sorry, I don't know what you're talking about." She sits up and swings her legs over the side of the table so she's facing me. "I can't believe you've been so rude as to barge in here and interrupt our afternoon. If you've got some issue with the development, take it up with council."

"No." That screeching voice coming out of me is getting louder. "I want to take it up with you. Norm told me you were behind this. I'm going to finish what he started."

Everyone's listening now. The girl doing the pedicures has her scalpel poised in the air and is staring at us.

"I hardly think the ravings of some filthy old junk man are anything to rely on." She looks around at her friends, who half-nod and half-smile, not knowing what else to do. "And coming in here like this is completely inappropriate. Please take your concerns up with the council." She waves an indolent hand at the girl near the counter. "Tran, can you show this person to the door."

"No, Tran. Don't bother. I'm not leaving."

The salon, usually full of chatter and the rush of water and the hum of hair dryers, is so still I can almost hear the guttering of the candles. Tran holds on to the counter.

Samantha looks around at her friends, but they're staring at the floor or the wall. I recognize one of them from the creative-writing class at the Neighbourhood House. She seemed like a kind person. Her list of pleasing things included hugging her granddaughter and smelling the flowery scent of her flyaway hair. Why would she be friends with this nasty woman?

"My friend Norm died. He was a good man."

"I'm sure he was." Samantha relaxes her shoulders, rolling the left, then the right, and brings her hands to rest in her lap. "I'm very sorry. I am really very sorry."

As soon as she says this everyone in the room starts to breathe again. Relief ripples through the salon. I start to see the funny side of this. Samantha's face is covered in cream. It's like talking to a pavlova.

"Should I call the council and make an appointment for you? Tran, could you please bring my handbag here?"

"No." I will not be put off. Norm is dead and I owe him.

Tran hurries past me with her head down and passes Samantha a red leather bag.

"You're obviously grieving. I'm very sorry about your friend. Go home and rest and we can organize an appointment with the council for you." She pulls a gold notebook and matching pencil from her handbag. "Now, what's your name and phone number? I'll get my assistant onto it first thing tomorrow."

I can hear murmurs of approval from the front of the salon. So her friends think she is doing the right thing. Perhaps I *am* blowing things out of proportion. Samantha has her pencil poised over the open notebook.

But no. Grief, stubbornness, anger, whatever it is, she's not getting rid of me this easily. "I want you to tell me about the development and your connection with it."

From her small pink mouth I hear a tiny *tsk*. She turns to

the woman at the next table and rolls her eyes. "For heaven's sake," she mutters.

I am not sure exactly why this sets me off the way it does. It's not only about Norm, or the development, or the council. It's everything about who Samantha Patterson is and who I am and who Norm was. It's Samantha Patterson rolling her eyes as if I'm some annoying bug that got inside her big air-conditioned house. It's the way she said, "For heaven's sake," as if my life and Norm's life and the lives of most of the people I know in this town are a waste of time. It's enough to make me take a step forward and do something I've never done in my life.

I slap her face.

Even as my hand connects, I realize what a stupid thing I'm doing. Not because it won't give me satisfaction—it will—but because her face is covered in cream. What should have been a resounding smack that leaves her with a stinging cheek and a good dose of humiliation becomes a slithering swipe that unbalances me and leaves my hand greasy and Samantha with the look of a half-eaten cream bun. A giggle rises in me.

"Tran, lock the door," the cream bun says through gritted teeth. "Call the police. I've been assaulted."

"Geez, Loretta, what do you think you're playing at?" Bill asks when I'm sitting in the passenger seat of the police car heading for the station.

I shrug.

"Samantha Patterson is not a person to get offside."

I shrug again. I don't care.

It's only a ten-minute drive from the salon to the police station, a small brick office at the front of Bill's house. We should drive past the CWA Hall and the school on the way, but Bill swings the car around the corner at the supermarket and heads along Grevillea Street. He says he doesn't want my children to look out of the window of their schoolroom and see me in a police car. I tell him I would probably go up ten points in Jake's estimation if he did see me in a police car. We drop by the doctor's surgery, where I run inside to ask Helen to pick up the kids after school and take them to her house. When she asks why and I explain I'm under arrest for assaulting Samantha Patterson, I think I go up ten points in her estimation too. An old lady I know from the Neighbourhood House hauls herself out of her chair in the waiting room and asks to shake my hand. Unfortunately my hand is still greasy from Samantha's face cream.

At the station, Bill sits across the desk and gazes at me with the sorrowful expression of a disappointed father. He shakes his head as he reaches into the drawer and pulls out a form with several colored copies attached.

"Full name?"

"Loretta Judith Boskovic."

"Address?"

"You know that perfectly well, Bill."

"Answer please, Loretta. This is serious. Mrs. Patterson has insisted I charge you with assault."

"Fine. I'm glad I slapped her. Do you have a tissue?"

"You know you could lose your job if you get a conviction?"

That shuts me up.

"You'll be charged on summons. You'll come up in front of a magistrate. You'll be a criminal if you're convicted, Loretta. It's not a joke."

31

THE KIDS SIT quietly in the back on the way home from Helen's place. It's likely they can see the steam pouring from my head and they're worried it's about them. I keep thinking about Samantha Patterson calling Norm a filthy old junk man, and each time that phrase goes through my head another surge of steam builds up. Sure, Norm was the local junk man, and I do admit that on occasion he was filthy, but that's not for her to say. And now I might lose my job.

"If you're looking down—or up—from somewhere, Norm Stevens, I'll show you what a battler I am. Nothing is going to stop me bringing that woman down."

"Mum!" Melissa says crossly. "You're talking to yourself again. And you missed our street."

"All right, all right, no need to blow your top."

"Not like some people," she says, pursing her lips in that special Gunapan way.

I swing the car into the next street, then do a blockie, heading for our road. With the silence broken, Jake can't help himself.

"Our class got a mouse today and the teacher said if anyone screamed she'd send them home and Jamie wet his pants and he had to wear the spare ones and they were blue and I got—"

He's stopped midstream for the same reason I'm applying the brakes. Sitting outside our house on a trailer behind an old Bedford truck is a massive yellow machine with a bucket at the front. It has caterpillar treads and a square cabin on the top with a seat in the shape of an upturned hand perched above the engine and levers sticking up from the floor. From this angle it looks like it could scoop up the whole house.

I'm expecting Justin to jump out of the truck, but when we pull up in the driveway, it's Merv Bull who ambles up beside the car. He leans in, shading his eyes against the sun.

"G'day, Loretta." He taps on the glass of the back window. "G'day, mate," he says to Jake.

Jake scrambles to get out of the car so fast he nearly knocks Merv over with the car door. I try to emerge in a more seemly manner. Melissa gets out of the car on her side and looks hard at Merv, then shouts across the car roof to me.

"I'll check the letter box and see if Dad's sent a card. Remember Dad? Your husband?"

I smile brightly at Merv Bull. "I used to be married. Kids can't let things go, can they?"

He laughs. Jake is welded to his left leg, gazing up adoringly. I think about how strange it is that he didn't react this way with his own father.

"Mr. Bull, can I pleeeeeeeese look at the yellow machine?"

"Sure, mate."

Melissa pushes the mail at me and storms inside. I watch as Merv lifts Jake onto the seat of the bulldozer and lets him try to move the gear levers. Jake's so excited he's laughing like a hyena. I hope he didn't get that laugh from me.

When we all get inside and sit down at the table for tea and lemonade and biscuits, Merv tells Jake about the different types of bulldozer he's worked on. He turns to Melissa, who has been sipping her lemonade and nibbling her biscuits with her face turned aside, as though even the sight of Merv Bull could ruin her appetite.

"I met your dad. Worked on his car. He seemed like a great bloke," Merv says.

It's as if he has turned on the sun.

"Yeah, my dad's great." Melissa nods vigorously. "Even though some people don't think so." She glares at me. I glare back. I know she's putting this on for Merv. She's as disappointed in her father as I am. The other night she took the postcard off her bedroom wall and put it in her secret box in the wardrobe. It made me sad when I found it.

"Anyway, I did want to have a word with your mum about some stuff," Merv says pointedly.

Now she's been appeased, Melissa gets up and herds her brother off to his room before settling into her room to do her homework.

"So," Merv says when the kitchen is quiet. "I wanted to say I'm sorry about Norm. He was a champion. I know I haven't been in town that long, but it was clear from the get-go that Norm was a bloke you could rely on."

I have to wrinkle up my face to keep the tears from coming.

"He did a couple of favors for me and I won't forget that," Merv goes on. "Which is why I'm here."

"Oh?"

"That Unsightly Property Notice business was out of line. Everyone knew it was dodgy."

"It was Samantha Patterson. I heard this morning. I don't

know how she's involved with that development, but I'm going to find out."

"I might be able to help. I'm not allowed to talk about the development, because I signed that confidentiality agreement. But I can talk about some other things I've noticed."

This is so exciting I feel a hyena laugh coming on. "Such as?"

"Such as the 'dozer I'm towing into town today. Do you know where it's going?"

I shrug, still trying to keep the hyena laugh inside.

"It's going to the house of John Ponty," Merv says triumphantly. "The heavy-equipment moving firm that does a lot of work for the place I'm not allowed to talk about was supposed to pick it up and deliver it, but they had a breakdown and I said I'd do it instead. Then I found out where it was going."

"John Ponty? The name sounds familiar."

"Council officer? Planning Department? Currently having major renovations done on his house?"

"Ah."

"And commonly known to be bonking a certain married female councillor."

"No!" How come I never know any of the real gossip in this town? "You mean Samantha Patterson?"

"Oh, yes. And here's the icing on the cake. I know my machines, right? I often work on them myself, don't only leave them to the apprentices. And I can tell you that someone has been swapping plates around on the 'dozers and the trenchers and the other machines. We note it all down, of course, for our records. Plate number and engine number on the repair sheet. And back when they started the shire swimming pool renos, I saw this very 'dozer on that site. Different plate, same 'dozer."

"I don't get it. What's the swimming pool got to do with it?"

"I'm no wiser than you. I can only tell you what I've seen. But those machines belong to a big company with fingers in a lot of different pies, and I've seen them on jobs that shouldn't be connected."

How can I start to figure this out? It's so complicated. No wonder they've been getting away with it, whatever it is.

"Thanks, Merv. I really didn't know anything much, so this is a great start."

"Happy to help, Loretta."

We teeter into a sudden, awkward silence. I can hear Jake singing to himself in his room, and the tapping and beeps of Melissa on the computer. Terror and Panic clatter up the steps of the back veranda and peer in the back window. They must be hungry.

"Liss," I call. "Did you feed Terror and Panic?"

Merv raises his eyebrows when I say "Terror and Panic," then looks behind him and jumps when he sees the two long bearded faces in the window.

"Lawn mowers from Norm," I explain.

"Maaaaaaa, maaaaaa," Terror calls. It works far better than my call and Melissa trots through the kitchen and out to the veranda in the automatic manner of a mother summoned by her baby's cry.

"Suppose I'd better deliver this 'dozer," Merv says, standing and stretching.

I follow him out to the truck.

"Thanks again, Merv." I'm getting that same feeling I had when I went to his garage ages ago. Something hanging in the air. His gaze resting a moment too long on the footpath, then the horizon.

He stands beside the door of the truck. Brushes his hand through his straight shiny brown hair. Turns to the truck and turns back again.

"I'm heading to Halstead for a drink and some dinner on Saturday. Don't suppose you'd like to come?"

He speaks so fast I want to ask him to say it again. Slowly. I think he asked me on a date.

"Halstead? Saturday?" I mumble. A thought occurs to me. "Aren't you . . . ? Isn't . . . ? Maxine . . . ?"

"Maxine's great," he says. "She's a good mate. Kind of turned out that way."

I open my mouth and wait for the yes to come out, but it doesn't. The silence becomes uncomfortable. I should say yes. I'm being asked on a date. But as I keep failing to answer, the realization dawns on me. He's not what I want.

"If you're busy," Merv says. He reaches for the truck handle.

"It's a bit hard to find babysitters. You know."

"Yeah, sure. It must be a problem. Well, maybe another time."

"Yep. Maybe another time," I reply. My heart is beating fast. If I tell Helen about this she'll kill me.

He climbs into the truck and starts the engine, which shakes and grunts as it strains away from the curb, pulling the 'dozer on its trailer. His arm reaches out and waves from the cabin of the truck, and I feel a small twinge of regret.

But I could never go for a man who drives a Bedford.

32

THE MAIL MELISSA brought in is fatter than usual. I sit back down at the kitchen table and open an envelope from the council. Inside is a letter and a wad of paper.

> *In response to your Freedom of Information Application*
> *No. 2/84/556, please find enclosed council documents*
> *relating to the Forest Springs Leisure Resort area*
> *rezoning and building application.*
>   *Please note that the protection of the public interest*
> *and private and business affairs may cause some*
> *information to be exempted from access.*

It's signed by Bree Howarth, another girl who used to babysit my kids while she was at school. I didn't know she was an admin assistant at the council now. How handy.

The wad of paper is thick. I think about putting it aside until after tea, but I can't wait so I start to leaf through, which is when I find out what they mean by "some information to be exempted from access." About two-thirds of every page is blacked out. They've left phrases like "from the zoning regulations" and "pertaining to the regulatory framework" and "in the" and "with reference to."

This makes me madder than ever.

Next afternoon I leave the Neighbourhood House at lunchtime, jump in the car, and race to Halstead. After a quick appointment at the Legal Aid office about my assault charge, I scoot over to the park across the road from the shire offices in Halstead to eat my sandwich. Around me a few pigeons burble. The fountain sits dry and empty in the center of the park, shut down by water restrictions. The plants are struggling and the grass is brown, but people still sit here in the dappled shade of the gum trees, eating and chatting and reading newspapers. At half past one, Bree trots down the council steps and heads in the direction of the shops.

"Hi, Bree," I say chirpily as I hurry up beside her. I hope I haven't got curried egg on my face. It wouldn't be the first time.

"Oh, Mrs. Boskovic." She looks at me in shock and starts to walk faster. I have to trot to keep up. Kids these days have beanpole legs. She's probably also heard that I'm a maniac who goes around assaulting people.

"Got your letter, thanks, Bree."

"Oh?" she says. She's starting to breathe faster now with the exertion of running away from me. The shops are within sight. "I send out so many letters. They're not really from me, they're from the bosses."

"Ah, I see. So you weren't the one who blacked out everything."

"I do what I'm told, Mrs. Boskovic. The documents come to me marked up by hand and I do it on the computer. I don't read anything."

"All I need to know is who gave you the marked-up documents."

"I don't know if I should say, Mrs. Boskovic. Isn't council business private?"

"No, Bree, it's not. The council is supposed to be working for us. It's our business."

We're outside the fish and chip shop. The colored straps of the fly curtain are flapping in the breeze. Three young men in blue overalls lean against the walls inside the shop, leafing through car mags as they wait for their orders.

"Who did the blacking out? You will never be mentioned, Bree. Not one word. You can trust me."

"I do trust you, Mrs. B, but . . ."

"If there's corruption in the council you have to make sure no one can accuse you of being involved, Bree. When it comes out, I can only back you up if you've been honest with me." I don't want to frighten her, but this is urgent.

Bree begins to sniffle. "I don't want to get into trouble. That horrible John Ponty made me do it and he's not even my boss! He's always telling me to do things and not to mention it to anyone. It makes me feel like I'm doing something wrong."

"No one will know you told me, Bree, unless you need me to stand by you when it comes out. I promise."

It's starting to fit together. I need to sit down and work it out properly, and I need space to concentrate. Child-free space. Helen's busy minding the Tim Tams. Brianna already has Kyleen's little girl because Kyleen's working in Halstead. In the past I would have had Norm as my emergency baby-sitter. After I've dabbed away the tears that welled up at the thought of Norm, I decide to call Justin.

"You don't need to do anything," I tell him. "If you come

over and sit with the kids in the lounge to watch TV and I can have some time to myself, that'll do the trick. Two hours maximum." I nod at the phone encouragingly, as if he can see me. "Or three or four," I add, realizing how many years it is since I attempted sustained intelligent thought.

"I don't know anything about children," he warns me. "I've spent the last fourteen years living in close quarters with violent, damaged men."

"Well, this will obviously be a bit more of a challenge, but I'm sure you're up to it."

He arrives bearing lollipops and a teen fashion magazine. He's a natural. I usher him into the lounge room, where the zombie children are watching a cartoon, and when he sits down on the couch Jake scoots across and snuggles up against him exactly the way he used to with Norm.

Next day after work, I hop in the car and race over to Vaughan's shop in Halstead. These trips are costing me a fortune in petrol. I wait until the customer in the shop leaves with a kettle under her arm, then wander in, peeling a banana. The shelves are stacked with the kind of labor-saving devices and luxury electrical goods people buy as presents for Mother's Day that end up in the back of the cupboard until they're discovered, twenty years later, by a grandchild who thinks they're fabulous and retro.

A young salesman comes to offer assistance, but Vaughan has seen me and he sends the salesman away.

"Need a word with you, Vaughan."

I've never seen Vaughan angry. He's a good mayor because he doesn't get riled up. He sits like a Buddha through the stormy meetings where councillors are throwing accusations at each other, and when they've worn themselves out, he stops patting his stomach and starts negotiating.

Today, I am seeing the mayor angry. He's a gorgeous pinky orange, the same color as a cocktail I had once called a Tequila Sunset, and he's patting his poor stomach so fast it's like watching the flitter of butterfly wings.

"No food in the shop, Loretta. And I'm not sure I should be talking to you. Aren't you being charged with assault?"

I wrap the banana back in its skin and drop it into my handbag. "I've been to Legal Aid. They're going to try to get me a bond."

"Yes, well, don't start on me now, Loretta. You've already ruined my reputation with that article. I have never taken an inappropriate trip. I haven't had time to take a bloody trip at all since I've been mayor, except to Melbourne in the car."

"I didn't give the information to the newspaper, Vaughan. It was Norm."

He shrugs. "What does it matter who did it? It made me look like a fool. Anyway, we've had an investigation and it's all been explained. So you can get off your high horse. The report will be out next month."

"Who investigated?"

"Leave it alone, Loretta. Why are you always stirring up trouble?"

"The whole thing stinks, Vaughan, and you know it. Why would you approve a development in beautiful local bushland that takes drinking water out of the ground to use in a bloody spa?"

He's patting his stomach so fast now it looks like he's got a motorized hand. The gorgeous pink has faded. He's dead white. I hope he isn't getting pains in his chest. I had to take a first aid course when I started work at the Neighbourhood

House, but the dummy was half the size of Vaughan. I don't think I'd even be able to turn him on his side.

"I didn't approve it. It didn't need to come to council because it met all the requirements of the code, so it was automatically approved in the shire offices. You don't know what you're talking about, Loretta."

"Let's sit down in your office." I'm really worried. He's about to keel over.

He swings around and stumbles to his glassed-in office. I call the salesman and ask him for water.

"You're killing me, Loretta." Vaughan collapses into his office chair, which creaks and sinks an inch.

Once he's taken a sip of water and his color is back to normal, I pull out the diagram I sketched last night. At school I did a subject we called veggie maths, for the less mathematically endowed, and I excelled at these diagrams. They are pretty and easy to understand. Overlapping colored bubbles show things that are connected. There are bubbles inside bubbles. Bubbles inside other bubbles connected to different bubbles. A great big bubble picture like soapsuds mixing up in the wash.

"What's this?" Vaughan says crossly, glancing over my carefully drawn and colored-in bubbles.

"See this bubble? This is Samantha Patterson. She is touching every other bubble in some way."

"Bubbles?"

"It's a Venn diagram, Vaughan."

He stares at it for a moment. "Why is the John Ponty bubble sitting almost on top of the Samantha Patterson bubble?" he asks.

"Don't make me say it, Vaughan." I'm glad I'm not the only one who didn't know.

"You're sure?"

"I've heard that if you drive to the motel at the Bendigo turnoff on a Thursday afternoon you can see for yourself."

"Jesus." He looks off to the side. "So I am a fool." He looks again at the diagram. "Who told you this? And what's the swimming pool got to do with it?"

"See the crosshatching of the linking bubbles here, here, and here?" I'm so proud of this diagram. It took me hours. "Same equipment used to do all these works. Equipment owned by the development company building the resort. No bets taken that John Ponty's renovations are gratis and that the work for the pool renovations went to a favored contractor with a parent company based in Western Australia."

"And that Samantha has some interest somewhere in this company or its development." Vaughan lets out a resigned sigh. "I'm an idiot. I didn't see any of this."

"Norm thought she was too smart to have shares or anything obvious like that. But she's involved. It's clear from the diagram."

"How could I have been such a fool? I didn't have a clue."

"You couldn't have known. John Ponty must have made sure none of it ever reached a council meeting by approving it at staff level."

"I hate it that you're right, Loretta."

"It wasn't me, Vaughan. It was Norm. He knew something was up when he got the Unsightly Property Notice."

Vaughan nods. "I was a bit surprised by that myself. But I thought it was a genuine complaint."

"Will you do something now, Vaughan? We can't let this go on. Samantha Patterson called Norm a filthy old junk man. And anyway, you'll look good because you'll be the one who exposes the corruption in the shire council."

"Oh, hell." Vaughan presses his hand against his belly and burps. "I get it now. Samantha's husband told me they'd bought into some new businesses. The one I can remember was aromatherapy oils and soaps and cosmetics."

33

AT SIX THIRTY, the Gunapan pub, once called the Criterion, now renamed the Toad and Bucket Bar and Grill for reasons no one can explain, is filling up. Jake, dressed in an oversized black suit we found at the Halstead charity shop yesterday, and Melissa, wearing her halter-neck dress and a splendid amount of pink eye shadow, are welcoming people to the auction and handing them tickets for the door prize. Every now and then Jake tells someone that Norm is decomposing at the cemetery. I see them flinch when he does it.

We've been talking for weeks about what being "dead" means. I think Jake still expects Norm to drop in one day soon, so I have been trying gently to introduce the concept of "gone forever." If his father hadn't turned up for that week it would have been a lot easier.

I had hoped Jake would be satisfied with the "Norm's gone to heaven" idea, but Jake likes bugs and tennis balls and things he can touch. He's not interested in heaven or life and death or abstract ideas. He was particularly intrigued when he heard that Norm is buried at the cemetery. "What will happen to him in the ground?" Jake asked, and I foolishly answered.

A small stage has been erected at the front of the pub

lounge. A microphone and gavel sit on a podium on the stage. We borrowed them from the local stock auctioneer, who is also a part-time barman here at the pub. Waiting to be hoisted above the stage is the banner Helen and I made last night.

Norm Stevens Snr Memorial Auction and SOS Eveni

We hadn't realized how long the title would be. It was ten o'clock when we got to "i" and there was no way I was going back to Brenda to ask her for more of that roll of beige silk she'd bought at a fire sale just in case one day she learned to sew. She did offer it in the first place, like everyone else who came out of nowhere after Norm died. They apologized for missing SOS meetings and promised to donate time and stuff for the auction. Hell, they pretty much offered me their firstborn children. I have enough trouble with my own to want more.

"We know how much Norm meant to you," Kyleen said. "He was like a husband, kind of. Oh, except he didn't . . ."

"No, he didn't. He certainly did not. He was like a father to me."

"Yeah, that's what I meant."

It's been so long for most of the single mothers in this town we've forgotten what husbands do to make us mothers in the first place.

Helen holds the sign up, admiring the finely wrought lettering. "They'll get what it means. When we hang it we'll let the end drape, as if the last letters are hidden in the folds."

Justin is kneeling at the front of the room fixing the microphone lead to the floor with gaffer tape. He was the one who insisted we go ahead with the auction. He said Norm had been excited about it, had been working hard on restoring the stationary engine and was even talking about buying a new shirt for the occasion.

He would have needed that shirt. The auction and dinner is a classy event. Ninety-four people have paid twenty dollars for adults—or five for children—for a set menu with a choice of chicken or beef. Mario Morelli's daughter is a vegetarian, due to the trauma of a summer job at the abattoir when she was fourteen, but she's only getting roast vegetables because the pub's cook is hysterical at the thought of cooking for more than ten people at a time. I've already made a quiet call to the Halstead pizza shop as a backup measure.

By eight thirty, the main meals—which ended up being a weight-loss version of a pub meal: two slices of beef or chicken, a carrot, a potato, and a teaspoon of gravy—have been served and thirty pizzas delivered and divided among the crowd. Mario's daughter was thrilled to get a vegetarian pizza to herself. The desserts are OK because the cook made the pavlovas and cheesecakes yesterday using a very reliable brand of packet mix. His kids are in the kitchen whipping cream and chopping strawberries and passion fruit as if they are getting paid for it.

With the beer and wine and whisky flowing, the auction is about to start. Or so I thought. I'm waiting for the auctioneer to come out from behind the bar when the lights go out and everyone looks up at the screen that normally shows the footy or the racing channel.

"Ladies and gentlemen," a voice issues from the speakers around the ceiling of the pub. I think that voice belongs to Vaughan.

Sure enough, he appears on the screen dressed in his rather tight-fitting scarlet robes and chain. In the real world he's sitting at the table next to ours, staring up at the screen.

I can hear his wife murmuring, "See, you've lost some of that chub around the tummy already." She's very much the proud wife now Vaughan is the honest mayor who exposed Samantha Patterson and John Ponty's schemes. She even nodded hello to me the other day.

"Norm Stevens Senior was a pillar of our community. He took part in many of our town-building activities, was a member of the Save Our School Committee—"

"That's my mum on that committee!" Jake screams. He's had three glasses of lemonade, it's past his bedtime, and if he has one more sip from that glass I think his head will start spinning like the girl in *The Exorcist*.

"Sssh." I quickly switch his lemonade for water while he stares up at the screen. Melissa's on the other side of Jake. She's gazing in the opposite direction to the screen. It's still school holidays and Kyleen's sister's kids are staying with her. One of them is a boy of fifteen, which is where Melissa's adoring gaze is directed. I think Helen's influence is starting to show. I notice Mersiha's girl is looking in the same direction. A couple of weeks ago we got Mersiha's children and my children together and they apologized to each other. If they'd done it with any less grace, baseball bats and chains would have been involved, but once it was done I did think I felt the tension in the air ease a little. Mersiha and I have been working together on a plan for the revitalization of the Neighbourhood House and a few days ago I finally got up the courage to ask about her husband. She thanked me, and she cried as she told me about his work during the war, transporting artworks and religious relics under cover of darkness out of their besieged town. One day he risked a run in the heavy fog of a winter morning. He was driving a truck loaded with illustrated manuscripts when the mist cleared long enough for a sniper to take him.

I thought then about how we don't have much here in Gunapan, but at least we are safe.

"—donated countless hours of labor as well as goods to community projects, was always around when a man needed an ear, offered excellent racing tips, and could be relied upon, with adequate notice, to source almost any spare part for any kind of mechanical device you could imagine. If he couldn't find it he'd make it. Given time, that is. Plenty of time."

The screen mayor pauses and the real-life mayor claps, looking around the room. Everyone joins in. I wish they'd hurry up. I hate these things. I hope they don't start with the soppy music and misty pictures of Norm as a baby through to old age. As much as I hate that sort of stuff, if they put it on the big screen now I'm sure it would undo me.

Across the room, Kyleen's on her feet with her two little fingers to her mouth. She lets out a piercing whistle and calls out, "We love Norm!" and the crowd cheers.

"Now," our on-screen mayor says, "on with Norm's auction. But keep your eye on the screen because you'll find out something about Norm during the night that probably very few of you knew. In fact, it was a secret held by a government department that even I only found out about last week. Enjoy!"

The barman edges out from behind the bar and pulls off his apron, leaving the owner serving drinks. Under the apron he's in tails. He leaps onto the stage and bows deeply. Beside him, the headmaster, Justin, and Mario Morelli pull the red velvet covering off the table with the goods to be auctioned. We stand up and peer at the table, but it's hard to see what's what because everything is piled up higgledy-piggledy.

A picture of a multicolored flower is on the screen. I wonder what that's got to do with Norm, or if it's a test pattern. I can't read the tiny text at the bottom of the screen.

"Without further ado," the auctioneer calls, "let the auction begin. Lot One. A stationary engine, part-repaired by the magic hands of the good man himself, wanting only a flattop piston, gudgeon pin, and ring set. Do I have one hundred dollars?"

Silence. I knew this wouldn't work. Across the room I can see Brenda leaning across her table, probably saying to her kids, "I knew this wouldn't work."

Justin stands behind the stationary engine, his arm resting on it.

"Do I hear fifty dollars?" the auctioneer calls.

Nothing.

"One hundred dollars!" a voice calls out. It's a very familiar voice. It's Melissa's voice. I almost fall out of my seat.

"One hundred and twenty," a voice calls from the back.

Everyone turns. It's Bowden with his new girlfriend, a hairdresser from Halstead. She's given him a haircut that, together with his ultrathin pencil moustache, makes him look as though he's come to sell you the Sydney Harbour Bridge.

"One hundred and fifty," Melissa responds.

"One hundred and fifty from the little lady at the front table, and we'll have to get your mother's OK on the bidding, darling. How about it, Mum?"

How about it? I'm wondering why I didn't drop those children off at the orphanage when I had the chance. As if I can say no when it's an auction to raise money for SOS and it's the engine Norm was fixing for us. I nod at the auctioneer even as I rack my brain for a punishment large and long enough to make up for this.

"One thousand dollars!" Jake screams.

"No!" I call out quick smart, and everyone in the pub lounge laughs, including the auctioneer.

"OK, we're at one hundred and fifty from the lovely Melissa. Any more bids?"

The heat of Melissa's blush almost sets fire to the tablecloth.

"One sixty."

"One eighty."

"Two hundred."

"This is more like it. Come on, ladies and gents, let's have some more bids for Norm Stevens's very own stationary engine. Remember, it's for a good cause—the education of our kids."

In a few seconds the bidding shoots up to four hundred and twenty dollars.

"Sold! To number twenty-six. Thank you, Gabrielle and Geoffrey. I'm sure you'll have many hours of pleasure from the putt-putting of this fine engine."

Amazingly, it's Gabrielle from the Neighbourhood House Committee who has bought the engine. I wave to her and she nods.

The auction continues while more images flash up on the screen: what could be a model of the Gunapan town square fountain, although it's missing the bunch of schoolkids who usually sit there from four till five daring each other to shoplift something, anything, from the milk bar; an outline of a pig that looks like it's done in mosaic. In fact, all the pictures look like mosaic.

"Did Norm do mosaic?" I ask Helen.

"How would I know? Mosaic doesn't sound very Norm."

When the donations for the auction first came in, it seemed as if everyone in Gunapan thought that bikes with broken chains, Scrabble sets with missing letters, one-armed action figures, and dolls with their hair cut off that their own kids wouldn't play with would be a real treat for someone else's kids. Ditto for adults with broken tools and electrical appliances, clothes covered in stains, three-legged chairs, books that had been dropped in the bath, dented bumper bars, cracked plastic containers of every shape and size. I could imagine Norm telling me to take them and dump them back in the yards of the idiots who'd dropped them off.

Instead I filled the Gunapan tip—luckily, tip fees were waived for the special occasion. They'll have to dig a new hole in the ground for the rest of Gunapan's rubbish. It's incredible how this town can generate so much landfill from so little income.

We're up to Lot 24. The auctioneer has knocked down two of the big-ticket items: Norm's engine and a side of beef from Mario. The mayor won the donation from Leonora, our entrepreneurial witch.

"What's it to be, Vaughan?" the auctioneer asked. "Hex or charm?"

"If I say it's for a certain ex-councillor, can you guess?" Vaughan called back, and the crowd cheered and whistled.

Helen, with the grade-three teacher egging her on, won the weekend for two at the alpaca homestay farm—I wonder if a demonstration of the rutting alpacas is part of the package. I paid ten dollars for a newish white dinner set that the charity shop couldn't sell. A picture of Kung Fu Jesus donated by a member of the Church of Goodwill has been bought by another member of the Church of Goodwill. A motor mower and brush cutter set from the local hardware shop got knocked down to Brianna, whose yard does a fair imitation of a Peruvian jungle. And dinner for two at the pub has been passed in unsold.

By nine o'clock Jake's asleep on my lap and Melissa is

yawning. Justin, Mario, and the headmaster, who started the evening lifting the goods above their heads and parading them around the room as they were auctioned, are now pointing to the next item on the table like lazy game-show hosts. Only two things are left: Tina's hand-sewn quilt, and a packet of vacuum cleaner bags for an unknown brand and size of vacuum cleaner.

I love that quilt. I've seen the ones Tina made on commission for the Neighbourhood House Committee members. They're thick and soft and made with gorgeous materials in patterns that could send you into a state of meditation.

"Now you can bid," I whisper to Melissa. "Up to two hundred and three dollars, then stop, OK?"

The bidding starts and, like a pro, Melissa waits till the bid reaches a hundred before she jumps in and tries to knock out the competition with a jump to one fifty.

I look at the screen again. The shots that were on before are repeating, but linking photographs have been inserted between them. It's like a stop-motion film where the pieces are moved around between takes to create movement. I watch with my mouth open as I begin to understand.

The quilt sells to another House Committee member for four hundred and ten dollars. I barely hear the applause for the end of the auction as the film speeds up and repeats one more time. The mayor hurries to the podium and waves his arm at the screen.

"Did anyone guess what it was?" he asks.

"We got it!" several tables call out.

The mayor points a remote control to freeze the screen. He thanks me, the auctioneer, the pub, Justin, and the headmaster, everyone who donated goods, the Save Our School Committee, and the audience. When he's finished his mayoral duties, he turns back to the screen.

"We always knew Norm was a bit crazy. Here's the proof, courtesy of the Department of Lands aerial surveying team and their shots taken over twelve years."

The final cycle of the photos shows the outline of the flower morph into the outline of a car, a Christmas tree, the town fountain, an airplane, a head with a Roman nose, a star, a tree, an arrow, a cat, and, lastly, the three letters *SOS*. If I peer very hard at the screen I can make out the shape of the individual mosaic pieces. There are tractor bodies and harvester parts, old engines, pallets of bricks, corrugated iron, doors, and windows.

It's Norm's yard from the air, a new image made from junk for each year.

34

NORM STEVENS JUNIOR (aka Justin) says I'll never sell my Holden. He says it's too old. Someone will come to test-drive the thing, and as they power down the highway at maximum speed, eighty clicks, bits of the car will fall away until the driver is sitting in a chassis with wheels and not a lot else.

"Leave it to me. I'll sell it for scrap. Send it to the compactor where it belongs." He looks around the yard. "Half the junk in this place should be sent to the compactor."

"It's more than junk, Justin. It's a memorial. It's an icon. It's the art of junk. And it's where people come to get things off their chest."

"Too right they do. I have no idea how Dad made a living. No one ever buys anything. All they want to do is stare at broken machinery and talk for hours."

"I don't think he did make a living here." As executor of the will, I received the paperwork for Norm's telephone betting account yesterday. It's got sixty thousand dollars in it. And that's apart from the money in his bank accounts. "That's what I'm here to tell you, Justin. Norm made quite a bit of money on the track."

Justin leans so far back in his chair I'm worried he's going to topple over. When Norm's will was read we found out he had left the yard to Justin. Any cash was to be divided three ways between Justin, Marg, and me and the kids. We thought he might have a bit put away because he hardly spent anything. The man could build a working machine out of tinfoil, a ribbon, and lemon peel. So I guessed I might get a few thousand dollars.

The minute I heard that money was coming, I drove straight to Merv Bull's Motor and Machinery Maintenance and Repairs, and asked Merv to find me a car for five thousand dollars. Norm's money might not come through for some time, but I still have the money from Mum.

"What kind of car?" Merv asked.

"Small, but with four doors. Automatic. Yes, automatic. And with a little cup holder that flips out of the dashboard."

"Engine size? Performance and handling? Warranty?"

"No, I just want a cup holder."

"Color?"

"A black or gray cup holder would be fine." I can't count the number of hours I've spent trying to get the morning school-run coffee stains out of my clothes.

"Right," Merv said.

He's going to call me when he's found a good one. Meanwhile, I'm thrashing this brute of a Holden like it deserves. Melissa and Jake have cinched their seat belts very tight and occasionally hold hands when we take a corner.

Justin drops his chair back to vertical and picks up another spanner from the table to work at the rusty nut and bolt he's fiddling with.

"What do you mean by quite a bit of money?" He's not looking at me. That's Justin's way. He manages to have entire conversations while gazing at a rock or a tree or a camshaft.

"Seventy-seven thousand four hundred and twenty-nine dollars and eleven cents." I can't help laughing. "The sly bugger. He'd be cracking up at the idiot looks on our faces." My breath does a quick intake of its own accord, a kind of hiccup. "I miss him."

Justin nods. He leans back in his chair again to flick on the kettle.

"Cup of tea?"

I sniff a yes and watch the steam fog up the shed window while Justin makes the tea.

"Milk?" He lifts the opened carton of milk, but I shake my head.

I take the cup he passes me and sip the strong brew. Outside in the yard, the rusted tractors and car bodies, the harvester combs and the sheets of corrugated iron, the motors and trays and wheel rims and cyclone wire and steel drums and sheep skulls and windows and metal lockers and a single broken vending machine crack and sigh as the morning sun evaporates the dew from their hides.

"By the way." I've suddenly remembered. "Did you know Samantha Patterson was bonking that council officer?"

"Of course."

"But you've only been here half a minute! How come you knew and I didn't?"

"Dad told me. So, what will happen with the development now?"

"They have to resubmit the application to council because, of course, it broke every regulation in the planning book. There's some court case going on. Not sure what will happen. I hope I don't have to start painting placards again. I've still got marine paint on my shirt."

I take another sip of tea. This is my life, I think. My ordinary life with tea and company and two unruly children. I don't need a Merc or an Audi, or even a Harley.

"When's the court date?"

Everyone's been asking me this. The SOS supporters have threatened to hire a bus and travel to Halstead Magistrates' Court. They said it's for support, but I'm fairly certain it's for the entertainment value. I told them we still need to save the school, so to stop playing around and start thinking about how to use the money we raised at the auction. The words "party" and "beach holiday" did come up, but in the end we decided on a media campaign. Whatever that is.

"Two weeks. The Legal Aid lawyer says I'll probably get off with a bond."

Melissa appears at the door of the shed, dragging her brother behind her. "I'm not looking after him anymore. He won't listen to me. He put an old paint tin on his head and I can't get it off."

She swings Jake in through the shed door. His tin head bangs against the doorjamb.

"Ow," Jake says from inside the tin.

"What are you doing, Jake?" I shout so he can hear me.

"I'm Ned Kelly."

"Hold your breath, Ned." When I give the paint tin a quick firm twist, Jake is too surprised to scream. He squeaks, then rubs his ears.

"This is a nice blue." I wonder how the kitchen would look painted this color.

"When are we going home?" Jake says.

I don't know why I put up with these children. Apparently there's still a white slave trade in the Middle East. I wonder how much I'd get for two.

"In a minute. Go and get some lemons and we'll head off."

They race to the tree in the middle of the yard and jump up and down, trying to grab the lemons off the high branches. I stand and stretch.

"Thanks for the tea." I put the cup on the table.

"I'm glad you knew my dad. I'm glad you're still here." Justin's voice is soft as he continues examining the thread on the bolt before placing it carefully on the bench. He stands up.

I hesitate before I say, "Actually, we're having sausages for dinner tonight. Top quality from the supermarket. You're welcome to come." I am almost fifty percent sure I didn't leave them sitting on the car seat in the sun.

He looks down at me and smiles. It's a rare thing, a Justin smile. He has beautiful teeth. Natural ones.

"That'd be great."

"See you at six, then." I might even put on the new green jersey dress I got from the charity shop last week.

As the kids hare off to the car with lemons aproned in their shirts, I take a long look over Norm Stevens Junior's yard.

The art of junk.

Acknowledgments

I am grateful that the writing of this novel was assisted by residencies from Varuna: The Writers' House, Litlink, and the Tasmanian Writers' Centre. Thanks also to my talented friends whose belief and support have helped to keep all manner of projects afloat: Janet Hutchinson, Jane Watson, Mary Manning, Janey Runci, Pam Baker, Penny Gibson.

THE FINE COLOR OF RUST

P. A. O'REILLY

A Readers Club Guide

INTRODUCTION

Loretta Boskovic is a woman struck with the Gunapan curse—her husband, Tony, ran off after ten years, leaving her with only two resources to bring up her children in this small Australian town: a part-time job and a robust sense of humor. When the government threatens to shut down Gunapan's only school, Loretta leaps into action to rally the community around the cause. And when she and her unlikely friend, the old junk man Norm, sense suspicious activity within the city council, Loretta finds her way through the corruption to uncover the real truth. She may be short on money, influence, and glamorous outfits, but with the help of her devoted friends and unflagging spirit, Loretta is ready to defend the true beauty of her imperfect home.

QUESTIONS AND TOPICS FOR DISCUSSION

1. O'Reilly describes the Japanese word *sabi* in the book's epigraph as "the simple beauty of worn and imperfect and impermanent things." How does this theme manifest itself in *The Fine Color of Rust*?

2. What are your first reactions to Gunapan as a community? Consider the positive aspects of the town (everyone knowing everyone else, people helping each other, a sense of all being "in the same boat") as well as the negative ones (economic depression, drought, welfare dependency). In your opinion, what is the value of a small town or community? Consider where you live and how you participate in your local community in your response.

3. What do you think is Loretta's greatest strength? Her greatest weakness? What is Loretta's greatest value to others?

4. Loretta has frequent fantasies of transformation: "The pudge has magically fallen from my hips and I'm wearing a long, slinky silk dress. I'm in the function room of the golf course, tossing my newly blond-streaked hair and full of ennui or some other French feeling . . ." (p. 75) Will she ever do anything about these fantasies? Why do we have fantasies like this? Are they helpful, or do they only make us long for things we can never have?

5. When Loretta reads her "List of Pleasing Things" aloud in writing class, it's clear that her pleasing things are completely different from those of the other women. Is this a

reflection of their different backgrounds? Is it a matter of working class versus upper class? Do you think the other women are being perfectly honest in their lists?

6. Loretta says her sister Tammy "thinks her wealthy lifestyle exemplifies cultured good taste and mine has degenerated into hillbilly destitution, whereas I think Tammy is living a nouveau riche nightmare while I represent a dignified insufficiency." (p. 54) Whose version do you agree with? Why?

7. What do you think was the real cause of Melissa and Jake's bullying behavior? Did Loretta do the right thing in the way she tried to short-circuit the bullying? Have you or members of your family ever been bullied? Or have you been the bully? What makes people become bullies?

8. Loretta's sister Patsy says, "You've got no reason to stay here [in Gunapan]. . . . That bastard's not coming back and the kids are young enough to move schools. Mum's gone to the Gold Coast, so she won't bother you. Come back to the real world." (pp. 61–62) Why do you think Loretta chooses to stay in Gunapan?

9. Most of the residents of Gunapan seem pleased and excited about the resort development. Why do you think they want the resort? Discuss the tension between gritty authenticity and out-of-reach luxury in *The Fine Color of Rust*.

10. When Loretta jokes about dropping her kids off at the orphanage, she's expressing the feelings most parents

have at some point: of being overwhelmed, exhausted, frustrated. She is also fiercely protective of her children. What do you think of the way motherhood is portrayed in the book?

11. Loretta's mom offers the following advice: "[You] should give up that political hocus-pocus you've got yourself into. Put your energy into finding a partner and a father for those children." (p. 57) What do you think is the best use of Loretta's energy, for herself, for Melissa and Jake, for the community? Whose needs are most important for Loretta to meet?

12. For both Loretta and Norm, humor is one of the ways they deal with adversity and pain. (Loretta also gets assistance from a dose of chocolate.) Do you think humor makes life easier or harder? How do you cope in difficult times?

13. What is the greatest injustice in *The Fine Color of Rust*? The greatest moment of justice restored?

ENHANCE YOUR BOOK CLUB

1. Write out your own "List of Pleasing Things" and bring it to your book club meeting. Read them aloud. Do you tend toward poetic, intangible things or simple, down-to-earth items? What do you think your list of "pleasing things" says about you as an individual? Were you surprised by any of your fellow book club members' lists?

2. Loretta is a firm believer in the power of local organization and fighting for the underdog. According to Loretta, "No one cares about us in the small towns. We have to fight or we'll go under." (p. 184) Channel Loretta's energy for change in your book club and spend an afternoon working together for a local cause that you all believe in. This could range from volunteering at a school, a shelter, or a residential care facility to canvassing or making phone calls for a local political or nonprofit organization. How does spending time in your community change your relationship to or perspective of your surroundings?

3. The local natural water resources are very important to Gunapan's community. What natural resources play a similar role in your community? Take a trip with your book club members to a local park. Consider packing a picnic, bringing some sports gear, or dusting off your camera and binoculars and taking some time to appreciate the outdoors together. To browse National Parks by state, visit en.wikipedia.org/wiki/List_of_national_parks_of_the_United_States. If you don't live near a National Park, try searching the National Park Service's state-by-state registry of places to visit instead: www.nps.gov/communities/states.htm.

Praise for MUDBOUND

"A compelling family tragedy, a confluence of romantic attraction and racial hatred that eventually falls like an avalanche . . . The last third of the book is downright breathless."

—*The Washington Post Book World*

"[A] supremely readable debut novel . . . *Mudbound* is packed with drama. Pick it up, then pass it on."

—*People*, Critics Choice, 4-star review

"*Mudbound* argues for humanity and equality, while high-lighting the effects of war . . . [The] mixture of the predictable and the unpredictable will keep readers turning the pages . . . It feels like a classic tragedy, whirling toward a climax. [An] ambitious first novel." —*The Dallas Morning News*

"By the end of the very short first chapter, I was completely hooked . . . [*Mudbound* is] so carefully considered and so full of weight . . . This is a book in which love and rage cohabit. This is a book that made me cry." —*Minneapolis Star Tribune*

"[A] tremendous gift, a story that challenges the 1950s text-book version of our history and leaves its readers completely in the thrall of her characters . . . *Mudbound* may well become a staple of syllabi for courses in Southern literature."

—*Paste* magazine, 4-star review

"Does an excellent job of capturing the impacts of racism both casual and deliberate." —*The Denver Post*

"[An] impressive first novel . . . Jordan is an author to watch."

—*Rocky Mountain News*

"This is storytelling at the height of its powers: the ache of wrongs not yet made right, the fierce attendance of history made as real as rain, as true as this minute. Hillary Jordan writes with the force of a Delta storm. Her characters walked straight out of 1940s Mississippi and into the part of my brain where sympathy and anger and love reside, leaving my heart racing. They are with me still."   —Barbara Kingsolver

"Is it too early to say, after just one book, that here's a voice that will echo for years to come? . . . Jordan picks at the scabs of racial inequality that will perhaps never fully heal and brings just enough heartbreak to this intimate, universal tale, just enough suspense, to leave us contemplating how the lives and motives of these vivid characters might have been different."

—*San Antonio Express-News*

"This book packs an emotional wallop that will engage adult and adolescent readers . . . The six narrators here have enough time and space to develop a complicated set of relationships. The fault lines among them converge into a crackling gunpoint confrontation, a stunning scene that ranks as my personal favorite of this year."   —*The Cleveland Plain Dealer*

"Refusing to turn the page is not an option. Jordan is able to make her painful subject matter irresistible by putting the breath of life in these people."   —*Richmond Times-Dispatch*

"Jordan has an uncanny knack for nailing the voices of characters she has no business knowing, but know them she does. *Mudbound* also reminds us of the sacrifices made by all soldiers, and how the home front isn't always as appreciative as it should be."   —MSNBC.com, Can't Miss column

"Luminous . . . The power of *Mudbound* is that the characters speak directly to the reader. And they will stay with you long after you put the book down." —*Jackson Free Press*

"A page-turning read that conveys a serious message without preaching." —*The Observer* (U.K.)

"*Mudbound* dramatizes the human cost of unthinking hatred . . . That [she] makes a hopeful ending seem possible, after the violence and injustice that precede it, is a tribute to the novel's voices . . . The characters live in the novel as individuals, black and white, which gives *Mudbound* its impact." —*The Atlanta Journal-Constitution*

"If Hillary Jordan's new book, *Mudbound*, is ever made into a movie, the odds are very good that it will end up on the short list for an Academy Award. Not just because of the quality of Jordan's writing . . . but also because she tackles some of this country's most enduring and well-trodden emotional and historical territory." —*Albany Times Union*

"The recognition [Jordan]'s received for the work has been nothing short of sparkling . . . *Mudbound* is as much a tale of racism as it is the transcending powers of love and friendship." —*Austin American-Statesman*

"Full of rich details and dimensional, engaging characters, and it sucks readers in like quicksand from its opening scene." —*Creative Loafing, Atlanta*

"[A] heart-rending debut novel . . . Jordan's beautiful, haunting prose makes it a seductive page-turner." —*DailyCandy*

"A meticulous, moving narrative." —*Texas Monthly*

"Jordan has crafted a story that shines . . . A good historical novel with a twist of an ending."
—*The Oklahoman*

"This is one of the most extraordinary novels I've read all year . . . Set against the pull of the land—and of the lonely heart—the ensuing tragedy is both inevitable and heart shattering."
—*Dame* magazine

"Stunning and disturbing . . . A story of heroism, loyalty, respect and abiding love."
—*Rocky Mount Telegram*

"No denying that readers in search of straightforward storytelling will be hooked."
—*Memphis Flyer*

"Debut novelist Hillary Jordan has crafted an unforgettable tale of family loyalties, the spiraling after-effects of war and the unfathomable human behavior generated by racism."
—*BookPage*

"[A] beautiful debut . . . A superbly rendered depiction of the fury and terror wrought by racism."
—*Publishers Weekly*

"[A] poignant and moving debut novel . . . Jordan faultlessly portrays the values of the 1940s as she builds to a stunning conclusion. Highly recommended."
—*Library Journal,* starred review

"*Mudbound* is a real page-turner—a tangle of history, tragedy, and romance powered by guilt, moral indignation, and a near chorus of unstoppable voices."
—Stewart O'Nan, author of *A Prayer for the Dying* and *Last Night at the Lobster*

MUDBOUND

A NOVEL BY

HILLARY JORDAN

ALGONQUIN BOOKS OF CHAPEL HILL.

2009

Published by
ALGONQUIN BOOKS OF CHAPEL HILL
Post Office Box 2225
Chapel Hill, North Carolina 27515-2225

a division of
WORKMAN PUBLISHING
225 Varick Street
New York, New York 10014

This is a work of fiction. While, as in all fiction, the literary perceptions
and insights are based on experience, all names, characters, places, and
incidents either are products of the author's imagination or are used
fictitiously.

Library of Congress Cataloging-in-Publication Data
Jordan, Hillary, [date]
    Mudbound : a novel / by Hillary Jordan.— 1st ed.
      p. cm.
    ISBN-13: 978-1-56512-569-8 (HC)
    1. Farm life—Mississippi—Fiction.   2. World War, 1939–1945—
Veterans—Fiction.   3. African American veterans—Fiction.
    4. Race relations—Mississippi—Fiction.   I. Title.

PS3610.O6556M83 2008
813'.6—dc22   2007044471

    ISBN-13: 978-1-56512-677-0 (PB)

18 17 16 15 14 13 12 11

To Mother, Gay and Nana,
for the stories

If I could do it, I'd do no writing at all here. It would be photographs; the rest would be fragments of cloth, bits of cotton, lumps of earth, records of speech, pieces of wood and iron, phials of odors, plates of food and of excrement. . . .

A piece of the body torn out by the roots might be more to the point.

—JAMES AGEE, *Let Us Now Praise Famous Men*

I.

JAMIE

HENRY AND I DUG the hole seven feet deep. Any shallower and the corpse was liable to come rising up during the next big flood: *Howdy boys! Remember me?* The thought of it kept us digging even after the blisters on our palms had burst, re-formed and burst again. Every shovelful was an agony— the old man, getting in his last licks. Still, I was glad of the pain. It shoved away thought and memory.

When the hole got too deep for our shovels to reach bottom, I climbed down into it and kept digging while Henry paced and watched the sky. The soil was so wet from all the rain it was like digging into raw meat. I scraped it off the blade by hand, cursing at the delay. This was the first break we'd had in the weather in three days and could be our last chance for some while to get the body in the ground.

"Better hurry it up," Henry said.

I looked at the sky. The clouds overhead were the color of ash, but there was a vast black mass of them to the north, and it was headed our way. Fast.

"We're not gonna make it," I said.

"We will," he said.

That was Henry for you: absolutely certain that whatever he wanted to happen *would* happen. The body would get buried before the storm hit. The weather would dry out in time to resow the cotton. Next year would be a better year. His little brother would never betray him.

I dug faster, wincing with every stroke. I knew I could stop at any time and Henry would take my place without a word of complaint—never mind he had nearly fifty years on his bones to my twenty-nine. Out of pride or stubbornness or both, I kept digging. By the time he said, "All right, my turn," my muscles were on fire and I was wheezing like an engine full of old gas. When he pulled me up out of the hole, I gritted my teeth so I wouldn't cry out. My body still ached in a dozen places from all the kicks and blows, but Henry didn't know about that.

Henry could never know about that.

I knelt by the side of the hole and watched him dig. His face and hands were so caked with mud a passerby might have taken him for a Negro. No doubt I was just as filthy, but in my case the red hair would have given me away. My father's hair, copper spun so fine women's fingers itch to run through it. I've always hated it. It might as well be a pyre blazing on top of my head, shouting to the world that he's in me. Shouting it to me every time I look in the mirror.

Around four feet, Henry's blade hit something hard.

"What is it?" I asked.

"Piece of rock, I think."

But it wasn't rock, it was bone—a human skull, missing a

big chunk in back. "Damn," Henry said, holding it up to the light.

"What do we do now?"

"I don't know."

We both looked to the north. The black was growing, eating up the sky.

"We can't start over," I said. "It could be days before the rain lets up again."

"I don't like it," Henry said. "It's not right."

He kept digging anyway, using his hands, passing the bones up to me as he unearthed them: ribs, arms, pelvis. When he got to the lower legs, there was a clink of metal. He held up a tibia and I saw the crude, rusted iron shackle encircling the bone. A broken chain dangled from it.

"Jesus Christ," Henry said. "This is a slave's grave."

"You don't know that."

He picked up the broken skull. "See here? He was shot in the head. Must've been a runaway." Henry shook his head. "That settles it."

"Settles what?"

"We can't bury our father in a nigger's grave," Henry said. "There's nothing he'd have hated more. Now help me out of here." He extended one grimy hand.

"It could have been an escaped convict," I said. "A white man." It could have been, but I was betting it wasn't. Henry hesitated, and I said, "The penitentiary's what, just six or seven miles from here?"

"More like ten," he said. But he let his hand fall to his side.

"Come on," I said, holding out my own hand. "Take a break. I'll dig awhile." When he reached up and clasped it, I had to stop myself from smiling. Henry was right: there was nothing our father would have hated more.

HENRY WAS BACK to digging again when I saw Laura coming toward us, picking her way across the drowned fields with a bucket in each hand. I fished in my pocket for my handkerchief and used it to wipe some of the mud off my face. Vanity—that's another thing I got from my father.

"Laura's coming," I said.

"Pull me up," Henry said.

I grabbed his hands and pulled, grunting with the effort, dragging him over the lip of the grave. He struggled to his knees, breathing harshly. He bent his head and his hat came off, revealing a wide swath of pink skin on top. The sight of it gave me a sharp, unexpected pang. *He's getting old,* I thought. *I won't always have him.*

He looked up, searching for Laura. When his eyes found her they lit with emotions so private I was embarrassed to see them: longing, hope, a tinge of worry. "I'd better keep at it," I said, turning away and picking up the shovel. I half jumped, half slid down into the hole. It was deep enough now that I couldn't see out. Just as well.

"How's it coming?" I heard Laura say. As always, her voice coursed through me like cold, clear water. It was a voice that belonged rightfully to some ethereal creature, a siren or an angel, not to a middle-aged Mississippi farmwife.

"We're almost finished," said Henry. "Another foot or so will see it done."

"I've brought food and water," she said.

"Water!" Henry let out a bitter laugh. "That's just what we need, is more water." I heard the scrape of the dipper against the pail and the sound of him swallowing, then Laura's head appeared over the side of the hole. She handed the dipper down to me.

"Here," she said, "have a drink."

I gulped it down, wishing it were whiskey instead. I'd run out three days ago, just before the bridge flooded, cutting us off from town. I reckoned the river had gone down enough by now that I could have gotten across—if I hadn't been stuck in that damned hole.

I thanked her and handed the dipper back up to her, but Laura wasn't looking at me. Her eyes were fixed on the other side of the grave, where we'd laid the bones.

"Good Lord, are those human?" she said.

"It couldn't be helped," Henry said. "We were already four feet down when we found them."

I saw her lips twitch as her eyes took in the shackles and chains. She covered her mouth with her hand, then turned to Henry. "Make sure you move them so the children don't see," she said.

WHEN THE TOP of the grave was more than a foot over my head, I stopped digging. "Come take a look," I called out. "I think this is plenty deep."

Henry's face appeared above me, upside down. He nodded. "Yep. That should do it." I handed him the shovel, but when he tried to pull me up, it was no use. I was too far down, and our hands and the walls of the hole were too slick.

"I'll fetch the ladder," he said.

"Hurry."

I waited in the hole. Around me was mud, stinking and oozing. Overhead a rectangle of darkening gray. I stood with my neck bent back, listening for the returning squelch of Henry's boots, wondering what was taking him so goddamn long. *If something happened to him and Laura*, I thought, *no one would know I was here*. I clutched the edge of the hole and tried to pull myself up, but my fingers just slid through the mud.

Then I felt the first drops of rain hit my face. "Henry!" I yelled.

The rain was falling lightly now, but before long it would be a downpour. The water would start filling up the hole. I'd feel it creeping up my legs to my thighs. To my chest. To my neck. "Henry! Laura!"

I threw myself at the walls of the grave like a maddened bear in a pit. Part of me was outside myself, shaking my head at my own foolishness, but the man was powerless to help the bear. It wasn't the confinement; I'd spent hundreds of hours in cockpits with no problem at all. It was the water. During the war I'd avoided flying over the open ocean whenever I could, even if it meant facing flak from the ground. It was how I won all those medals for bravery: from being so scared of that vast, hungry blue that I drove straight into the thick of German antiaircraft fire.

I was yelling so hard I didn't hear Henry until he was standing right over me. "I'm here, Jamie! I'm here!" he shouted.

He lowered the ladder into the hole and I scrambled up it. He tried to take hold of my arm, but I waved him off. I bent over, my hands on my knees, trying to slow the tripping of my heart.

"You all right?" he asked.

I didn't look at him, but I didn't have to. I knew his forehead would be puckered and his mouth pursed—his "my brother, the lunatic" look.

"I thought maybe you'd decided to leave me down there," I said, with a forced laugh.

"Why would I do that?"

"I'm just kidding, Henry." I went and took up the ladder, tucking it under one arm. "Come on, let's get this over with."

We hurried across the fields, stopping at the pump to wash the mud off our hands and faces, then headed to the barn to get the coffin. It was a sorry-looking thing, made of mismatched scrap wood, but it was the best we'd been able to do with the materials we had. Henry frowned as he picked up one end. "I wish to hell we'd been able to get to town," he said.

"Me too," I said, thinking of the whiskey.

We carried the coffin up onto the porch. When we went past the open window Laura called out, "You'll want hot coffee and a change of clothes before we bury him."

"No," said Henry. "There's no time. Storm's coming."

We took the coffin into the lean-to and set it on the rough plank floor. Henry lifted the sheet to look at our father's face one last time. Pappy's expression was tranquil. There was nothing to show that his death was anything other than the natural, timely passing of an old man.

I lifted the feet and Henry took the head. "Gently now," he said.

"Right," I said, "we wouldn't want to hurt him."

"That's not the point," Henry snapped.

"Sorry, brother. I'm just tired."

With ludicrous care, we lowered the corpse into the coffin. Henry reached for the lid. "I'll finish up here," he said. "You go make sure Laura and the girls are ready."

"All right."

As I walked into the house I heard the hammer strike the first nail, a sweet and final sound. It made the children jump.

"What's that banging, Mama?" asked Amanda Leigh.

"That's your daddy, nailing Pappy's coffin shut," Laura said.

"Will it make him mad?" Bella's voice was a scared whisper.

Laura shot me a quick, fierce glance. "No, darling," she said. "Pappy's dead. He can't get mad at anyone ever again. Now, let's get you into your coats and boots. It's time to lay your grandfather to rest."

I was glad Henry wasn't there to hear the satisfaction in her voice.

LAURA

When I think of the farm, I think of mud. Limning my husband's fingernails and encrusting the children's knees and hair. Sucking at my feet like a greedy newborn on the breast. Marching in boot-shaped patches across the plank floors of the house. There was no defeating it. The mud coated everything. I dreamed in brown.

When it rained, as it often did, the yard turned into a thick gumbo, with the house floating in it like a soggy cracker. When the rains came hard, the river rose and swallowed the bridge that was the only way across. The world was on the other side of that bridge, the world of light bulbs and paved roads and shirts that stayed white. When the river rose, the world was lost to us and we to it.

One day slid into the next. My hands did what was necessary: pumping, churning, scouring, scraping. And cooking, always cooking. Snapping beans and the necks of chickens. Kneading dough, shucking corn and digging the eyes out of potatoes. No sooner was breakfast over and the mess cleaned up than it was time to start on dinner. After dinner came supper, then breakfast again the next morning.

Get up at first light. Go to the outhouse. Do your business, shivering in the winter, sweating in the summer, breathing through your mouth year-round. Steal the eggs from under the hens. Haul in wood from the pile and light the stove. Make the biscuits, slice the bacon and fry it up with the eggs and grits. Rouse your daughters from their bed, brush their teeth, guide arms into sleeves and feet into socks and boots. Take your youngest out to the porch and hold her up so she can clang the bell that will summon your husband from the fields and wake his hateful father in the lean-to next door. Feed them all and yourself. Scrub the iron skillet, the children's faces, the mud off the floors day after day while the old man sits and watches. He is always on you: "You better stir them greens, gal. You better sweep that floor now. Better teach them brats some manners. Wash them clothes. Feed them chickens. Fetch me my cane." His voice, clotted from smoking. His sly pale eyes with their hard black centers, on you.

He scared the children, especially my youngest, who was a little chubby.

"Come here, little piglet," he'd say to her.

She peered at him from behind my legs. At his long yellow teeth. At his bony yellow fingers with their thick curved nails like pieces of ancient horn.

"Come here and sit on my lap."

He had no interest in holding her or any other child, he just liked knowing she was afraid of him. When she wouldn't come, he told her she was too fat to sit on his lap anyway, she might break his bones. She started to cry, and I imagined that old man in his coffin. Pictured the lid closing on his face, the box being lowered into the hole. Heard the dirt striking the wood.

"Pappy," I said, smiling sweetly at him, "how about a nice cup of coffee?"

BUT I MUST START at the beginning, if I can find it. Beginnings are elusive things. Just when you think you have hold of one, you look back and see another, earlier beginning, and an earlier one before that. Even if you start with "Chapter One: I Am Born," you still have the problem of antecedents, of cause and effect. Why is young David fatherless? Because, Dickens tells us, his father died of a delicate constitution. Yes, but where did this mortal delicacy come from? Dickens doesn't say, so we're left to speculate. A congenital defect, perhaps, inherited from his mother, whose own mother had married beneath her to spite her cruel father, who'd been beaten as a child by a nursemaid who was forced into service when her faithless husband abandoned her for a woman he chanced to meet when his carriage wheel broke in front of the milliner's where she'd gone to have her hat trimmed. If we begin there, young David is fatherless because his great-great-grandfather's nursemaid's husband's future mistress's hat needed adornment.

By the same logic, my father-in-law was murdered because I was born plain rather than pretty. That's one possible beginning. There are others: Because Henry saved Jamie from drowning in the Great Mississippi Flood of 1927. Because Pappy sold the land that should have been Henry's. Because

Jamie flew too many bombing missions in the war. Because a Negro named Ronsel Jackson shone too brightly. Because a man neglected his wife, and a father betrayed his son, and a mother exacted vengeance. I suppose the beginning depends on who's telling the story. No doubt the others would start somewhere different, but they'd still wind up at the same place in the end.

It's tempting to believe that what happened on the farm was inevitable; that in fact all the events of our lives are as pre-determined as the moves in a game of tic-tac-toe: Start in the middle square and no one wins. Start in one of the corners and the game is yours. And if you don't start, if you let the other person start? You lose, simple as that.

The truth isn't so simple. Death may be inevitable, but love is not. Love, you have to choose.

I'll begin with that. With love.

THERE'S A LOT of talk in the Bible about cleaving. Men and women cleaving unto God. Husbands cleaving to wives. Bones cleaving to skin. Cleaving, we are to understand, is a good thing. The righteous cleave; the wicked do not.

On my wedding day, my mother—in a vague attempt to prepare me for the indignities of the marriage bed—told me to cleave to Henry no matter what. "It will hurt at first," she said, as she fastened her pearls around my neck. "But it will get easier in time."

Mother was only half-right.

I was a thirty-one-year-old virgin when I met Henry McAllan in the spring of 1939, a spinster well on my way to petrifaction. My world was small, and everything in it was known. I lived with my parents in the house where I'd been born. I slept in the room that had once been mine and my sisters' and was now mine alone. I taught English at a private school for boys, sang in the Calvary Episcopal Church choir, babysat my nieces and nephews. Monday nights I played bridge with my married friends.

I was never beautiful like my sisters. Fanny and Etta have the delicate blonde good looks of the Fairbairns, my mother's people, but I'm all Chappell: small and dark, with strong Gallic features and a full figure that was ill-suited to the flapper dresses and slim silhouettes of my youth. When my mother's friends came to visit, they remarked on the loveliness of my hands, the curliness of my hair, the cheerfulness of my disposition; I was that sort of young woman. And then one day—quite suddenly, it seemed to me—I was no longer young. Mother wept the night of my thirtieth birthday, after the dishes from the family party had been cleaned and put away and my brothers and sisters and their spouses and children had kissed me and gone home to their beds. The sound of her crying, muffled by a pillow or my father's shoulder perhaps, drifted down the hallway to my room, where I lay awake listening to the whippoorwills, cicadas and peepers speak to one another. *I am! I am!* they seemed to say.

"I am," I whispered. The words sounded hollow to my ears, as pointless as the frantic rubbings of a cricket in a matchbox. It was hours before I slept.

But when I woke the next morning I felt a kind of relief. I was no longer just unmarried; I was officially unmarriageable. Everyone could stop hoping and shift the weight of their attention elsewhere, to some other, worthier project, leaving me to get on with my life. I was a respected teacher, a beloved daughter, sister, niece and aunt. I would be content with that.

Would I have been, I wonder? Would I have found happiness there in the narrow, blank margins of the page, habitat of maiden aunts and childless schoolteachers? I can't say, because a little over a year later, Henry came into my life and pulled me squarely into the ink-filled center.

My brother Teddy brought him to dinner at our house one Sunday. Teddy worked as a civilian land appraiser for the Army Corps of Engineers, and Henry was his new boss. He was that rare and marvelous creature, a forty-one-year-old bachelor. He looked his age, mostly because of his hair, which was stark white. He wasn't an especially large man, but he had density. He walked with a noticeable limp which I later learned he'd gotten in the war, but it didn't detract from his air of confidence. His movements were slow and deliberate, as if his limbs were weighted, and it was a matter of great consequence where he placed them. His hands were strong-looking and finely made, and the nails wanted cutting. I was struck by their stillness, by the way they remained folded calmly in his lap or planted on either side of his plate, even when he talked politics. He spoke with the lovely garble of the Delta—like he had a mouthful of some rich, luscious dessert. He addressed most of his remarks to Teddy and my parents, but I felt his gray eyes on my face all through dinner, lighting there briefly, moving away and then returning again. I remember my skin prickling with heat and damp beneath my clothes, my hand trembling slightly when I reached for my water glass.

My mother, whose nose was ever attuned to the scent of male admiration, began wedging my feminine virtues into the conversation with excruciating frequency: "Oh, so you're a college graduate, Mr. McAllan? Laura went to college, you know. She got her teaching certificate from West Tennessee State. Yes, Mr. McAllan, we all play the piano, but Laura is by far the best musician in the family. She sings beautifully too, doesn't she Teddy? And you should taste her peach chess pie." And so on. I spent most of dinner staring at my plate. Every time I tried to retreat to the kitchen on some errand or another, Mother insisted on going herself or sending Teddy's wife, Eliza, who shot me sympathetic glances as she obeyed. Teddy's eyes were dancing; by the end of the meal he was choking back laughter, and I was ready to strangle him and my mother both.

When Henry took his leave of us, Mother invited him back the following Sunday. He looked at me before he agreed, a measuring look I did my best to meet with a polite smile.

In the week that followed, my mother could talk of little else but that charming Mr. McAllan: how soft-spoken he was, how gentlemanly and—highest praise of all from her—how he did not take wine with dinner. Daddy liked him too, but that was hardly a surprise given that Henry was a College Man. For my father, a retired history professor, there was no greater proof of a person's worth than a college education. The Son of God

Himself, come again in glory but lacking a diploma, would not have found favor with Daddy.

My parents' hopefulness grated on me. It threatened to kindle my own, and that, I couldn't allow. I told myself that Henry McAllan and his gentlemanly, scholarly ways had nothing to do with me. He was newly arrived in Memphis and had no other society; that was why he'd accepted Mother's invitation.

How pathetic my defenses were, and how paper-thin! They shredded easily enough the following Sunday, when Henry showed up with lilies for me as well as for my mother. After dinner he suggested we go for a walk. I took him to Overton Park. The dogwoods were blooming, and as we strolled beneath them the wind blew flurries of white petals down on our heads. It was like a scene out of the movies, with me as the unlikely heroine. Henry plucked a petal from my hair, his fingers lightly grazing my cheek.

"Pretty, aren't they?" he said.

"Yes, but sad."

"Why sad?"

"Because they remind us of Christ's suffering."

Henry's brows drew together, forming a deep vertical furrow between them. I could tell how much it bothered him, not knowing something, and I liked him for admitting his ignorance rather than pretending to know as so many men would have done. I showed him the marks like bloody nail holes on each of the four petals.

"Ah," he said, and took my hand.

He held it all the way back to my house, and when we got

there he asked me to a performance of *The Chocolate Soldier* at the Memphis Open Air Theatre the following Saturday. The female members of my family mobilized to beautify me for the occasion. Mother took me to Lowenstein's department store and bought me a new dress with a frothy white collar and puffed sleeves. On Saturday morning my sisters came to the house with pots of color for my cheeks and eyes, and lipsticks in every shade of red and pink, testing them out on me with the swift, high-handed authority of master chefs choosing seasonings for the sauce. When I was plucked, painted and powdered to their satisfaction, they held a mirror to my face, presenting me with my own reflection like a gift. I looked strange to myself and told them so.

"Just wait till Henry sees you," laughed Fanny.

When he came to pick me up, Henry merely told me that I looked nice. But later that day he kissed me for the first time, taking my face in his hands as naturally and familiarly as if it were a favorite hat or a shaving bowl he'd owned for years. Never before had a man kissed me with that degree of possession, either of himself or of me, and it thrilled me.

Henry had all the self-confidence that I lacked. He was certain of an astonishing number of things: Packards are the best-made American cars. Meat ought not to be eaten rare. Irving Berlin's "God Bless America" should be the national anthem instead of "The Star-Spangled Banner," which is too difficult to sing. The Yankees will win the World Series. There will be another Great War in Europe, and the United States would do well to stay out of it. Blue is your color, Laura.

I wore blue. Gradually, over the course of the next several months, I unspooled my life for him. I told him about my favorite students, my summer jobs as a camp counselor in Myrtle Beach and my family, down to the second and third cousins. I spoke of my two years at college, how I'd loved Dickens and the Brontës and hated Melville and mathematics. Henry listened with grave attention to everything I chose to share with him, nodding from time to time to indicate his approval. I soon found myself looking for those nods, making mental notes on when they were bestowed and withheld, and inevitably, presenting him with the version of myself that seemed most likely to elicit them. This wasn't a deliberate exercise of feminine wiles on my part. I was unused to male admiration and knew only that I wanted more of it, and all that came with it.

And there was so much that came with it. Having a beau — my mother's word, which she used at every possible opportunity—gave me cachet among my friends and relations that I'd never before enjoyed. I became prettier and more interesting, worthier somehow of every good thing.

How lovely you look today, my dear, they would say. And, *I declare, you're positively glowing!* And, *Come and sit by me, Laura, and tell me all about this Mr. McAllan of yours.*

I wasn't at all sure that he was my Mr. McAllan, but as spring turned to summer and Henry's attentions showed no sign of slacking, I began to allow myself to hope that he might be. He took me to restaurants and the picture show, for walks along the Mississippi and day trips to the surrounding countryside, where he pointed out features of the land and the farms we passed. He was very knowledgeable about crops, livestock and such. When I remarked on it, he told me he'd grown up on a farm.

"Do your parents still live there?" I asked.

"No. They sold the place after the '27 flood."

I heard the wistfulness in his voice but put it down to nostalgia. I didn't think to ask if he was interested in farming his own land someday. Henry was a College Man, a successful engineer with a job that allowed him to live in Memphis—the center of civilization. Why in the world would he want to scratch out a living as a farmer?

"MY BROTHER'S COMING UP from Oxford this weekend," Henry announced one day in July. "I'd like for him to meet you."

For *him* to meet *me*. My heart fluttered. Jamie was Henry's favorite sibling. Henry spoke of him often, with a mixture of fondness and exasperation that made me smile. Jamie was at Ole Miss studying fine arts ("a subject of no practical use whatever") and modeling men's clothing on the side ("an undignified occupation for a man"). He wanted to be an actor ("that's no way to support a family") and spent all his spare time doing thespian productions ("he just likes the attention"). Yet despite these criticisms, it was obvious that Henry adored his little brother. Something quickened in his eyes whenever he talked about Jamie, and his hands, normally so impassive, rose from his sides to make large, swooping shapes in the air. That he wanted Jamie to meet me surely meant that he was considering a more permanent attachment between us. Out of long habit, I tried to stifle the thought, but it stayed stubbornly alive in my mind. That night, as I peeled the potatoes for supper, I imagined Henry's proposal, pictured him kneeling before me in the parlor, his face earnest and slightly worried—what if I didn't accept him? As I made my narrow bed the next morning, I envisioned myself smoothing the covers of a double bed with a white, candlewick-patterned spread and two pillows bearing the imprints of two heads. In class the next day, as I quizzed my boys on prepositional phrases, I pictured a child with Henry's gray eyes staring up at me from a wicker bassinet. These visions bloomed in my mind like exotic flowers, opulent and jewel-toned, undoing years of strict pruning of my desires.

The Saturday I was to meet Jamie I dressed with extra care, wearing the navy linen suit I knew Henry liked and sitting patiently while my mother tortured my unruly hair into an upswept do worthy of a magazine advertisement. Henry picked me up and we drove to the station to meet his brother's train. As we stood in the flow of disembarking passengers, I scanned the crowd for a younger copy of Henry. But the young man who came bounding up to us looked nothing like him. I studied the two of them as they embraced: one weathered and solid, the other tall, fair and lanky, with hair the color of a newly minted penny. After a time they clapped each other on the back, as men will do to break the intimacy of such a moment, then pulled apart and searched each other's face.

"You look good, brother," said Jamie. "The Tennessee air seems to agree with you. Or is it something else?"

He turned to me then, grinning widely. He was beautiful; there was no other word for him. He had fine, sharp features and skin so translucent I could see the small veins in his temples. His eyes were the pale green of beryl stones and seemed lit from the inside. He was just twenty-two then, nine years younger than myself and nineteen years younger than Henry.

"This is Miss Chappell," said Henry. "My brother, Jamie."

"Pleased to meet you," I managed.

"The pleasure's mine," he said, taking my offered hand and kissing the back of it with exaggerated gallantry.

Henry rolled his eyes. "My brother thinks he's a character in one of his plays."

"Ah, but which one?" Jamie said, raising a forefinger in the air. "Hamlet? Faust? Prince Hal? What do you think, Miss Chappell?"

I blurted out the first thing that came into my head. "Actually, I think you're more of a Puck."

I was rewarded with a dazzling smile. "Dear lady, thou speakest aright, I *am* that merry wanderer of the night."

"Who's Puck?" asked Henry.

Jamie shook his head in mock despair. "Lord, what fools these mortals be," he said.

I saw Henry's lips tighten. I suddenly felt sorry for him, standing there in his brother's shadow. "Puck's a kind of mischievous sprite," I said. "A troublemaker."

"A hobgoblin," Jamie said contritely. "Forgive me, brother, I'm only trying to impress her."

Henry put his arm around me. "Laura's not the impressionable type."

"Good for her!" Jamie said. "Now why don't you two show me this fine city of yours?"

We took him to the Peabody Hotel, which had the best restaurant in Memphis and a swing band on weekends. At Jamie's insistence we ordered a bottle of champagne. I'd had it only once before, at my brother Pearce's wedding, and I was light-headed after one glass. When the band started up, Jamie asked Henry if he could have a dance with me (Henry didn't dance, that night or any other, because of his limp). We whirled round and round to Duke Ellington, Benny Goodman and Tommy Dorsey, music I'd heard on the radio and danced to in the parlor with my brothers and young nephews. How different this was, and how exhilarating! I was aware of Henry's eyes following us, and others' too—women's eyes, watching me enviously. It was a novel sensation for me, and I couldn't help but revel in it. After several numbers, Jamie escorted me back to our table and excused himself. I sat down, flushed and out of breath.

"You look especially pretty tonight," Henry said.

"Thank you."

"Jamie has that effect on girls. They sparkle for him." His expression was bland, his tone matter-of-fact. If he was jealous of his brother, I couldn't detect it. "He likes you, I can tell," he added.

"I'm sure he doesn't dislike anyone."

"Well, at least not anyone in a skirt," Henry said, with a wry smile. "Look." He gestured toward the dance floor, and I saw Jamie with a willowy brunette in his arms. She was wearing a satin dress with a low-cut back, and Jamie's hand rested on her bare skin. As she followed him effortlessly through a series of complicated turns and dips, I realized what a clumsy partner I must have been. I wanted to cover my face with my hands; I knew everything I felt was there for Henry to see. My envy and embarrassment. My foolish yearning.

I stood up. I don't know what I would have said to him, because at that moment he rose and took my hand. "It's late," he said, "and I know you have church in the morning. Come on, I'll take you home."

He was so gentle, so kind. I felt a rush of shame. But later, as I lay sleepless in my bed, it occurred to me that what I'd shown Henry so nakedly wasn't new to him. He must have seen it before, must have felt it himself a hundred times in Jamie's presence: a longing for a brightness that would never be his.

JAMIE RETURNED TO Oxford, and I put him out of my thoughts. I was no fool; I knew a man like him could never desire a woman like me. It was marvel enough that Henry desired me. I can't say whether I was truly in love with him then; I was so grateful to him that it dwarfed everything else. He was my rescuer from life in the margins, from the pity, scorn and crabbed kindness that are the portion of old maids. I should say, he was my potential rescuer. I was by no means sure of him, and for good reason.

One night at choir practice, I looked up from my hymnal and saw him watching me from one of the rear pews, his face solemn with intent. *This is it,* I thought. *He's going to propose.*

Somehow I got through the rest of the practice, though the director had to chide me twice for missing my entrance. In the choir room afterward, as I unbuttoned my robe with clumsy fingers, I had a sudden vision of Henry's hands undoing the buttons of my nightgown on our wedding night. I wondered what it would be like to lie with him, to have him touch my body as intimately as though it were his own flesh. My sister Etta, who was a registered nurse, had told me about the sexual act when I turned twenty-one. Her explanation was strictly factual; she never once referred to her own relations with her husband, Jack, but I gathered from her private smile that the marriage bed was not an altogether unpleasant place.

Henry was waiting for me outside the church, leaning against his car in his familiar white shirt, gray pants and gray fedora. That was all he ever wore. Clothes didn't matter to him, and his were often ill-fitting—pants drooping at the waist, hems dragging in the dirt, sleeves too long or too short. I laugh now when I think of the feelings his wardrobe aroused in me. I practically throbbed with the desire to sew for him.

"Hello, my dear," he said. And then, "I've come to say goodbye."

Goodbye. The word billowed in the space between us before settling around me in soft black folds.

"They're building a new airfield in Alabama, and they want me to oversee the project. I'll be gone for several months, possibly longer."

"I see," I said.

I waited for him to say something more: How he would miss me. How he would write to me. How he hoped I'd be here when he returned. But he said nothing, and as the silence stretched on I felt myself fill with self-loathing. I was not meant for marriage and children and the rest of it. These things were not for me, had never been for me. I'd been a fool to think otherwise.

I felt myself receding from him, and from myself too, our images shrinking in my mind's eye. I heard him offer to give me a lift home. Heard myself decline politely, telling him I needed the fresh air, then wish him the best of luck in Alabama. Saw him lean toward me. Saw myself turn my head so his kiss found my cheek instead of my lips. Watched as I walked away from him, my back as straight as pride could make it.

Mother pounced on me as soon as I came in the door. "Henry stopped by earlier," she said. "Did he find you at church?"

I nodded.

"He seemed eager to speak with you."

It was hard to look at her face, to see the hope trembling just beneath the surface of her bright smile. "Henry's going away," I said. "He doesn't know for how long."

"Is that . . . all he said?"

"Yes, that's all." I started up the stairs to my room.

"He'll be back," she called out after me. "I know he will."

I turned and looked down at her, so lovely in her distress. One pale, slender hand lay on the banister. The other clenched the fabric of her skirt, crumpling it.

"Oh, Laura," she said, with a telltale quaver.

"Don't you dare cry, Mother."

She didn't. It must have been a Herculean effort. My mother

weeps over anything at all: dead butterflies, curdled sauce. "I'm so sorry, darling," she said.

My legs went suddenly boneless. I sank down onto the top step and put my head on my knees. I heard the creak of her footsteps and felt her sit beside me. Her arm went around me, and her lips touched my hair. "We won't speak of him," she said. "We won't mention his name ever again."

She kept her promise, and she must have passed the word to the rest of the family, because no one said a thing about Henry, not even my sisters. They were just overly kind, all of them, complimenting me more often than I deserved and concocting ways to keep me busy. I was in great demand as a dinner guest, bridge partner and shopping companion. Outwardly I was cheerful, and after a time they began to treat me normally again, believing I was over it. I wasn't. I was furious—with myself, with Henry. With the cruel natural order that had made me simultaneously undesirable to men and unable to feel complete without one. I saw that my former contentment had been a lie. This was the truth at the core of my existence: this yawning emptiness, scantily clad in rage. It had been there all along. Henry had merely been the one who'd shown it to me.

I didn't hear from him for nearly two months. And then one day, I came home to find my mother waiting anxiously in the foyer. "Henry McAllan's come back," she said. "He's in the parlor. Here, your hair's mussed, let me fix it for you."

"I'll see him as I am," I said, lifting my chin.

I regretted that little bit of defiance as soon as I laid eyes on him. Henry looked tan and fit, more handsome than he ever had. Why hadn't I at least put on some lipstick? No—that was foolishness. This man had led me on, then abandoned me. I hadn't gotten so much as a postcard from him in all these weeks. What did I care whether I looked pretty for him?

"Laura, it's good to see you," he said. "How have you been?"

"Just fine. And you?"

"I've missed you," he said.

I was silent. Henry came and took my hands in his. My palms were damp, but his were cool and dry.

"I had to be sure of my feelings," he said. "But now I am. I love you, and I want you to be my wife. Will you marry me."

And there it was, just like that: the question I'd thought I would never hear. Granted, the scene didn't play out quite like I'd pictured it. Henry wasn't kneeling, and the question had actually come out as more of a statement. If he felt any worry over my answer, he hid it well. That stung a little. How dared he be so sure of himself, after such a long absence? Did he think he could simply walk back into my house and claim me like a forgotten coat? And yet, beside the enormity of his wanting me, my anger seemed a paltry thing. If Henry was certain of me, I told myself, it was because that was his way. *Meat should not be eaten rare. Blue is your color. Will you marry me.*

As I looked into his frank gray eyes, I had a sudden, unbidden image of Jamie grinning down at me as he'd spun me around the ballroom of the Peabody. Henry was neither dashing nor romantic; like me, he was made of sturdier, plainer stuff. But he loved me, and I knew that he would provide for me and be true to me and give me children who were strong and bright. And for all of that, I could certainly love him in return.

"Yes, Henry," I said. "I will marry you."

He nodded his head once, then he kissed me, opening my mouth with his thumb and putting his tongue inside. I clamped my mouth shut, more out of surprise than anything; it had been years since I'd been French-kissed, and his tongue felt foreign, thick and strange. Henry let out a little grunt, and I realized I'd bitten him.

"I'm sorry," I stammered. "I didn't know you were going to do that."

He didn't speak. He merely reopened my mouth and kissed me again exactly the same as before. This time I accepted his invasion without protest, and that seemed to satisfy him, because after a few minutes he left me to go and speak to Daddy.

WE WERE MARRIED six weeks later in a simple Episcopal ceremony. Jamie was the best man. When Henry brought him to the house he greeted me with a bear hug and a dozen pink roses.

"Sweet Laura," he said. "I'm so glad Henry finally came to his senses. I told him he was an idiot if he didn't marry you."

Jamie had spoiled me for the rest of the McAllans, whom I met for the first time two days before the wedding. From the moment they arrived it was clear they felt superior to us Chappells, who (it must be said) had French blood on my father's side and a Union general on my mother's. I didn't see much of Henry's father that weekend—Pappy and the other men were off doing whatever men do when there's a wedding on—but I spent enough time with the McAllan women to know we'd never be close, as I'd naïvely hoped. Henry's mother was cold, haughty and full of opinions, most of them negative, about everyone and everything. His two sisters, Eboline and Thalia, were former Cotton Queens of Greenville who'd married into money and made sure everybody knew it. The day before the wedding my mother gave a luncheon for the ladies of both families, and Fanny asked them whether they'd gone to college.

Thalia arched her perfectly plucked brows and said, "What good is college to a woman? I confess I can't see the need for it."

"Unless of course you're poor, or plain," said Eboline.

She gave a little laugh, and Thalia giggled with her. My sisters and I looked at each other uncertainly. Had Henry not told them we were all college girls? Surely they didn't know, Fanny said to me later; surely the slight had been unintentional. But I knew better.

Still, not even Henry's disagreeable relations could dampen the happiness I felt on my wedding day. We honeymooned in Charleston, then returned to a little house Henry had rented for us on Evergreen Street, not far from where my parents lived. And so my time of cleaving began. I loved the smallness of domestic life, the sense of belonging it gave me. I was Henry's now. Yielding to him—cooking the foods he liked, washing and ironing his shirts, waiting for him to come home to me each day—was what I'd been put on the earth to do. And then Amanda Leigh was born in November of 1940, followed two years later by Isabelle, and I became theirs more utterly even than I was their father's.

It would be six years into my marriage before I remembered that cleave has a second meaning, which is "to divide with a blow, as with an axe."

JAMIE

IN THE DREAM I'm alone on the roof of Eboline's old house in Greenville, watching the water rise. Usually I'm ten, but sometimes I'm grown and once I was an old man. I straddle the peak of the roof, my legs hanging down on either side. Snatched objects race toward and then around me, churning in the current. A chinaberry tree. A crystal chandelier. A dead cow. I try to guess which side of the house each item will be steered to by the water. The four-poster bed with its tail of mosquito netting will go to the left. The outhouse will go to the right, along with Mr. Wilhoit's Stutz Bearcat. The stakes of the game are high: every time I guess wrong the water rises another foot. When it reaches my ankles I draw my knees up as much as I can without losing my balance. I jockey the house, riding it north into the oncoming flood while the water urges me on in its terrible voice. I don't speak its language but I know what it's saying: It wants me. Not because I have any significance, but because it wants everything. Who am I, a skinny kid in torn britches, to deny it?

When the river takes me I don't try to swim or stay afloat. I open my eyes and my mouth and let the water fill me up. I feel my lungs spasm but there's no pain, and I stop being afraid. The current carries me along. I'm flotsam, and I understand that flotsam is all I've ever been.

Something glows in the murk ahead of me, getting brighter as I get closer to it. The light hurts my eyes. *Has a star fallen in the river?* I wonder. *Has the river swallowed everything, even the sky?* Five rays emanate from the star's center. They're moving back and forth, like they're seeking something. As I pass by them I see that they're fingers, and that what I thought was a star is a big white hand. I don't want it to find me. I'm part of the river now.

And then I'm not. I feel a sharp pain in my head and am yanked up, back onto the roof, or into a boat—the dream varies. But the hand is always Henry's, and it's always holding a bloody hank of my hair.

More than a thousand people died in that flood. I survived it, because of Henry. I wasn't alone on Eboline's roof, she and my parents were there with me, along with her husband, Virgil, and their maid, Dessie. The water didn't come and take me, I fell into it. I fell into it because I stood up. I stood up because I saw Henry approaching in the boat, coming to rescue us.

Because of Henry. So much of who I am and what I've done is because of Henry. My earliest memory is of meeting him for the first time. My mother was holding me, rocking me, and then she handed me to a large, white-haired stranger. I was afraid, and then I wasn't—that's all I remember. The way Mama always told it, I started to pitch a fit, but when Henry held me up in front of him and said, "Hello, little brother," I stopped crying at once and stuck my fingers in his mouth. I, who howled like a red Indian whenever my father or any other male tried to pick me up, went meekly into my brother's hands. I was one and a half. He was twenty-one and just returned from the Great War.

Because of Henry, I grew up hating Huns. Huns had tried to kill him in a forest somewhere in France. They'd given him his limp and his white hair. They'd taken things from him too—I didn't know what exactly but I could sense his lack of them. He never talked about the war. Pappy was always prodding him about it, wanting to know how many men Henry had killed and how he'd killed them. "Was it more than ten? More than fifty?" Pappy would ask. "Did you get any with your bayonet, or did you shoot em all from a distance?"

But Henry would never say. The only time I ever heard him refer to the war was on my eighth birthday. He came home for the weekend and took me deer hunting. It was my first time getting to carry an actual weapon (if you can call a Daisy Model 25 BB gun an actual weapon) and I was bursting with manly pride. I didn't manage to hit anything besides a few trees, but Henry brought down an eight-point buck. It wasn't a clean kill. When we got to where the buck had fallen we found it still alive, struggling futilely to get up. Splintered bone poked out of a wound in its thigh. Its eyes were wild and uncomprehending.

Henry passed a hand over his face, then gripped my shoulder hard. "If you ever have to be a soldier," he said, "promise me you'll try and get up to the sky. They say battle is a lot cleaner up there."

I promised. Then he knelt and cut its throat.

From that day on, whenever the crop dusters flew over our farm, I pretended I was the pilot. Only it wasn't boll weevils I was killing, it was Huns. I must have shot down hundreds of German aces in my imagination, sitting in the topmost branches of the sweet gum tree behind our house.

But if Henry sparked my desire to fly, Lindbergh ignited it with his solo flight across the Atlantic. It was less than a month after the flood. Greenville and our farm were still under ten feet of water, so we were staying with my aunt and uncle in Carthage. The house was full, and I was stuck sleeping in a three-quarter bed in the attic with my cousins Albin and Avery, strapping bullies with pimply faces and buckteeth. Crammed between the two of them, I dreamed of the flood: the guessing game, the voice of the water, the big white hand. My moaning woke them, and they punched and kicked me awake, calling me a pansy and a titty baby. But not even their threats—to smother me, to throw me out the window, to stake me out over an anthill and pour molasses in my eyes—could stop the flood from coming to get me in my sleep. It came almost every night, and I always gave in to it. That was the part I dreaded: the part where I just let the water have me. It seemed a shameful weakness, the kind my brother would never give in to, even in a dream. Henry would fight with everything he had, and when his last bit of strength was gone he'd fight some more—like I hadn't done. At least, I was pretty sure I hadn't. That was the hell of it, I had no memory of what had happened between the time I fell in the water and when Henry pulled me out. All I had was the dream, which seemed to confirm my worst fears about myself. As the days passed and it kept recurring, I became more and more convinced it was true. I'd given myself willingly to the water, and would do it again if I had the chance.

I started refusing to take baths. Albin and Avery added "pig boy" to the list of endearments they had for me, and Pappy whipped my butt bloody with a switch, yelling that he wouldn't have a son who went around stinking like a nigger. Finally my mother threatened to bathe me herself if I wouldn't. The thought of Mama seeing me naked was enough to send me straightaway into the tub, though I never filled it more than a few inches.

It was during this time that stories about Lindbergh started to crop up in the papers and on the radio. He was going after the twenty-five-thousand-dollar Orteig Prize, offered by a Frenchman named Raymond Orteig to the first aviator to fly nonstop from New York to Paris, or vice versa. The purse had been up for grabs since 1919. A bunch of pilots had tried to win it. All of them had failed, and six had died trying.

Lindbergh would be the one to make it, I was positive. So what if he was younger and greener than the other pilots who'd tried? He was a god—fearless, immortal. There was no way he would fail. My confidence wasn't shared by the local papers, which dubbed him "the Flying Fool" for attempting it without a copilot. I told myself they were the fools.

The day of the flight, our entire family gathered around

the radio and listened to the reports of Lindbergh's progress. His plane was sighted over New England, then Newfoundland. Then he vanished, for sixteen of the longest hours of my life.

"He's dead," Albin taunted. "He fell asleep, and his plane crashed into the ocean."

"He did not!" I said. "Lindy would never fall asleep while he was flying."

"Maybe he got lost," said Avery.

"Yeah," said Albin, "maybe he was just too stupid to find his way."

This was a reference to the fact that I'd gotten lost a few days before. The two of them were supposed to take me fishing, but they'd led me in circles and then disappeared snickering into the woods. I was unfamiliar with the country around Carthage and it took me three hours to find my way back to the house, by which time my mother was out of her mind with worry. Albin and Avery had gotten a whipping, but that didn't make me feel any better. They'd bested me again.

They wouldn't this time. Lindbergh would show them. He would win for both of us.

And of course, he did. "The Flying Fool" became "the Lone Eagle," and Lindy's triumph became mine. Even my cousins cheered when he landed safely at Le Bourget Field. It was impossible not to feel proud of what he'd done. Impossible not to want to be like him.

That night after supper, I went outside and lay on the wet grass and stared up at the sky. It was twilight—that impossible shade of purple-blue that only lasts a few minutes before dulling into ordinary dark. I wanted to dive up into that blue and lose myself in it. I remember thinking there was nothing bad up there. No muck or stink or killing brown water. No ugliness or hate. Just blue and gray and ten thousand shades in between, all of them beautiful.

I would be a pilot like Lindbergh. I would have great adventures and perform acts of daring and defend my country, and it would be glorious. And I would be a god.

Fifteen years later the Army granted my wish. And it was not. And I was not.

RONSEL

THEY CALLED US "Eleanor Roosevelt's niggers." They said we wouldn't fight, that we'd turn tail and run the minute we got into real combat. They said we didn't have the discipline to make good soldiers. That we didn't have brains enough to man tanks. That we were inclined by nature to all kind of wickedness—lying, stealing, raping white women. They said we could see better than white GIs in the dark because we were closer to the beasts. When we were in Wimbourne an English gal I never laid eyes on before came up and patted me right on the butt. I asked her what she was doing and she said, "Checking to see if you've got a tail."

"Why would you think that?" I said.

She said the white GIs had been telling all the English girls that Negroes were more monkey than human.

We slept in separate barracks, ate in separate mess halls, shit in separate latrines. We even had us a separate blood supply—God forbid any wounded white boys would end up with Negro blood in their veins.

They gave us the dregs of everything, including officers. Our lieutenants were mostly Southerners who'd washed out in some other post. Drunkards, yellow bellies, bigoted no-count crackers who couldn't have led their way out of a one-room shack in broad daylight. Putting them over black troops was the Army's way of punishing them. They had nothing but contempt for us and they made sure we knew it. At the Officers' Club they liked to sing "We're dreaming of a white battalion" to the tune of "White Christmas." We heard about it from the colored staff, who had to wait on their sorry white asses while they sang it.

If they'd all been like that I probably would've ended up fertilizing some farmer's field in France or Belgium, along with every other man in my unit. Lucky for us we had a few good white officers. The ones out of West Point were mostly fair and decent, and our CO always treated us respectful.

"They say you're not as clean as other people," he told us. "There's a simple answer to that. Make damn sure you're cleaner than anybody else you ever saw in your life, especially all those white bastards out there. Make your uniforms look neater than theirs. Make your boots shine brighter."

And that's exactly what we did. We aimed to make the 761st the best tank battalion in the whole Army.

We trained hard, first at Camp Claiborne, then at Camp Hood. There were five men to a tank, each with his own job to do, but we all had to learn each other's jobs too. I was the driver, had a feel for it from the very first day. Funny how many of us farm boys ended up in the driver's seat. Reckon if you can get a mule to go where you want it to, you can steer a Sherman tank.

We spent a lot of time at the range, shooting all kind of weapons—.45s, machine guns, cannons. We went on maneuvers in the Kisatchie National Forest and did combat simulations with live ammo. We knew they were testing our courage and we passed with flying colors. Hell, most of us were more scared of getting snakebit than getting hit by a bullet. Some of the water moccasins they had down there were ten feet long, and that's no lie.

In July of '42 we got our first black lieutenants. There were only three of them but we all walked with our heads a little bit higher after that, at least on the base. Off base, in the towns where we took our liberty, we walked real careful. In Killeen they put up a big sign for us at the end of Main Street: NIGGERS HAVE TO LEAVE THIS TOWN BY 9 PM. The paint was blood red in case we missed the point. Killeen didn't have a colored section, only about half of them little towns did. The one in Alexandria near Camp Claiborne was typical—nothing to it but a falling-down movie theater and two shabby juke joints. Wasn't no place to buy anything or set and eat a meal. The rest of the town was off limits to us. If the MPs or the local law caught you in the white part of town they'd beat the shit out of you.

Our uniforms didn't mean a damn to the local white citizens. Not that I expected them to, but my buddies from up north and out west were thunderstruck by the way we were treated. Reading about Jim Crow in the paper is a mighty different thing from having a civilian bus driver wave a pistol in your face and tell you to get your coon hide off the bus to make room for a fat white farmer. They just couldn't understand it, no matter how many times we tried to explain it to them. You got to go along to get along, we told them, got to humble down and play shut-mouthed when you around white folks, but a lot of them just couldn't do it. There was this Yankee private in Fort Knox, that's where most of the guys in the battalion did their basic training. He got into an argument with a white storekeeper who wouldn't sell him a pack of smokes and ended up tied with a rope to the fender of a car and dragged up and down the street. That was just one killing, out of dozens we heard about.

The longer I spent around guys from other parts of the country, the madder I got myself. Here we were, about to risk our lives for people who hated us as bad as they hated the Krauts or the Japs, and maybe even worse. The Army didn't do nothing to protect us from the locals. When local cops beat up colored GIs, the Army looked the other way. When the bodies of dead black soldiers turned up outside of camp, the MPs didn't even try to find out who did it. It didn't take a genius to see why. The beatings, the lousy food and whatall, the piss-poor officers—they all added up to one thing. The Army wanted us to fail.

WE TRAINED FOR two long years. By the summer of '44, we'd about gave up hope that they were ever going to let us fight. According to the *Courier* there were over a hundred thousand of us serving overseas, but only one colored unit in combat. The rest were peeling potatoes, digging trenches and cleaning latrines.

But then, in August, word came down that General Patton had sent for us. He'd seen us on maneuvers at Kisatchie and wanted us to fight at the head of his Third Army. Damn, we were proud! Here was our chance to show the world something it'd never seen before. To hell with God and country, we'd fight for our people and our own self-respect.

We left Camp Hood in late August. I ain't never been so glad to see the back of a place. Only thing I'd miss about that hellhole was Mallie Simpson, she was a schoolteacher I kept company with in Killeen. Mallie was considerable older than me. She might've been thirty even, I never asked and didn't care. She was a tiny little gal with a big full-bellied laugh. She knew things the girls back home didn't have the first idea about, things to do with what my daddy calls "nature activity." Some weekends we didn't hardly leave her bed, except to go to the package store. Mallie liked her gin. She drank it straight up, one shot at a time, downing it in one gulp. She used to say a half-full glass of gin was a invitation to the devil. Seemed to me there was plenty of devilment going on with the glasses being empty, but I wasn't complaining. I said goodbye to her with real sadness. I reckoned it'd be a long while before I had another woman—from what I'd heard, Europe had nothing but white people in it.

But I reckoned wrong. There were plenty of white people over there all right, but they weren't like the ones back home. Wasn't no hate in them. In England, where we spent our first month, some of the folks had never seen a black man before and they were curious more than anything. Once they figured out we were just like everybody else, that's how they treated us. The gals too. The first time a white gal asked me to dance I about fell out of the box.

"Go on," whispered my buddy Jimmy, he was from Los Angeles.

"Jimmy," I said, "you must be plumb out of your mind."

"If you don't I will," he said, so I went on and danced with her. I can't say I enjoyed it much, not that first time anyway. I was sweating so bad I might as well to been chopping cotton. I hardly even looked at her, I was too busy watching every white guy in the place. Meantime my hand was on her waist and her hand was wrapped around my sweaty neck. I kept my arms as stiff as I could but the dance floor was crowded and her body kept on bumping up against mine.

"What's the matter," she asked me after awhile, "don't you like me?" Her eyes were full of puzzlement. That's when it hit me: She didn't care that I was colored. To her I was just a man who was acting like a damn fool. I pulled her close.

"Course I like you," I said. "I think you just about the prettiest gal I ever laid eyes on."

We didn't stay in their country long, but I'll always be grateful to those English folks for how they welcomed us. First time in my life I ever felt like a man first and a black man second.

In October they finally sent us over to where the fighting was, in France. We crossed the Channel and landed at Omaha Beach. We couldn't believe the mess we seen there. Sunken ships, blasted tanks, jeeps, gliders and trucks. No bodies, but we could see them in our heads just the same, sprawled all over the sand. Up till then we'd thought of our country, and ourselves, as unbeatable. On that beach we came face-to-face with the fact that we weren't, and it hit us all hard.

Normandy stayed with us during the four-hundred-mile trip east to the front. It took us six days to get there, to this little town called Saint-Nicholas-de-Port. We could hear the battle going on a few miles away but they didn't send us in. We waited there for three more days, edgy as cats. Then one afternoon we got the order to man all guns. A bunch of MPs in jeeps mounted with machine guns rolled up and parked themselves around our tanks. Then a single jeep came screeching up. A three-star general hopped out of it and got up onto the hood of a half-track. When I seen his ivory-handled pistols I knew I was looking at Ole Blood and Guts himself.

"Men," he said, "you're the first Negro tankers to ever fight in the American Army. I'd have never asked for you if you weren't the best. I have nothing but the best in my Army. I don't give a damn what color you are as long as you go up there and kill those Kraut sonsabitches."

Gave me a shock when I heard his voice, it was as high-pitched as a woman's. I reckon that's why he cussed so much—he didn't want nobody to take him for a sissy.

"Everybody's got their eyes on you and is expecting great things from you," he went on. "Most of all, your race is count-ing on you. Don't let them down, and damn you, don't let me down! They say it's patriotic to die for your country. Well, let's see how many patriots we can make out of those German bastards."

Course we'd all heard the scuttlebutt about Patton. How he'd hauled off and hit a sick GI at a hospital in Italy. How he was crazy as a coot and hated colored people besides. I don't care what anybody says, that man was a real soldier, and he took us when nobody else thought we were worth a damn. I'd have gone to hell and back for him, and I think every one of us Panthers felt the same. That's what we called ourselves: the 761st Black Panther Battalion. Our motto was "Come Out Fighting." That day at Saint-Nicolas-de-Port they were just words on a flag, but we were about to find out what they meant.

A TANK CREW's like a small family. With five of you in there day after day, ain't no choice but to get close. After awhile you move like five fingers on a hand. A guy says, *Do this,* and before he can even get the words out it's already done.

We didn't take baths, wasn't no time for them and it was too damn cold besides, and I mean to tell you the smell in that tank could get ripe. One time we were in the middle of battle and our cannoneer, a big awkward guy from Oklahoma named Warren Weeks, got the runs. There he was, squatting over his upturned helmet, grunting and firing away at the German Panzers. The air was so foul I almost lost my breakfast.

Sergeant Cleve hollered out, "Goddamn, Weeks! We oughta load you in the gun and fire you at the Jerries, they'd surrender in no time."

We all about busted our guts laughing. The next day an armor-piercing shell blew most of Warren's head off. His blood and brains went all over me and the other guys, and all over the white walls. Why the Army decided to make the walls white I could never understand. That day they were red but we kept right on fighting, wearing pieces of Warren, till the sun went down and the firing stopped. I don't remember what battle that was, it was somewhere in Belgium—Bastogne maybe, or Tillet. I got to where I didn't know what time it was or what day of the week. There was just the fighting, on and on, the crack of rifles and the *ack ack ack* of machine guns, bazookas firing, shells and mines exploding, men screaming and groaning and dying. And every day knowing you could be next, it could be your blood spattered all over your buddies.

Sometimes the shelling was so ferocious guys from the infantry would beg to get in the tank with us. Sometimes we let them, depending. Once we were parked up on a rise and this white GI with no helmet on came running up to us. Ain't nothing worse for a foot soldier than losing your helmet in battle.

"Hey, you fellas got room for one more?" he yelled.

Sergeant Cleve yelled back, "Where you from, boy?"

"Baton Rouge, Louisiana!"

We all started hooting and laughing. We knew what that meant.

"Sorry, cracker," said Sarge, "we full up today."

"I got some hooch I took off a dead Jerry," said the soldier. He pulled a nice-sized silver flask out of his jacket and held it up. "This stuff'll peel the paint off a barn, sure enough. You can have it if you let me in."

Sarge cocked an eyebrow and looked around at all of us.

"I'm a Baptist, myself," I said.

"Me, too," said Sam.

Sarge hollered, "You want us to burn in hell, boy?"

"Course not, sir!"

"Cause you know drinking's a sin."

We all had plenty of reasons to hate crackers but Sarge hated them more than all of us put together. Word was he had a sister who was raped by a bunch of white boys in Tuscaloosa, that's where he was from.

"Please!" begged the soldier. "Just let me in!"

"Get lost, cracker!"

Reckon that soldier died that day. Reckon I should've felt bad about it but I didn't. I was so worn out it was hard to feel much of anything.

I didn't talk about none of that when I wrote home. Even if the censors would've let it through, I didn't want to fret Mama and Daddy. Instead I told them what snow felt like and how nice the locals were treating us (leaving out a few details about the French girls). I told them about the funny food they had over there and the glittery dress Lena Horne wore when she came and sang to us at the USO. Daddy wrote back with news from home: The skeeters were bad this year. Ruel and Marlon had grown two whole inches. Lilly May sang a solo in church. The mule got into the cockleburs again.

Mississippi felt far, far away.

LAURA

DECEMBER 7, 1941, changed everything for all of us. Within a few days of the attack on Pearl Harbor, Jamie and both of my brothers had enlisted. Teddy stayed with the Engineers, Pearce joined the Marines and Jamie signed up for pilot training with the Air Corps. He wanted to be an ace, but the Army had other plans for him. They made him a bomber pilot, teaching him to fly the giant B-24s called Liberators. He trained for two years before leaving for England. My brothers were already overseas by then, Teddy in France and Pearce in the Pacific.

I stayed in Memphis, worrying about them all, while Henry traveled around the South building bases and airfields for the Army. He remained a civilian; as a wounded veteran of the Great War he was exempt from the draft, for which I was grateful. I didn't mind his absences once I got used to them. I soon realized they made me more interesting to him when he was home. Besides, I had Amanda Leigh for company, and then Isabelle in February of '43. The two of them were as different as they could be. Amanda was Henry's child: quiet, serious-minded, self-contained. Isabelle was something else altogether. From the day she was born she wanted to be held all of the time and would start wailing as soon as I laid her in her crib. Her demanding nature exasperated Henry, but for me her sweetness more than made up for it.

I was bewitched by both of them, and by the beauty of ordinary life, which went on despite the war and seemed all the more precious because of it. When I wasn't changing diapers and weeding my victory garden, I was rolling bandages and sewing for the Red Cross. My sisters, cousins and I organized drives for scrap metal and for silk and nylon stockings, which the Army turned into powder bags. It was a frightening and sorrowful time, but it was also exhilarating. For the first time in our lives, we had a purpose greater than ourselves.

Our family was luckier than many. I lost two cousins and an uncle, but my brothers survived. Pearce was wounded in the thigh and sent home before the fighting turned savage in the Pacific, and Teddy returned safe and sound in the fall of '45. Jamie lost a finger to frostbite but was otherwise unharmed. He didn't come home after he was discharged, but stayed in Europe—to travel, he said, and see the place from the ground for a change. This baffled Henry, who was convinced there was something wrong with him, something he wasn't telling us about. Jamie's letters were breezy and carefree, full of witty descriptions of the places he'd seen and the people he'd met. Henry thought they had a forced quality, but I didn't see it. I thought it was natural Jamie would want to enjoy his freedom after four years of being told where to go and what to do.

Those months after the war were jubilant ones for us and for the whole country. We'd pulled together and been victorious. Our men were home, and we had sugar, coffee and gasoline again. Henry was spending more time in Memphis, and I was hoping to get pregnant. I was thirty-seven; I wanted to give him a son while I still could.

I never saw the axe blow coming. The downstroke came that Christmas. As we usually did, we spent Christmas Eve with my people in Memphis, then drove down to Greenville the next morning. Eboline and her husband, Virgil, hosted a grand family dinner every year in their fancy house on Washington Street. How I hated those trips! Eboline never failed to make me feel dull and unfashionable, or her children to make mine cry. This year would be even worse than usual, because Thalia and her family were driving down from Virginia. The two sisters together were Regan and Goneril to my hapless Cordelia.

When we pulled up at Eboline's, Henry's father came and met us at the car. Pappy had been living with Eboline since Mother McAllan died in the fall of '43. One look at his grim face and we knew something was wrong.

"Well," he said to Henry by way of greeting, "that stuck-up husband of your sister's has gone and killed himself."

"Good God," Henry said. "When?"

"Sometime last night, after we'd all gone to bed. Eboline found the body a little while ago."

"Where?"

"In the attic. He hanged himself," Pappy said. "Merry Christmas."

"Did he leave a note saying why?" I asked.

Pappy pulled a sheet of paper from his pocket and handed it to me. The ink had run where someone's tears had fallen on it. It was addressed to "My darling wife." In a quavering hand, Virgil confessed to Eboline that he'd lost the bulk of their money in a confidence scheme involving a Bolivian silver mine and the rest on a horse named Barclay's Bravado. He said he was ending his life because he couldn't bear the thought of telling her. (Later, when I was better acquainted with my father-in-law, I would wonder if what Virgil really couldn't bear was the thought of spending one more night under the same roof as Pappy.)

Eboline wouldn't leave her bed, even to soothe her children. That job fell to me, along with most of the cooking for a house full of people; Henry had kept the maid on for the time being, but he'd had to let the gardener and cook go. I did what I could. As much as I disliked Eboline, I couldn't help feeling terribly sorry for her.

After the funeral, the girls and I drove home to Memphis while Henry stayed on to help his sister sort out her affairs. He would just be a few days, he said. But a few days turned into a week, then two. The situation was complicated, he told me on the phone. He needed more time to settle things.

He took the train home in mid-January. He was cheerful, almost ebullient, and unusually passionate that night in our bed. Afterward he threaded his fingers through mine and cleared his throat.

"Honey, by the way," he said.

I braced myself. That particular phrase, coming out of Henry's mouth, could lead to anything at all, I never knew what: *Honey, by the way, we're out of mustard, could you pick some up at the store? Honey, by the way, I had a car accident this morning.*

Or in this case, "Honey, by the way, I bought a farm in Mississippi. We'll be moving there in two weeks."

The farm, he went on to tell me, was located forty miles from Greenville, near a little town I'd never heard of called Marietta. We'd live in town, in a house he'd rented for us there, and he'd drive to the farm every day to work.

"Is this because of Eboline?" I asked, when I could speak calmly.

"Partly," he said, giving my hand a squeeze. "Virgil's estate is a mess. It'll take months to untangle, and I need to be close by." I must have given him a dubious look. "Eboline and the children are all alone now," he said, his voice rising a little. "It's my duty to help them."

"What about your father?" I asked. Meaning, can't he help them?

"Eboline can't be expected to look after him now. Pappy will have to come and live with us." Henry paused, then added, "He'll be driving the truck up next week."

"What truck?"

"The pickup truck I bought to use on the farm. We'll need it to move the furniture. We won't be able to take everything at once, but I can make a second trip when we're settled."

Settled. In rural Mississippi. In two weeks' time.

"I bought a tractor too," he said. "A John Deere Model B. It's one hell of a machine—you won't believe how fast it can get a field plowed. I'll be able to farm a hundred and twenty acres by myself. Imagine that!"

When I said nothing, Henry propped himself up on one elbow and peered down at my face. "You're mighty quiet," he said.

"I'm mighty surprised."

He gave me a puzzled frown. "But you knew I always intended to have my own farm someday."

"No, Henry. I had no idea."

"I'm sure I must have mentioned it."

"No, you never did."

"Well," he said, "I'm telling you now."

Just like that, my life was overturned. Henry didn't ask me how I felt about leaving my home of thirty-seven years and moving with his cantankerous father in tow to a hick town in the middle of Mississippi, and I didn't tell him. This was his territory, as the children and the kitchen and the church were mine, and we were careful not to trespass in each other's territories. When it was absolutely necessary we did it discreetly, on the furthermost borders.

MOTHER CRIED WHEN I told her we were leaving, but it was hardly the squall I'd expected. It was more of a light summer shower, quickly over, followed by admonitions to buck up and make the best of it. Daddy merely sighed. "Well," he said,

"I guess we've had you with us longer than we had any right to expect." This was what happened to daughters, their expressions seemed to say. You raised them, and if you were lucky they found husbands who might then take them off anywhere at all, and it was not only to be expected, but borne cheerfully.

I tried to be cheerful, but it was hard. Every day I said good-bye to some beloved person or thing. The porch swing of my parents' house, where Billy Escue had given me my first real kiss the night of my seventeenth birthday. My own little house on Evergreen Street, with its lace curtains and flowered wallpaper. The roaring of the lions at the nearby zoo, which had made me uneasy when we first moved in but now provided a familiar punctuation to my days. The light at my church, which fell in shafts of brilliant color upon the upturned faces of the congregation.

My own family's faces I could hardly bear to look at. My mother and sisters, with their high Fairbairn foreheads and surprised blue eyes. My father, with his wide, kind smile and sloping nose that never could hold up his spectacles properly.

"It'll be an adventure," said Daddy.

"It's not that far away," said Etta.

"There are bound to be nice people there," said Mother.

"I'm sure you're right," I told them.

But I didn't believe a word of it. Marietta was a Delta town; its population—a grand total of four hundred and twelve souls, as I later learned—would consist mostly of farmers, wives of farmers and children of farmers, half of whom were probably Negroes and all of whom were undoubtedly Baptists. We would be miles from civilization among bumpkins who drank grape juice at church every Sunday and talked of nothing but the weather and the crops.

And as if that weren't bad enough, Pappy would be there with us. I'd never spent much time around my father-in-law, a blessing I didn't fully appreciate until that last week in Memphis, when I was forced to spend all day every day alone with him while Henry was at work. Pappy was sour, bossy and vain. His pants had to be creased, his handkerchiefs folded a certain way, his shirts starched. He changed them twice a day, not that they were ever soiled by anything but spilled food; he exerted himself only to roll cigarettes and instruct me on how to pack. I dug up some books I thought he'd like, hoping to distract him, but he waved them away contemptuously. Reading was a waste of time, he said, and education was for prigs and sissies. I wondered how he'd ever managed to produce two sons like Henry and Jamie. I hoped that once we got to Marietta, he'd be spending his days with Henry at the farm, leaving the house to me and the girls.

The house was the only bright spot in this otherwise bleak picture. Henry had rented it from a couple who'd lost their son in the war and were moving out west. He described it as a two-story antebellum with four bedrooms, a wraparound porch and, most enticing to me, a fig tree. I've always been crazy for figs. As I wrapped dishes in newspaper and boxed up lamps and books and linens, I spent many not entirely unpleasant moments picturing myself walking out my back door, plucking the ripe fruit from the branches and eating it unrinsed, like a greedy child. I imagined the pies and minces I would make, the preserves I would lay in for the winter. I said nothing of this to Henry; I wasn't about to give him the satisfaction. But every night at supper, he'd bring up some pleasing detail about the house that he'd neglected to mention before. Had he told me it had a modern electric stove? Did I know it was just three blocks from the elementary school where Amanda Leigh would start first grade the following year?

"That's nice, Henry," I would reply noncommittally.

The day of our departure, we rose before dawn. Teddy and Pearce came and helped Henry load the truck with our furniture, including my most prized possession—an 1859 Steiff upright piano with a rosewood case carved in the Eastlake style. It had belonged to my grandmother, who'd taught me to play. I'd just started giving lessons to Amanda Leigh.

Daddy arrived as I was making my last check of the house. I was surprised to see him; we'd said our goodbyes the night before. He brought biscuits from Mother and a crock of her apple butter. The eight of us ate the hot biscuits standing in the mostly empty living room, shivering in the chill, licking our sticky fingers between bites. When we were done my father and brothers walked us out to the car. Daddy shook Pappy's hand, then Henry's, then hugged the children. At last he turned to me.

Softly, in a voice meant for my ears alone, he said, "When you were a year old and you came down with rubella, the doctor told us you were likely to die of it. Said he didn't expect you'd live another forty-eight hours. Your mother was frantic, but I told her that doctor didn't know what he was talking about. Our Laura's a fighter, I said, and she's going to be just fine. I never doubted it, not for one minute, then or since. You keep that in your pocket and take it out when you need it, hear?"

Swallowing the lump in my throat, I nodded and embraced him. Then I hugged my brothers one last time.

"Well," Henry said, "the day's getting on."

"You take good care of my three girls," Daddy said.

"I will. They're my three girls too."

The children and I sang as we left Memphis. They sat beside me in the front seat of the DeSoto. Henry, Pappy, and all our belongings were in the truck in front of us. The Mississippi River was a vast, indifferent presence on our right.

"You've got to ac-cent-tchu-ate the positive," we sang, but the words felt as foolish and empty as I did.

IT WAS NEARING dusk when we turned onto Tupelo Lane. This, I knew, was the name of our street, and I felt a little ripple of excitement each time Henry slowed down. Finally he pulled the truck over and stopped, and I saw the house: a charming old place much as he'd described, but with many agreeable particulars he'd neglected to mention—probably because, being Henry, he hadn't noticed them in the first place. There was a large pecan tree in the front yard, and one side of the house was entirely covered in wisteria, like a nubby green cloak. In the spring, when it bloomed, its perfume would carry us down into sleep every night, and in the summer the lawn would be dotted with fallen purple blossoms. There were two bay windows on either side of the front door, and under them, clumps of mature azalea bushes.

"You didn't tell me we had azaleas, Henry," I chided him when I'd gotten the girls bundled up and out of the car.

"So we do," he said with a smile. I could tell he was feeling pleased with himself. I didn't begrudge him that. The house was truly lovely.

Amanda Leigh sneezed. She was leaning heavily against my leg, and her sister was half-asleep in my arms. Both of them had head colds. "The children are done in," I said. "Let's get them in the house."

"The key should be under the mat," he said.

As we started up the walk, the porch light went on and the front door opened. A man stepped out onto the porch. He was huge, with hunched shoulders like a bear's. A small woman came up behind him, peering from around his shoulder.

"Who are you?" he said. His tone wasn't friendly.

"We're the McAllans," Henry replied. "The new tenants of this house. Who are you?"

The man widened his stance, crossing his arms over his chest. "Orris Stokes. The new owner of this house."

"New owner? I rented this place from George Suddeth just three weeks ago."

"Well, Suddeth sold me the house last week, and he didn't say nothing to me about any renters."

"Is that a fact," Henry said. "Looks like I need to refresh his memory."

"You won't find him. He left town three days ago."

"I gave him a hundred-dollar deposit!"

"I don't know nothing about that," Orris Stokes said.

"You get anything in writing?" Pappy asked Henry.

"No. We shook on the deal."

The old man spat into the street. "How a son of mine could be such a fool, I'll never know."

I watched my husband's face fill with the knowledge that he'd been cheated, and worse, that he was powerless to make it right. He turned to me. "I paid him a hundred dollars cash," he said, "right there in the living room of that house. Afterward I sat down to dinner with him and his wife. I showed her pictures of you and the girls."

"You'd best be getting on," said Orris Stokes. "Ain't nothing for you here."

"Mama, I have to tinkle," Amanda Leigh said in a child's loud whisper.

"Hush now," I said.

The woman moved then, coming out from behind her husband. She was a tiny bird-boned thing with freckled skin and small, fluttering hands. No steel in her, I thought, until I saw her chin. That chin—sharply pointed and jutting forward like a trowel—told a different story. I imagined Orris had felt the sting of her defiance on more than one occasion.

"I'm Alice Stokes," she said. "Why don't y'all come in and have a little supper before you go?"

"Now, Alice," said her husband.

She ignored him, addressing herself to me as if the three men weren't there. "We've got stew and cornbread. It ain't fancy but we'd be pleased to share it with you."

"Thank you," I said, before Henry could refuse. "We'd be most grateful."

The house was cheaply furnished and deserved better. The ceilings were high and the rooms spacious, with lovely period details. I couldn't help but imagine my own things in place of the Stokeses': my piano beside the bay window in the living room, my Victorian love seat in front of the hand-carved mantel in the parlor. As I sat down to supper at Alice's crude pine table, I thought how much better my own dining set would have looked beneath the ornate ceiling medallion.

Over supper we learned that Orris owned the local feed store. That perked Henry up a bit. The two of them talked livestock for a while, discussing the merits of various breeds of pigs—a subject on which Henry was astonishingly well versed. Then the talk turned to farm labor.

"Damn niggers," Orris said. "Moving up north, leaving folks with no way to make a crop. Ought to be a law against it."

"In my day we didn't let em leave," Pappy said. "And the ones that tried sneaking off in the middle of the night ended up sorry they had."

Orris nodded approvingly. "My brother has a farm down to Yazoo City. Do you know, last October he had cotton rotting in the fields because he couldn't find enough niggers to pick it? And the ones he did find were wanting two dollars and fifty cents per hundred pounds."

"Two-fifty per hundred!" Henry exclaimed. "At that rate

they'll put every planter in the Delta out of business. And then what'll they do, when there's nobody to hire them and give them a roof over their heads?"

"If you're expecting sense from a nigger, you're gonna be waiting a good long while," said Pappy.

"You mark my words," said Orris, "they're gonna be asking for even more this year, now the government's done away with the price controls."

"Damn niggers," said Pappy.

It was eight o'clock by the time we finished supper, and the children were nodding into their bowls. When Alice offered to let us stay the night, I accepted quickly; it was a two-hour drive to Eboline's in Greenville, and I wasn't about to chance our flimsy wartime tires on those pothole-filled roads in the dark. Henry and Orris both looked like they wanted to object, but neither of them did. The three men went outside to cover the furniture in the truck against the dew, while Alice cleaned up and I put the girls to bed. After I got them tucked in, I helped her make up the bed Henry and I would share.

"This is a big house," I said. "Is it just you and Mr. Stokes?"

"Yes," she said in a low, sad voice. "Diphtheria took Orris Jr. in the fall of '42, and our daughter Mary died of pneumonia last year. Your girls are sleeping in their beds."

"I'm sorry." I busied myself with the pillowcases, not knowing what else to say.

"I'm expecting," she confided shyly after a moment. "I haven't told Orris yet. I wanted to be sure it took."

"I hope you have a fine strong baby, Alice."

"So do I. I pray for it every night."

She left me then, wishing me a good sleep. I went to the window, which looked out over the backyard. I could see the promised fig tree, its branches naked of leaves but still graceful in the moonlight. *If he had just signed a lease,* I thought. *If he were just a different sort of man.* Henry was never good at reading people. He always assumed everybody was just like him: that they said what they meant and would do what they said.

When the door opened I didn't turn around. He walked up behind me and laid his hand on my shoulder. I hesitated, then reached up and touched it with my own. The skin on top was soft and papery. I felt a rush of tenderness for him, for his aging hands and his wounded pride. He kissed the top of my head, and I sighed and leaned into him. How could I wish him to be other than he was? To be hard and suspicious, like his father? I couldn't, and I felt ashamed of myself for having had such thoughts.

"We'll find another house," I said.

I felt him shake his head. "This was the only place for rent in town. It's all the returning soldiers, they've taken all the housing. We'll have to live out on the farm."

"What about one of the other towns nearby?" I asked.

"I've got no time to look elsewhere," he said. "I have to get the fields broken. I'm already starting a month late."

He stepped away from me. I heard the snap of the suitcase opening. "The farmhouse isn't much, but I know you'll make it nice," he said. "I'm going to brush my teeth now. Why don't you get into bed?"

There was a brief pause, then the door opened and shut. As his footsteps receded down the hall, I looked at the fig tree and thought of the fruit that would begin ripening there come summer. I wondered if Alice Stokes liked figs; if she would gather up the fruit eagerly or let it fall to the ground and rot.

IN THE MORNING we said goodbye to the Stokeses and headed to the general store to buy food, kerosene, buckets, candles and the other provisions we would need on the farm. That's when I learned there was no electricity or running water in the house.

"There's a pump in the front yard," Henry said, "and some kind of stove in the kitchen."

"A pump? There's no indoor plumbing?"

"No."

"What about the bathroom?" I said.

"There is no bathroom," he said, with a hint of impatience. "Just an outhouse."

Honey, by the way.

A stout-bodied woman in a man's checked shirt and overalls spoke from behind the counter. "You the new owners of the Conley place?"

"That's right," said Henry.

"You'll be wanting wood for that stove. I'm Rose Trickle-bank, and this is my store, mine and my husband Bill's."

She stuck her hand out, and we all shook it in turn. She

had a strong, callused grip; I saw Henry's eyes widen when her hand grasped his. Yet for all her mannish ways, from the neck up Rose Tricklebank resembled nothing so much as the flower whose name she bore. She had a Cupid's-bow mouth and a round face surrounded by a mop of curly auburn hair. A cigarette tucked behind one ear spoiled the picture, but only a little.

"You'll want to stock up good on supplies today," she said. "Big storm's coming in tonight, could rain all week."

"Why should that matter?" Pappy asked.

"When it rains and that river rises, the Conley place can be cut off for days."

"It's the McAllan place now," Henry said.

After we paid, Rose hefted one of our boxes herself and carried it out to the car, over Henry's protests. She pulled two licorice ropes out of her pocket and handed them to Amanda Leigh and Isabelle. "I've got two girls of my own, and my Ruth Ann is about your age," she said to Amanda, tousling her hair. "She and Caroline are in school right now, but I hope you'll come back and visit us soon."

I promised we would, thinking it would be nice to have a friend in town, and some playmates for the girls. As soon as she was out of earshot, Henry muttered, "That woman acts like she thinks she's a man."

"Maybe she is a man, and her husband hasn't cottoned to it yet," Pappy said.

The two of them laughed. It irritated me. "Well, I like her," I said, "and I plan on visiting her once we get settled in."

Henry's brows went up. I wondered if he would forbid me

to see her, and what I would say if he did. But all he said was, "You'll have a whole lot to do on the farm."

THE FARM WAS about a twenty-minute drive from town, but it seemed longer because the road was so rutted and the view so monotonous. The land was flat and mostly featureless, as farmers will inevitably make it. Negroes dotted the fields, tilling the earth with mule-drawn plows. Without the green of crops to bring it alive, the land looked bleak, an ocean of unrelieved brown in which we'd been set adrift.

We crossed over a creaky bridge spanning a small river lined with cypresses and willows. Henry stuck his head out the window of the truck and shouted back at me, "This is it, honey! We're on our land now!"

I mustered a smile and a wave. To me, it looked no different from the other land we'd passed. There were brown fields and unpainted sharecroppers' shacks with dirt yards. Women who might have been any age from thirty to sixty hung laundry from sagging clotheslines while gaggles of dirty barefoot children watched listlessly from the porch. After a time we came to a shack that was larger than the others, though no less decrepit. It had a deserted air. The truck stopped in front of it, and Henry and his father got out.

"Why are we stopping?" I called out.

"We're here," Henry said.

Here was a long, rickety house with a warped tin roof and shuttered windows that had neither glass nor screens. Here was a porch that ran the length of the house, connecting it to a small lean-to. Here was a dirt yard with a pump in the middle of it, shaded by a large oak tree that had somehow managed to escape razing by the original steaders. Here was a barn, a pasture, a cotton house, a corncrib, a pig wallow, a chicken coop and an outhouse.

Here was our new home.

Amanda Leigh and Isabelle scrambled out of the car and ran around the yard, delighted with everything they saw. I followed, stepping up to my ankles in muck. It would be weeks before I learned that on a farm, you always look before you step, because you never know what you might be stepping in or on: a mud puddle, a pile of excrement, a rattlesnake.

"Will we have chickens, Daddy? And pigs?" Amanda Leigh asked. "Will we have a cow?"

"We sure will," Henry said. "You know what else?" He pointed back to the line of trees that marked the river. "See that river we crossed over? I bet it's full of catfish and crawdads."

There was some kind of structure on the river, about a mile away. Even from a distance I could tell it was much larger than the house. "What's that building?" I asked Henry.

"An old sawmill, dates back to before the Civil War. You and the girls stay out of there, it's liable to fall down any minute."

"It ain't the only thing," said Pappy, gesturing at the house. "That roof needs repairing, and them steps look rotten. And some of the shutters are missing, you better replace em quick or we're liable to freeze to death."

"We'll get the place fixed up," Henry said. "It'll be all right. You'll see."

He wasn't speaking to Pappy, but to me. *Make the best of it,* his eyes urged. *Don't shame me in front of my father and the girls.* I felt a stirring of anger. Of course I would make the best of it, for the children's sake if nothing else.

With the help of one of the tenants, a talkative light-skinned Negro named Hap Jackson, Henry unloaded the truck and moved the furniture in. I saw right away that we wouldn't be able to bring much more from Memphis. The house had just three rooms: a large main room that encompassed the kitchen and living area, and two bedrooms barely big enough to hold a bed and a chest of drawers each. There were no closets, just pegs hammered at intervals along the walls. Like the floors, the walls were rough plank, with gaps between the boards through which the wind and all manner of insects could enter freely. Every surface was filthy. I felt another surge of anger. How could Henry have brought us to such a place?

I wasn't the only one displeased with the accommodations. "Where am I gonna sleep?" demanded Pappy.

Henry looked at me. I shrugged. He had laid this egg all by himself; he could figure out how to hatch it.

"I guess we'll have to put you out in the lean-to," Henry said.

"I ain't sleeping out there. It don't even have a floor."

"I don't know where else to put you," Henry said. "There's no room in the house."

"There would be, if you got rid of that piano," Pappy said.

The piano just barely fit in one corner of the main room.

"If you got rid of that piano," Pappy said, "we could put a bed there."

"We could," Henry agreed.

"No," I said. "We need the piano. I'm teaching the girls to play, you know that. Besides, I don't want a bed in the middle of the living room."

"We could rig a curtain around it," Pappy said.

"True," Henry said.

They were both looking at me: Henry unhappily, his father wearing a smirk. Henry was going to agree. I could see it in his face, and so could Pappy.

"I need to speak to you in private," I said, looking at Henry. I went out onto the front porch. Henry followed, shutting the door behind him.

In a low voice, I said, "When you told me you were bringing me here, away from my people and everything I've ever known, I didn't say a word. When you informed me your father was coming to live with us, I went along. When Orris Stokes stood there and told you you'd been fleeced by that man you rented the house from, I kept my mouth shut. But I'm telling you now, Henry, we're not getting rid of that piano. It's the one civilized thing in this place, and I want it for the girls and myself, and we're keeping it. So you can just go back in there and tell your father he can sleep in the lean-to. Either that or he can sleep in the bed with you, because I am *not* staying here without my piano."

Henry was looking at me like I'd just sprouted antlers. I stared back, resisting the urge to drop my gaze.

"You're overtired," he said.

"No. I'm fine."

How my heart thumped as I waited him out! I'd never defied my husband so openly, or anyone else for that matter. It felt dangerous, heady. Inside the house I could hear the girls squabbling over something. Isabelle started crying, but I didn't take my eyes off Henry's.

"You'd better go to them," he said finally.

"And the piano?"

"I'll put a floor in the lean-to. Fix it up for him."

"Thank you, honey."

That night in our bed he took me hard, from behind, without any of the usual preliminaries. It hurt, but I didn't make a sound.

HENRY

When I was six years old, my grandfather called me into the bedroom where he was dying. I didn't like to go in there—the room stank of sickness and old man, and the skeleton look of him scared me—but I was reared to be obedient so I went.

"Run outside and get a handful of dirt, then bring it back here," he said.

"What for?"

"Just do it." He waved one gnarled hand. "Go on now."

"Yes, sir."

I went and got the dirt. When I returned with it, he asked me what I was holding.

"Dirt," I said.

"That's right. Now give it to me."

He cupped his hands. They shook with palsy. I poured the dirt into them, trying not to spill any on the sheets.

"What am I holding?" he asked.

"Dirt."

"No."

"Earth?"

"No, boy. This is *land* I've got. Do you know why?" His eyebrows shot up. They were gray and bushy, tangled like wire.

I shook my head, not understanding.

"Because it's *mine*," he said. "One day this'll be your land, your farm. But in the meantime, to you and every other person who don't own it, it's just dirt. Here, take it on back outside before your mama catches you with it."

He poured it back into my hands. As I turned to leave, he grabbed ahold of my sleeve and fixed me with his rheumy eyes. "Remember this, boy. You can put your faith in a whole lot of things—in God, in money, in other people—but land's the only thing you can count on to be there tomorrow. It's the only thing that's really yours."

A week later he was dead, and his land passed to my mother. That land was where I grew to manhood, and though I left it at nineteen to see what lay outside its borders, I always knew I'd return to it someday. I knew it during the weeks I spent overseas with my face pressed in alien mud soaked in the blood of people not my own, and during the long months after, lying on my back in Army hospitals while my leg stank and throbbed and itched and finally healed. I knew it while I was a student up in Oxford, where the land doesn't lie flat, but heaves itself up and down like seawater. I knew it when I went to work for the Corps of Engineers, a job that took me many places that were strange to me, and some others that looked like home but weren't. Even when the flood came in '27, overrunning Greenville and destroying our house and that year's cotton crop, it never occurred to me that my father would do other than rebuild and replant. That land had been in my mother's family for nearly a hundred years. My great-great-grandfather and his slaves had cleared it, wresting it acre by acre from the seething mass of cane and brush that covered it. Rebuild and replant: that's what farmers do in the Delta.

My father did neither. He sold the farm in January of '28, nine months after the flood. I was living down to Vicksburg at the time and traveling a great deal for work. I didn't find out what he'd done till after it was too late.

"That damned river wiped me out," Pappy liked to tell people after he'd moved to town and started working for the railroad. "Never would've sold otherwise."

That was a lie, one of many that made up his story of himself. The truth was he walked away from that land gladly, because he feared and hated farming. Feared the weather and the floods, hated the work and the sweat and the long hours alone with his own thoughts. Even as a boy I saw how small he got when he looked at the sky, how he brushed the soil from his hands at the end of the day like it was dung. The flood was just an excuse to sell.

Took me nearly twenty years to save enough to buy my own land. There was the Depression to get through, and then the war. I had a wife and two children to provide for. I put by what I could and waited.

By V-J Day, I had the money. I figured I'd work one more year to give us a cushion and start looking for property the following summer. That would give me plenty of time to learn the land, purchase seed and equipment, find tenants and so on before the new planting season started in January. It would also give me time to work on my wife, who I knew would be reluctant to leave Memphis.

That's how it was supposed to be, nice and orderly, and it would have been if that good-for-nothing husband of Eboline's hadn't gone and hanged himself that Christmas. I never trusted my brother-in-law, or any man comfortable in a suit. Virgil was a great drinker and a great talker besides, and those are stains enough on anybody's character, but what sort of man ends his life with no thought for the shame and misfortune his actions will bring upon his family? He left my sister flat broke and my nephew and nieces fatherless. If he hadn't already been dead, I would have killed him myself.

Eboline and the children needed looking after, and there was no one to do it but me. As soon as we buried Virgil, I started searching for property nearby. There was nothing suitable for sale around Greenville, but I heard about a two-hundred-acre farm in Marietta, forty miles to the southeast. It belonged to a widow named Conley whose husband had died at Normandy. She had no sons to inherit the place and was eager to sell.

From the minute I set foot on the property, I had a good feeling about it. The land was completely cleared, with a small river running along the southern border. The soil was rich and black—Conley had had the sense to rotate his crops. The barn and cotton house looked sound, and there was a ramshackle house on the property that would serve me well as a camp, though it wouldn't do as a home for Laura and the girls.

The farm was everything I wanted. Mrs. Conley was asking ninety-five hundred for it—mostly, I reckoned, because I'd driven up in Eboline's Cadillac. I bargained her down to eighty-seven hundred, plus a hundred and fifty each for her cow and two mules.

I was a landowner at last. I could hardly wait to tell my wife.

But first, I had some things to take care of. Had to find us a rent house in town. Had to buy a tractor—I wasn't about to be a mule farmer like my father had been—and a truck. And I had to decide which tenants to keep on and which to put off. With the tractor I could farm more than half the acreage myself, so I'd only need three of the six tenants who were living there. I interviewed them all, checking their accounts of themselves against Conley's books, then asked the ones with the smallest yields per acre and the greatest talent for exaggeration to leave.

I kept on the Atwoods, the Cottrills, and the Jacksons. The Jacksons looked to be the best of the bunch, even though they were colored. They were share tenants, not sharecroppers, so they only paid me a quarter of their crop as opposed to half. You don't see many colored share tenants. Aren't many of them have the discipline to save for their own mule and equipment. But Hap Jackson wasn't your typical Negro. For one thing, he could read. The first time I met him, before he signed his contract, he asked to see his page in Conley's account book.

"Sure," I said, "I'll show it to you, but how will you know what it says?"

"I been reading going on seven years now," he said. "My

boy Ronsel learned me. I wasn't much good at it at first but he kept after me till I could get through Genesis and Exodus on my own. Teached me my numbers too. Yessuh, Ronsel's plenty smart. He's a sergeant in the Army. Fought under General Patton hisself, won him a whole bunch of medals over there. Reckon he'll be coming home any day now, yessuh."

I handed him the account book, as much to shut him up as anything. Underneath Hap's name, Conley had written, *A hardworking nigger who picks a clean bale.*

"Mr. Conley seemed to have a good opinion of you," I said.

Hap didn't answer. He was concentrating on the figures, running his finger down the columns. His lips moved as he read. He scowled and shook his head. "My wife was right," he said. "She was right all along."

"Right about what?"

"See here, where it says twenty bales next to my name? Mist Conley only paid me for eighteen. Told me that was all my cotton graded out to. Florence said he was cheating us, but I didn't want to believe her."

"You never saw this book before?"

"No suh. One time I asked Mist Conley to look in it, that was the first year we was here, and he got to hollering at me till it was a pity. Told me he'd put me off if I questioned his word again."

"Well I don't know, Hap. It says here he paid you for twenty."

"I ain't telling no part of a lie," he declared.

I believed him. A Negro is like a little child, when he tries to lie it's stamped on his face plain as day. Hap's face held nothing but honest frustration. Besides, I know it's common practice for planters to cheat their colored tenants. I don't hold with it myself. Whatever else the colored man may be, he's our brother. A younger brother, to be sure, undisciplined and driven by his appetites, but also kindly and tragic and humble before God. For good or ill, he's been given into our care. If we care for him badly or not at all, if we use our natural superiority to harm him, we're damned as surely as Cain.

"Tell you what, Hap," I said. "You stay on and I'll let you look in this account book any time you want. You can even come with me to the gin for the grading."

He gave me a measuring look and I saw that his eyes, which I'd thought were brown, were actually a muddy green. Between that and his light skin, I figured he must have had two white grandfathers. It explained a lot.

He was still looking at me. I raised my eyebrows, and he dropped his gaze. I was glad to see that. Smart is well and good, but I won't have a disrespectful nigger working for me.

"Thank you, Mist McAllan. That'd be just fine."

"Good, it's settled then," I said. "One more thing. I understand your wife and daughter don't do field work. Is that true?"

"Yessuh. Well, they help out at picking time but they don't do no plowing or chopping. Ain't no need for em to, me and my sons get along just fine without em. Florence is a granny midwife, she brings in a little extra thataway."

"But you could farm another five acres with them helping you in the fields," I said.

"I don't want no wife of mine chopping cotton, or Lilly May neither," he said. "Womenfolks ain't meant for that kind of labor."

I feel that way myself, but I'd never heard a Negro say so before. Most of them use their women harder than their mules. I've seen colored women out in the fields so big with child they could barely bend over to hoe the cotton. Of course, a colored woman is sturdier than a white woman to begin with.

Laura wouldn't have lasted a week in the fields, but I thought she'd make a fine farmwife once she got used to the idea. Shows you how smart I was.

SHE WAS AGAINST the move from the minute I told her about it. She didn't say so directly, but she didn't have to. I could tell from the way she started humming whenever I walked in the room. A woman will make her feelings known one way or another. Laura's way is with music: singing when she's content, humming when she isn't, whistling tunelessly when she's thinking a thing over and deciding whether to sing or hum about it.

The music got a lot less pleasant once we got to the farm. Slamming doors and banging pans, raising her voice to Pappy and me. Defying me. It was as if somebody had come in the night and stolen my sweet, biddable wife, leaving behind a shrew in her place. Everything I did or said was wrong. I knew she blamed me for losing that house in town, but was it my fault the girls got so sick? And the storm—I suppose that was my doing too?

It hit the middle of the night we arrived, making an ungodly racket on the tin roof. The girls' room was leaking, so we brought them into the bed with us. By morning they were both coughing and hot to the touch. They'd been sniffling for a few days but I hadn't thought much of it, kids are always catching something. The rain kept up all that day and the next, coming down in heavy sheets. Late that second afternoon I was out in the barn mending tack when Pappy came to fetch me.

"Your wife wants you," he said. "Your daughters are worse."

I hurried to the house. Amanda Leigh was coughing, high, cracking sounds like shots from a .22. Isabelle lay in the bed beside her, making a terrible wheezing noise with each indrawn breath. Their lips and fingernails were blue.

"It's whooping cough," Laura said. "Go and fetch the doctor at once. And tell your father to put a pot of water on to boil." I wanted to comfort her but her eyes stopped me. "Just go," she said.

I told Pappy to put the water on and ran out to the truck. The road was a muddy churn. Somehow I made it to the bridge without skidding off into a ditch. I heard the river before I saw it: a roar of pure power. The bridge was two feet underwater. I stood with the rain lashing my face and looked at the swollen brown water and cursed George Suddeth for a liar, and myself for a gullible fool. Never should have trusted him to begin with, that's what Pappy said, and I reckoned he was right. Still, it's a sorry world if you can't count on a man to keep his given word after you've sat at his table and broken bread with him.

It was on the way back to the house that I thought of Hap Jackson's wife, Florence. Hap had said she was a midwife, she might know something of children's ailments. Even if she didn't, she'd be able to help with the cooking and housework while Laura nursed the girls.

Florence herself answered my knock. I hadn't met her before, and her appearance took me aback. She was a tall, strapping Negress with sooty black skin and muscles ropy as a man's—an Amazon of her kind. I had to look up at her to talk to her. Woman must have been near to six feet tall.

"May I help you?" she said.

"I'm Henry McAllan."

She nodded. "How do. I'm Florence Jackson. If you looking for Hap, he's out in the shed, tending to the mule."

"Actually, I came to see you. My little girls, they're three and five, they've taken sick with whooping cough. I can't get to town because the bridge is washed out, and my wife . . ." *My wife is liable to kill me if I come home with no doctor and no help.*

"When they start the whooping?"

"This afternoon."

She shook her head. "They still catching then. I can give you some remedies to take to em but I can't go with you."

"I'll pay you," I said.

"I wouldn't be able to come home for three or four days at least. And then who gone look after my own family, and my mothers?"

"I'm asking you," I said.

As I locked eyes with her, I was struck by the sheer force of her. That force was banked now but I could sense it underneath, ready to come alive at need. This wasn't your commonplace Negro vitality—the animal spirits they spend so recklessly in music and fornication. This was a deep-running fierceness that was almost warriorlike, if you can imagine a colored farmwife in a flour-sack dress as a warrior.

Florence shifted, and I saw a girl of maybe nine or ten in the room behind her, white to the elbows with flour from kneading dough. Had to be the daughter, Lilly May. She was watching us, waiting like I was for her mother's answer.

"I got to ask Hap," Florence said finally.

The girl ducked her head and went back to her kneading, and I knew that Florence was lying. The decision was hers to make, not Hap's, and she'd just made it.

"Please," I said. "My wife is afraid." I felt my face get hot as she considered me. If she said no, I wouldn't ask her again. I wouldn't stoop to beg a nigger for help. If she said no—

"All right then," she said. "Wait here while I get my things."

"I'll wait in the truck."

A few minutes later she came out carrying a battered leather case, a rolled-up bundle of clothes and an empty burlap bag. She opened the passenger door and set the case and the clothes inside.

"You got you any chickens yet?" she asked.

"No."

She closed the truck door and walked around to the chicken coop on the side of the house, moving unhurriedly in spite of the pouring rain. She stepped over the wire fence and tucked the bag under one arm. Then she reached into the henhouse, pulled out a flapping bird and, with one sure twist of her big hands, wrung its neck. She put the chicken in the bag and walked back to the truck, still moving at that same steady, deliberate pace.

She opened the door. "Them girls gone need broth," she said, as she climbed inside. She didn't ask my permission, just got in like she had every right to sit in the cab with me. Under normal circumstances I wouldn't have stood for it, but I didn't dare ask her to ride in back.

FLORENCE

FIRST TIME I LAID eyes on Laura McAllan she was out of her head with mama worry. When that mama worry takes ahold of a woman you can't expect no sense from her. She'll do or say anything at all and you just better hope you ain't in her way. That's the Lord's doing right there. He made mothers to be like that on account of children need protecting and the men ain't around to do it most of the time. Something bad happen to a child, you can be sure his daddy gone be off somewhere else. Helping that child be up to the mama. But God never gives us a task without giving us the means to see it through. That mama worry come straight from Him, it make it so she can't help but look after that child. Every once in awhile you see a mother who ain't got it, who just don't care for her own baby that came out of her own body. And you try and get her to hold that baby and feed that baby but she won't have none of it. She just staring off, letting that baby lay there and cry, letting other people do for it. And you know that poor child gone grow up wrong-headed, if it grows up at all.

Laura McAllan was tending to them two sick little girls when I come in with her husband. One of em was bent over a pot of steaming water with a sheet over her head. The other one was just laying there in the bed making that awful whooping sound. When Miz McAllan looked up and seen us her eyes just about scorched us both to a crisp.

"Who's this, Henry? Where's the doctor?"

"The bridge is washed out," he said. "I couldn't get to town. This is Florence Jackson, she's a midwife. I thought she might be able to help."

"Do you see anybody giving birth here?" she said. "These children need a medical doctor, not some granny with a bag full of potions."

Just then the little one started gagging like they do when the whooping takes em real bad. I went right over to her. I turned that child onto her side and held her head over the bowl, but all that come out was some yellow bile. "I seen this with my own children," I told her. "We need to get some liquid down em. But first we got to clear some of that phlegm out."

She glared at me a minute, then said, "How?"

"We'll make em up some horehound tea, and we'll keep after em with the steam like you been doing. That was real good, making that steam for em."

Mist McAllan was just standing there dripping water all over the floor, looking like somebody stabbed him whenever one of them little girls coughed. Times like that, you got to give the men something to do. I asked him to go boil some more water.

"That tea'll draw the phlegm right on out of there," I told Miz McAllan. "Then once they get to breathing better we'll make em some chicken broth and put a little ground-up willow bark in it for the fever."

"I've got aspirin somewhere, if I can find it in all this mess."

"Don't fret yourself over it. Aspirin's made out of willow bark, they do the same work."

"I should have taken them to the doctor yesterday, as soon as they started coughing. If anything happens to them . . ."

"Listen to me," I said, "your girls gone be just fine. Jesus is watching over em and I'm here too, and ain't neither one of us going nowhere till they feeling better. Give em a week or so, they'll be right as rain, you'll see." I talked to her just like I talk to a laboring woman. Mothers need to hear them soothing words. They just as important as the medicines, sometimes even more.

"Thank you for coming," she said after awhile.

"You welcome."

After they had some tea and was quieted down some I went and started plucking the chicken I'd brought. I hadn't been in the house since the Conleys left and it was filthy from standing empty. Well, not altogether empty—plenty of creatures had been in and out of there. There was mouse droppings and snail tracks on the floor, cicada husks stuck to the walls and dirt all over everything. When Miz McAllan come in and seen me looking, I could tell she was ashamed.

"I haven't had time to clean," she said. "The children took sick as soon as we got here."

"We'll set it to rights, don't you worry."

Whole time I was plucking that chicken and cutting up the onions and carrots for the broth, that ole man was setting at the table watching me. Mist McAllan's father, that they called Pappy. He was a bald-headed fellow with hardly any meat on him, but he still had all his teeth—a whole mouthful of em, long and yellow as corn. His eyes was so pale they was hardly any color at all. There was something bout them eyes of his, gave me the willies whenever they was on me.

Mist McAllan had gone outside and Miz McAllan was back in the bedroom with the children, so it was just me and Pappy for a spell.

"Say, gal, I'm thirsty," he said. "Why don't you run on out to the pump and fetch me some water?"

"I got to finish this broth for the children," I said.

"That broth can do without you for a few minutes."

I had my back to him, didn't say nothing. Just lingered along, stirring that pot.

"Did you hear me, gal?" he said.

Now, my mama and daddy raised me up to be respectful to elderly folks and help em along, but I sure didn't want to fetch that water for that ole man. It was like my body got real heavy all of a sudden and didn't want to budge. Probably I would a made myself do it but then Miz McAllan come in and said, "Pappy, there's drinking water right there, in the pail by the sink. You ought to know, you pumped it yourself this morning."

He held his cup out to me without a word. Without a word

I took it and filled it from the pail. But before I turned around and gave it back to him I stuck my finger in it.

For supper I fried up some ham and taters they had and made biscuits and milk gravy. After I served em I started to make up a plate for myself to take out to the porch.

"Florence, you can go on home now," Miz McAllan said. "I'm sure you've got your own family to see to."

"Yes'm, I do," I said, "but I can't go home to em. It's like I told your husband when he come to fetch me. That whooping cough is catching, specially at the start like your girls is. They gone be contagious till the end of the week at least. If I went home now I could pass it to my own children, or to one of my mothers' babies."

"I ain't sleeping under the same roof as a nigger," Pappy said.

"Florence, why don't you go check on the girls?" Miz McAllan said.

I left the room but it was a small house and there wasn't nothing wrong with my ears.

"She ain't sleeping here," Pappy said.

"Well, we can't send her home to infect her own family," Miz McAllan said. "It wouldn't be right."

There was a good long pause, then Mist McAllan said, "No, it wouldn't be."

"Well then," Pappy said, "she can damn well sleep out in the barn with the rest of the animals."

"How could you suggest such a thing, in this cold?" Miz McAllan said.

"Niggers need to know their place," Pappy said.

"For the last few hours," she said, "her *place* has been by your granddaughters' bedside, doing everything she could to help them get better. Which is more than I can say for you."

"Now Laura," Mist McAllan said.

"We'll make up a pallet for her here, in the main room," Miz McAllan said. "Or you can sleep in here and we can put Florence out in the lean-to."

"And have her stinking up my room?"

"Fine then. We'll put her in here."

I heard a chair scrape.

"Where are you going?" Mist McAllan asked.

"To the privy," she said. "If that's all right with you."

The front door opened and then banged shut.

"I don't know what's gotten into your wife," Pappy said, "but you better get a handle on her right quick."

I listened hard, but if Mist McAllan said anything back I didn't hear it.

SLEPT FOUR NIGHTS in that house and by the end of em I'd a bet money there was gone be trouble in it. Soft citybred woman like Laura McAllan weren't meant for living in the Delta. Delta'll take a woman like that and suck all the sap out of her till there ain't nothing left but bone and grudge, against him that brung her here and the land that holds him and her with him. Henry McAllan was as landsick as any man I ever seen and I seen plenty of em, white and colored both. It's in their eyes, the way they look at the land like a woman they's itching for. White men already got her, they thinking, *You mine now, just you wait and see what I'm gone do to you.* Colored men ain't got her and ain't never gone get her but they dreaming bout her just the same, with every push of that plow and every chop of that hoe. White or colored, none of em got sense enough to see that she the one owns them. She takes their sweat and blood and the sweat and blood of their women and children and when she done took it all she takes their bodies too, churning and churning em up till they one and the same, them and her.

I knew she'd take me and Hap someday, and Ruel and Marlon and Lilly May. Only one she wasn't gone get was my eldest boy, Ronsel. He wasn't like his daddy and his brothers, he knowed farming was no way to raise hisself up in the world. Just had to look at me and Hap to see that. Spent our lives moving from farm to farm, hoping to find a better situation and a boss that wouldn't cheat us. Longest we ever stayed anywhere was the Conley place, we'd been there going on seven years. Mist Conley cheated us some too but he was better than most of em. He let us put in a little vegetable patch of our own, and from time to time his wife gave us some of their old clothes and shoes. So when Miz Conley told us she'd up and sold the farm we was real anxious. You never know what you getting into with a new landlord.

"I wonder if this McAllan fellow ever farmed before," Hap fretted. "He's from up to Memphis. Bet he don't know the eating end of a mule from the crapping end."

"It don't matter," I told him. "We'll get by like we always do."

"He could put us off."

"He won't, not this close to planting time."

But he could a done it if he'd had a mind to, that was the plain truth. Landlords can do just about anything they want. I seen em put families off after the cotton was laid by and that family worked all spring and summer to make that crop for em. And if they say you owe em for furnishings you don't get nothing for your labor. Ain't nobody to make em do right by you. You might as well not even go to the sheriff, he gone take the boss man's side every time.

"Even if he wants us to stay," Hap said, "we still might have to move on, depending on what type a man he is."

"I don't care if he's the Dark Man hisself, I ain't moving if we don't have to. Took me this long to get the house fit to live in and the garden putting out decent tomatoes and greens. Besides, I can't just go off and leave my mothers." I had four mothers due in the next two months and one of em, little Renie Atwood, was just a baby herself. Couldn't nary one of em afford a doctor and I was the only granny midwife for miles around.

"You'll move if I say so," Hap said. "For the husband is the head of the wife, even as Christ is the head of the church."

"Only so long as he alive," I said. "For if the husband be dead the wife is loosed from his law. Says so in Romans."

Hap gave me a sharp look and I gave him one right back. He's never once laid a hand to me and I always speak my mind to him. Some men need to beat a woman to get her to do what they want, but not Hap. All he has to do is talk at you. You can start off clear on the other side of something, and then he'll get to talking, and talking some more, and before long you'll find yourself nodding and agreeing with him. That was how I started loving him, was through his words. Before I ever knowed the feel of his hands on me or the smell of him in the dark, I used to lay my head on his shoulder and close my eyes and let his words lift me up like water.

Henry McAllan turned out not to be the Dark Man after all, but wasn't no use telling that to my husband. "Do you know what that man is doing?" Hap said. "He's bringing in one of them infernal tractors! Using a machine to work his land instead of the hands God gave him, and putting three families off on account of it too."

"Who?"

"The Fikeses, the Byrds and the Stinnets."

That surprised me about the Fikeses and the Stinnets, on account of them being white. Lot of times a landlord'll put the colored families off first.

"But he's keeping us on," I said.

"Yes."

"Well, we can thank the Almighty for that."

Hap just shook his head. "It's devilry, plain and simple."

That night after supper he read to us from the Revelations. When he got to the part about the beast with seven heads and ten horns, and upon his horns ten crowns and upon his heads the name of blasphemy, I knowed he was talking bout that tractor.

THE REAL DEVIL was that ole man. When Miz McAllan asked me to keep house for her like I done for Miz Conley,

I almost said no on account of Pappy. But Lilly May needed a special kind of boot for her clubfoot and Ruel and Marlon needed new clothes, they was growing so fast they was about to split the seams of their old ones, and Hap was wanting a second mule so he could work more acres so he could save enough to buy his own land, so I said I'd do it. I worked for Laura McAllan Monday to Friday unless I had a birthing or a mother who needed looking in on. My midwifing came first, I told her that when I took the job. She didn't like it much but she said all right.

That ole man never gave her a minute's peace, or me neither. Just set there all day long finding fault with everything and everybody. When he was in the house I thought up chores to do outside and when he was out on the porch I worked in the house. Still, sometimes I had to be in the same room with him and no help for it. Like one time I had ironing to do, mostly his ironing, he wore Sunday clothes every day of the week. He was setting at the kitchen table like always, smoking and cleaning the dirt from under his fingernails with a buck knife. Cept he couldn't a been getting em too clean cause he was too busy eyeballing me.

"You better be careful, gal, or you're gonna burn them sheets," he said.

"Ain't never burnt nothing yet, Mist McAllan."

"See that you don't."

"Yessuh."

He admired the dirt on the tip of the knife awhile, then he said, "How come that son of yours ain't home from the war yet?"

"He ain't been discharged yet," I said.

"Guess they still need some more ditches dug over there, huh?"

"Ronsel ain't digging ditches," I said. "He's a tank commander. He fought in a whole lot of battles."

"That what he told you?"

"That what he done."

The ole man laughed. "That boy's pulling your leg, gal. Ain't no way the Army would turn a tank worth thousands of dollars over to a nigger. No, ditch digger's more like it. Course that don't sound as good as 'tank commander' when you're writing the folks back home."

"My son's a sergeant in the 761st Tank Battalion," I said. "That's the truth, whether you want to believe it or not."

He gave a loud snort. I answered the only way I could, by starching his sheets till they was as stiff and scratchy as raw planks.

LAURA

FAIR FIELDS. That's what Henry wanted to call the farm. He announced this to me and the children one day after church, clearing his throat first with the self-consciousness of a small-town politician about to unveil a new statue for the town square.

"I think it has a nice ring to it, without being too fancy," he said. "What do you girls think?"

"Fair Fields?" I said. "Mudbound is more like it."

"Mudbound! Mudbound!" the girls cried.

They couldn't stop laughing and saying the name. Mudbound stuck; I made sure of it. It was a petty form of revenge, but the only kind available to me at the time. I was never so angry as those first months on the farm, watching Henry be happy. Becoming a landowner had transformed him, bringing out a childlike eagerness I'd rarely seen in him. He would come in bursting with the exciting doings of his day: his decision to plant thirty acres in soybeans, his purchase of a fine sow from a neighbor, the new weed killer he'd read about in the *Progressive Farmer*. I listened, responding with as much enthusiasm as I could muster. I tried to shape my happiness out of the fabric of his, like a good wife ought to, but his contentment tore at me. I would see him standing at the edge of the fields with his hands in his pockets, looking out over the land with fierce pride of possession, and think, *He's never looked at me like that, not once.*

For the children's sakes, and for the sake of my marriage, I hid my feelings, maintaining a desperate cheerfulness. Some days I didn't even have to pretend. Days when the weather was clear and mild, and the wind blew the smell of the outhouse away from us rather than toward us. Days when the old man went off with Henry, leaving the house to me, the girls and Florence. I depended on her a great deal, and for far more than housework, though I wouldn't have admitted it then. Each time I heard her brisk knock on the back door, I felt a loosening in myself, an unclenching. Some mornings I would hear Lilly May's more hesitant rapping instead, and I would know that Florence had been called away to another woman's house. Or I'd open the door to find an agitated husband standing on my porch, twisting his soiled straw hat in his hands, saying the pains had started, could she come right now? Florence would take her leather case and go, bustling with purpose and importance, leaving me alone with the girls and the old man. I accepted these absences because I had no choice.

"I got to look after the mothers and the babies," she told me. "I reckon that's why the Lawd put me on this earth."

She had four children of her own: Ronsel, her eldest, who was still overseas with the Army; the twins, Marlon and Ruel, shy, sturdy boys of twelve who worked in the fields with their father; and Lilly May, who was nine. There had been another boy, Landry, who'd died when he was only a few weeks old. Florence wore a leather pouch on a thong around her neck containing the dried remains of the caul in which he'd been born.

"A caul round a child mean he marked for Jesus," she told me. "Jesus seen the sign and taken Landry for His own self. But my son'll be watching over me from heaven, long as I wear his caul."

Like many Negroes, Florence was highly superstitious and full of well-meaning advice about supernatural matters. She urged me to burn my nail clippings and every strand of hair left in my brush to prevent my enemies from using them to hex me. When I assured her that wouldn't be necessary, as I had no enemies, she looked pointedly at Pappy across the room and replied that the Dark Man had many minions, and you had to be vigilant against them all the time. One day I smelled something rotten in the bedroom and found a broken egg in a saucer under the bed. It looked to have been there for at least a week. When I confronted Florence with it, she told me it was for warding off the evil eye.

"There are no evil eyes here," I said.

"Just cause you can't see em don't mean they ain't there."

"Florence, you're a Christian woman," I said. "How can you believe in all these curses and spirits?"

"They right there in the Bible. Cain was cursed for killing his brother. Womenfolks cursed on account of Eve listened to that ole snake. And we got the Holy Spirit in every one of us."

"That's not the same thing at all," I said.

She replied with a loud sniff. Later I saw her give the dish to Lilly May, who went and buried the egg at the base of the oak tree. Lord knows what that was supposed to accomplish.

There was no colored school during planting season, so Florence often brought Lilly May to work with her. She was a fey child, tall for her age, with purple-black skin like her mother's. The girls adored Lilly May, though she didn't talk much. She had a clubfoot, so she lacked Florence's slow heavy grace, but her voice more than made up for it. I've never heard anyone sing like that child. Her voice soared, and it took you along with it, and when it stopped and the last high, yearning note had shivered out, you ached for its passing and for your return to your own lonely, mortal sack of flesh. The first time I heard her, I was playing the piano and teaching the girls the words to "Amazing Grace" when Lilly May joined in from the front porch, where she was shelling peas. I've always prided myself on my singing voice, but when I heard hers, I was so humbled I was struck dumb. Her voice had no earthly clay in it, just a sure, sweet grace that was both a yielding and a promise. Anyone who believes that Negroes are not God's children never heard Lilly May Jackson sing to Him.

This is not to say that I thought of Florence and her family as equal to me and mine. I called her Florence and she called me Miz McAllan. She and Lilly May didn't use our outhouse, but did their business in the bushes out back. And when we sat down to the noon meal, the two of them ate outside on the porch.

• • •

EVEN WITH FLORENCE'S help, I often felt overwhelmed: by the work and the heat, the mosquitoes and the mud, and most of all, the brutality of rural life. Like most city people, I'd had a ridiculous, goldenlit idea of the country. I'd pictured rain falling softly upon verdant fields, barefoot boys fishing with thistles dangling from their mouths, women quilting in cozy little log cabins while their men smoked corncob pipes on the porch. You have to get closer to the picture to see the wretched shacks scattered throughout those fields, where families clad in ragged flour-sack clothes sleep ten to a room on dirt floors; the hookworm rashes on the boys' feet and the hideous red pellagra scales on their hands and arms; the bruises on the faces of the women, and the rage and hopelessness in the eyes of the men.

Violence is part and parcel of country life. You're forever being assailed by dead things: dead mice, dead rabbits, dead possums, dead birds. You find them in the yard, crawling with maggots, and smell them rotting under the house. Then there are the creatures you kill for food: chickens, hogs, deer, quail, wild turkeys, catfish, rabbits, frogs and squirrels, which you pluck, skin, disembowel, debone and fry up in a pan.

I learned how to load and fire a shotgun, how to stitch up a bleeding wound, how to reach into the womb of a heaving sow to deliver a breached piglet. My hands did these things, but I was never easy in my mind. Life felt perilous, like anything at all might happen. At the end of March, several things did.

One night near to dawn, I woke to the sound of gunshots. I was alone with the children; Henry and Pappy had gone to

Greenville to help Eboline move into her new and considerably more humble abode—the big house on Washington Street had been sold to pay off Virgil's debts. I checked on the girls, but the shots hadn't wakened them. I went out to the porch and peered into the graydark. A half mile away, in the direction of the Atwood place, I saw a light moving. Then it stopped. Then, from that same direction, came two more gunshots. Thirty seconds later there was another. Then another. Then silence.

I must have stood on the porch for twenty minutes, hands clenched in a death grip around our shotgun. The sun rose. Finally I saw someone coming up the road. I tensed, but then I recognized Hap's slightly stooped gait. He was out of breath when he reached me. His clothes were covered with dirt, and he too was carrying a shotgun.

"Miz McAllan," he said. "Is your husband here?"

"No, he and Pappy went to Greenville. What's going on? Was that you firing your gun?"

"No, ma'am, it was Carl Atwood. He done shot his plow horse in the head."

"Good heavens! Why would he do that?"

"He been messing with that whiskey. Ain't no devilment a man won't get hisself into when he's full of drink."

"Please, Hap. Just tell me what happened."

"Well, Florence and I was asleep when we heard them first two gunshots. Both of us like to jump right out of our skins. I got up and looked out the window but I couldn't see nothing. Then we heard another two shots, sound like they coming from the Atwood place. I got my gun and went over there but I know

them Atwoods is crazy so I snuck up on em. First thing I seen
was that plow horse of Carl's, haring through the fields like
the devil hisself was after it. I could hear Carl a-cussing that
horse, hollering, 'You oughten not to done it, damn your hide!'
Then here he come chasing after it with his shotgun. I could
tell he'd been at the whiskey and I was afraid he was gone see
me and shoot me too so I dropped down on the ground and
laid there real still. He pointed the gun at that horse and bam!
He missed again and fell over backwards. That horse let into
whinnying, I could a swore it was laughing at him. Carl kept
trying to get up and falling back down again, all the while just
a-cussing that horse up and down. Finally he got up and aimed
again and bam! This time that horse went down, wasn't twenty
feet from where I was laying. Carl went over to it and said,
'Damn you to hell, horse, you oughten not to done it.' And then
he pissed—begging your pardon Miz McAllan, I mean to say
he done his business on that horse, right on its shot-up head,
cussing and crying like a baby the whole time."

I hugged myself. "Is he still out there?" I asked.

"No, ma'am. He went on back home. Reckon he'll be sleeping it off most of the day."

Carl Atwood was my least favorite of all our tenants. He
was a banty rooster of a man, spindly legged and sway backed,
with little muddy eyes that crowded his nose on either side.
His lips were dark red, like the gills of a bass, and his tongue
was constantly darting out to moisten them. He was always
polite to me, but there was a sly, avid quality about him that
made me uneasy.

I looked in the direction of the Atwood place. Hap said, "You want me to stay here till Mist McAllan come back?"

As tempted as I was to say yes, I couldn't ask him to lose an entire day in the fields during planting season. "No, Hap," I said. "We'll be fine."

"Florence will be over in a little while. And I'll keep a sharp eye out for Carl."

"Thank you."

I spent the day pacing and looking anxiously out the windows. The Atwoods would have to go. As soon as Henry got home, I'd tell him so. I wouldn't have my children living near such a man.

Later that afternoon, I was at the pump getting water when I saw two figures coming up the road. They walked slowly and unsteadily, one leaning on the other. As they got closer I recognized Vera Atwood and one of her daughters. Vera was huge with child. Except for the jutting mound of her belly, she was little more than skin stretched over bone. One eye was swollen shut, and she had a split lip. The girl had the look of a frightened fawn. Her eyes were large, brown and wide-set, and her dark blonde hair wanted washing. I guessed her to be ten or eleven at most. This, then, wasn't the Atwood girl who'd had an out-of-wedlock baby in February. That child was fourteen, Florence had told me, and her baby had lived only a few days.

"Howdy, Miz McAllan," Vera called out. Her voice was soft and eerily childlike.

"Hello, Vera."

"This here's my youngest girl, Alma."

"How do you do, Alma," I said.

"How do," she replied, with a dip of her head. She had a long, elegant neck that looked incongruous sprouting from her ragged dress. Her face under the grime that covered it was fine-boned and sorrowful. I wondered if she ever smiled. If she ever had reason to.

"I come to speak with you woman to woman," Vera said. She swayed on her feet, and Alma staggered under the extra weight. The two of them looked ready to collapse right there in the yard.

I gestured to the chairs on the porch. "Please, come and sit."

As we made our way up the steps, Florence appeared in the doorway. "What you doing walking all this way, Miz Atwood?" she said. "I done told you, you got to stay off a your feet." Then Florence saw the state of Vera's face. She scowled and shook her head, but she held her tongue.

"Had to come," said Vera. "Got business with Miz McAllan."

I handed Florence the bucket. "Bring us a pitcher of water, will you?" I said. "And some of that shortbread I made yesterday. And keep an eye on Amanda Leigh for me."

"Yes'm."

Vera half sat, half lay in the chair with one hand curled over her upthrust belly. The faded fabric of her dress was stretched so taut I could see the nipple-like lump her navel made. I felt a wave of longing to have a child growing inside of me again. To be full to bursting with life.

"You wanna touch it?" she asked.

Embarrassed, I looked away. "No, thank you."

"You can if you want." When I hesitated, she said, "Go on. He's kicking now, you can feel it."

I went over to her. As I laid my palm against her belly, her scent enveloped me. Everyone smelled a little ripe on the farm, but Vera's odor was positively eye-watering. I stood there holding my breath and waited. For a long moment nothing happened. Then I felt two sharp kicks against my hand. I smiled, and Vera smiled back at me, and I saw the ghost of the girl she'd once been. A pretty girl, much like Alma.

"He's a feisty un," she said proudly.

"You think it's a boy?"

"I pray for it. I pray to God every day He's done sending me girls."

Florence brought out a tray with the food and drinks. Vera accepted a glass of water but waved the shortbread away. Alma looked to her mother for permission before taking a piece off the plate. I expected her to cram it in her mouth, but she nibbled at it delicately.

"Go on now," her mother said. "I need to have a word with Miz McAllan."

"There's a mockingbird's nest in that bush over there," I said.

Alma went obediently down the steps and over to the bush, and Florence went back in the house. Her footsteps didn't go far, though, and I knew she was listening.

"Your Alma's a good girl," I said.

"Thankee. You got two of your own, ain't you?"

"Yes. Isabelle's three and Amanda Leigh's five."

"I reckon they're good girls too. Reckon you'd do anything for em."

"Yes, of course I would."

Vera leaned forward. Her eyes seemed to leap out from her haggard face and grab hold of me. "Don't put us off then," she said.

"What?"

"I expect you're wanting to, on account of what Carl done last night."

"I don't know what you mean," I stammered.

"I seen that nigger walking this way earlier. I know he must a told you."

I nodded reluctantly.

"We ain't got nowhere to go if you put us off. Nobody'll hire us this late in the season."

"It's not up to me, Vera, it's up to my husband."

She laid a hand on her belly. "For this un's sake, and my other younguns', I'm asking you to keep us on."

"I'm telling you, it's not my decision."

"And if it was?"

If her eyes had accused me, I might have been able to look away from them, but they didn't. They just hoped, blindly and fiercely.

"I don't know, Vera," I said. "I have my own children to think about."

She stood up, stomach first, grunting with the effort. I stood too but didn't move to help her. I sensed she wouldn't have wanted it. "Carl never hurt nothing that weren't his own," she said. "It ain't his way. You tell that to your husband when you tell him the rest." She turned away. "Alma!" she called. "We got to be going now."

Alma came at once and helped her mother down the steps, and together they tottered across the yard to the road. I went inside. I needed to see my girls, badly. As I walked past Florence, she muttered, "That man gone burn in hell someday, but it won't be soon enough."

Amanda Leigh was reading quietly on the couch. I scooped her up and carried her into the bedroom where her sister was taking her nap. Isabelle's features looked blurred and insubstantial under the mosquito netting. I jerked it back, startling her awake, then sat down with Amanda on the bed and crushed them both to me, breathing in their little girl scent.

"What is it, Mama?" Amanda Leigh asked.

"Nothing, darling," I said. "Give your mother a kiss."

BAD NEWS IS about the only thing that travels fast in the country. I was giving Amanda Leigh her piano lesson when I heard the car pull up out front, followed by the sound of running feet. The door flew open and Henry came in, looking a little wild. "I stopped at the feed store and heard what happened," he said. "Are you all right?"

"We're fine, Henry."

The girls pelted over to him. "Daddy! Daddy!"

He knelt down and hugged them both so hard they squealed, then came over to me and took me in his arms. "I'm sorry, honey. I know you must have been scared. I'll go over there right now and tell the Atwoods they have to leave."

I hadn't known what I was going to say to him until that moment, when I found myself shaking my head. "Don't put them off," I said.

He stared at me as though I'd gone crazy. Which I undoubtedly had.

"Vera Atwood came by this morning, Henry. She's eight and a half months pregnant. If we put them off now, where would they go? How would they survive?"

A burst of harsh laughter came from the doorway. I looked up and saw Pappy standing there with a box of groceries. He came in and set them on the table. "Well ain't this a touching scene," he said. "Saint Laura, protector of women and children, begging her husband for mercy. Let me ask you this, gal. When Atwood decides to come after you, what are you gonna do then, huh?"

"He won't," I said.

"And how do you figure that?"

"Vera swore he wouldn't. She said he never hurt anything that wasn't his own."

The old man laughed again. Henry's jaw was tight as he looked at me. "This is farm business," he said.

"Honey, please. Just think it over."

"I'll go have a word with Carl tomorrow morning, see what he has to say for himself. That's all I'll promise."

"That's all I'm asking."

Henry walked toward the front door. "Next thing you know she'll be telling you what to plant," Pappy said.

"Shut up," Henry said.

I don't know who was more astonished, me or Pappy.

The next day at dinnertime, Henry told us about his meeting with Carl Atwood. Apparently the horse had gotten into the drying shed and had eaten all of Carl's tobacco. Which explained why the creature had gone so berserk, and why Carl had been so furious.

"I told him I'd keep him on through the harvest," Henry said. "But come October, they'll have to leave. A man who'll do that, who'll kill the hardworking creature that saves him from toil and puts food on his table, is a man who can't be trusted."

I thanked him and reached for his hand to give it a squeeze, but he pulled it away. "Now that Carl's got no plow horse," he said, "he'll have to use one of our mules and pay us a half share like the Cottrills. It'll mean extra money in our pocket. That's the main reason I'm keeping them on." His eyes met mine and held them. "There's no room for pity on a farm," he said.

"Yes, Henry. I understand."

I didn't understand, not at all, but I was about to go to school on the subject.

HAP

PRIDE GOETH BEFORE destruction, and a haughty spirit before a fall. Many's the time I'd sermoned on it. Many's the time I'd stood in front of a church or a tent full of people and praised the meek amongst em while warning the prideful their day of reckoning was coming sooner than they thought, oh yes, it was a-coming right quick and they would pay for their impudent ways. I should a been telling it to the mirror is what I should a been doing, if I'd a listened to my own preaching I wouldn't a ended up in such a mess. Ain't no doubt in my mind God had a hand in it. He was trying to instruct me whatall I'd been doing wrong and thinking wrong. He was saying, *Hap, you better humble down now, you been taking the blessings I've given you for granted. You been walking around thinking you better than some folks cause you ain't working on halves like they is. You been forgetting Who's in charge and who ain't. So here's what I'm gone do: I'm gone send a storm so big it rips the roof off the shed where you keep that mule you so proud of. Then I'm gone send hail big as walnuts down on that mule, making that mule crazy, making it break its leg trying to bust*

out of there. Then, just so you know for sure it's Me you deal-
ing with, the next morning after you put that mule down and
buried it and you up on the ladder trying to nail the roof back
onto the shed I'm gone let that weak top rung, the one you ain't
got around to fixing yet, I'm gone let it rot all the way through so
you fall off and break your own leg, and I'm gone send Florence
and Lilly May to a birthing and the twins out to the far end of
the field so you laying there half the day. That'll give you time
to think real hard on what I been trying to tell you.

A dead mule, a busted shed and a broke leg. That's what
pride'll get you.

I must a laid there two three hours, tried to drag myself to
the house but the pain was too bad. The sun climbed up in the
sky till it was right overhead. I closed my eyes against it and
when I opened em again there was a scowling red face hanging
over me with fire all around the edges of it, looked like a devil
face to me. I wondered if I was in hell. I must a said it out loud
cause the devil answered me.

"No, Hap," he said, "you're in Mississippi." He pulled back
some and I seen it was Henry McAllan. "I stopped by to see if
you had any storm damage."

If my leg hadn't a been hurting so bad I'd a laughed at that.
Yessuh, I guess you could say we had us a little damage.

He went and fetched Ruel and Marlon from the fields. When
they picked me up to carry me in the house I must a blacked
out cause the next thing I remember is waking up in the bed
with Florence leaning over me, tying something around my
neck.

"What you doing?" I said.

"Somebody must a worked a trick on you. We got to turn it back on em."

I looked down under my chin and seen one of her red flannel bags laying there full of God knew what, a lizard's tail or a fish eye or a nickel with a hole in it, no telling whatall she had in there. "You take that thing off a me," I told her, "I don't want none of your hoodoo devilment."

"You get well, you can take it off yourself."

"Damnit, woman!" I tried to lift myself up so I could get the bag off and pain lit out from my leg, felt like somebody taken a dull saw to it and was working it back and forth, back and forth.

"Hush now," Florence said. "You got to lay still till the doctor gets here."

"What doctor?

"Doc Turpin. Mist McAllan went to town to fetch him."

"He won't come out here," I said. "You know that man don't like to treat colored folks."

"He will if Mist McAllan asks him to," Florence said. "Meantime I want you to drink some of this tea I made you, it'll help with the pain and the fever."

I swallowed a few spoonfuls but my belly wasn't having it and I brung it right back up again. The fellow sawing away at my leg picked up his pace and I went back out.

When I come to it was nighttime. Florence was sleeping in a chair next to the bed with a lit lantern by her feet. Her face looked beautiful and stern with the light shining up from underneath it. My wife ain't pretty in the average female way but

I like her looks just fine. Strong jaw, strong bones and a will to match em, oh yes, I seen that back when we was courting. My brothers Heck and Luther made fun of me for marrying her on account of her being taller than me and her skin being so dark. They was just like our daddy, never did think of nothing but nature affairs in choosing a woman. I tried to tell em, you don't wed a gal just to linger between her legs, there's a lot more to a married life than that, but they just laughed at me. Fools, both of em. A man can't prosper by hisself. Unless he can hold onto his wife and she holds onto him too, he won't never amount to nothing. Before I married Florence I told her, "I aim to make this a lifetime journey so if you ain't up for it just say so now and we'll stop right here."

And she said, "Let's go." So we went on and got married, that was back in '23.

She must a felt me thinking bout her cause her eyes opened. "You wasting kerosene," I said.

"I reckoned you was worth it." She reached over and felt my forehead. "You running a fever. Let's get a little food in you, then we'll try some more willowbark tea."

Her touch was gentle but I could tell by the hard set of her mouth she was vexed, and I could guess the reason for it.

"Doc Turpin never showed up, huh?" I said.

"No. Told Mist McAllan he'd try to come out tomorrow after he was done with his other patients."

I looked down at my leg. It was covered with a blanket and Florence had propped it up on a sack of cornmeal. I shifted a little and was sorry I had.

"He sent poppy juice for the pain," she said, holding up a

brown bottle. "I gave you some just before sundown. You want some more?"

"Not yet, we got to talk first. How bad is it?"

"The skin ain't broke, but still. It needs to be set by a doctor."

"I'd trust you to do it."

She shook her head. "If I did it wrong . . ." She didn't finish the thought but she didn't have to. A cripple can't make a crop, and a one-legged man ain't good for much of anything at all.

"What'd you tell Henry McAllan?" I said.

"Bout what?"

"Bout that mule."

"The truth. He could see for hisself it wasn't in the shed."

"And what did he say?"

"He asked if we'd be wanting to use one of his mules and I said what if we did for awhile. And he said then we'd have to pay him a half share instead of a quarter and I said but the fields is already broke. And he said but you still got to lay em off and fertilize and plant and if you using my mule to do it you got to pay me a full half. And I said we wouldn't be needing his mule, we'd get along just fine without it. And he said we'll see about that."

Meaning, if we couldn't get the seed in quick enough to suit him he'd make us use his mule anyway and charge us half our crop for it. Half a crop would hardly be enough to keep us all fed for a year, much less buy seed and fertilizer, much less buy us another mule. You got to have your own mule, elseways you lost. Working on halves there ain't nothing left over, end of the year come around and you got nothing in your pocket

and nothing put by for the lean times. Start getting into debt
with the boss, borrowing for this, borrowing for that, fore you
know it he owns you. You working just to pay him back, and
the harder you work the more you end up owing him.

"We ain't using Henry McAllan's mule," I said. Big words,
but they was just words and we both knew it. Ruel and Marlon couldn't make a twenty-five-acre crop by themselves, they
was strong hardworking boys but they was just twelve, hadn't
come into their full growth yet. If Ronsel was home the three
of em could a managed it, but it was too much work for two
boys with no mule and I didn't have nearly enough put by for
another one. Paid a hundred and thirty dollars for the one
that died, reckoned on having him another ten twelve years
at least.

"That's what I told him," Florence said. "I also told him I
couldn't keep house for his wife no more cause I'd need to be
out in the fields with the twins."

I opened my mouth to tell her no but she covered it up with
her hand. "Hap, there ain't no other way and you know it. It
won't kill me to do a little planting and chopping till you get
to feeling better."

"I promised you I'd never ask you to do field work again."

"You ain't asking, I'm offering," she said.

"If I'd a just fixed that ladder."

"Ain't your fault," she said.

But it was my fault, for holding my head so high I couldn't
see the rotted board right under my foot. Laying there in that
bed, I never felt so low. The tears started to rise up and I shut

my eyes to hold em in. Damned if I was gone let into eye-shedding in front of my wife.

By the time Doc Turpin finally showed up late the next day my leg was swole up bad. I'd been to him twice before, once when I got lockjaw from stepping on a rusty nail and the second time when Lilly May taken sick with lung fever. He wasn't from Marietta, he'd moved up from Florida bout five years ago, word was he was in the Klan down there. We didn't have the Klan in our part of Mississippi. They tried to come into Greenville back in '22 but Senator Percy ran em off. He was a real gentleman, Mr. Leroy Percy was, a good sort of white man. Doc Turpin was the other sort. He hated the colored race, just hated us for being alive on this earth. Problem was he was the only doctor anywhere around. You had to go all the way to Belzoni or Tchula for another doctor, either way it was a two-hour wagon ride. Sometimes you had to, depending on when you got sick. Doc Turpin only treated colored people on certain days of the week and it wasn't always the same. Time I had that lockjaw it was on a Monday and he said he couldn't see me till Wednesday, but when I took Lilly May to him it was a Friday and he told me it was my lucky day cause Friday was nigger day.

When Florence brung him in to me he told her to go wait in the other room. "Is there any way I can help you, doctor?" she asked.

"If I want something I'll tell you," he said.

I would a liked her to stay and I knew she wanted to but she

went on and left. Doc Turpin shut the door behind her and
came over to the bed. He was a fat fellow with yellow-brown
eyes and a funny little tilted-up nose, looked like it belonged
on a lady's face. "Well, boy," he said, "I heard you went and
broke your leg."

"Yessuh, I did."

"Henry McAllan sure does want to see you get well, so I
spose I'd better fix you up. You know how lucky you are to have
a landlord like Mr. McAllan?"

Seemed like every time I seen that man he was telling me
how lucky I was. I didn't feel too lucky right at that moment
but I nodded my head. He pulled the cover off a my leg and
whistled. "You sure did bust yourself up good. You been taking
that pain medicine I sent you?"

"Yessuh."

He poked my leg and I jumped. "When was the last time you
had some of it?" he said.

"Right after dinner, bout four five hours ago."

"Well, in that case, this is gonna hurt some." He reached
down into his bag and pulled out some pieces of wood and
some strips of cloth.

"Can't you give me some more medicine?" I said.

"Sure I can," he said, "but it won't take effect for another
fifteen or twenty minutes. And I don't have time to sit here and
wait on it. Mrs. Turpin's expecting me home for supper." He
handed me one of the pieces of wood, smaller than the others.
There were marks all over it in curved rows. "Put that between
your teeth," he said.

I put it in my mouth and clamped down on it. Sweat broke out all over me and I could smell my own fear, and if I could smell it I knew Doc Turpin could too. Couldn't do nothing bout that but I told myself I wasn't gone cry out, no matter what. God would see me through this like He seen me through so much else, if I just had faith in Him.

What time I am afraid, I will trust in Thee.

"Now, boy," he said, "I'd shut my eyes if I was you. And don't you move. Not if you want to keep that leg a yours." He winked at me and grabbed my leg by the knee and the ankle.

In God I will praise His word, in God I have put my trust. I will not fear what flesh can do unto me.

He pulled up sharp on my ankle and the pain come, pain so bad it made whatall I had before seem like stubbing a toe. I screamed into the stick.

Then nothing.

LAURA

WHEN HENRY TOLD ME Florence wouldn't be coming back, I felt something close to panic. It wasn't just her help around the house I'd miss, it was her company, her calm, womanly presence in my house. Yes, I had the children, and Henry in the evenings, but all three of them were unspeakably happy on the farm. Without Florence, I would be all alone with my anger, doubt and fear.

"It's only till July," Henry said. "Once the cotton's laid by, she should be able to come back."

July was three months away—an eternity. I spoke without thinking. "Can't we lend them one of our mules?"

As soon as the words were out of my mouth I regretted them. "Lend" is a dirty word for Henry, akin to the foulest profanity. He distrusts banks and pays cash for absolutely everything. At Mudbound he kept our money in a strongbox under the floorboards of our bedroom. I had no idea how much was in there, but he'd shown me where it was and told me the combination of the lock: 8-30-62, the date Confederate forces under the command of Robert E. Lee crushed the Union Army in the Battle of Richmond.

"No, we can't 'lend' them a mule," he snapped. "You don't just 'lend' somebody a mule. And I'll tell you something else, if Florence and those boys don't get that seed in real quick, they'll be using our mule all right, and paying us for the privilege."

"What do you mean?"

"Well, it's just like with the Atwoods. If they don't have a mule and they can't get the work done on time, they'll have to use one of ours. Which means they'll have to pay us a half share in cotton. It's hard luck for them, but good for us."

"We can't take advantage of them like that, Henry!"

His face reddened with outrage. "Take advantage? I'm about to let Hap Jackson use my stock to make his crop. A mule I paid good money for, that I'm still paying to keep fed. And you think I ought to let him use it for free? Maybe you think I should just give him that mule outright, on account of Hap being sick and all. Why don't we give him our car while we're at it? Hell, why don't we just give him this whole place?"

Sounded like a fine plan to me.

"I just think we owe it to them to help them, honey," I said. "After all, Hap hurt himself working for us, trying to repair our property."

"No. Hap hurt himself working for Hap. If he didn't repair that shed, *his* tools would rust, and *his* income would suffer for it. Farming's a business, Laura. And like any business, it carries risks. Hap understands that, and you need to understand it too."

"I do, but—"

"Let me put it another way," he said. "I sank everything we had into this place. Everything. We need to make some money this year. If we don't, *our* family's in trouble. Do you understand that?"

Like the Union Army at Richmond, I was utterly defeated. "Yes, Henry," I said.

He softened a little, gracious in victory. "Honey, I know this has been hard on you. We'll see about finding you a new maid just as soon as the planting's done. In the meantime, why don't you go to Greenville tomorrow and do a little shopping. Buy yourself a new hat and some Easter dresses for the girls. Take Eboline to lunch. Pappy and I can fend for ourselves for a day."

I didn't want a new hat, I didn't want to see Eboline and I especially didn't want a new maid. "All right, Henry," I said. "That sounds nice."

THE GIRLS AND I set out early the next morning. On the way I stopped at the Jacksons' to check on Hap and drop off some more food for them. I hadn't seen Florence since the day of the accident, and her haggard, unkempt appearance alarmed me.

"Hap's terrible sickly," she said. "His leg ain't healing straight and he been running a fever for three days now. I've tried everything but I can't get it to come down."

"Do you want us to get Doc Turpin back?"

"That devil! Never should a let him lay a hand on Hap in the first place. Half the colored folks who go to him end up sicker than they was before. If Hap loses his leg on account of that man . . ." She trailed off, no doubt contemplating various gruesome ends for Doc Turpin. My mind was racing in a different direction: If Hap lost his leg, I'd never get Florence back.

And so I went shopping in Greenville—not for hats and Easter dresses, but for a doctor willing to drive two hours each way to treat a colored tenant. It would have been easier to find an elephant with wings. The first two doctors I saw acted like I'd asked them to do my laundry. The third, an old man in his seventies, told me he didn't drive anymore. But as I turned to leave, he said, "There's Dr. Pearlman over on Clay Street. He might do it, he's a foreigner and a Jew. Or you could go to niggertown, they've got a doctor there."

I decided to take my chances with the Jewish foreigner, though I was unsure what to expect. Would he be competent? Would he try to cheat me? Would he even agree to treat a Negro? But my fears proved foolish. Dr. Pearlman seemed kindly and learned, and his office, though empty of patients, was well-kept. I'd barely finished explaining the situation to him before he was getting his bag and hurrying out the door. He followed me and the girls to Hap and Florence's house, where I paid him the very reasonable fee he asked and left him.

By the time we got home it was almost dark. Henry was waiting on the porch. "You girls must have bought out half of Greenville," he called out.

"Oh, we didn't find much," I said.

He walked over to the car. When he saw there were no packages, his eyebrows went up. "Didn't you get anything?"

"We got a doctor," said Amanda Leigh. "He talked funny."

"A doctor? Is somebody sick?"

I felt a flutter of nervousness. "Yes, Henry, it's Hap. His leg's not healing. The doctor was for him."

"That's what you spent your whole day doing?" he said. "Looking for a doctor for Hap Jackson?"

"I didn't set out to look for one. But there was a doctor's office right next to the dress shop, and I thought—"

"Amanda Leigh, take your sister in the house," said Henry.

They knew that tone and obeyed with alacrity, leaving me alone with him. Well, not quite alone; I saw the old man at the window, lapping up every word.

"Why didn't you come to me?" Henry asked. "Hap is my tenant, my responsibility. If he's sick, I need to know about it."

"I just happened to stop by their place on my way to town. And Florence said he'd gotten much worse, so I—"

"Did you think I wouldn't have taken care of it? That I wouldn't have gone and fetched Doc Turpin?"

He wasn't so much angry as hurt; I saw that suddenly. "No, honey, of course not," I said. "But Florence doesn't trust Doc Turpin, and since I was already in Greenville . . ."

"What do you mean, she doesn't trust him?"

"She said he didn't set Hap's leg properly."

"And you just took her word for that. The word of a colored midwife with a fifth-grade education over a medical doctor's."

Put like that, it sounded ridiculous. I had taken her word, unquestioningly. And yet, as I stood withering under the heat of my husband's gaze, I knew I'd do it again.

"Yes, Henry. I did."

"Well, I need you to do the same thing for me, your husband. To take my word for it that I'm going to do what's best for the tenants, and for you and the children. I need you to trust me, Laura." In a thick voice he added, "I never thought I'd have to ask you that."

He left me standing by the car. The sun had slipped below the horizon, and the temperature had dropped. I shivered and leaned against the hood of the DeSoto, grateful for its warmth.

HAP

WHEN I COME TO, Doc Turpin was gone and I was still alive, that was the good news. The bad news was my leg hurt like the dickens. It was all bandaged up so I couldn't see it, but I could feel it all right. Heat was coming off it and the skin felt dry and tight. That was a bad sign, I knew that from tending to mules.

"Doctor said you should get to feeling better in a day or two," Florence said.

But I didn't feel better, I felt worse and worse. The throbbing got real bad and I was in and out of sense. I remember faces floating over me, Florence's, the children's. My mama's, and she'd been laying in the clay going on twenty years. Then come a strange white man bending over me, a settle-aged man with a gray beard and one long eyebrow thick as a mustache.

"This is Doc Pearlman," Florence said. "He gone fix your leg."

He picked up my wrist and held it while he looked at his pocket watch. Then he shined a light in my eyes and put his eyeball right up next to mine and looked in there. "Your husband is in shock," he said, in a funny accent. He started shaking his head like he seen something that disgusted him, I reckoned he was mad on account of having to doctor a nigger. I didn't want no angry white man doctoring me and I told him so but he went ahead anyway and started taking the bandages off a my leg. I let into thrashing.

"Hold him still," he said to Florence.

She came and held my shoulders down. I tried to push her off me but I was too weak. I couldn't see what the doctor was doing and I had a bad feeling.

"Has he got a saw?" I asked her.

"No, Hap."

"Don't you let him cut my leg off. I know he's mad but don't you let him."

"You got to lay still now," Florence said.

The doctor bent down to me again, so close I could smell the pipeweed on his breath. "Your leg wasn't set properly, and it's in flames," he said.

"What?" I started fighting Florence again, trying to get up, but I might as well to been wrestling Goliath.

"Shh," she said. "It's just swole up is all. That's what's causing your fever."

"I'm going to make you sleep now," said the doctor. He put a little basket over my nose and mouth and dribbled some liquid on there. It had a sickly sweet smell.

"Please, Doc, I need my leg."

"Rest now, Mr. Jackson. And don't worry."

I tried to stay awake, but sleep was tugging, tugging. The

last thing I remember is him bending down to get something
out of his bag. There was a little knitted cap on the back of his
bald head, looked like a doily, and I wondered how he got it
to stay on there. Then sleep took ahold of me and swallowed
me up.

WHEN I WOKE UP it was morning and my leg still hurt,
but less than before. This time I was glad of the pain till I remembered ole Waldo Murch and his arm that had to be took
off back in '29. Waldo swore that arm still ached even though
it wasn't there no more. I'd seen him myself plenty of times,
rubbing at the air, and I wondered if it was that kind of imagine pain I was feeling. But I guess God must a decided He'd
humbled me enough cause when I pulled the blanket off there
was my leg, all bandaged and splinted up. I'm here to tell you,
seeing you got two legs when you thought you was down to just
one is a mighty glad feeling.

I could hear Florence moving around in the other room and
I called out to her.

"I'm fixing your breakfast," she said. "Be right there."

She brung me a plate of brains and eggs. Soon as I smelled
it my stomach let into growling, felt like I hadn't et in a week.
"Take this first," she said, handing me a pill.

"What is it?"

"Pencil pills. They to keep away the infection. You got to
take em twice a day till they all gone."

I swallowed the pill and tucked into the food. Florence put

her hand on my forehead. "Fever's down," she said. "You was plumb out of your head yesterday. Sure is a good thing that doctor showed up. Miz McAllan brung him all the way from Greenville."

"She went and fetched him by herself?"

"Yeah. Drove up in the car with him following her."

"When you see her, tell her we're much obliged."

She snorted. "You lucky you still got your leg after the job that butcher done on it. Doc Pearlman was considerable mad about it, I mean to tell you. Said Doc Turpin didn't deserve to be called a doctor."

"Reckon Doc Pearlman ain't from around here," I said.

"No, he's from somewhere over to Europe. Australia, I think he said."

"You mean Austria. That's the place Ronsel was where it snowed all the time."

Florence shrugged. "Whatever it's called, I'm mighty glad he ended up here instead of there."

"How long am I gone be laid up?"

"Eight to ten weeks, if there's no infection."

"Eight weeks! I can't lay here till June!"

She went on like I hadn't said a word. "Doc said we got to keep a sharp eye out for it. And you got to keep that leg real still. He's coming back on Monday to check on you, said if the swelling was down he'd make you a cast."

"How am I gone chop cotton in a cast? How am I gone preach on Sundays?"

"You ain't," Florence said. "The children and me gone do the chopping, and Junius Lee gone drive over from Tchula and do the preaching, and you gone keep your weight off a that leg like the doctor told you to. If you don't, you could wind up a cripple, or worse."

"And if I do and we have to go back to sharecropping, we'll never get out from under Henry McAllan."

"Can't worry bout that now," Florence said. "God'll see to that, one way or another. Meantime you gone do what the doctor told you."

"The contentions of a wife are a continual dropping," I said. "Proverbs 19:13."

"And a prudent wife is straight from the Lord," she shot back. "Proverbs 19:14."

Woman knows her Scripture, I'll give her that. Got no book-learning but there ain't nothing wrong with her memory.

"I better get out to the fields," she said. "Lilly May will be here if you need anything. You rest now."

Lingered along, lingered along. Laid in that bed knowing my wife was out doing my work for me. Couldn't even do my business without one of em helping me. I tried to put it off till Florence and the boys got home but one day I couldn't wait and I had to ask Lilly May to come help me with the pan. There's some things a daughter should never have to do for her daddy. Made me wish I'd a just crapped myself and set in it till Florence got home.

Meantime she and the twins was just about done in from working in the fields. Florence's hands was all blistered up and I seen her rubbing her back when she thought I wasn't looking.

She didn't complain though, nary a word, just went on and did what had to be done. They worked straight through, even on Sunday, and Florence don't hold with working on the Sabbath. They had to do it though. Had to get them fields planted before Henry McAllan decided to bring in his mule.

Monday rolled around and Doc Pearlman come back just like he said he would. He took the bandages off a my leg and looked at it. "Goot," he said, which I took to mean good. "The swelling is gone. We must make the cast now. For that I will need boiled water."

Florence sent Lilly May to do it. Meantime, Doc Pearlman was checking me all over, looking in my eyes and listening to my heart and wiggling my toes. He didn't seem to mind touching me. I wondered if all the white people in his country were like him.

"Florence says you from over to Austria," I said.

"Ya," he said. "My wife and I came here eight years ago."

Fore I could think what I was saying I said, "Our son Ronsel was there. He's a tanker, fought under General Patton."

"Then I'm grateful to him."

I shot a glance at Florence. She looked as fuddled as I was. Speaking real slow to be sure he understood me, I said, "Ronsel fought against Austrian folks."

He got a kindling look in his eye, made all the hairs on my arms stand straight up. "I hope he killed a great many of them," he said. Then he left the room to go wash his hands.

"Well, what do you make of that?" I said to Florence.

She shook her head. "All kind a crazy white people in the world."

THE RAIN CAME the next day, a big hard rain that packed the fields down tight as wax. Nothing we could do but set there and watch it and fret for two days till it finally cleared up. Florence and the children went back out to the fields, even Lilly May. Field work was hard for her with her bad foot and all but there wasn't no help for it.

I laid in the bed with my leg propped up, itching and cussing. Felt like I had a bunch of ants crawling around under my cast, looking for their next meal. There was no way to scratch either, the cast went all the way from my ankle to the top of my thigh.

I was weaving a basket out of a river birch trunk, trying to take my mind off the itching, when I heard a infernal noise and I looked out the window and seen Henry McAllan driving up on that tractor. He turned it off and got down.

"Hap?" he called out.

"Over here," I called back.

He come to the bedroom window and looked in. We howdyed and he asked how I was feeling.

"Whole lot better, thanks to that doctor Miz McAllan brung me," I said. "Sure am grateful to her for fetching him."

"I expect you are," he said. He lit a cigarette. "How much longer you gonna be in that cast?"

Behind him off in the distance I could see Florence and the children out plowing. I mean to tell you, setting there jawing with Henry McAllan while my family was toiling in the hot sun hurt me a lot worse than my leg. "Another month or so is all," I said.

"Is that a fact."

"Yessuh."

"You know, I broke my leg in the Great War. As I recollect, it was a couple of months before the cast came off, and longer than that before I could do any real work."

"I'm a fast healer, always have been," I said.

He took a drag off his cigarette. I waited, knowing what was coming. "The thing is, Hap, it's the second week of April," he said. "Y'all ought to be well into planting by now but you haven't even gotten your fields laid off."

"Soil has to be rebroke first on account of the rain."

"I'm aware of that. But if they were using a mule they'd be done in no time. As it is it'll be the end of the week before they even start fertilizing, much less getting that seed in the ground. There's just the three of them, Hap. I can't afford to wait any longer. You're a farmer, you understand that."

"It won't take that long. We got Lilly May helping too."

"A crippled little girl's not going to make the difference and you know it." He flicked his cigarette into the dirt. "You tell one of your boys to come fetch that mule after dinner today."

Then I looked on all the works that my hands had wrought, and on the labor that I had labored to do: and behold, all was vanity and vexation of spirit, and there was no profit under the sun.

"Yessuh," I said. The word stuck in my throat, but wasn't nothing else I could say. *That's it, Hap,* I told myself, *you a sharecropper again now, might as well get used to it.*

When Florence come in for dinner with the children I didn't even have to tell her, she took one look at my face and said, "He sending that mule, ain't he."

"Yeah. Starting this afternoon."

"Well," she said, "it'll make the plowing go faster anyway."

We set down to eat. It wasn't much of a meal, just fatback and grits one of the sisters from church had brung by earlier, but I said the blessing like always. When I was through Florence kept her head bent for a good long while. I knew what she was praying for. It was the same thing I'd been asking Him for every day since I fell off a that ladder: for Ronsel to come home and deliver us.

II.

LAURA

HENRY STAYED MAD at me, and he showed it by ignoring me in our bed. My husband was never an especially passionate man, but he'd always made love to me at least twice a week. In the first months of our marriage I'd felt awkward and reluctant (though I never refused him—I wouldn't have dreamed of it). But eventually we settled into an intimacy that was sweet and familiar, if not entirely fulfilling. He liked to do it at night, with one lamp on. At Mudbound it was one candle. That was his signal: the sound of the match head rasping against the striker. Joined with Henry, his body shuddering against mine, I felt very close to him and miles distant from him at the same time. He was experiencing sensations I wasn't, that much was plain to me, but I didn't expect ecstasy. I had no idea it was even possible for a woman. I hadn't always enjoyed Henry's lovemaking, but it made me feel like a true wife. I never realized how much I needed that until he turned away from me.

If my bed that April was cold, my days were hot, sweaty and grueling without Florence to help me. Henry hired Kester Cottrill's daughter Mattie Jane to come and clean for me, but she was slovenly and a chatterbox to boot, so after the first day I restricted her to laundry and other outdoor tasks. I saw Florence mostly from a distance, bent over a hoe, chopping out the weeds that threatened the tender cotton plants. Once I ran into her in town and started to complain about Mattie Jane. Florence gave me a look of incredulous scorn—*This is your idea of a problem?*—that shamed me into silence. I knew I should be grateful I wasn't spending twelve or more hours a day in the cotton fields, but it was poor consolation.

One Saturday at the end of April, the five of us went into town to do errands and have dinner at Dex's Diner, famed for its fried catfish and the sign outside that read:

JESUS LOVES YOU

MONDAY - FRIDAY 6:00-2:00

SATURDAYS 6:00-8:00

After we ate we stopped at Tricklebank's to get the week's provisions. Henry and Pappy lingered on the front porch with Orris Stokes and some other men, and the girls and I went inside to visit with the ladies. While I chatted with Rose, Amanda Leigh and Isabelle ran off to play with her two girls. Alice Stokes was there, radiantly pregnant, buying a length of poplin for a maternity dress. Wretched as I was, I couldn't bring myself to begrudge her happiness. We'd been chatting for a few minutes when a Negro soldier came in the back door. He was a tall young man with skin the color of strong tea. There were sergeant's stripes on his sleeves and a great many medals on his chest. He had a duffel bag slung over one broad shoulder.

"Howdy, Miz Tricklebank," he said. "Been a long time." His voice was sonorous and full of music. It rang out loudly in the confines of the store, startling the ladies.

"Is that you, Ronsel?" Rose said wonderingly.

He grinned. "Yes, ma'am, last time I looked."

So this was Florence's son. She'd told me all about him, of course. How smart he was, how handsome and brave. How he'd taken to book-learning like a fish to water. How he drew people to him like bees to honey, and so on. "Ain't just me talking mama nonsense," she'd declared. "Ronsel's got a shine to him, you'll see it the minute you lay eyes on him. The gals all want to be with him, and the men all want to be like him. They can't help it, they drawn to that shine."

I had thought it was mama nonsense, though I hadn't said so. What mother doesn't believe her firstborn son has more than his fair share of God's gifts? But when I saw Ronsel standing there in Tricklebank's, I understood exactly what she meant.

He dipped his head politely to me and the other ladies. "Afternoon," he said.

"Well, I declare," said Rose. "Aren't you grown up."

"How you been doing, Miz Tricklebank?"

"Getting along fine. You seen your folks yet?"

"No, ma'am," he said. "Bus just got in. I stopped to buy a few things for em."

I studied him as Rose helped him with his purchases. He

looked more like Hap, but he had Florence's way of filling up a room, and then some. You couldn't help but watch him; he had that kind of force. He glanced over at me curiously, and I realized he'd caught me staring. "I'm Mrs. McAllan," I said, a little embarrassed. "Your parents work on our farm."

"How do," he said. His eyes only met mine briefly, but in those few seconds I had the feeling I'd been thoroughly assessed.

"Do Hap and Florence know you're coming home?" I said.

"No, ma'am. I wanted to surprise em."

"Well, I know they'll be mighty glad to see you."

His forehead wrinkled in concern. "Are they all right?"

He didn't miss much, this son of Florence's. I hesitated, then told him about Hap's accident, emphasizing the positive. "He's using crutches now, and the doctor said he should be walking again by June."

"Thank God for that. He can't stand to be idle. He's probably driving Mama crazy, being underfoot all day."

Uneasily, I looked away from him. "What is it?" he asked.

I realized suddenly that the other women had gone dead silent and were watching us, making no effort at discretion. Some looked shocked, others hostile. Rose looked concerned, and her eyes held a warning.

I turned back to Ronsel. "Your parents lost their mule," I said, "and then we had a spell of bad weather. They're using our stock now. And your mother's working in the fields with your brothers."

His jaw tightened and his eyes turned cold. "Thank you for

telling me," he said. The ironic emphasis on the first two words was impossible to miss. I heard a sharp intake of breath from Alice Stokes.

"Excuse me," I said to Ronsel. "I have shopping to do."

As I walked away from him, I heard him say, "I'll come back for that cloth later, Miz Tricklebank. I better get on home now."

He paid Rose hurriedly and headed for the front door with his purchases and his duffel bag. Just before he reached the door, it opened and Pappy came in, followed by Orris Stokes and Doc Turpin. Ronsel stopped just short of running into them.

"Beg pardon," he said.

He tried to step around them, but Orris moved to stand in his way. "Well, looky here. A jig in uniform."

Ronsel's body went very still, and his eyes locked with Orris's. But then he dropped his gaze and said, "Sorry, suh. I wasn't paying attention."

"Where do you think you're going, boy?" said Doc Turpin.

"Just trying to get home to see my folks."

The door opened again, and Henry and a few other men came inside, crowding behind Pappy, Orris and Doc Turpin. All of them wore unfriendly expressions. I felt a flicker of fear.

"Honey," I called out to Henry, "this is Hap and Florence's son Ronsel, just returned from overseas."

"Well, that explains it then," drawled Pappy.

"Explains what?" said Ronsel.

"Why you're trying to leave by the front door. You must be confused as to your whereabouts."

"I ain't confused, suh."

"Oh, I think you are, boy," Pappy said. "I don't know what they let you do over there, but you're in Mississippi now. Niggers don't use the front here."

"Why don't you go out the back where you belong," said Orris.

"I think you'd better," said Henry. "Go on now."

It got very quiet. The air fairly crackled with hostility. I saw muscles tense and hands clench into fists. But if Ronsel was afraid, he didn't show it. He looked slowly around the store, meeting the eyes of every man and woman there, mine included. *Just go,* I pleaded with him silently. He let the moment drag out, waiting until just before the breaking point to speak.

"You know, suh, you're right," he said to Pappy. "We didn't go in the back over there, they put us right out in front. Right there on the front lines, face-to-face with the enemy. And that's where we stayed, the whole time we were there. The Jerries killed some of us, but in the end we kicked the hell out of em. Yessuh, we sure did."

With a nod to Rose, he turned and strode out the back door.

"Did you hear what he just said?" sputtered Pappy.

"Nigger like that ain't gonna last long around here," said Orris.

"Maybe we ought to teach him better manners," said Doc Turpin.

Things might have turned ugly, but Henry stepped forward and faced them, hands up and palms out. "No need for that. I'll have a word with his father."

For a moment I was afraid they wouldn't back down, but then Orris said, "See that you do, McAllan."

The men dispersed, and the tension lifted. I did my shopping and rounded up the girls, and we left Tricklebank's. On the way back to Mudbound, we came upon Ronsel walking down the middle of the road. He moved to one side to let us pass. As we went by him, I traded another glance with him through the open window of the car. His eyes were defiant, and they were shining.

RONSEL

HOME AGAIN, HOME AGAIN, jiggety-jig. Coon, spade, darky, nigger. Went off to fight for my country and came back to find it hadn't changed a bit. Black folks still riding in the back of the bus and coming in the back door, still picking the white folks' cotton and begging the white folks' pardon. Nevermind we'd answered their call and fought their war, to them we were still just niggers. And the black soldiers who'd died were just dead niggers.

Standing there in Tricklebank's, I knew exactly how much hot water I was in but I still couldn't shut my mouth long enough to keep myself from drowning. I was acting just like my buddy Jimmy back in our training days. I told him and told him he'd better humble down if he knew what was good for him, but Jimmy just shook his head and said he'd rather get beat up than act like a scared nigger. And he did get beat up, once in Louisiana and twice in Texas. The last time a bunch of local MPs roughed him up so bad he was in the infirmary for ten days, but Jimmy never did humble down. If we hadn't shipped out I think they might've killed him. When I told him that he just laughed and said, "I'd have liked to seen em try."

Jimmy would've been proud of me that day at Tricklebank's, but my daddy would've blistered my ears. All he knew was the Delta. He'd never walked down the street with his head held high, much less had folks lined up on either side cheering him and throwing flowers at him. The battles he'd fought were the kind nobody cheers you for winning, against sore feet and aching bones, too little rain or too much, heat and cotton worms and buried rocks that could break the blade of a plow. Ain't never a lull or a cease-fire. Win today, you got to get up tomorrow and fight the same battles all over again. Lose and you can lose everything. Only a fool fights a war with them kind of odds, or a man who ain't got no other choice.

Daddy had aged a considerable bit in the two years since I'd last seen him. There was white in his hair and new worry lines around his eyes. He'd lost weight he didn't need to lose too, Mama said that was since he broke his leg. But his voice was as strong and sure as ever. The day I got home I could hear it from way out in the yard, thanking God for the food they were about to eat and the sun He'd been sending lately to make the cotton grow, and for the health of all here present including the laying hens and the pregnant sow, and for watching over me wherever in creation I was. Which by that time was standing right in the doorway.

"Amen," I said.

For a minute nobody moved, they all just set there gawping at me like they didn't recognize me. "Well?" I said. "Ain't nobody gone offer me some supper?"

"Ronsel!" yelled Ruel, with Marlon a half second behind him like always.

Then they were up and hugging me, and Mama and Lilly May were kissing my face and carrying on about how big and handsome I was and asking me how was my trip and when did I get back to the States and how come I hadn't wrote to tell them I was on my way home. Finally Daddy hollered, "Quit fussing over him now and let him say hello to his father."

He was setting there with his leg propped up on a stool. He held out his arms and I went and gave him a big hug, then knelt down by him so he wouldn't have to look up at me.

"I knew you'd come," he said. "I prayed for it, and here you are."

"And here you are with your leg in a cast. How'd you manage to do that?"

"It's a long story. Why don't you set down and eat and I'll tell you all about it."

I couldn't help smiling. With my daddy, everything's a long story. I heaped my plate. There was salt pork and beans and pickled okra, with Mama's biscuits to sop up the juice.

"I used to daydream about these biscuits," I said. "I'd be setting on top of my tank eating my C rations—"

"What's a sea ration?" said Ruel.

"Is that some kind of fish?" said Marlon.

"C like the letter C, not like the ocean. It's Army food. I brought some home so you could try them. They're in my bag. Go on, you can look."

The twins ran over to my duffel bag, opening it and pulling everything out onto the floor. Still a couple of kids, though they were near as tall as me. Made me a little sad to watch them, so young and eager. I knew they wouldn't stay that way much longer.

"Anyway," I said to Mama, "I told all the guys about your biscuits. By the time the Jerries surrendered I had every man in the company dreaming of them, even the Yankee lieutenants."

"I dreamed about you," Mama said.

"What did you dream?"

She shook her head, running her hands up over her arms like she was cold.

"Tell me, Mama."

"It don't matter, none of it come true. You back with us now, safe and sound."

"Back where you belong," Daddy said.

AFTER DINNER THE two of us were having a jaw on the porch when we seen a truck coming down the road. It pulled up in our yard and Henry McAllan got out.

"Wonder what that man wants now?" said Daddy.

I got to my feet. "I reckon he wants to talk to me."

"Why in the world would Henry McAllan want to talk to you?" said Daddy.

I didn't answer. McAllan was already at the foot of the steps.

"Afternoon, Mist McAllan," said Daddy.

"Afternoon, Hap."

"Ronsel, this is our landlord. This here's my son Ronsel that I been telling you bout."

"We've met," said McAllan.

Daddy turned to me, worried now.

"I better speak with you alone, Hap," said McAllan.

"I ain't a child, sir," I said. "If you got something to say, you can say it to my face."

"All right then. Let me ask you a question. You planning on staying here and helping your father?"

"Yes, sir."

"Well, you're not helping him, acting like you did earlier at Tricklebank's. You're just helping yourself to a heap of trouble, and your family too."

"What'd you do?" asked Daddy.

"Nothing," I said. "Just tried to walk out the door is all."

"The front door," McAllan said, "and when my father and some other men objected to it he made a fine speech. Put us all in our place, didn't you?"

"Is that true?" said Daddy.

I nodded.

"Then I reckon you better apologize."

McAllan waited, his pale eyes fixed on me. I didn't have a choice and he knew it. He might as well to been God Almighty as far as we were concerned. I made myself say the words. "I'm sorry, Mr. McAllan."

"My father will want to hear it too."

"Ronsel will pay him a visit after church tomorrow," said Daddy. "Won't you, son?"

"Yes, Daddy."

"That's fine then," said McAllan. "Let me tell you something else, Ronsel. I don't hold with everything my father says, but he's right about one thing. You're back in Mississippi now, and you better start remembering it. I'm sure Hap would like to have you around here for a good long while."

"Yessuh, I would," said Daddy.

"Well then. Y'all enjoy your Saturday."

As he turned to leave, I said, "One more thing, sir."

"What?"

"We won't be needing that mule of yours much longer."

"How's that?"

"I aim to buy us one of our own just as soon as I can find a good one."

Daddy's jaw dropped. I heard a little gasp from inside the house and knew Mama was listening too. I'd wanted to buy it first and surprise them with it, but I wanted to knock Henry McAllan down a peg even more.

"Mules cost a lot of money," he said.

"I know what they cost."

McAllan looked at my father. "All right, Hap, you let me know when he finds one. In the meantime I'll rent you mine on a day-to-day basis. I'll just put it on your account and we can settle after the harvest."

"I'll settle with you in cash soon as I get that mule," I told him.

I could tell Henry McAllan didn't like that, not one bit. His voice had a sharp edge to it when he answered. "Like I said, Hap, I'll just put it on your account."

Daddy laid a hand on my arm. "Yessuh, that'll be fine," he said.

McAllan got in his truck and started up the engine. As he

was about to pull away, he called out, "Don't forget to stop by the house tomorrow, boy."

I watched the truck disappear into the falling dusk. The whippoorwills had started their pleading and the lightning bugs were winking in and out over the purpling fields. The land looked soft and welcoming, but I knew what a lie that was.

"No point in fighting em," said Daddy. "They just gone win every time."

"I ain't used to walking away from a fight. Not anymore."

"You better get used to it, son. For all our sakes."

WE FOUGHT FOR six months straight across France, Belgium, Luxembourg, Holland, Germany and Austria. With the different infantry battalions we were attached to, we killed thousands of German soldiers. It wasn't personal. The Jerries were the enemy, and while I tried to account for as many as I could, I didn't hate them. Not till the twenty-ninth of April 1945. That was the day we got to Dachau.

We didn't know what it was even, just that it was in our way. Nary one of us had ever heard of a concentration camp before. There'd been rumors floating around about Germans mistreating POWs, but we thought they were just tall tales meant to scare us into fighting harder.

By then I'd gotten my own tank command. Sam was my bow gunner. We were driving toward Munich a few miles ahead of the infantry when we caught the smell, a stink worse than any-

thing I'd ever smelled in my life, and by that time I'd smelled
plenty of corpses. About a mile later we came to a compound
fenced all around by a concrete wall, looked like a regular
military post from the outside. There was a big iron gate set
in the wall with German writing on the top. Then we seen the
people lined up in front of the gate, naked people with sticks
for arms and legs. SS soldiers were walking up and down the
lines, shooting them with machine guns. They were falling in
waves, falling down dead right in front of us. Sam took out the
soldiers while Captain Scott's tank busted down the gate.

Hundreds of people—if you can call skin scraped over a
pile of bones a person—came staggering out of there. Their
heads were shaved and they were filthy and covered with sores.
Some of them ran off down the road but most of them were
just walking around in a daze. Then they caught sight of this
dead horse that'd been hit by a shell. It was like watching ants
on a watermelon rind. They swarmed the carcass, ripping off
pieces of it and eating them. It was horrible to see, horrible. I
heard one of the guys retching behind me.

We followed the sound of gunshots to this big barnlike
building. It was on fire and I could smell roasting flesh. We
came around the corner and seen more SS soldiers shooting
at people inside. The building was full of bodies stacked six
foot high on top of one another, smoking and burning. Some
of them were still alive and they were crawling over the dead
ones, trying to get out. The SS soldiers were standing there
just as calm as they could be, shooting anybody that moved.

We opened fire on those motherfuckers. Some of them ran and we got out of the tank and chased them down and shot them. I took out two myself, shooting them in the back as they were running away from me, and I felt nothing but glad.

I was walking back to my tank when a woman tottered over to me with her hands stretched out toward me. She had on a ragged striped shirt but she was naked from the waist down—that's the only way I could tell she was a woman. Her eyes were sunk way back in the sockets and she had sores all over her legs. She looked like a walking corpse. I started backing away from her but I stepped in a hole and fell and then she was on me, clutching me, jabbering nonstop in whatever language she spoke. I was pushing her away, yelling at her to get the fuck off me, when all the strength seemed to go out of her and she went limp. I laid there underneath her and stared up at the sky—such a pale pretty blue, like nothing bad had ever happened under it or ever could happen. Her weight on me was light as a blanket, so light she was hardly there at all. But then I felt the warmth of her body through my uniform. I ain't never been so ashamed of myself. It wasn't her fault if she seemed less than human, it was the fault of them that did this to her, and them that didn't raise a voice against it.

I sat up, trying to be careful. Her head was laying in my lap and she was looking up at me like I was her sweetheart, like the sight of me was everything she ever hoped for in this world. I rooted around in my pockets and found a chocolate bar. I unwrapped it and gave it to her. She sat up and crammed the whole thing in her mouth, like she was afraid I was going

to change my mind and take it away from her. I felt a shadow
on me and looked up and seen other prisoners surrounding
us, dozens of them, ragged and stinking and pitiful. Some
were talking and making eating motions with their hands and
mouths, and some were just standing there quiet as ghosts. I
was feeling around in my pockets to see what other food I had
when the woman in my lap curled up into a ball, moaning and
grabbing her stomach.

"What's the matter?" I said. "What's the matter with you?"
But she just laid there jerking and moaning like she was gut-
shot. It went on a long while and there wasn't nothing I could
do. Finally she went still. I put my head on her chest and listened but I couldn't hear a heartbeat. Her eyes were wide and
staring. They were blue, the same pale blue as the sky.

"Ronsel!"

I looked through the stick-thin legs of the prisoners and
seen Sam walking toward me. Tears were running down his
face. "Medic says not to feed em," he said. "Says it can kill em
since they ain't eaten in so long."

I looked back down at her, the woman I'd just killed with
a chocolate bar. I wondered what her name was and who her
people were. I wondered whether anybody ever held her like
I was doing, whether anybody ever stroked her hair. I hoped
somebody did, before she came to this place.

I NEVER THOUGHT I'd miss it so much. I don't mean
Nazi Germany, you'd have to be crazy to miss a place like that.

I mean who I was when I was over there. There I was a libera-
tor, a hero. In Mississippi I was just another nigger pushing a
plow. And the longer I stayed, the more that's all I was.

I was in town picking up some feed for the new mule when
I ran into Josie Hayes. Well, she was Josie Dupock now—she'd
gone and married Lem Dupock last September. Josie and me
used to walk out together before the war. I was real sweet on
her, even thought about marrying her. But when I joined up
she was so vexed with me she wouldn't see me or speak to me,
and I ended up leaving Marietta without saying goodbye to
her. I sent her a few letters but she never wrote back, and after
awhile I just let it go. So when I seen her there on Main Street,
I wasn't sure what to expect.

"Heard you was back," she said.

"Yeah. Got home about two months ago. How you been?"

"Been fine. I'm married now."

"Yeah, Daddy wrote and told me."

A silence came down between us. Time I knew Josie we
were always laughing and jollying. I used to tickle her till she
squealed but she never tried to get away, just wriggled and
giggled and if I stopped she'd tease me till I started up again.
She didn't look like she did much laughing now. She was still
a fine-looking gal but her eyes had hardened up, and I had a
good idea of why. Lem and me went to school together. He
was the kind always starting trouble and never ending up with
the blame, just setting off to the side smiling while the rest of
us were getting our butts switched. When we got older he was
always slipping around at the gals, had him two or three at a

time. Lem Dupock wouldn't never give a woman nothing but tears, I could've told Josie that a long time ago.

"Ain't seen you in church," I said.

"Ain't been there. Lem ain't the church-going kind."

I hesitated, then asked, "He treating you all right?"

"What's it to you, how he's treating me?"

Not a damn thing I could say to that. "Well," I said, "I'd best be getting on home, Josie. You take care of yourself."

I started to head back to the wagon but she grabbed ahold of my arm. "Don't go, Ronsel. I need to talk to you."

"What about?"

"Bout us."

"Ain't no us, Josie. You seen to that five years ago."

"Please. There's some things I want to say to you."

"I'm listening."

"Not here. Meet me tonight."

"Where?"

"My house. Lem's gone, he went down to Jackson. I ain't expecting him back till next week."

"I don't know, Josie," I said.

"Please."

I knew I shouldn't have gone over there but I went anyway. Ate the supper she fixed me and talked about old times. Let her tell me how sorry she was. Let her show me. Josie and me used to fool around some but we never laid down together. I'd imagined it plenty of times though, how it would feel to have her and to let her have me. Afterward we'd snuggle up and talk and laugh together, that was how I always pictured it.

It wasn't nothing like that. It was sad and lonesome during and stone quiet after. I thought Josie was asleep but then in a husky voice she said, "Where you gone to, Ronsel? Who you thinking bout?"

I didn't tell her the truth: that I was all the way to Germany, thinking about a white woman named Resl, and the man I was when I was with her.

HER FULL NAME was Theresia Huber, Resl was just a nickname. That surprised me at first, that the Germans would have nicknames like we did. Shows you how well the Army trained us not to think of them as human.

Resl's husband was a tanker too, he got killed at Strasbourg. That was one of the first things she asked me: "Vas you at Strasbourg?" I was glad I could tell her no. She had a six-year-old daughter, name of Maria, a shy little thing with dark blue eyes and hair white as cotton. That was how I met Resl in the first place, was through Maria. When we rolled into a town the women would send their children out to beg us for food. German or not, it was a hard thing watching hungry kids rooting around in garbage cans, so we always kept some extra rations in our mess kits. The day we got to Teisendorf there were more kids than usual swarming around our tanks. Maria was hanging back a little like she was afraid. I went over to her and asked her name. She didn't answer, I reckoned she didn't understand me, so I pointed at my chest and said "Ronsel" then pointed at hers. But she just stood there looking up at me

with eyes too big for her face. Child that age should've still had
baby fat in her cheeks but hers were hollowed out. I gave her
all my extra rations that day and the next. The third day she
took me by the hand and led me back to her house. Sam went
with me. We always went in pairs, just in case. Even though
the Jerries had surrendered, you could still run into trouble in
some of them little Bavarian towns—SS soldiers hiding out in
somebody's cellar, that kind of thing. But when we got to the
house all we found was Resl, waiting for us with hot soup and
a little old loaf of brown bread about the size of my hand. We
gave her our rations and told her we weren't hungry but she
kept on pushing the food at us. We could tell it was hurting her
feelings that we wouldn't eat so finally we had some. The soup
was mostly water with a few potatoes and onions floating in
it and the bread like to broke our teeth, but we made "mmm"
sounds and told her it was good.

"Goot!" she said. Then she smiled for the first time and my
breath caught. Resl was that sorrowful kind of pretty that's
even prettier than the happy kind. Some women get like that,
hard times just pares them down till all that's left is their
beauty. I'd seen it at home amongst my own people too but
somehow it was different over there, and not just because the
faces were white. Here was a woman who'd never wanted for a
thing in her life and now all of a sudden she had nothing—no
husband, no food, no hope. Well, not nothing, she had her
daughter and her pride, and those were the two things she
lived for.

Resl's English wasn't too good and I hardly spoke ten words

of German, but that don't matter between a man and a woman
who understand each other. Up to that point I'd stayed away
from the fräuleins—after whatall I seen at Dachau I just
didn't want to mess with them—but plenty of the other guys
had German sweethearts. Jimmy taken up with this gal, she
wasn't even a fräulein, she was a frau, meaning a missus with a
live husband. Jimmy met her up in Bissingen, the first town we
occupied after the cease-fire, and when we left there to go to
Teisendorf she followed after him. There were plenty of others
like her too. I used to wonder what would make a woman want
to transact herself that way, want to leave her husband and
take up with a colored man who'd laid waste to her country
and killed her people. But after knowing Resl awhile I started
to understand it better. It wasn't just that she'd been without a
man for two years and here I was giving her food and whatever
else she wanted from me. That was part of it, sure, but there
was more to it than that. The two of us had something in common. Her people were conquered and despised, just like mine
were. And just like me, Resl was hungry to be treated like a
human being.

I spent every spare minute I had at her house. With the
money and provisions I gave her, she made dumplings and
sauerkraut and rye bread, and sausage when we could get it.
Every night after she put Maria to bed, Resl and me would set
on the couch for a spell. Sometimes she'd talk in German in a
low sad voice—remembering how things used to be, I guessed.
Sometimes I'd tell her about the Delta: how the sky was so big
it shrank you to nothing, and how in the summertime the lint

from the cotton laid a fuzzy coat of white over everything in
the house. Then after awhile I'd feel her tug at my hand and
we'd go upstairs. I'd been with a fair number of women by that
time, I never made a dog of myself like some of the guys but I'd
had my share of romances. But I never felt nothing like I felt
with Resl in the nights. She gave her whole self to me, didn't
hold back, and before too long I didn't either. When I was on
duty I'd be thinking about her the whole time, got to where I
could smell her scent even when I wasn't with her. One time in
the quiet after, she put her hand on my chest and whispered,
"Mein Mann." I was happy to be her man and I told her so,
but later I found out from Jimmy it also meant "my husband."
That fretted me for a few days, till I made myself see the truth.
The way we were together, we might as well to been man and
wife.

So in September when most of the other guys took their dis-
charges and headed home, I volunteered to stay in Teisendorf.
Lot of greenhorns were coming over from the States to replace
the guys who'd shipped out, and the Army needed seasoned
men to show them the ropes. Jimmy and Sam told me I was
crazy for staying, but I couldn't stand to leave Resl. First time
I ever lied to my mama and daddy was when I wrote and told
them the Army wasn't ready to let me go yet. I didn't like to do
it but Daddy wouldn't have understood the truth. Me loving
a white woman, he might've come around to that, though he
would've told me I was a damn fool. But me not jumping at the
first chance to come home—that, he never would've understood, not if he had a hundred years to think about it.

But then in March the Army gave me a choice: either re-enlist or ship out for the States. I wasn't about to sign up for four more years of soldiering so I took my discharge. Lot of tears over it but there wasn't nothing else I could do. I couldn't stay in Germany, and I damn sure couldn't bring Resl and Maria home with me. On the boat to New York I told myself it was just one of them things, just a wartime romance that was never meant to last, between two people who didn't have nobody else.

Till that night with Josie I even believed it.

FLORENCE

EVERY DAY I asked God, *Please send him home to us.*
Send him home whole and right in his mind. And if that's too
much to ask of You just let him be right in his mind and not
like my uncle Zeb, who come back from the Great War with all
his parts but touched in the head. One morning my mama and
I went out to the yard and found all six of our hens laid out
in a neat row with their necks wrung and Uncle Zeb laying
sound asleep at the end of the row like he was number seven.
Few weeks later he wandered off and we never laid eyes on
him again.

Four years I prayed for my son to come home. The first two
years we only seen him twice, that was when he was still in
training in Louisiana and Texas. We was hoping he'd miss out
on all the fighting but then in the summer of '44 they sent him
over there, smack dab in the middle of it. Every now and then
there'd be an article about his battalion in the *AFRO American*
and Hap would read it out loud to me. Course by the time we
got ahold of the paper it was usually a month old or more and
Ronsel was long gone from wherever they was writing about.

Same with his letters, it took em forever to reach us. Whenever we got one I'd hold it in my hand and wonder if he was being shot at or lying somewhere bleeding or dead right at that moment, but the marks on the paper didn't tell me. And when the war was over and he didn't come home, them marks didn't tell me why. Ronsel was always after me to learn how to read but I don't see the point of it myself. Writing on a paper ain't flesh and blood under your roof.

But there's a old word that goes, "Be careful what you wish for or you might just get it." God answered all my prayers. He sent my son home safe and with enough money for a new mule too. We was back to working on a quarter share and I was keeping house again for Miz McAllan while Lilly May stayed home and looked after her father. (Well, I didn't exactly pray to keep Laura McAllan's house but I sure did like the extra money.) Hap was getting around good on his crutches, preaching again on Sundays and spinning his old dreams, talking bout getting a second mule and taking on more acres and saving up to buy his own land. Marlon and Ruel loved having their big brother back. They followed him around like puppies, pestering him for stories about the places he seen and the battles he was in. Oh yes, we all got our wishes, all on account of Ronsel, and all except for him.

What he wanted was to leave. He never said so—I didn't raise my children to be complainers—but I could tell he wasn't happy from the day he got home. At first I thought he was just vexed on account of that ugly business at Tricklebank's with ole Mist McAllan and them other no-count white men. Told myself he'd been away a long while and just needed to get hisself settled back in, but that didn't happen. He was jumpy and broody, and he twitched and moaned in his sleep. When he wasn't working in the fields he was writing letters to his Army friends or setting on the porch steps staring off at nothing. Didn't talk at mealtimes, wasn't chatting up the gals at church. That fretted me more than anything. What man don't want a woman's arms around him after he's just got done fighting a war?

Part of him was still fighting it, I knowed that from his sleep talk. I reckoned he seen some pretty terrible things over there and maybe done some too, things that wasn't setting easy with him. But I also knowed it wasn't just the war troubling him. It was the Delta, pressing in on him and squeezing the life right out of him. And we was too, by wanting him to stay.

Hap said that was hooey. Said I worried too much about Ronsel and always had. Maybe that was true and maybe not but I knowed my son and it wasn't like him to be so quiet. Four of my five children come peaceful into the world, but not Ronsel. When I was carrying him he squirmed all day and kicked all night. My aunt Sarah, she taught me midwifing, she said all that ruckus was a good sign, it meant the baby was healthy. "Well," I told her, "I sure am glad somebody's feeling good cause I'm plumb wore out." Then when I went into labor, Ronsel decided he was just gone stay put. I labored thirty-two hours with him. He like to tore me in two coming out and when he finally did he bout busted our ears with his squalling. Aunt Sarah didn't even have to turn him upside down and swat him, his lungs already knowed what to do.

After all that I thought I was gone have a devil baby on my hands but Ronsel was just as sweet as he could be. Strong too. Before he was even a year old he was walking. I'd set him on a pallet at the end of the row I was picking and here he'd come, toddling down that row, wanting my breast. He was always babbling and singing to hisself. His first word was *Ha!* and he said it fifty times a day, pointing at his foot or a cloud or a cotton worm, any little thing that caught his eye. By the time he was three he was talking up a storm, wanting to know everything bout everything. Come time to go to school he was always itching to go, and always hangdogging around during planting and picking time when school was closed. When he finished eighth grade his teacher come to see me, said Ronsel had a gift. Well, she wasn't telling me nothing I didn't already know. She said if we'd let him come in the afternoons she'd keep on teaching him. I had a wrangle with Hap over that, he wanted Ronsel helping him full-time in the fields. But I stood my ground, told Hap we had to let our son use whatall the Lord seen fit to give him, not just his strong back and his strong arms.

"You sure this is what you want?" Hap asked him.

"Yes, Daddy."

"You'll still have to help me till two o'clock every day and get all your chores done besides. Won't leave you no time for fishing or having fun."

"I don't mind," Ronsel said.

Hap just shook his head and let him go. And when the war come and Ronsel was hell-bent on joining the white man's army, Hap didn't understand that either but he let him.

When I looked at my children I could see me and Hap in all of em. And I loved my husband and myself too, and so I loved our children. But when I looked at Ronsel I seen something more, something me and Hap couldn't a gave him cause we ain't got it. A shine so bright it hurt your eyes sometimes but you still had to look at it.

I loved all my children, but I loved Ronsel the most. If that was a sin I reckoned God would forgive me for it, seeing as how He the one stacked the cards in the first place.

LAURA

THE COTTON BLOOMED at the end of May. It was magical, like being surrounded by thousands of little white fairies, shimmering in the sunlight. The blooms turned pink after a few days and fell off, revealing green bolls no bigger than my fingertip. They would ripen over the summer and burst open in August. My own time would come right around the new year. My morning sickness had started in early May, so I reckoned I was about two months pregnant.

I wanted to be certain before I told Henry. There was no obstetrician in Marietta, much less a hospital; most women had their babies at home with Doc Turpin. I had no intention of going that route if I could help it. I was about to ask Eboline for the name of her doctor in Greenville when I received a timely invitation from Pearce to attend Lucy's confirmation at Calvary at the end of June. Lucy was my goddaughter as well as my niece; of course I had to go. And while I was in Memphis, I would pay a visit to my old obstetrician, Dr. Brownlee.

Henry couldn't spare the time to accompany me, but he agreed to let me and the girls go for a week. Seven days in civilization! Seven days with no mud, no outhouse and no Pappy. It was a heady prospect. I would have a hot bath every day, twice a day if I wanted to. I would call people on the telephone and have afternoon tea at the Peabody and visit the Renoirs at the museum. I might even lie awake in bed at night and read a book by lamplight that didn't flicker.

Henry drove us to the train station. He went at his usual leisurely pace, slowing often to look at the farms we passed and compare the growth of their cotton, soybeans, and corn to ours. I wanted to tell him to hurry up or we'd miss the train, but I knew he couldn't help himself. Henry never had much use for nature in its untouched state. Forests didn't move him, nor mountains, nor even the sea, but show him a well-tended farm and he was breathless with excitement.

We arrived at the station with ten whole minutes to spare. Henry kissed the girls and exacted solemn promises from them to be good and mind me. Then he turned to me. "I'll miss you," he said. Time and the daily sight of his cotton thriving had thawed him considerably, though he was still touchy about his authority and had only just resumed our intimate relations in the last week.

"I wish you could come with us," I said.

As soon as the words were out of my mouth I realized they weren't true. I wanted some time away from him, not just from Pappy and the farm. I wondered if Henry suspected how I felt.

"You know I can't be away for that long, not this time of year," he said. "Besides, you girls will have more fun without me along."

"I'll write to you every day."

He bent and kissed me. "You just make sure and come back, hear? I couldn't do without you."

He said it lightly, with a smile, but I thought I detected a faint undercurrent of worry in his voice. I felt a twinge of guilt at that, but not nearly enough to make myself say, *I'm not going after all, not without you.*

The train ride seemed interminable to me. It was stiflingly hot, and the sooty air that blew through the open windows made me queasy. But to the children, who had never been on a train before, it was a grand adventure. My parents met us at the station, Daddy with a big hug and Mother with the expected flood of tears.

It was wonderful, after five months of exile, to be among my own people again. To stand in church and hear the voices of my family, young and old and in-between, ringing out on every side of me. To sit between my sisters on Etta's wicker glider and sip sweet tea while our children chased lightning bugs together in the slowgathering dusk. And best of all, to share my joyful news, once Dr. Brownlee had confirmed it, with all of them, and be the object of their tender fussing. At any other time, I might have padlocked myself to my old bed in my parents' house and thrown away the key rather than return to Mudbound. But within a few days, I began to want Henry: the groan of his weight settling onto the mattress beside me at night; the damp, heavy press of his arm across my waist; the rasp of his breathing as I fell asleep. I never felt more in love with my husband than when I was carrying his children.

I reckon that's the Lawd's doing—that's what Florence would have said.

The night before we were to return, just as I was about to turn off the bedside lamp, I heard a soft drumming of fingernails on my door. My mother came in and sat on the edge of the bed, bringing the familiar smell of Shalimar with her. It was Daddy's favorite scent and she never wore any other, just like she never cut her hair because he liked it long. During the day she wore it pinned up, but now it hung like a girl's in a long silver plait down her back. She was seventy-one years old, and to me, as lovely as ever. And as maddeningly indirect.

"I've been thinking about your brother," she said.

"Pearce?" Pearce was the one of us she worried the most about, because he was entirely too serious and had married into money.

"No, Teddy," she said. Teddy was her favorite, though she'd always tried valiantly to hide the fact. Teddy was everybody's favorite. He was a natural clown; he didn't hesitate to spend his dignity, and we all loved him for it, even Pearce.

"What about him?"

"I was just about your age when I was carrying him, you know."

I'd heard the story many times: How she'd conceived at thirty-eight, after the doctor had told her she'd never have another child. How it had been the most trouble-free pregnancy and shortest labor of them all.

"The last baby came the easiest," I said, quoting the familiar ending to the story. "I hope it'll be the same for me."

"Except Teddy wasn't the last baby," my mother said in a low voice.

"What do you mean?"

"He was a twin. His little sister was stillborn ten minutes after him. She barely weighed four pounds."

"Oh, Mother. Does Teddy know?"

"No, and don't you ever tell him," she said. "I don't want it haunting him like it has me. I should have listened to the doctor, he warned me not to get pregnant again. He said I was too old, that my body couldn't take the strain, but I thought I knew better. And so that poor little child, your sister—" She broke off and looked down at her hands.

"Is that why you're telling me this?" I asked. "Because you're afraid for me?" She nodded. "But Mother, if you hadn't gotten pregnant again, you wouldn't have had Teddy. And how could any of us bear it without him? We couldn't."

She gave my hand a hard squeeze. "You just be extra careful not to strain yourself," she said. "Let Henry and your colored girl do for you, and if you feel tired, rest. You rest even if you aren't tired, for a couple of hours every afternoon. Promise me."

"I will, Mother, I promise. But you're worrying for nothing. I feel fine."

She reached out and stroked my hair just as she had when I was a child. I closed my eyes and let sleep take me, feeling utterly safe.

• • •

THE NEXT DAY, I returned to the farm, if not quite eagerly, then at least willingly. Henry was thrilled by my news. "This one will be a boy," he said. "I feel it in my bones."

I hoped his bones were right. Not that I didn't adore my girls, but I wanted the fiercer, less complicated love, unsullied by judgment and comparisons to one's own self, that my sisters had for their sons, and my brothers for their daughters.

"Well, one thing's for sure," said Florence, the day I told her I was pregnant. "You definitely carrying a male child."

"What makes you say that?"

"I've knowed for almost two months now. The signs are all there, plain as the nose on your face."

I ignored the implication that she'd known I was pregnant before I had. "What signs?" I asked.

"Well, you ain't had much morning sickness, that's one way you can tell it's a boy. And you craving meat and cheese more than sweets."

"I always do."

"Besides," she said, with a decisive wave of her hand, "the pillows on your bed are to the north."

"What difference does that make?"

The lift of her eyebrows sent a clear message: How could I possibly be so ignorant of such a universally known fact? "You'll see, six months from now," she said.

Things between the two of us were much the same as they had been, but she was noticeably stiffer around Pappy and, to a lesser extent, Henry. That was because of the trouble with Ronsel, I knew. We hadn't seen much of him since the day he'd come to apologize to the old man, and for Ronsel's sake I was glad. He and Pappy weren't oil and water, they were oil and flame. Best for all concerned if they stayed far apart.

Unfortunately I had no such option with respect to my father-in-law. He was constantly underfoot and more cantankerous than ever once Henry put him to work helping me and Florence around the house. Henry was always protective of me when I was pregnant, but this time he was positively Draconian: under no circumstances was I to risk any sort of exertion. Florence could do only so much in a day, so it fell to Pappy to help with the hauling, milking, churning and so on.

"You'd think a man would be allowed to enjoy the fruits of his labor in his old age," he said. "You'd think his family wouldn't put him to work like a nigger."

"It's only for a little while, Pappy," I said. "Just to make sure you have a healthy grandchild."

He snorted. "Just what I need. Another granddaughter."

JULY SPED BY. The weather got hotter and the cotton grew. I wasn't showing much yet, but I could feel the baby's presence inside of me, a tiny spark I fed with prayers and whispered exhortations to grow and be well. My pregnancy had completely healed the breach between Henry and me, unraveling our anger and knitting us back together again. We began to talk about what we would do when the baby was born. There was no question of our staying on the farm with an infant. Henry promised we'd look for a house to rent right after the

harvest. If necessary, he said, we'd live in one of the neigh-
boring towns, Tchula or Belzoni, even though it would mean
a longer drive for him. The thought of being in a real house
again was exhilarating. I began to feel a certain wistful nostalgia for Mudbound—now that I knew I was leaving it—and
even occasionally to enjoy its rustic charms.

It was on such a day, an unusually balmy Saturday toward
the end of July, that disaster struck. As usual when anything
bad happened, Henry was away. He and Pappy had gone to
Lake Village to see about some hogs, so I was alone with the
girls. They were making mud pies by the pump and I was sitting under the oak mending one of Henry's shirts. There was
a nice breeze and a sweet smell of poison in the air; the crop
dusters had flown over that morning. I must have nodded off,
because I didn't see Vera Atwood come into the yard. I woke
to the sound of her girlish voice, loud and shrill. "Where's your
mama at?" she was saying. "Where is she?"

"I'm right here, Vera," I said.

She whirled and looked at me. Her breath was coming in
whistling gasps, and her dress was drenched with sweat. She
must have run all the way to our house.

"What's the matter?" I said.

"You got to take me to town," she said. "I'm gonna kill
Carl."

It was then that I saw the butcher knife in her hand. I felt a
surge of raw fear. The girls were standing just a few feet away
from her. I stood and said, "Come here, Vera. Come and tell
me what's happened."

She came, staggering a little. The girls started to follow, but I made a shooing motion with my fingers. Amanda Leigh took her sister's hand and held her back.

"He's started in on Alma," said Vera.

"What do you mean?"

"He's started in on her just like he done with Renie. I got to stop him. You got to take me."

"He beat her?"

"No."

When I took her meaning my body went cold despite the heat. Renie was the eldest Atwood girl, the one whose baby Florence had delivered in February, just two months before Vera's own. Both children had died within a few days of being born—crib death, Florence had told me.

"He ain't gonna have Alma too, not if I can help it," Vera said.

"Where is he now?"

"He went to town to get some shotgun shells. Said he's taking her hunting this afternoon."

Just keep her talking, I thought. Henry and Pappy were due back any time now. "Hunting?" I said.

"That's how he started with Renie, taking her out to the woods with him."

"How can you be sure? That he . . .?"

"Renie wouldn't eat nothing they brought back. Deer, rabbit, squirrel—didn't matter what it was, she wouldn't touch it. Said she wasn't hungry. But Carl sure was. Set there gobbling that food like he hadn't et in a week, gnawing on the bones and talking about how nothing tastes better than meat you hunted and brought down yourself. 'Ain't that right, Renie,' he says to her. And her setting there skinny as a rail, staring at that food like it was full of maggots."

Vera was rocking back and forth on the balls of her bare feet, the knife swinging at her side. Her head was tilted, and her eyes were wide and unfocused. She looked like a woman I'd seen once at a hypnotist's show at the state fair.

Just keep her talking. "Did you say anything to him about it?" I asked.

"No. He would have just denied it. When Renie started to show I asked her who done it but she wouldn't say, not even when I got after her with the switch. Just stood there real quiet and took it like she deserved a whupping. I knew right then but I didn't want to know. I told myself if it was a boy then it wasn't but if it was a girl then it was, that would be the proof cause Carl ain't got nothing in him but girls. And when that baby came out and I seen its parts, I knew it for his seed."

I stole a glance at Amanda Leigh and Isabelle. Their gingham dresses were spattered with mud. A streak of it ran across Isabelle's forehead where she'd brushed her bangs out of her eyes, and she was sucking on her thumb, watching us.

"Look at me," Vera demanded.

I obeyed instantly.

"You look at me," she said.

"I'm looking, Vera. I see you."

"A few days after it was born I came in the bedroom and found Carl holding it. He had his finger in its mouth and the baby was sucking on it, and Renie was laying there watching em. Right then I decided to do it."

"What?" I asked. But I knew.

"I waited till they was all asleep that night. And then I took a pillow and I sent that baby out of his reach, like I hadn't done for Renie."

"And your own baby?"

Her face contorted, and then she was standing right beside me and the knife was touching the side of my neck. I could hear my heart thundering in my ears. "You got to drive me to town *now*," she said.

Her breath smelled of rotting teeth. Fighting back nausea, I said, "Vera, listen to me. My husband will be back soon. When he gets here, we'll talk to him. Henry will know what to do."

"No," said Vera, "I can't wait. We got to go now. Come on."

She jerked me by the arm, pulling me toward the truck, but the key wasn't in it; it was hanging on a nail by the front door. Amanda Leigh and Isabelle were watching us with big frightened eyes. What would I do with them? I couldn't leave them alone on the farm—they were too little, anything might happen to them. But how could I take them with us? I didn't think Vera would harm them, but in the wild state she was in I couldn't be sure. I pictured Carl's red lips pressed to Alma's. Pictured Vera sitting next to my children in the truck with the butcher knife in her hand.

"I can't, Vera," I said.

"Why not?"

"Henry doesn't let me drive the truck. I'm not even sure where he keeps the key."

"You're lying."

"I swear it's true. The one time I tried to drive it I almost wrecked it. See that big dent there, on the front fender? I did that. Henry was so mad he took the key away."

Vera grabbed my shoulder hard. Her eyes bulged, the pupils dilated despite the brightness of the day. "I got to stop him!" she said, giving me a shake. "You got to help me stop him!"

I felt another swell of nausea. I sagged in her grip. "Vera, I can't. I don't have the key. For all I know Henry took it with him."

She let go of me, and I sank to the ground. She threw her head back and gave a keening cry. It was a sound of such desolation that I had to stop myself from running into the house and getting the key.

"Mama?" Amanda Leigh's voice, thin with fear. I glanced over at them, then back at Vera. I saw the madness drain from her face.

"Don't be scared," she said to the girls. "I ain't gonna hurt you or your mama." She turned to me. Her eyes were serene and terrible. "I'm going now," she said.

"I'll speak to Henry as soon as he gets home. He'll help you, I promise."

"It'll be too late then."

"Vera—"

"You look after them girls of yourn," she said.

She set off down the road toward town, moving at a steady lope, the knife glinting in the sun. As the girls ran over to me, I felt the first cramp hit—a mocking imitation of labor pains. I sank to my knees and pressed my hands to my stomach.

"What's the matter, Mama?" asked Amanda Leigh.

"I need you to be a big girl, and go and fetch Florence from her house. Do you know how to get there?"

She nodded solemnly.

"Hurry now," I said. "Run as fast as you can."

She went. I felt another cramp, like a fist grabbing my insides and squeezing hard, then wetness between my legs. Isabelle clung to me, sobbing. I lay in the dirt and curled my body around hers, letting her cry for both of us, and for the child who would never be her brother.

THEY FOUND CARL'S body lying in the road halfway between the farm and town. Vera had stabbed him seventeen times, then gone on to Marietta and turned herself in to Sheriff Tacker. Rose and Bill saw her walking down Main Street. They said she was covered in blood, like she'd bathed in it.

I learned these details later. At the time, I was too lost in my own agony to care about anyone else's. I lay in the bed, sleeping as many hours a day as my body would permit, waking reluctantly to lie with my face turned to the wall. I got up only to use the outhouse. Florence nursed me, cajoling me to eat and pushing clean nightgowns over my head. The children brought me gifts: wildflowers, drawings they'd made, a molted rattlesnake skin that I feigned delight with, though it repelled me. Rose paid me a couple of visits, offering news from town between awkward throat-clearings. Henry tried to comfort me when he came to bed at night, but I lay stiff against him, and after a few days he kept to his side.

A week passed in this way, then two. The children grew fretful, and Henry's compassion turned to impatience. "What's the matter with her?" I overheard him say to Florence. "Why doesn't she get up?"

"You got to give her time, Mist McAllan. That baby left a hollow place that ain't been filled back up yet."

But Florence was wrong about that. It had been filled up, and to the bursting, with rage—toward Vera and Carl, toward Henry and God, and most of all, myself. It blazed inside of me, and I fed it just like I'd fed the baby, keeping it alive with what-ifs and recriminations. If it hadn't been Florence's day off. If Henry hadn't left me alone with the girls. If he hadn't brought me to this brutal place to begin with. If I'd just listened to him when he told me there was no room for pity on a farm. I played that phrase over and over in my head like a fugue, cudgeling myself with it. Thinking of Henry's face when he walked in and found me lying in the bed, empty of our child; of the way he'd schooled his features, packing away his sorrow so I wouldn't see it and be hurt by it, letting only his tenderness show. Tenderness for me, the woman who had just lost his baby through her own stubborn foolishness. Yes, I knew miscarriages were common, especially in women my age, but I still couldn't shake the idea that the stress of Vera's assault had caused mine; that if I'd let Henry put the Atwoods off like he'd wanted to, I wouldn't have lost the baby. It had been a boy, just as we'd hoped. Florence didn't tell me and she wouldn't let me look at it, but I saw it in her face, and in Henry's.

I resumed my life some three weeks after the miscarriage, on a Monday. There was no fanfare, no scene between me

and Henry, or me and Florence, in which I was lectured on
my responsibilities and dragged, flailing and cursing, from my
sickbed. I simply got up and went on. I bathed my sour body,
combed my hair, put on a clean dress and took up my roles of
wife and mother again, though without really inhabiting them.
After a time I realized that inhabiting them wasn't required.
As long as I did what was expected of me—cooked the meals,
kissed the cuts and scrapes and made them better, accepted
Henry's renewed nocturnal attentions—my family was content. I hated them for that, a little. Sometimes, in the small
hours of the night, I would wake in the stifling airless heat
with Henry's skin hot as a brand against mine and imagine
myself getting up, dressing swiftly, going into the girls' room
and brushing my lips softly against their foreheads, then taking the car key from the nail by the door, walking across the
muddy yard, getting in the DeSoto and driving off—down the
dirt road, across the bridge, to the gravel road, to the highway,
and then straight east until the road ran into the sand. It had
been so long since I'd smelled the ocean and immersed myself
in that cool bluegreen.

I didn't act on this impulse, of course. But I sometimes wonder if I might have, in another week or another month, if Jamie
hadn't come to live with us.

WE WEREN'T EXPECTING him; the last we'd heard he
was in Rome. We'd gotten a postcard back in May with a picture of the Colosseum on the front and a hastily scrawled mes-

sage on the back about how the Italian girls were almost as beautiful as Southern girls. It had made me smile, but not Henry.

"It's not right," he said, "Jamie wandering all over and not coming home."

"I know you find this hard to believe, but not everybody longs to be in rural Mississippi," I said. "Besides, he's a young man, with no responsibilities. Why shouldn't he travel if he wants to?"

"I'm telling you, it's not right," Henry repeated. "I know my brother. Something's the matter with him."

I didn't want to believe it, and so I didn't. Nothing could ever be the matter with Jamie.

He came to us in late August, in the hot, slow days before the harvest. I was the first to see him: an indistinct form, shimmering slightly in the heat, striding up the dusty road with a suitcase in each hand. He wore a hat, so I couldn't see his red hair, but I knew it was Jamie by the way he walked—back straight, shoulders steady, hips absorbing all the motion. A movie star's walk.

"Who's that?" asked Pappy, squinting through the haze of smoke that surrounded him. The two of us were sitting on the porch, me churning butter and the old man back to doing his usual nothing. The girls were playing in the yard. Henry was out in the barn, feeding the livestock.

I shook my head in answer to Pappy's question, pretending ignorance for reasons I couldn't have explained, even to myself. As Jamie got closer I began to make out details: aviator sunglasses, oval patches darkening the armpits of his white shirt, baggy trousers sagging around his narrow hips. He spotted us and lifted one suitcase in greeting.

"It's Jamie!" said Pappy, waving his cane at his son. There was nothing wrong with the old man's legs; he was spry as a fox. The cane was purely for effect, a prop he used whenever he wanted to appear patriarchal or get out of working.

"Yes, I think you're right."

"Well don't just sit there, gal! Go and greet him!"

I stood, swallowing a tart response—for once, I wanted to obey him—and walked down the steps and across the yard. I was painfully conscious of the sweat staining my own dress, of my sun-browned skin and unwashed hair. I ran my hands through it, feeling it catch on the calluses on my palms. Farmwife's hands, that's what I had now.

I was about a hundred feet away from him when Pappy hollered, "Henry! Your brother's home! Henry!"

Henry emerged from the barn holding a feed bucket. "What?" he yelled. Then he saw Jamie. He whooped, dropped the bucket and broke into a run, and so did Jamie. Henry's bad leg made him awkward, but he seemed not to notice it. He pelted forward with the joyous abandon of a schoolboy. I realized I'd never seen my husband run before. It was like glimpsing another side of him, secret and unsuspected.

They came together ten feet in front of me. Clapped each other on the back, pulled apart, searched each other's faces: ritual. I stood outside of it and waited.

"You look good, brother," Jamie said. "You always did love farming."

"You look like hell," Henry replied.

"Don't sugarcoat it, now."

"You need to put some meat on those bones of yours, get some good Mississippi sun on your face."

"That's why I'm here."

"How'd you get out here?"

"I hitched my way from Greenville. I met one of your neighbors at the general store in town. He dropped me off at the bridge."

"Why didn't Eboline drive you?"

"One of the girls wasn't feeling well. Sick headache or some such thing. Eboline said they'd be down this weekend."

"I'm glad you didn't wait," Henry said.

Jamie turned to me then, looking at me in that way he had— as if he were really seeing me and taking me in whole. He held his hands out. "Laura," he said.

I went to him and gave him a hug. He felt light against me, insubstantial. His ribs protruded like the black keys of a piano. *I could pick him up,* I thought, and had a sudden irrational urge to do so. I stepped back hastily, flustered. Aware of his eyes on me.

"Welcome home, Jamie," I said. "It's good to see you."

"You too, sweet sister-in-law. How are you liking it here in Henry's version of paradise?"

I was spared from lying by the old man. "You'd think a son would see fit to greet his father," he bellowed from the porch.

"Ah, the dear, sweet voice of our pappy," said Jamie. "I'd forgotten how much I missed hearing it."

Henry picked up one of Jamie's suitcases and we headed

toward the house. "I think he's lonely here," Henry said. "He misses Mama, and Greenville."

"Oh, is that the excuse he's using these days?"

"No. He doesn't make excuses, you know that," Henry said. "He's missed you too, Jamie."

"I just bet he has. I bet he's quit smoking and joined the NAACP, too."

I laughed at that, but Henry's reply was serious. "I'm telling you, he's missed you. He'd never admit it, but it's true."

"If you say so, brother," Jamie said, throwing an arm around Henry's shoulder. "I'm not gonna argue with you today. But I have to say, it's mighty good of you to have taken him in and put up with him all these months."

Henry shrugged. "He's our father," he said.

I felt a ripple of envy, which I saw echoed on Jamie's face. How simple things were for Henry! How I wished sometimes that I could join him in his stark, right-angled world, where everything was either right or wrong and there was no doubt which was which. What unimaginable luxury, never to wrestle with whether or why, never to lie awake nights wondering what if.

AT SUPPER THAT NIGHT, Jamie regaled us with stories about his travels overseas. He'd been as far north as Norway and as far south as Portugal, mostly by train but sometimes by bicycle or on foot. He told us about snow-skiing in the Swiss Alps: how the mountains were so tall the tops of them pierced the clouds, and the snow so thick and soft that when you fell it was like sinking into a feather bed. He took us to the sidewalk cafés of Paris, where waiters in crisp white shirts and black aprons served pastries made of a hundred layers, each thinner than a fingernail; to the bullfights in Barcelona, where the matadors were hailed as gods by roaring crowds of thousands; to the casino in Monaco, where he'd won a hundred dollars on a single hand of baccarat and sent Rita Hayworth a bottle of champagne with the winnings. He made it all sound grand and marvelous, but I couldn't help noticing how drawn he looked, and how his hands shook each time he lit one of his Lucky Strikes. He ate little, preferring to smoke one cigarette after another until the room was so hazy the children's eyes were red and watery. They didn't complain, though. They were completely under their uncle's spell, especially Isabelle, who made eyes at him all through dinner and demanded to sit in his lap afterward. I'd never seen her so smitten with anyone.

Henry was the only one of us who seemed impatient with Jamie's stories. I could tell by the crease between his eyebrows, which got deeper and deeper as the evening wore on. Finally he blurted out, "And that's what you've been doing all these months, instead of coming home?"

"I needed some time," said Jamie.

"To play in the snow and eat fancy foreign bread."

"We all heal in our own ways, brother."

Henry made a gesture that took in Jamie's appearance. "Well, if this is what you call healing, I'd hate to see what hurting is."

Jamie sighed and passed a hand across his face. The veins on the back of his hand stood out like blue cords.

"Are you hurt, Uncle Jamie?" asked Isabelle worriedly.

"Everybody was hurt some in the war, little Bella. But I'll be all right. Do you know what *bella* means?" She shook her head. "It's Italian for 'beautiful one.' I think that's what I'll call you from now on. Would you like that, Bella?"

"Yes, Uncle Jamie!"

I would heal him, I thought. I would cook food to strengthen him, play music to soothe him, tell stories to make him smile. Not the weary smile he wore tonight, but the radiant, reckless grin he'd given me on the dance floor of the Peabody Hotel so many years before.

The war had dimmed him, but I would bring him back to himself.

HENRY

THE WAR BROKE my brother—in his head, where no one could see it. Never mind all his clever banter, his flirting with Laura and the girls. I could tell he wasn't right the second I saw him. He was thin and jittery, and his eyes had a haunted look I recognized from my own time in the Army. I knew too well what kind of sights they were seeing when he shut them at night.

Jamie was thin-skinned to begin with, had been all his life. He was always looking for praise, then getting his feelings hurt when he didn't get it, or enough of it. And he never knew his own worth, not in his guts where a man needs to know it. Our father was to blame for that. He was always whittling away at Jamie, trying to make him smaller. Pappy thought he had everybody fooled, but I knew why he did it. He did it because he loved my brother like he never loved anybody else in his whole life, not even Mama, and he wanted Jamie to be just like him. And when Jamie couldn't be or wouldn't be, which was most of the time, Pappy punished him. It was a hard thing to watch, but I learned not to get in the middle of it. We all did, even Mama. Defending Jamie just made Pappy whittle harder.

Once when I was home for Christmas, Jamie must have been six or seven, we were hauling wood and we flushed a copperhead out from under the woodpile. I grabbed the axe and chopped its head off, and Jamie screamed.

"Stop acting like a goddamn sissy," Pappy said, cuffing him on the head. "You'd think I had three daughters instead of two."

Jamie squared his shoulders and pretended he didn't care— even that young, he was good at acting—but I could tell how hurt he was.

"Why do you do that?" I asked Pappy when we were alone.

"Do what?"

"Cut him down like that."

"It's for his own good," Pappy said. "You and your mother and sisters have near to ruined him with your mollycoddling. Somebody needs to toughen him up."

"He's going to hate you if you're not careful," I said.

Pappy gave me a scornful look. "When he's a man, he'll understand. And he'll thank me, you wait and see."

My father died waiting for that thanks. It gives me no satisfaction to say so.

Jamie didn't talk to me about the war. Most men don't, who've seen real combat. It's the ones who spent their tours well behind the lines who want to tell you all about it, and the ones who never served who want to know. Our father didn't waste any time before he started in with the questions. Jamie's first night home, as soon as Laura and the girls had gone to bed, Pappy said, "So what's it like, being a big hero?"

"I wouldn't know," Jamie said.

Pappy snorted. "Don't give me that. They wrote me about your fancy medals."

Jamie's "fancy medals" included the Silver Star and the Distinguished Flying Cross, two of the highest honors an airman can receive. He never mentioned them in his letters. If the Army hadn't notified Pappy, we wouldn't have known about them.

"I was lucky," Jamie said. "A lot of guys weren't."

"Bet you got plenty of tail out of it too."

My brother just shrugged.

"Jamie never needed medals to get girls," I said.

"Damn right, he don't," Pappy said. "Takes after me that way. I didn't have two cents to rub together when your mama married me. Prettiest girl in Greenville, could've had any fellow in town, but it was me she wanted."

That was true, as far as I knew. At least, Mama had never contradicted his version of their courtship. I believe they married each other almost entirely for their looks.

"She wasn't the only one either," Pappy went on. "I had em all sniffing after me, just like you do, son."

Jamie shifted in his chair. He hated being compared to our father.

"Well one thing's for sure," Pappy said. "You must've killed a whole lot of Krauts to get all them medals."

Jamie ignored him and looked at me. "You got anything to drink around here?"

"I think I've got some whiskey somewhere."

"That'll do just fine."

I found the bottle and poured two fingers all around. Jamie downed his and refilled his glass again, twice as full as before. That surprised me. I'd never known my brother to be a drinker.

"Well?" Pappy asked. "How many'd you take out?"

"I don't know."

"Take a guess."

"I don't know," Jamie repeated. "What does it matter?"

"A man ought to know how many men he's killed."

Jamie took a hefty swig of his whiskey, then smiled unpleasantly. "I can tell you this," he said. "It was more than one."

Pappy's eyes narrowed, and I swore under my breath. Back in '34, when he was still working for the railroad, Pappy had killed a man, an escaped convict from Parchman who'd tried to rob some passengers at gunpoint. Pappy pulled his own pistol and shot him right in the eyeball. A single shot, delivered with deadeye accuracy—at least, that was how he always told it. Over the years the elements of the story had hardened into myth. The terrified women and children, and the cool-headed conductor who never felt a moment's fear. The onlookers who cheered as he carried the body off the train and dumped it at the feet of the grateful sheriff. Killing that convict was the proudest moment of our father's life. Jamie knew better than to belittle it.

"Well," Pappy said with a smirk, "at least I looked my *one* in the eye before I shot him. Not like dropping bombs from a mile up in the air."

Jamie stared tight-jawed into his glass.

"Well," I said, "time to hit the hay. We've got an early day tomorrow."

"I'll just finish my drink," Jamie said.

Pappy got up with a grunt and took one of the lanterns. "Don't wake me up when you come in," he said to Jamie.

I sat with my brother while he finished his whiskey. It didn't take him long, and when he was done his eyes flickered to the bottle like he wanted more. I took it and put it back in the cupboard. "What you need is a good night's sleep," I said. "Come on, Laura made up your bed for you."

I took the other lantern and walked him out to the lean-to. At the door I gave him a quick hug. "Welcome home, little brother."

"Thanks, Henry. I'm grateful to you and Laura for having me."

"Don't talk nonsense. We're your family, and this is your home for as long as you want, hear?"

"I can't stay long," he said.

"Why not? Where else have you got to go?"

He shook his head again and looked up at the sky. It was a cloudless night, which I was glad to see. I wanted the cotton to stay nice and dry till after the harvest. Then it could rain all it wanted to.

"Actually," Jamie said, "it was more like four miles up in the air."

"What was?"

"The altitude we dropped the bombs from."

"How can you even see anything from that high up?"

"You can see more than you'd think," he said. "Roads, cities, factories. Just not the people. From twenty thousand feet, they're not even ants." He let out a harsh laugh. It sounded exactly like our father. "How many did you kill, Henry? In the Great War?"

"I don't know exactly. Fifty, maybe sixty men."

"That's all?"

"I was only in France for six weeks before I got wounded. I was lucky, I guess."

For a long time Jamie was silent. "Pappy's right," he said finally. "A man ought to know."

After he'd gone in I shuttered the lantern and sat on the porch awhile, listening to the cotton plants rustle in the night wind. Jamie needed more than a good night's sleep, I thought. He needed a home of his own, and a sweet Southern gal to give him children and coax his roots back down into his native soil. All of that would come in good time, I had no doubt of it. But right now he needed hard work to draw the poison from his wounds. Hard work and quiet nights at home with a loving family. Laura and the girls and I would give him that. We'd help him get better.

When I went in to bed I thought she was asleep, but as soon as I was settled under the covers, her voice came soft in the dark. "How long is he planning to stay?" she asked.

"Not for long, is what he says. But I aim to change his mind."

Laura sighed, a warm gust on the back of my neck.

• • •

THE HARVEST STARTED two weeks later. The cotton plants were so heavy with bolls they could barely stand up. There must have been a hundred bolls per plant, fat and bursting with lint. The air prickled with the smell of it. Looking out over the fields, breathing that dusty cotton smell, I felt a sense of rightness I hadn't known in years, and maybe not ever. This was my land, my crop, that I'd drawn forth from the earth with my wits and labor. There's no knowledge in the world as satisfying to a man as that.

I hired eight colored families to pick for me, which was as many as I could find. Orris Stokes had been right—field labor was hard to come by, though why anybody, colored or white, would prefer the infernal stink of a factory and the squalor of a city slum to a life lived under the sun, I will never understand. The talk at Tricklebank's was all about these new picking machines they were using on some of the big plantations, but even if I could have afforded one I wouldn't have wanted it. Give me a colored picker every time. There's nothing and no one can harvest a cotton crop better. Cotton picking's been bred into the Southern Negro, bred right into his bones. You just have to watch the colored children in the fields to see that. Before they're even knee-high their fingers know what to do. Of course, picking's like any other task you give one of them, you've got to keep a close eye on them, make sure they're not snapping on you, taking the boll along with the lint to increase the weight of their haul. You take that trash to the gin, you'll get your crop downgraded right quick. Any picker we caught snapping got his pay docked by half. You better believe we had them all picking clean cotton before long.

Jamie was a big help to me. He threw himself into every task I gave him, never once complaining about the work or the heat. He pushed himself hard, too hard sometimes, but I didn't try to stop him. Moodwise, he was up and down. He'd go along fine for three or four days, then he'd have one of his nightmares and wake us all with his shouting. I'd go out there and calm him down while our father grumbled about being kept awake. Pappy thought it was a weakness of character, something Jamie could fix if he just put his mind to it. I tried to explain to Pappy what it was like, reminding him how I'd once had those same kind of nightmares myself, and I was in combat for a lot less time than Jamie.

"Your brother needs to toughen up," Pappy said. "You wouldn't see me quaking and screaming like a girl."

On the weekends Jamie would take the car and disappear for a night, sometimes two. I was pretty sure he was going to Greenville to drink and mess around with cheap women. I didn't try to stop that either. I figured he was old enough to make his own decisions. He didn't need his big brother telling him what to do anymore.

But I figured wrong. One Monday in October I was on the tractor in the south field harvesting the last of the soybeans when I saw Bill Tricklebank's truck coming up the road in a hurry. Jamie had been gone since Saturday, and I was starting to worry. When I saw Bill's truck I knew something must have happened. We didn't have a phone, so when somebody needed to reach us they called Tricklebank's.

I got down off the tractor and ran across the field to the

road. I was out of breath by the time I reached Bill. "What is it?" I said. "What's the matter?"

"The Greenville sheriff's office called," Bill said. "Your brother's been arrested. They got him in the county jail."

"What for?"

He looked away from me and mumbled something.

"Speak up, Bill!"

"Driving drunk. He hit a cow."

"A *cow*?"

"That's what they said."

"Is he hurt?"

"Just a bump on the head and some bruises, is what the deputy told me."

Relief flooded me. I gripped Bill by the shoulder and saw him wince a little. The man was thin as a dandelion stalk and about as sturdy. "Thank you, Bill. Thank you for coming out and telling me."

"That ain't all," he said. "There was a . . . young lady in the car with him."

"Was she hurt?"

"Concussion and a broke arm. Deputy said she'd be all right though."

"I'd be obliged if you and Rose would keep this to yourselves," I said.

"Sure thing, Henry. But you ought to know, Mercy's the one who placed the call."

"Damn." Mercy Ivers was the nosiest of the town's operators, with the biggest mouth. If everybody in Marietta didn't already know Jamie was in jail, I had no doubt they would by nightfall.

Bill dropped me at the house and went on his way. Laura and Pappy were waiting on the porch. I filled them in, leaving out the part about the young lady. I was sorry my wife had to know about any of it, but with the Tricklebanks and Mercy Ivers involved there was no help for it. I figured Laura would be angry, and she was—just not in the way I expected.

"After all he's done for his country," she said, "to throw him in jail like a common criminal! They ought to be ashamed."

"Well, honey, he was blind drunk."

"We don't know that," she said. "And even if he was, I'm sure he had reason to be, after all he's been through."

"What if he'd hit another car instead of a cow? Somebody could have been badly hurt."

"But nobody was," she said.

Her defending him like that nettled me. My wife was a sensible woman, but where Jamie was concerned she was as blind as every other female who ever breathed. If it had been me out driving drunk and killing livestock, you can bet she wouldn't have been nearly so forgiving.

"Henry? Was someone else hurt?"

It was on the tip of my tongue to tell her and knock him off the pedestal she'd built for him—I was that mad at both of them. Lucky for Jamie I'm no rat. "No, just him," I said.

"Well then," Laura said, "let me get some supper for you to take to him. I'm sure they haven't fed him properly." She went inside.

"You want me to come with you?" Pappy asked.

"No," I said. "I'll take care of it."

"You'll need money for bail."

"I've got enough in the strongbox."

Pappy pulled his wallet out of his pants pocket, took out a worn hundred-dollar bill and held it out to me. I gaped at it, then at him. My father was a Scot to the marrow. Parting him from money was like trying to get milk out of a mule.

"Go on, take it," he said gruffly. "But don't you tell him I gave it to you."

"Why not?"

"I don't want him expecting more."

"Whatever you say, Pappy."

At the Greenville jail I asked to see Sheriff Partain. I knew him slightly. He and my sister Thalia had been high school sweethearts. He'd wanted to marry her, but she had her sights set higher. Caught herself a rich tobacco planter from Virginia and moved up north with him. Told everybody she'd broken Charlie Partain's heart beyond repair. For Jamie's sake, I hoped she'd been wrong. Thalia always did have an exaggerated idea of her own importance.

When the deputy led me into Charlie's office he came out from behind his desk and shook my hand, a little too hard. "Henry McAllan. How long's it been?"

"About fifteen years, give or take."

Charlie hadn't changed much in that time. He had a little

belly on him, but he was still a good-looking fellow, big and affable, with an aw-shucks smile that couldn't quite hide the ambition underneath it. A born politician.

"How you been?" he asked.

"Just fine. I'm living over to Marietta now. Got me a cotton farm there."

"So I heard."

"You've done well for yourself," I said, gesturing at the badge on his shirt. "Congratulations on winning sheriff."

"Thanks. I was an MP in the war, guess I just got a taste for the law."

"About my brother," I said.

He shook his head gravely. "Yeah, it's a bad business."

"How is he?"

"He's all right, but he's got one helluva headache. Course, drinking a whole fifth of bourbon'll do that to you."

"Can you tell me what happened, Charlie? I got the story secondhand."

He walked back behind his desk, taking his time about it, and sat down. "You know," he said, "I like to be called sheriff when I'm working. Helps me keep the job separate. You understand." His face stayed friendly, but I didn't miss the sharp glint in his eye.

"Of course. Sheriff."

"Have a seat."

I sat in the chair he gestured to, facing the desk.

"Seems your brother and a female companion were parked out east of town on Saturday night. Watching the moon is what she said." Charlie's tone indicated how much he believed that.

"Who is this gal?"

"Her name's Dottie Tipton. She's a waitress over at the Levee Hotel. Her husband Joe was a friend of mine. He died at Bastogne."

"Sorry to hear it. Jamie fought in the Battle of the Bulge too. It's where he won his Silver Star. He was a bomber pilot, you know."

"You don't say," Charlie said, crossing his arms over his chest.

So much for my efforts to impress him. I decided I'd better stick to the business at hand. "So the two of them were parked, and then what happened?"

"Well, that's where it gets kinda fuzzy. Your brother don't remember a thing, or so he claims."

"And the woman?"

"Dottie says he ran into that cow by accident when they were driving back to town. Which I might believe if we'd found it laying in the road instead of smack-dab in the middle of Tom Easterly's pasture."

"You said yourself Jamie was drunk. He probably just lost track of the road."

Charlie leaned back in his chair, putting his feet up on the desk. Enjoying himself. "Uh-huh. There's just two problems with that."

"What?"

"One, he busted through a split-rail fence. And two, he hit

that cow dead on, like he was aiming for it. Had to been going fast too. That was some mighty tenderized beef."

I shook my head, unable to imagine why Jamie would deliberately run into a cow. It made no sense at all.

"Your brother got something against livestock?" Charlie asked, with a lift of his eyebrow.

I decided to level with him. "Jamie isn't well. He hasn't been himself since he got home from the war."

"That may be," Charlie said. "But it don't give him the right to do whatever the hell he wants. To just *take* whatever he wants. He ain't in the almighty Air Corps anymore." He ground out his cigarette. "All those flyboys, thought they were such hot stuff. Strutting around in their leather jackets like they owned the world and everything in it. The way the girls chased after em, you'd have thought they were the only ones putting their necks on the line. But if you ask me, it was the men on the ground who were the real heroes. Men like Joe Tipton. Course they didn't give Joe a Silver Star. He was just an ordinary soldier."

"There's honor in that too," I said.

Charlie's lip curled. "Mighty big of you to say so, McAllan."

I wanted to punch the sneer right off his face. What stopped me was the thought of Jamie in that cell on the other side of the wall. I locked eyes with Charlie Partain. "My brother flew sixty missions into German territory," I said. "Risked his life sixty times so more of our boys could come home in one piece. Maybe not your friend Joe, but Jamie saved a whole lot of others. And now—now he's messed up in the head and he needs some time to get himself straightened out. I think he deserves that, don't you?"

"I think Joe Tipton's widow deserves better than to be treated like a whore."

Then she shouldn't act like one, I thought. "I'm sure my brother never meant her any disrespect," I said. "Like I told you, he isn't himself. But I give you my word, sheriff, if you'll drop the charges and send him home with me, you won't have any more trouble from him."

"What about Dottie's hospital bills and Tom's cow?"

"I'll take care of it. I'll do it today."

Charlie shook out a cigarette from the pack on his desk and lit it. He took three leisurely drags without saying a word. Finally he got up and walked to the door. "Dobbs!" he yelled. "Go fetch Jamie McAllan. We're releasing him."

I got up and held my hand out to him. "Thank you, sheriff. I'm much obliged."

He ignored my hand and my thanks both. "Tell your brother to stay away from Dottie, and from Greenville," he said. "If I catch him making trouble here again, he'll be the one who needs saving."

WHEN THEY BROUGHT him out to me he wouldn't meet my eyes, just stammered an apology while Charlie Partain and his deputy watched. He reeked of whiskey and vomit. He looked like hell too. There was a bad gash on his forehead and one eye was swollen nearly shut.

Still, he was in better shape than the DeSoto, which they'd taken to the municipal pound. We went there first, intending to pick it up, but I didn't need a mechanic to tell me it was undrivable. The front end was collapsed like an overripe pumpkin, and the engine was a mangled mess. Jamie's face went white when he saw it.

"Jesus, did I do that?"

"Yeah, you did," I said. "What the hell happened?"

"I don't know. The last thing I remember is Dolly telling me to slow down."

"Her name's Dottie. And you put her in the hospital."

"I know, they told me," he said in a low voice. "But I'm gonna make it up to her, and to you. I swear it."

"You can make it up to me all you want, but you're never to see her again."

"Says who?"

"Charlie Partain. Her husband was a friend of his."

"I wondered why he was so pissed off. He gave me this shiner, you know."

"He hit you? That son of a bitch."

"I reckon I deserved it."

He looked so hunched and miserable. "Next time, do me a favor," I said.

"What?"

"Go after a rabbit, will you?"

It took him a few seconds but then he started laughing, and so did I. The two of us laughed till tears ran down our faces, like we hadn't done in years. And if Jamie's face stayed wet for a time after we were done, I pretended not to notice.

I dropped him at the Levee Hotel, where he'd been staying. While he was getting cleaned up I drove over to the hospital and paid Dottie Tipton's bill. They were sending her home that afternoon, which I was glad to hear. I didn't visit her—what in the world would I have said?—but I asked one of the nurses to tell her Jamie was sorry and hoped she'd get better soon.

When I picked him up he looked and smelled a little better. We stopped at Tom Easterly's place on the way out of town. Bastard wanted two hundred dollars for his cow, which was a good fifty dollars more than it or any other cow was worth, but I thought of Charlie Partain and paid it. The whole thing ended up costing me close to three hundred dollars, not count-ing the car. Figured I was looking at another four hundred minimum to fix it, and double that if I had to replace it. I'd planned on spending that money on a rent house for Laura and the girls, but now that wouldn't be possible.

All the way home I dreaded telling her, dreaded seeing that disappointed look on her face.

"We're tapped out," I said, when we were alone in bed. "Even with a good harvest, there won't be enough for a house in town this year. I'm sorry, honey."

She didn't say a word, and I couldn't see her expression in the dark.

"The good news is, Jamie's promised to stay another six months to make it up to us. With his help, I should be able to put enough by that we can get a house next year."

She sighed and got out of bed. I heard her bare feet scuff-ing on the floor, down to the foot of the bed and around to my side. Then I heard a familiar scraping sound and saw a match flare. She lit the candle, parted the mosquito netting and got in, squeezing in next to me. Her arm went around me.

"It's all right, Henry," she whispered. "I don't mind it so much."

I felt her lips on my neck, and her hand slip down into my pajamas.

JAMIE

BECAUSE OF HENRY. Somehow it always comes back to that.

There I was again, indebted to him for pulling my ass out of the sling I'd custom-made to hold it. He wouldn't tell me how much he was out on my account, but I figured it was close to a thousand bucks.

Henry wasn't the only one I owed. Thanks to me, Laura didn't get her house in town, her indoor toilet and grass lawn. Instead she got another year of stink and muck. She never reproached me for it, though, never even raised an eyebrow at me. She welcomed me home as sweetly as if I were returning from church and not the county jail. A lot of women act sweet, but with most of them that's all it is, an act they learn young and hone to perfection by the time they're twenty-one. My sisters were both masters of the craft, but Laura was something else altogether. She was sweet to the core.

Then there was Dottie Tipton. I snuck into Greenville to see her a week after the accident. (That's how everybody except my father referred to it—"the accident." Pappy referred to it as "your drunken rampage" and took to calling me "the cow-slayer.") Dottie was tickled pink to see me. Nothing was too good for the man who'd given her a concussion and put her arm in a cast. She changed her dress and put on lipstick, one-handedly fixed me a drink in a crystal highball, fussed over my bruises. Was I sure I wasn't hungry? She'd be happy to whip up a little something, it would be no trouble at all. I pictured us sitting at her dining room table eating supper off her wedding china, no doubt with dessert afterward in her bedroom. The urge to leap up and run out the door was as powerful as anything I'd ever felt before battle. It was Dottie's dead husband who stopped me. Joe Tipton stared out at me from his silver frame on the mantel, his expression stern under the cap of his uniform. *Don't you do it, you craven son of a bitch*, that expression said. So I stayed awhile and had a few drinks and laughs with her. The drinks made the laughs come easier, and the lies too. When it was time to say goodbye, I was tender and rueful—Antony to her Cleopatra. *Bravo*, said Joe. *Now get the fuck out.* Dottie clung to me a little when I told her I could never see her again, but she didn't cry. Another thing I owed her for.

All those people whose lives I'd careened into—just like that, they let me off the hook. All that was left was for me to do the same, and that wasn't hard. Booze helped, and remembering: Flaming planes trailing black smoke, falling from the sky. Men falling from the planes, falling with their chutes on fire, falling with no chutes at all, throwing themselves out of the planes rather than be burned alive. The *wuff wuff wuff* of enemy flak, ripping them all to pieces, the falling planes and falling men and pieces of men.

They say you have to hate to be in the infantry, but that wasn't true in the Air Corps. We never saw the faces of our enemies. When I thought of them at all, I pictured blank white ovals framed by blond crew cuts—never bangs or curls or pigtails, though I knew our bombs fell on plenty of women and kids too. Sometimes we just picked a big city and blasted the hell out of it. Other times, if we couldn't get to our primary target, usually a military installation or factory, we went after a "target of opportunity" instead. We called them AWMs, short for "Auf Wiedersehen, Motherfuckers." There was an unspoken rule never to bring the bombs back home. My last run, thunderstorms kept us from reaching the munitions depot we were supposed to hit, so we ended up dumping our full load on a big park full of refugees. We knew from our intelligence briefing that there were SS soldiers there, seeking cover among the civilians. Still, we killed thousands of innocent people along with them. When we got back to base and made our strike report to the CO, he congratulated us on a job well done.

A few seconds before I hit that cow it turned its head and looked straight at me. It could have moved, but it didn't. It just stood there watching me as I bore down on it.

I GUESS I COULD have talked to Henry about the war, but whenever I started to bring it up I found myself cracking a joke or making up a story instead. He wouldn't have understood what I felt. The horror, yes, but not the guilt, and certainly not the urge I'd sometimes had to drive my plane into an enemy fighter and turn us both into a small sun. Henry, longing for oblivion—the very idea of it was laughable. What my brother longed for was right under his feet. He scraped it from his boots every night with tender care. The farm was his element, just as the sky had once been mine. That was the other reason I didn't confide in him: I didn't want to muddy his happiness.

Whiskey was the only thing that kept the nightmares at bay. After the accident I knew Henry, Laura and Pappy were all keeping a close eye on me, so I was careful never to have more than a couple of beers in front of them. I did my real drinking in secret. I had bottles stashed everywhere—on top of the outhouse, out in the barn, under a floorboard on the front porch—and I always carried a tin of lemon drops to hide the smell on my breath. I never got falling-down drunk, just maintained a nice steady infusion throughout the day. A lot of it I sweated out. The rest I put to use. I was the designated charmer of the household, the one responsible for keeping everybody else's spirits up. To play my part I needed booze.

I played it brilliantly, if I do say so myself. None of them guessed my secret, except for Florence Jackson. Her sharp eyes didn't miss much. One time I discovered a half-full bottle of Jack Daniel's tucked underneath my pillow, like a gift from the Bourbon Fairy. I knew it was Florence who'd put it there because it was washing day and the sheets had been changed. I must have left it somewhere, and she'd found it and returned it to me. This one act of kindness aside, she didn't much like me.

I tried to win her over, but she was immune to my charm—one of the only women I'd ever met who was. I think she must have sensed the part I would play in the events to come. Henry would scoff at me for saying so, but I believe Negroes have an innate ability that us white people lack to sense things, a kind of bone-sense. It's different from head-sense, which we have more of than they do, and it comes from an older, darker place.

Florence may have sensed something, but I had no idea of what I was setting in motion the day I gave Ronsel Jackson a lift from town. It was just after the new year. I'd been back in Mississippi for four months, but it felt more like four years. I drove into Marietta to get my hair cut and pick up some groceries for Laura, and some bourbon for me. Usually I bought my liquor in Tchula or Belzoni, but that day I didn't have time. I was coming out of Tricklebank's with my purchases when I heard a loud explosion off to my left. I hit the ground, covering my head with my hands and dropping the box of groceries, which spilled out into the street.

"It's all right," said a deep voice behind me. "It was just a car." A tall Negro in overalls stepped out from behind a parked truck. He pointed at an old Ford Model A moving away from us down the street. "It backfired, is all," he said. "Must've had a stuck intake valve." Belatedly I recognized Ronsel Jackson. I'd only spoken to him a couple of times and only about farm business, but I knew from Henry that he'd fought in one of the colored battalions.

Somebody chuckled, and I looked up to see a dozen pairs of

eyes staring at us from under hat brims. All the Saturday afternoon regulars were on the porch at Tricklebank's, exchang-
ing opinions on whatever passed for news in Marietta—at the
moment, no doubt, that crazy brother of Henry McAllan's, the
one who killed that cow over to Greenville. Hot-faced, I bent
down and started putting the groceries back in the box. Ronsel
helped me, handing me some oranges that had rolled his way.
The flour sack had come untied, spilling half its contents onto
the dirt, but the whiskey was mercifully intact. When I picked
it up, my hands were shaking so hard I dropped it again.

If Ronsel had said anything, if he'd even made a sound that
was meant to be sympathetic or soothing, I might have hauled
off and hit him—God knows I wanted to hit somebody. He
didn't give me the excuse, though. He just held his own hand
out, palm down, so I could see it was shaking every bit as bad
as mine. I saw the same frustration in his face that I was feeling, and the same rage, maybe more.

"Reckon it'll ever stop?" he asked, looking down at his
hand.

"They say it does eventually," I said. "Did you walk here?"

"Yessuh. Daddy's using the mule to break the fields."

"Come on, I'll give you a lift."

He headed for the bed of the truck. I was about to tell him
he could ride up front with me—it was cold out and starting
to drizzle—but then I saw the men on the porch watching us,
and I remembered Henry mentioning that Ronsel had gotten
into some trouble here awhile back. I waited till we were out
of town, then I pulled over, stuck my head out the window and
called out, "Why don't you come on up front?"

"I'm doing just fine back here," he called back.

The drizzle had turned into a steady rain. I couldn't see him, but he had to be cold and wet, and getting more so by the minute. "Get in, soldier!" I yelled. "That's an order!"

I felt the truck rock as he jumped off, then the passenger door opened and he got in, smelling of wet wool and sweat. I expected him to thank me. What he said was, "How do you know you outranked me?"

I laughed. "You obeyed my order, didn't you? Besides, I was a captain."

His chin came up. "There were Negro captains," he said. "I served under plenty of em."

"Let me guess. You were a sergeant."

"That's right," he said.

I reached into the box sitting between us, uncorked the whiskey and took a good long swallow. "Well, sergeant, how do you like being back here in the Delta?"

He didn't answer, just turned his head and stared out the side window. At first I thought I'd ruffled his feathers, but then I realized he was giving me privacy in which to drink. *A fine fellow, this Ronsel Jackson,* I thought, taking another swig. Then I had a second, more accurate realization: He wasn't looking at me because he figured I wasn't going to offer him any. He was protecting his dignity and giving me the leeway to be a son of a bitch at the same time. Annoyed, I thrust the bottle at him. "Here, have a snort."

"No thanks," he said.

"Are you always this stubborn, or is it just around white people who are trying to be nice to you?"

He accepted the bottle and took a quick sip, his eyes never leaving my face. The truth was, not that long ago I wouldn't have offered him any, not unless it was the last swig in the bottle. I wasn't sure whether it was a good or a bad thing that I didn't care anymore.

"What kind of an NCO are you?" I said, when he tried to hand the bottle back to me after that one little sip. This time he took a big snort, so big he choked and spilled some on his overalls. "Don't waste it, now," I said. "That's my medicine, I need every drop."

When I took the bottle back from him, I saw him notice my missing finger. "You get that in the war?" he asked.

"Yeah. Frostbite."

"How does a pilot manage to get frostbite?"

"You got any idea how cold it is at twenty thousand feet, with the wind blowing through like fury? I'm talking twenty, thirty below zero."

"Why'd you leave the window open?"

"Had to. There were no wipers. When it rained, you had to stick your head out the window to see."

He shook his head. "And I thought I had it bad, being stuck inside a rolling tin can."

"You were a tanker?"

"Sure was. Spearheaded for Patton."

"You ever piss in your helmet?"

"Yeah, plenty of times."

"We had relief tubes in the cockpit but sometimes it was easier just to use our flak helmets. And at twenty thousand feet that piss freezes solid in less than a minute. One time I went in my helmet and forgot all about it. It was a long haul. When we got close to the target I put the helmet back on. We did the bombing run and were dodging enemy flak when I felt something wet running down my face. And then I smelled it and realized what it was."

Ronsel gave a big booming laugh. "You must a caught hell back at the Officers' Club."

"My buddies never let me hear the end of it. The ones who survived, that is."

"Yeah. I hear you."

It was nearing dark and cold enough that I could see his breath and mine, mingling in the air. I put the truck in gear and we drove the rest of the way to the farm in silence, letting the bourbon be our conversation, back and forth. When we pulled up to the Jackson place, Hap was outside filling a bucket at the pump. The look of alarm on his face when he saw his son in the cab of the truck was so exaggerated it was comical.

I rolled down my window. "Evening, Hap."

"Everything all right, Mist Jamie?"

"Everything's fine. I just gave Ronsel here a lift from town."

Ronsel opened the door and got out, a bit unsteadily. "Thanks for the ride," he said.

"You're welcome." As he was about to shut the door, I said, "I expect I'll be heading into town again next Saturday afternoon. If you like I'll stop by here, see if you want a ride."

Ronsel glanced at his father, then back at me. He nodded

his head once, as solemnly as a judge. And in that moment, sealed his fate.

Maybe that's cowardly of me, making Ronsel's the trigger finger. There are other ways to look at it, other turning points I could pick, eeny, meeny, miny, moe: When that car backfired. When he got in the cab of the truck. When I handed him the whiskey. But I think it was right then, when he stood half-drunk in the rain and nodded his head. And I believe Ronsel would tell you the same thing, if you could ask him, and he could answer.

III.

LAURA

I FELL IN LOVE with my brother-in-law the way you fall asleep in the car when someone you trust is driving — gradually, by imperceptible degrees, letting the motion lull your eyes closed. *Letting*, that's the key word. I could have stopped myself. I could have shoved those feelings into some dark corner of my mind and locked them away, as I'd done with so many other feelings I'd found troubling. I tried to, for a time, but it was a halfhearted effort at best, doomed to failure.

Jamie set about making me love him from the first day he arrived. Complimenting me on my cooking and doing little things for me around the house. Things that said, *I see you. I think about what might please you.* I was starved for that kind of attention, and I soaked it up like a biscuit soaks up gravy. Henry was never a thoughtful man, not in the small, everyday ways that mean so much to a woman. In Memphis, surrounded by dozens of doting Chappells and Fairbairns, I hadn't minded so much, but at Mudbound I'd felt the lack of attention keenly. Henry was wholly preoccupied with the farm. I would have gotten more notice from him if I'd grown a tail and started to bray.

I want to make one thing clear: When I say that Jamie set about making me love him, I don't mean that he seduced me. Oh, he flirted with me plenty, but he flirted with everybody, even the men. He liked to win people. That makes it sound like a game, and perhaps to a certain type of man it is, but Jamie was no rake. He *needed* to win them. I didn't see that then. I saw only the way he leaned forward whenever I spoke, his head cocked slightly to one side as if to better catch my words. I saw the wildflowers he left for me in a milk bottle on the kitchen table, and the happy smiles of my children when he teased them.

Isabelle was his pet, and I was glad of it. I could never love her enough or give her enough attention. Jamie saw her need and met it with extravagant affection, which she returned in full measure. When he was in the room, none of the rest of us existed for her. He'd come in dirty and worn out from the fields, and she'd hold her chubby arms up to him like a Baptist preacher calling on the Almighty. Jamie would shake his head and say, "I'm too tired to hold you tonight, little Bella." She'd stamp her foot imperiously and reach for him, knowing better, and he'd swoop down and gather her into his arms, twirling her around and around while she squealed with delight. It wasn't just that he loved her; it was that he loved *her*, in particular. That was everything to her. Before long, she was insisting we all call her Bella. She refused to answer to Isabelle, even after Henry spanked her bottom for it. But she's his child as well as mine, at least in stubbornness, and eventually she got her way.

Even dimmed as he was, Jamie charmed and leavened us all. Pappy carped less, and Henry laughed more often and slept more soundly. I came alive again, like I hadn't been since before the miscarriage. I was less resentful of Henry and less mindful of the privations of the farm. He must have known Jamie was the cause of my improved spirits, but if it bothered him he didn't let on. He seemed to accept that Jamie "made the girls sparkle," as he'd told me all those years ago. It would have been unthinkable to Henry that his wife would have sexual feelings for his little brother.

And that's exactly what I was having: sexual feelings, of an intensity I'd never experienced in my life. Anything could bring them on: slicing a tomato, pulling weeds in the garden, running a comb through my hair. My senses were acute. Food was more succulent and smells more pungent. I was hungrier than usual and perspired more often. Not even pregnancy had made my body so strange to me.

Even so, it all might have come to nothing if Jamie hadn't built the shower for me. That shower became the crucible of my feelings for him. To understand why, you have to imagine life without running water or bathrooms. It was an all-day undertaking to get the whole family clean, so we bathed only on Saturdays. During the summer months I filled the tub and let the morning sun warm the water. I bathed the girls first, then myself, praying nobody would come calling while I was naked. For privacy we hung sheets from two clotheslines, placing the tub between them—an arrangement that left the bather exposed on two sides and gave the whole country an eyeful on windy days. After my bath I refilled the tub for Pappy. When he was done, I emptied and refilled it again—sometimes with the old man's grudging help, but more often by myself—for when Henry and Jamie came in from the fields. In the winter, the tub had to be dragged into the kitchen and the water hauled in and heated on the stove. Still, for all the work involved, Saturday was my favorite day of the week. It was the only day I felt truly clean.

The rest of the time, we stank. You can say all you want about honest sweat, but it smells just as bad as any other kind. Henry didn't seem to mind, but I never got used to it. I remembered my little bathroom on Evergreen Street with swooning nostalgia. I'd taken it completely for granted, even grumbled occasionally about the poor water pressure and the chips in the porcelain tub. Now, as I took my hasty spit baths from a pail of cold water in the kitchen, that little bathroom seemed a place of impossible luxury.

The worst time for me was during my menses. The musky-sweet reek of my blood on the cloths I wore seemed to fill the house until I could hardly breathe. I'd wait each night for the others to fall asleep, then tiptoe to the kitchen to wash the cloths and myself. One night, as I squatted over the basin with my nightgown bunched around my waist and my hand moving awkwardly between my legs, Henry walked in on me. He turned quickly and left, but oh, how ashamed I was!

Jamie must have guessed how I felt. One day in March, I returned from an overnight shopping trip to Greenville to discover a narrow wooden stall in back of the house, with a large bucket attached to a pulley contraption mounted on top. Jamie was just finishing it when the girls and I pulled up in the car.

"What is it, Uncle Jamie?" asked Amanda Leigh.

"It's a shower, little petunia."

"I don't like showers, I like baths!" cried Bella.

"I didn't build it for you, honey. I built it for your mama."

Bella frowned at that. Jamie tousled her hair, but his eyes were on me. "Well," he said, "what do you think?"

"I think it's the most marvelous thing I've ever seen."

And it was. Of course, like everything at Mudbound, the shower required some effort. You still had to heat water on the stove and haul it outside—two or three bucketfuls, depending on whether or not you were washing your hair. You lowered the big shower bucket, poured the hot water in, then raised it again by pulling on a rope attached to the pulley. Then you went in the stall and got undressed, draping your clothes over the walls. When you were ready, you tugged gently on a second rope attached to the bucket's lip, tilting it and releasing just enough water so you could soap yourself. Finally, you pulled on the rope again and rinsed until all the water was gone.

I had my first shower that very evening. It was one of those warm soft nights in early spring when the air itself seems like a living being, surrounding and gently supporting you. As soon as I stepped into the stall and closed the door, I was in a private universe. On the other side of the walls, I could hear the deep thrumming of insects and frogs, the constant music of the

Delta, and more distantly, the men's voices interwoven with the sound of Amanda Leigh practicing her piano scales. I took off my clothes and just stood there for several minutes in that warm, embracing air. Overhead floated large clouds, stained fantastic hues of pink and gold by the setting sun. I pulled the rope and felt the water stream down my body and thought of my brother-in-law, of his hands sawing the planks, fitting them together, nailing them down. He'd even made me a soap dish, I saw. It was slatted at the bottom and held a small bar of embossed purple soap, the kind they had in fancy stores in Memphis. When I brought it to my nose I smelled the dusky, pungent sweetness of lavender. It was my favorite scent; I'd mentioned it to Jamie once, years ago. And he had remembered.

I ran the soap across my body and wondered: as he was building the shower, had he imagined me in it like this, naked and free under the darkening sky? I don't know what shocked me more, the thought itself, or the heavy ripple of pleasure it sent through me.

Henry was the beneficiary of all this newfound ardor. He'd almost always been the one to initiate our lovemaking, but now I found myself seeking him out in our bed, to his surprise and my own. Sometimes he would refuse me. He never gave an explanation, just took my exploring hand and returned it to my own side of the bed, patting it dismissively before he turned away. The anger that filled me on those nights was so

hot and raw I was surprised it didn't set the bed ablaze. I'd
never refused him, not once in all the years of our marriage.
How dared he push me aside like an unwanted pet?

I tried to keep my feelings for Jamie secret, but I've never
been good at subterfuge; my father used to call me his little
trumpeter for the way my face proclaimed my every emotion.
One day Florence and I were working in the house together,
me cooking and her sorting laundry, and she said, "Mist Jamie
doing some better."

"Yes," I said, "I think he is."

Seven months on the farm had done him good. I had no il-
lusions that he was completely healed, but he was having fewer
nightmares, and physically he seemed stronger. My cooking
had put some meat on him; I was especially proud of that.

"He got hisself a woman, that's why," Florence said, with a
sly smile.

I felt a constriction in my throat, like a stone was lodged
there. "What are you talking about?"

"See here?" She held up one of his shirts. There was a
smudge of red on the collar.

"That's blood," I said. "He probably cut himself shaving."
But I knew better. Dried blood would have been brown.

"Well, it sure is some mighty sweet-smelling blood then,"
said Florence.

The stone in my throat seemed to swell until I could hardly
swallow.

"Ain't good for a man to be without a woman," she went on

conversationally. "Now a woman, she likes a man, but she can get along just fine without him. The Almighty seen to that. But a man ain't never gone thrive without a woman by his side. He be looking high and low till he find one. Course Mist Jamie, he the kind come by em easy. They be lined up like daisies on the side of the road, just waiting for him to pluck em. He just got to reach out his hand and—"

"Shut your mouth," I said. "I won't listen to another word of such low talk."

We stared at each other for a moment, then Florence dropped her gaze, but not before I saw the knowing look in her dark eyes. "Now go and fetch some water," I said. "I want to make some coffee."

She obeyed, moving with an unhurriedness that bordered on insolent. When the front door closed behind her, I went to the table and picked up the shirt. I raised it to my nose and smelled the cloying scent of lily-of-the-valley perfume. I tried to imagine the type of woman who would wear that scent. Her dresses would be low-cut and her fingernails would be painted the same shade of carmine as her lipstick. She'd have a throaty laugh and smoke cigarettes from a long holder and let her slip show on purpose when she crossed her legs. She'd be nothing but a cheap little tramp, I thought.

"Smell something you like, gal?" I turned and saw Pappy framed in the front window. I felt my cheeks flame. How long had he been standing there, and how much had he overheard? Long enough and plenty, judging by the smirk on his face.

Nonchalantly, or so I hoped, I dropped the shirt into the

basket. "Just sweat," I said. "You know, the odor that comes from a person's body when they do work of some kind? Perhaps you've heard of it."

I left the room before he could reply.

THE TROUBLE STARTED the first Saturday in April. I was driving the old man to town when we encountered Jamie coming the other way in the truck. As we drew closer I could see Ronsel Jackson in the passenger seat. He'd wisely kept his head down in the year since he'd been home. We rarely saw him, except as a distant figure in the fields, hunched over his plow. That view of him seemed to have appeased Pappy; at least, he'd stopped ranting about "that smart-mouthed nigger" on a daily basis.

"Who's that with Jamie?" Pappy said, squinting at them.

The old man was too vain to wear glasses in public, so he often depended on us to be his eyes. For once, I was glad. "I don't know," I said. "I can't make him out."

The road was too narrow for two vehicles to pass. Jamie pulled the truck over to let us by, and I was forced to slow to a crawl. As we passed them, Jamie raised his hand in greeting. Ronsel sat beside him, looking straight ahead.

"Stop the car!" Pappy ordered. I braked, but Jamie drove on. Pappy's head whipped around to follow the truck through the rear window. "Did you see that? I think he had that nigger with him."

"Who do you mean?"

"The Jackson boy, the one with the big mouth. You didn't see him?"

"No. The sun was in my eyes."

Pappy turned to me, fixing me with his basilisk stare. "You lying to me, gal?"

"Of course not, Pappy," I replied, with all the innocence I could muster.

He grunted and faced forward, crossing his arms over his chest. "I'll tell you one thing, it better not have been that nigger."

We ran our errands and returned to the farm several hours later. I was hoping for a word alone with Jamie before Pappy could speak to him, but as luck would have it, he and Henry were out front working on the truck when we pulled up. The children ran to meet us, clamoring for the candy I'd promised them.

"I'll give it to you inside," I said. "Jamie, would you help me carry these groceries in the house?"

"Wait just a goddamn minute," Pappy said to Jamie. "Who was that you had with you in the truck?"

Jamie's eyes flickered to me. I shook my head slightly, hoping he'd catch on and make something up.

"Well? Are you gonna answer me or not?" Pappy said.

"Girls, go inside," I said. "I'll be right there."

Reluctantly, they went. Jamie waited until they were out of earshot before answering Pappy. "As a matter of fact, it was Ronsel Jackson. What's it to you?" His voice was steady, but his cheeks had a hectic look. I wondered if he'd been drinking again.

"What's this?" asked Henry.

"I gave Ronsel a lift from town. Evidently our pappy doesn't approve."

"Not when he's sitting in the cab with you, I don't, and I bet your brother don't either," Pappy said.

Henry's expression was incredulous. "You let him sit inside the truck all the way from town?"

"What if I did?" Jamie said. "What does it matter?"

"Did anybody see you?"

"No, but I wouldn't care if they had."

They glared at each other, Jamie defiantly, Henry with a familiar mixture of anger, hurt and bewilderment that I'd last seen directed at me. Henry shook his head. "I don't know who you are anymore," he said. "I wonder if you do." He turned and walked toward the house. Jamie looked after him like he wanted to stop him, but he didn't move.

"Don't ever let me catch you giving that jigaboo a ride again," Pappy said.

"Or what?" Jamie said. "You gonna come after me with your cane?"

The old man grinned, revealing his long yellow teeth. He rarely smiled; when he did, the effect was both bizarre and repellent. "Oh, it ain't what I'll do to *you*."

Pappy followed Henry inside, leaving me alone with Jamie. His body looked tensed, poised for violence or flight. I was torn between wanting to soothe and chide him.

"I can't stay here," he said. "I'm going to town."

To his woman, I thought. "I wish you'd change your mind," I said. "I'm making rabbit stew for supper."

He reached out and lightly brushed my cheek with one finger. I swear I felt that touch in every nerve of my body. "Sweet Laura," he said.

I watched him go. As the truck and its wake of dust got smaller and smaller and finally disappeared, I thought, *Rabbit stew. That's what I'd been able to offer him.* It was all I would ever be able to offer him. The knowledge was as bitter as bile.

FLORENCE

I RAN THE BROOM over his foot three times. Said,
"Sorry, Mist Jamie, ain't I clumsy today." The third time Miz
McAllan gave me a scolding and sent me out of the house,
finished the sweeping her own self. I didn't care what she
thought, or him either. I just wanted him gone. But he didn't
go, not even after I threw salt in his tracks and put a mojo of
jimsonweed and gumelastin under his bed. He kept right on
coming back, turning up like the bad penny he was.

He was a shiny penny though, with his handsome face and
his littleboy smile. Folks just took to him natural, they couldn't
help themselves, like the way a child hankers for a holly berry.
He don't know it's poison, he just sees something pretty and
red and he wants it in his mouth. And when you take it away
from him he cries like you taking away his own heart. There's
a whole lot of evil in the world looks pretty on the outside.

Jamie McAllan wasn't evil, not like his pappy was, but he
did the Dark Man's business just the same. He was a weak
vessel. Whiskey on his breath at noon and womansmell all
over his clothes every Monday. Now a man can like his nature

activity and even his drink and still be the Lord's, but Jamie McAllan had a hole in his soul, the kind the devil loves to find. It's like a open doorway for him, lets him enter in and do his wicked work. I thought maybe he got it in the war and it would close on up in time but it just kept on getting bigger and bigger. None of em seen it but me. Jamie McAllan geehawsed em all, specially Miz McAllan. The way she looked at him you would a thought he was her husband and not his brother. But Henry McAllan didn't seem to mind, that's if he even noticed. Tell you one thing, if my sister ever stretched her eyes at Hap like that, I'd claw em right out.

Even my son was took in by him. I knowed about their Saturday afternoon drives and them other times too when Ronsel went out walking after dark. Only place colored folks round here go walking after dark is to and from the outhouse, if they know what's good for em anyway. No, I knowed exactly where he was. He was out in that ole falling-down sawmill by the river, getting drunk with Jamie McAllan. I seen Ronsel heading off that way plenty of times and heard him stumbling in late at night. I tried to tell him to keep away from that man but he wouldn't listen.

"What you doing, hanging around with that white man?" I asked him.

"Nothing. Just talking."

"You asking for trouble is what you doing."

Ronsel shook his head. "He ain't like the rest of em."

"You right about that," I said. "Jamie McAllan's got a snake in his pocket and he carries it along with him wherever he goes. But when that snake gets ready to bite, it ain't gone bite him, oh no. It's gone sink them fangs into whoever else is with him. You just better make sure it ain't you."

"You don't know him," Ronsel said.

"I know he's drinking whiskey every day and hiding it from his family."

Ronsel looked away. "He's just chasing off his ghosts," he said.

My son had plenty of em too, I knowed that, but he wouldn't talk to me bout em. He was like a boarded-up house since he come back from that war, nothing going into him or coming out of him—at least, nothing from or to us. Jamie McAllan had more of Ronsel than we did.

I didn't tell Hap about the two of em drinking together. I don't like to keep things from my husband but him and Ronsel was already butting heads all the time. That was Hap's doing, he was pushing Ronsel to talk to Henry McAllan bout taking over the Atwoods' old acres. There was a new cropper family in there but Mist McAllan wasn't happy with em, he'd said so to Hap. Ronsel told his daddy he'd think it over, but he wanted them acres like a cat wants a pond to swim in. And Hap just kept on pushing him and pushing him, that was the landsickness talking is what that was.

"You don't stop, you gone push him right out the door," I told him.

"He's a man grown," Hap said. "He needs to get his own place, start his own family. Might as well be here. One of the twins can help him. With the four of us working fifty acres, and if cotton prices stay above thirty cents a pound, in three four years we'll have enough to buy our own land."

Ronsel couldn't a cared less about having his own land, but there wasn't no point in telling that to my husband. Might as well to been singing songs to a dead hog. Once Hap gets a notion a something, he's deaf and blind to everything that don't mesh with it. It's what makes him a good preacher, his faith never wobbles. Folks see that in him and it bucks em up. But what works in the pulpit ain't always good at your own kitchen table. All Ronsel seen was his daddy not caring bout what he wanted. And what he wanted was to leave. I hated the thought of him going but I knowed he had to do it soon, just like I had to set back and let him.

By springtime he was getting drunk with Jamie McAllan every couple days. So when ole Mist McAllan seen the two of em together in the truck, I was glad. I thought it would put a stop to the whole business.

Ronsel didn't mention it to us. Just like the last time, we had to find out what happened from Henry McAllan. He come by one afternoon, all het up, wanting a word with Hap and Ronsel. And just like the last time, I listened in. Reckoned I had a right to know what was being said on my own front porch, whether the men thought so or not.

"I expect you know why I'm here, Ronsel," Mist McAllan said.

"No suh, I don't."

"My brother tells me he gave you a lift from town today."

"Yessuh."

"I reckon it wasn't the first time."

"No, not the first."

"Exactly how long has this been going on?"

"I can't rightly say."

"Hap, do you know what I'm talking about?"

"No, Mist McAllan."

"Well, let me tell you then," Henry McAllan said. "Apparently your son here and my brother have been riding around the countryside in my truck for God knows how long, sitting in the cab together like two peas in a pod. My father saw them today, coming back from town. You telling me you knew nothing about this?"

"No suh," Hap said. "Well, I knew Mist Jamie given Ronsel a ride every once in awhile, but I didn't know he was setting up in front with him."

But Hap did know, cause he'd seen em together that first time. You better believe he gave Ronsel a talking-to that day, told him never to sit in the front seat of a white man's car again unless he was the driver and wearing a black cap to prove it.

"And now that you do know," Mist McAllan said, "what have you got to say about it?"

A silence come down amongst em. I could feel Hap struggling, trying to decide how to answer. It wasn't right, Henry McAllan asking him to take sides against his own son like that. If Mist McAllan wanted Ronsel humbled down he should a done it his own self, instead of expecting Hap to do it for him. *Don't you do it, Hap,* I thought.

But before he could answer, Ronsel spoke up. "I don't reckon my father's got anything to say about it, seeing as how he didn't know nothing about it. It's me you should be asking."

"Well then?" Henry McAllan said. "What in the world were you thinking?"

"White man tells me to get in his truck, I get in." Ronsel's voice was pretend-humble though, even I could hear it.

"You mocking me, boy?" Henry McAllan said.

"No suh, course not," Hap said. "He just trying to explicate hisself."

"Well let me explicate something to you, Ronsel. If I catch you riding in the car with my brother again, you're going to be in a heap of trouble, and I don't mean a nice little talk like we're having right now. My pappy isn't much of a talker when he gets riled up, if you take my meaning. So the next time Jamie offers you a ride, you tell him you need the exercise, hear?"

"Yessuh," Ronsel said.

"You know, Hap," Henry McAllan said, "I expected better sense from a son of yours." In a louder voice he said, "And that goes for you too, Florence."

After he was gone I went to the front door and looked out. Ronsel was standing on the edge of the porch staring after Henry McAllan's truck, and Hap was setting in his rocking chair staring at Ronsel's back.

"Well, Daddy," Ronsel said, "ain't you gone say I told you so?"

"Got no need to say it."

"Come on, I know you're itching to. So say it."

"Got no need."

For a long while the only sound was the crickets and the tree frogs and the squeak of Hap's rocker. Then Ronsel cleared his throat. *Here it comes,* I thought.

"I'll stay till the cotton's laid by," he said. "Then I'm leaving."

"Where you gone go, son?" Hap said. "Some big city up north, where you got no home and no people? That ain't no way to live."

"Wherever I go and however I live," Ronsel said, "I reckon it'll be better than here."

HENRY

By planting time I was about ready to kill my brother, messed up in the head or not. It wasn't just that he was drinking again and lying about it after he swore to me he'd stop. It was his selfishness that really got my goat. Jamie did whatever he damn well pleased without a thought for how it might affect anybody else. There I was, working hard to make a place for myself and my family in Marietta, and having a drunk brother who consorted with whores and niggers sure wasn't helping me. And on top of everything I had to listen to Laura make excuses for him while my father sat there smirking. Pappy thought I was blind to it but he was wrong. Even if I hadn't had two perfectly good eyes in my head, my ears would have told me.

Whenever Jamie was around she sang. And when it was just me, she hummed.

Still, I didn't mean to say what I said, not like that. But Jamie pushed me too far and the words just spilled out, and once they were out I couldn't take them back.

The two of us were in the barn. Jamie had just milked the cow and was taking the pail to the house when he tripped and fell, spilling the milk all over the floor and himself. He started laughing, acted like it was nothing. And I guess in the scheme of things it wasn't but right at that moment it rankled me.

"You think it's funny, spilling good milk," I said.

"Well, you know what they say, no use crying over it."

By the way he ran the words together and lurched to his feet I could tell he'd been drinking. That rankled me even more. I said, "No, especially when it's somebody else's."

That wiped the grin off his face. "I see," he said, in a sarcastic tone. "What do I owe you, Henry?" He reached in his pocket and pulled out a handful of change. "Let's see, there must have been three gallons there, that'd run what, about two dollars? Let's say two and a quarter to be on the safe side. I wouldn't want to gyp you." He started to count out the money.

"Don't be an ass," I said.

"Oh no, brother, I insist." He held out the money. When I wouldn't take it, he reached over and tried to shove it in my shirt pocket. I batted his hand away, and the coins fell to the floor.

"For Christ's sake," I said. "This isn't about money and you know it."

"What's it about then? What would you have me do, Henry?"

"Sober up, for one thing," I said. "Take some responsibility for yourself and start acting like a grown man."

"One pail of spilled milk and I'm not a man?" he said.

"You're sure not acting like one lately."

His eyes got small and mean, just like our father's did when anybody crossed him. "And how should I act, brother—like you?" Jamie said. "Walking around here like God Almighty in his creation, laying down the law, so wrapped up in myself I can't see my wife is miserable? Is that the kind of man I should be? Huh?"

I'd never hit my brother before but right then I was mighty close to it. "Be whatever kind of man you want," I said. "Just do it someplace else."

"Fine. I'll go to town." He started to walk out.

"I don't mean for the night," I said.

I saw it in his face then, that look like he used to get as a boy when one of Pappy's gibes cut deep. Then it was gone, pasted over with indifference. He shrugged. "Yeah, well," he said. "I was getting tired of this place anyway."

He's got nothing, I thought. *No wife or kids, no home to call his own. No idea of himself he can shape his life around.* "Look," I said, "that didn't come out like I meant it to."

"Didn't it?" Jamie said. "Seemed to me it came out pretty easy, like you've been thinking it for a good long while."

"I just think you need a fresh start somewhere," I said. "We both know you're no farmer."

"I'll leave tomorrow, if that's soon enough for you."

I didn't want him going off mad and half-cocked. "There's no need for that," I said. "Besides, I'm counting on your help with the planting."

He acted like he hadn't heard me. "I'll catch the first bus out of here in the morning," he said.

"I'm asking you to stay a little longer," I said. "Just till we get the seed in."

He considered me for a long moment, then gave me a bitter smile. "Anything for my big brother," he said. He walked out then, back straight and rigid as a soldier's. Jamie would deny it but he's just like our pappy in one respect. He never forgets a slight, or forgives one.

LAURA

IF HENRY HADN'T been so stubborn.

If there hadn't been a ball game on.

If Eboline had taken better care of her trees.

It was the twelfth of April, a week after the incident with Ronsel. Henry, Jamie, Pappy and I were having dinner at Dex's. The girls were at Rose's, celebrating Ruth Ann's seventh birthday with a much-anticipated tea and slumber party.

Halfway through the meal, Bill Tricklebank came in looking for us. Eboline had called the store, frantic. A dead limb had cracked off her elm tree that morning and caved in her roof. No one was hurt, but the living room was exposed and there was a big storm headed our way. It was expected to hit Greenville sometime Monday.

"Damn," said Henry after Bill had left. "Wouldn't you know it'd be right in the middle of planting season."

"I'll go," Jamie offered.

"No," said Henry. "That's not a good idea."

Jamie's mouth tightened. "Why not?" he said.

Things were still tense between him and Henry. I was staying out of it; the two times I'd tried to talk to Henry about it he'd practically taken my head off.

"You know why," Henry said.

"Come on, it's been six months. Charlie Partain's not gonna do anything even if he does happen to see me. Which he won't."

"That's right," said Henry, "because you're not going."

"Who's Charlie Partain?" I asked.

"The sheriff of Greenville," said Pappy. "He ain't too fond of our family."

"After the accident, he told me to keep Jamie out of town," said Henry, "and that's exactly what I aim to do."

"This isn't about Charlie Partain," said Jamie. "You don't trust me to go. Do you, brother?"

Henry stood, took a ten-dollar bill out of his wallet and set it on the table. To me he said, "Telephone Eboline and let her know I'm on my way. Then get somebody at Tricklebank's to take you all home. I'll be back in a few days."

He bent and gave me a swift kiss. When he turned to leave, Jamie grabbed his arm. "Do you?" he asked again.

Henry looked down at the hand on his arm, then at Jamie. "Let the tenants know there's a storm coming," he said. "Get the tractor inside the barn and fix that loose shutter in the girls' bedroom. And you better check the roof of the house, nail down any loose edges."

Jamie gave him a curt nod, and Henry left. We finished eating and walked over to Tricklebank's. Jamie and Pappy stayed on the porch while I went inside and called Eboline. Afterward

I bought a few groceries from Bill. When I came out with them, Pappy was at one end of the porch, listening to a ball game on the radio with some other men. Jamie was sitting alone at the opposite end, smoking and staring moodily out at the street. I went over to him and asked if he'd found us a ride.

He nodded. "Tom Rossi's going to take us. He went to the feed store, said to meet him over there."

Tom owned the farm to the west of ours. He was also the part-time deputy sheriff of Marietta. I found it oddly dispiriting, living in a place whose citizens only misbehaved enough to warrant a police force of one and a half.

"You about ready to leave?" I called to Pappy.

"Do I look like I'm ready, gal? The game just started."

"I'll bring him," said one of the other men.

"Supper's at six," I said.

Pappy waved us off, and Jamie and I left to go find Tom.

I sat between them on the ride to the farm, making awkward small talk with Tom while Jamie brooded beside me. As soon as Tom dropped us off, Jamie took the truck and drove off to warn the tenants about the storm. When I heard him return, I went outside. He was striding angrily toward the barn, his hair ablaze in the sun. I called out to him.

He kept going, calling back, "I need to fetch the ladder and see to the roof."

"That can wait a little while," I said. "I want to talk to you."

He stopped but didn't turn around. His body was rigid, his hands balled into fists. I went and stood directly in front of him.

"You're wrong about Henry not trusting you," I said.

"You think so, huh?"

"Don't you see, that's what he was trying to tell you, when he asked you to warn the tenants and all the rest of it. That he trusts you."

"Yeah," Jamie said, with a harsh laugh, "he trusts me so much he wants me gone."

"Don't be silly. He's just sore at you over the Ronsel business. He'll get over it."

Jamie cocked his head. "So, he hasn't told you yet," he said. "I didn't think he had."

"Told me what?"

"He kicked me out."

"What are you talking about?"

"He asked me to leave yesterday. I'm going as soon as we're done planting. Next week, most likely."

I felt a sharp pain somewhere near the center of my body, followed by a draining sensation that made me a little dizzy. It reminded me of how I'd felt when I used to give blood for the war effort. Only now it was all going, all the life and color in me, seeping out into the dirt at my feet. When Jamie left and I was emptied, I would be invisible again, just like I'd been before he came. I couldn't go back to being that dutiful unseen woman, the one who played her roles without really inhabiting them. I wouldn't go back. *No.*

I realized I'd spoken the word out loud when Jamie said, "I have to, Laura. Henry's right about one thing, I need to make a new start. And I sure as hell can't do it here." He waved his hand to take it all in—the shabby house and outbuildings, the ugly brown fields. And me, of course, I was part of that dreary landscape too. Henry's landscape. Fury gathered in my belly, rising up, scalding my throat. I truly hated my husband at that moment.

"I'd better get busy on those chores," Jamie said.

I watched him walk to the barn. At the door, he stopped and looked back at me. "I never thought my brother would turn against me like this," he said. "I never thought he was capable of it."

I could think of nothing to say in answer. Nothing that would comfort him. Nothing that would keep him here.

I LISTENED TO HIM move the tractor, hammer the shutter, climb up on the ladder to check the roof. Mundane sounds, but they filled me with sadness. All I could think of was the silence to come.

When he was finished he popped his head in the front window. "The roof looks fine," he said. "I've taken care of the rest."

"You want some coffee?"

"No, thanks. I think I'll take a nap."

He'd been asleep for maybe twenty minutes when I heard him moaning and shouting. I hurried out to the lean-to, but at the door I found myself hesitating. I looked at my hand on the latch and thought of all the things it had proven capable of since I'd been at Mudbound, things that would have frightened or shocked me once. I looked at the ragged nails, the swollen red knuckles, the slender strip of gold across the fourth finger. I watched my hand lift the latch.

Jamie was sprawled on his back, his arms flung wide. He was still dressed, except for his shoes and socks. His feet were long, pale and slender, with a blue tracery of veins in the arches. I had the urge to press my mouth to them. He cried out and one arm flailed upward, as if he were warding something off. I sat on the edge of the bed and took hold of his arm, pushing it down against the sheet. With my other hand I smoothed his hair back from his damp forehead. "Jamie, wake up," I said.

He tore his arm from my grasp and grabbed my shoulders, his fingers digging into my skin. I said his name again and his eyes opened, darting around wildly before settling on my face. I watched sense come into them, then awareness of who I was, and where we were.

"Laura," he said.

I could have looked away then, but I didn't. I held myself very still, knowing he could see everything I felt and letting him see it. It was the most intimate act of my life, more intimate even than the acts that followed. Jamie didn't move, but I felt the change in the way his hands gripped me. His eyes dropped to my mouth and my heart lurched, slamming against the bone. I waited for him to pull me down to him, but he didn't, and I realized finally that he wouldn't; that it was up to me. I remembered the first time Henry had kissed me, how he'd taken my face in his hands as though it were something he had a right to. That was the difference between men and women, I thought: Men take for themselves the things they want, while women wait to be given them. I would not wait any longer. I bent down and touched my lips to Jamie's, tasting whiskey and cigarettes, anger and longing that I knew was not just for me. I didn't care. I took it all, no questions asked, either of him or myself. His hands pulled me on top of him, undid the buttons of my blouse, unsnapped my garters. Urgent, impatient, speeding us past whether and why. I went willingly, following the path of his desire.

And then, suddenly, he stopped. He rolled me to one side and got up out of the bed, and I thought, *He's changed his mind. Of course he has.* He took my hand and drew me up to stand in front of him. Mortified, I looked down and started to button my blouse back up. His hand reached out, raised my chin. "Look at me," he said.

I made myself look. His gaze was steady and fierce. He ran his thumb across my mouth, stroking the bottom lip open, then his hand dropped lower. He brushed the backs of his fingers across my breast, once, and then again in the opposite direction. My nipples stiffened and my legs trembled. My body felt dense and heavy, an unwieldy liquid mass. I would have fallen but his eyes held me up. There was a demand in them, and a gravity I'd never seen before. I understood then: We wouldn't be swept away by passion, as I'd always imagined. Jamie wouldn't let us be. This would be a deliberate act. A choosing.

Without looking away from him, I reached out with my hand, found his belt buckle and pulled the leather from it. When I released the catch he let out a long breath. His arms went around me and his mouth came down on mine.

When he was poised above me I didn't think of Henry or my children, of words like *adultery, sin, consequences.* I thought only of Jamie and myself. And when I drew him into me I thought of nothing at all.

HE FELL ASLEEP on top of me, as Henry sometimes did when he was tired, but I felt none of my usual irritation or restiveness. Jamie's weight on me was sweet. I closed my eyes, wanting to shut out every other sensation, wanting his weight to imprint the shape of him into my flesh.

It was the thought of Pappy that got me to move. By the golden tint of the light coming in the window, it was late afternoon; he'd be home any time now. Carefully, trying not to wake Jamie, I extricated myself from beneath him. He stirred and moaned but his eyes stayed closed. I picked up my clothes from the floor, dusted them off and got dressed. I went to the mirror. My hair was disheveled, but apart from that I looked like myself: Laura McAllan on a normal Saturday afternoon. Everything had changed; nothing had changed. Astonishing.

I heard the cot springs creak slightly behind me and knew that Jamie was awake and watching me. *I should turn around and face him,* I thought, but my body refused to do it. I left the room quickly, without looking at him or speaking. Afraid I would find shame in his eyes, or hear regret in his voice.

About half an hour later I heard the truck start up and pull away.

HAP

THAT MONDAY AFTERNOON I was out by the shed hitching the mule to the guano cart when Ronsel finally come back from town. By that point I was mighty vexed with him. He'd went in to run an errand for his mama but he was gone way too long for that. Mooning around again, I reckoned, thinking bout going off to New York or Chicago or one a them other faraway places he was always talking bout, meantime here I was trying to get the fields fertilized and needing every bit of help I could get.

"Where you been?" I said. "Half the day's gone."

He didn't answer, it was like he didn't hear me or even see me. He was just staring off with this funny look on his face, like he'd had the stuffing knocked out of him.

"Ronsel!" I hollered. "What's the matter with you?"

He jumped and looked at me. "Sorry, Daddy. I guess I was off somewhere else."

"Come help me load this fertilizer."

"I'll be right there," he said.

He went in the house. Bout a minute later he come charging

out onto the porch, looking all around like he'd lost something. "You seen a piece of paper anywhere?" he said.

"What kind of paper?"

"An envelope, with writing on the front."

"No, I ain't seen nothing like that," I said.

He looked all around the yard, getting more and more worked up every second. "It must a fell out of my pocket on the road from town. Goddamnit!"

"Ronsel! What's in this envelope?"

But he didn't answer me. His eyes lit on the road. "I bet it fell out in that ditch," he said. "I got to go fetch it."

"I thought you were gone help me with this fertilizer."

"This can't wait, Daddy," he said. He took off running down the road. That was the last time I ever heard my son's voice.

RONSEL

THE ENVELOPE HAD a German stamp in the corner of it. It was dirty and beat up from traveling so many miles and passing through so many hands. The writing was a woman's, fancy and slanted. Soon as I seen it I knew it had to been from Resl. The censors had opened it and taped it back up again. I hated the thought of them knowing what she'd wrote me before I did.

When I pulled out the letter a photograph fell out, right onto the floor of the post office. I picked it up and looked at it. Amazing, how a little piece of shiny paper can change your whole life forever. My mouth went dry and my heart sped up. I opened the letter, hoping the censors hadn't blacked anything out, but for once it was all there.

> Lieber Ronsel,
>
> This Letter I am writing with the Help of my Friend Berta on who you may remember. I do not know if it is arriving to you but I am hoping that it will. May be you are surprised to hearing from me. At first I am thinking I am not writing to you but then I have decided that I must do it, because it is

not right that a Mann does not know he is having a Son. That is what I want to say you—you have a Son. I name him after my Father und his Father, Franz Ronsel. He is born in the Nacht of the 14 November at 22:00, in the Hospital of Teisendorf. I ask myself what you is doing at that Moment. I am trying to imagine you in your flat Missippi but I can not make such a Picture in my Mind, only of your Face which I see everyday when I look at the little Franz. I am sending you a Foto so that you can see him. He have your Eyes und your Smile.

At your Leaving I did not know that I am carrying your Child in me and when I learned to know it my Proud did not let me write you. But now I have this beautiful Son and I am thinking on the Day on which he know he has no Father and his smiling will die. Compared to that my Proud is not important. For Franzl I ask you please, will you come back and stay with us hier, with me und Maria und your Son. I know it is not being easy but I have this Haus und I believe that together we are making a gut Life. Please answer quick and say me that you are coming back to us.

In Love,

Your Resl

The letter was dated 2 February 1947, more than two months ago. My heart was sore thinking of her waiting all that time for an answer and not getting one. I lifted the paper to my nose but if her scent had ever been on it, it was long gone. I looked at the photo again. There was Resl, looking as sweet and pretty as ever, with the baby bundled up in her arms. In the picture his skin was a medium gray, lighter than mine would've been, so I guessed he was gingercake-colored like my daddy. She was holding up one of his little hands and waving it at the camera.

My Resl. My son.

A SON, I HAVE A SON. That was the only thought in my head, walking back from town with that letter in my pocket. Knowing I was a father made the world sharper edged to my eye. The sky looked bluer and the shacks that squatted underneath it looked shabbier. The newly planted fields on either side of me seemed to stretch on and on like a brown ocean between me and him. But how in the hell could I get to Germany? And what would I do once I got there? I didn't speak the language, had no way to support a family there. But I couldn't just abandon them. Maybe I could bring the three of them back, not to Mississippi but someplace else where they wouldn't care that she was white and I was colored. Had to be a place like that somewhere, maybe in California or up north. I could ask Jimmy, he might know. Too damn many mights and maybes, that was the problem. I needed to think it through and make a plan. In the meantime I'd help them however I could. I didn't have much money left, maybe a few hundred dollars stuffed into the toes of my boots at the bottom of my duffel bag. I'd write to Captain Scott at Camp Hood, he'd know how to get it to Resl. But first I'd write and tell her I still loved her and was working on a plan, so she could whisper it to my son.

I was so busy thinking I didn't even hear the truck till it was almost on top of me. Turned around and there it was, coming straight at me. Soldier's instincts is all that saved me. I dived into the ditch on the side of the road and landed in mud. The truck passed so close to my head it like to gave me a crew cut, then it went off into the ditch right in front of me. I recognized it then, it was the McAllans' truck. For a minute I thought Old Man McAllan had tried to run me over but when the door opened Jamie got out. Well, fell out is more like it, he was drunker than I'd ever seen him, and that was saying something. He had a bottle in one hand and a cigarette in the other. He staggered over to where I was.

"That you, Ronshel?"

"Yeah, it's me."

"You all right?"

"I'm as muddy as a pig in a wallow, but other than that I'm fine."

"Shouldn't be walking in the middle of the road like that, you're liable to get yourself killed."

"It'll take more than a drunk white flyboy to kill me," I said.

He laughed and plopped down on the edge of the ditch, and I got up and sat beside him. He looked terrible sickly. Red-eyed, unshaven, skin all sweaty. He took a swig from the bottle and offered it to me. It was more than three-quarters empty already.

"No thanks, I better not," I said. "Maybe you better not either."

Jamie wagged his finger at me. "Do not think, gentlemen, I am drunk." He raised his left hand and said, "This is my ancient, this is my right hand." Then he raised the hand holding the bottle. A little whiskey sloshed out onto his pants leg but he didn't seem to notice. "And this is my left. Oh God, that men should put an enemy in their mouths to steal away their brains! That we should with joy, pleasure, revel and . . . revel and . . . what's the fourth thing, damnit?"

He looked at me like I was supposed to know. I just shrugged.

"With joy, pleasure, revel and . . . applause—that's it, applause!—transform ourselves into beasts!" He twirled his left hand in the air and bowed from the waist. He would've fell over into the ditch if I hadn't grabbed his shirt collar and yanked him back up.

"Hey," I said, "is something the matter?"

He shook his head and stared at the bottle, picking at the label with his fingernail. He was quiet a good long while, then he said, "What's the worst thing you ever did?"

"Killing Hollis, I guess." I'd told him about it one night at the sawmill: how I'd shot my buddy Hollis in the head after his legs got blown off by a grenade and he begged me to do it.

"No, I mean something that hurt somebody bad. Something you never forgave yourself for. You ever do anything like that?"

Yeah, I thought, *leaving Resl.* I was that close to telling him about her. I wanted to say the words out loud: *I'm a father, I have a son.* I'd already told him plenty of things, like about shooting Hollis and refusing to let the crackers in our tanks and the time me and Jimmy went to a cabaret in Paris where the dancing girls were all stark naked. But there was a mighty big difference between that and me having a child by a white woman. Jamie McAllan was born and bred in Mississippi. If he got fired up and decided to turn me in, I could get ten years in Parchman—that's if I didn't get lynched on the way there.

"No," I said, "nothing I can think of."

"Well I have. I've belied a lady, the princess of this country."

"What you talking bout? What princess?"

"And she, sweet lady, dotes, devoutly dotes, dotes in idolatry upon this spotted and inconstant man. Idolatry, idultery—ha!"

So that's what was troubling him. Thinking of Josie, I said, "Ain't good to mess with the married gals, you just looking for heartache there. Best thing to do is put it behind you, never see her again."

He nodded. "Yeah. I'm leaving here next week."

"Where you going?"

"I don't know. Maybe California. I always wanted to see it."

"I've got a buddy lives in Los Angeles. According to Jimmy, it never gets too hot or too cold there and it hardly ever rains. Course he could've been pulling my leg."

Jamie looked at me, a hard clear look like you get sometimes from somebody who's drunk, it's like they sober up just long enough to really see you. "You ought to leave here too, Ronsel," he said. "Hap can manage without you now."

"I am leaving, just as soon as the crop's laid by."

"Good. This is no place for you."

He finished the whiskey and tossed the bottle into the ditch.

When he tried to stand up his legs gave out. I got up and helped him to his feet. "Reckon you better let me drive you home," I said.

"Reckon I better."

Somehow we managed to push the truck out of the ditch, then I drove him as far as the bridge and got out. I figured he could make it from there, and I didn't want Henry McAllan or that old man seeing us.

"You drive careful the rest of the way," I told him. "Try not to run any more colored people off the road."

He smiled and held out his hand. We shook. "Doubt I'll see you again before I go," he said. "You take care of yourself, hear?"

"You too."

"You've been a friend. I want you to know that."

He didn't wait for me to say anything back, just waved and drove off. I followed the truck down the road toward home, watching it weave back and forth, thinking of how surprising a place the world could be sometimes.

MUST'VE BEEN HALF an hour later that I found the letter gone. The first thing I thought was it fell out in that ditch. Ran all the way back there and looked but all I found was Jamie's whiskey bottle. I kept on going all the way to town and still didn't find it. The post office was closed but I was sure I hadn't left it in there. Only two places it could be: in somebody's pocket who'd picked it up or in the McAllans' truck. I made myself keep calm. If I'd left it in the truck Jamie might've found it. He wouldn't show it to nobody, he'd keep it for me. Maybe he was over at my house right now looking to give it back to me. And if not and it was still in the truck, I could sneak over there after dark and get it before anybody saw it.

By the time I headed back home it was coming on to dark and raining hard. I'd left without my hat so I was soaking wet. I was about halfway there when I heard the sound of a vehicle bearing down on me for the second time that day. I turned around and seen two sets of headlights. I jumped down into the ditch but instead of passing me they stopped right beside me. I didn't recognize the car in front but I knew the truck behind it. There were white figures inside, four in the car and maybe another three in the truck. Seemed like they practically glowed in the dark. When they got out I seen why.

LAURA

JAMIE DIDN'T COME back on Saturday, or on Sunday. When Rose brought the girls home Sunday morning I asked if she'd seen him in town, and she said no. It was a long couple of days, waiting. The sweet ache between my legs was a constant reminder of what Jamie and I had done. I had a few pricks of conscience—seeing Henry's pajama bottoms hanging forlornly from a peg in our bedroom, his comb on the dresser, a stray white hair on his pillow—but real shame and regret were absent. In their place was a riotous sense of wonder. I'd never imagined myself capable of either great boldness or great passion, and the discovery that I had reservoirs of both astounded me. I couldn't stop picturing myself with Jamie. I burned the grits, forgot to feed the animals, scalded my arm on the stove.

Pappy was in a fouler mood than usual. He was low on cigarettes and furious at Jamie for leaving us with no transportation. He smoked his last one early Monday morning and spent the entire day punishing me for it. My biscuits were too dry, was I trying to choke him to death? My floors were so dirty they weren't fit for a nigger to walk on. My brats were making too much racket. My coffee was too weak, how many times had he told me he liked it strong?

Short of walking, there was no way to get to town until Henry or Jamie got home.

"Goddamnit, where is he?" Pappy called out for the tenth time.

"Mind your language," I said. "The children are right here."

He was out on the porch watching the road, which was preferable to having him in the house with us. Florence had gone home for the day. I was sewing new dresses for the girls, and they were making paper dolls. We could hear Pappy's boots clomping back and forth outside the window.

"It's just like him," said the old man, "pulling a stunt like this. Thinking only of himself, the hell with everybody else."

The irony of Pappy complaining about Jamie or any other person being selfish was too much, and I laughed out loud. The shutters banged open, revealing Pappy's scowling face at the window. I was reminded of a malevolent cuckoo clock.

"What are you snickering at?" he demanded.

"Something Bella just did."

"You think it's funny, an old man being without his cigarettes. Just you wait and see how you feel when you get old, and you have to do without your comforts because nobody cares enough to look after you."

"You could always ride one of the mules to town," I suggested, deadpan.

Pappy couldn't stand animals, especially large ones. I think he was afraid of them, though he never admitted as much. It was the reason we didn't have any pets on the farm; he wouldn't tolerate them.

"I ain't doing any such thing," he said. "Why don't you go ask that nigger gal if she'll go? Tell her I'll pay her two bits."

"I'm sure Florence has better things to do than fetch your cigarettes for you."

His face retreated as abruptly as it had appeared. "Never mind," he said. "I see the truck coming."

The girls ran out to the porch to wait for their uncle. I took a deep breath and followed them. I would need to be very careful around Jamie to avoid raising Pappy's suspicions.

"Drunk again," Pappy said scornfully.

The car was weaving all over the road. At one point it went off entirely and into the newly planted fields. I was glad Henry wasn't home to see that; he would have been apoplectic. Jamie pulled up in front of the house and got out of the truck. Bella started to run to him but I held her back. He was rumpled and unshaven. One shirt tail hung out of the front of his pants. "Afternoon Laura, Pappy, little petunias," he said, swaying on his feet.

"You got any cigarettes?" said the old man.

"Hello, son," said Jamie, slurring the words together. "I'm so glad to see you, how are you today? Why Pappy, thank you for asking, I'm fine, and how are you?"

"You can talk to yourself all you want, just give me a smoke first."

Jamie reached in his shirt pocket and pulled out a pack of

Lucky Strikes, tossing them to his father. The throw fell short, forcing Pappy to bend down and pick them up off the ground. "There's only one cigarette here," said the old man.

"Guess I smoked the rest."

"You ain't worth a damn, you know that?"

"Well, I'm worth one cigarette. That's something. Unless you don't want it."

"Just give me the truck keys."

Jamie held them up, dangling them. "Ask nice and maybe I will."

Pappy walked toward Jamie, his steps slow and menacing. "You trying to mess with me? Huh, mister big hero?" The old man's cane was in his left hand, but he wasn't leaning on it; he was gripping it like a club. "Just keep talking, and we'll find out which one of us is a man and which one ain't. See, I know the answer already, but I don't think you do. I think you're confused on the subject. That's why you keep giving me lip, is because you want to be straightened out. Ain't that right, boy?"

When he reached Jamie he stopped and leaned forward until their faces were inches apart. How strongly they resembled each other! I'd never seen it before—I'd always thought of Pappy as ugly—but their features were essentially the same: the arched sardonic brows, the slanting cheekbones, the full, slightly petulant mouth.

"Ain't that right?" said the old man again.

My muscles tensed; the urge to step between them was almost overwhelming. Suddenly Pappy raised his cane, thrusting it toward Jamie's face—a feint, but Jamie flinched and took a step back.

"That's what I thought," Pappy said. "Now give me the goddamn keys."

Jamie dropped them into his outstretched hand. The old man shook the cigarette out of the pack, lit it and blew the smoke in Jamie's face. Jamie crumpled to his knees and retched. Liquid gushed out, not a solid thing in it. I wondered when he'd last eaten. I went and knelt beside him, helpless to do anything but pat him gingerly on the back as his body convulsed. His shirt was soaked through with sweat.

I heard a bark of laughter and looked up. The old man was watching us from the cab of the truck. "Well, ain't you a pretty pair," he said.

"Just go," I said.

"Can't wait to have him all to yourself, eh gal? Too bad he's too liquored up to be any good to you."

"What are you talking about?"

"You know exactly what I mean."

"No, I don't."

"Then why's your face so red, huh?" Pappy started the truck. "Don't let him fall asleep on his back," he said. "If he throws up again he could choke to death."

He drove off. I looked down at Jamie. He'd stopped retching and was lying limp on his side in the dirt. "When he is best, he is a little worse than a man," Jamie said in a hoarse voice, "and when he is worst he is little better than a beast."

"What's the matter with Uncle Jamie?" Amanda Leigh called out.

I turned and saw the girls watching. I'd forgotten all about them. "He just has an upset tummy is all," I said. "Do me a favor, darling, fetch me a clean washrag. Dip it in the bucket, wring it out, then bring it here. And a glass of water too."

"Yes, Mama."

Somehow I got him to his bed in the lean-to. He fell onto it and lay on his back without moving. I took off his shoes. His socks were missing. A vivid and unwelcome picture of them lying abandoned under some woman's bed flashed into my mind. With some difficulty, I rolled him onto his side. When I'd gotten him settled I looked down to find him watching me with an unreadable expression.

"Sweet Laura," he said. "My angel of mercy." His hand lifted and cupped my breast, possessively, familiarly. I felt a stab of desire. His eyes fluttered closed and his hand fell to the bed. I heard a familiar tapping sound on the roof; gentle at first, then sharper and more insistent. It had begun to rain.

It MUST HAVE been about two hours later that the front door flew open and Florence came bursting in. The girls and I had just sat down to a late supper. Pappy still hadn't come home, and I wasn't going to wait on him any longer. The children were hungry and so was I.

"Where's Mist Jamie?" Florence said, without preamble. She was soaked to the skin and breathing harshly, like she'd been running.

"Taking a nap in the lean-to. What's the matter?"

"Where's the truck then?"

"Pappy took it to town. Now what in the world's gotten into you?"

"Ronsel went to town earlier and he ain't come back. What time did Mist Jamie get home?"

Her high-handed attitude was beginning to annoy me. "Shortly after you left," I said. "Not that it's any of your business."

"Something's happened to my son," Florence said, "and Mist Jamie's caught up in it somehow, I know it."

"You're talking nonsense. How long has Ronsel been gone?"

"Since bout five o'clock. He should a been home by now."

"Well, it's nothing to do with Jamie. Like I said, he's been here since around three-thirty. Ronsel probably ran into a friend in town and lost track of the time. You know how young men are."

Florence shook her head, just once, but I felt the weight of that negation as strongly as if she'd shoved me. "No. He ain't got no friends here, cept for Mist Jamie."

"What do you mean, they're friends?"

"You got to wake him up and ask him."

I stood up. "I'll do no such thing. Jamie's worn out, and he needs his rest."

Her nostrils flared, and her eyes flickered to the front door. *She means to force her way past me and go wake him,* I thought. I wouldn't be able to stop her; she was a foot taller than me and outweighed me by a good forty pounds. For the first time since I'd known her, I felt afraid of her.

"Best if you go on home," I said. "I bet Ronsel's there right now, wondering where you are."

There was real animosity in Florence's eyes, and it woke an answering flare in me. How dared she threaten me, and under my own roof? I remembered Pappy telling the girls one time that Lilly May wasn't their friend and never would be; that if it came down to a war between the niggers and the whites, she'd be on the side of the niggers and wouldn't hesitate to kill them both. It had angered me at the time, but now I wondered if there wasn't a brutal kernel of truth in what he'd said.

Bella started coughing; she'd swallowed her milk the wrong way. I went and whacked her on the back, then looked at Florence. I thought back to the first time we'd met; how crazy with worry I'd been for my children. The memory was like a clean blast of air, clearing my head of foolishness. This wasn't a murderous Negro in front of me, but an anxious mother.

"Watch the girls," I said. "I'll go and ask him."

I knocked on the door of the lean-to, but there was no answer, and when I opened it the lantern light revealed two empty beds. Jamie's pillowcase was cool to my hand. I checked the outhouse, but he wasn't there either, and there was no light in the barn. Where could he have gone, on foot and in such pitiful condition? He couldn't possibly have sobered up; it had been less than three hours since he got home. And where was Pappy? Tricklebank's was long closed, and it wasn't like the old man to miss supper and a chance to complain about my cooking.

It was with a growing feeling of dread that I went back to the house. "Jamie's not here," I told Florence. "He must have gone for a walk to clear his head. He sometimes does that in the evenings. I'm sure it's nothing to do with Ronsel."

Florence headed swiftly out the door. I followed her to the edge of the porch. "I'll send Jamie to your house as soon as he gets back," I called, "just to set your mind at ease. I'm sure you're worrying for nothing."

But I was talking to the air. The darkness had swallowed her up.

JAMIE

THE RAIN STARTLED me awake. The din of a Delta thunderstorm hitting a tin roof is about as close as you can get to the sound of battle without actually being in it. For a heart-pounding minute I was back in the skies over Germany, surrounded by enemy Messerschmitts. Then I realized where I was, and why.

I lay in the dark of the lean-to and took stock of my condition. My head hurt and my mouth was full of cotton. I was still a little tipsy, but not nearly lit enough to face Pappy and Laura. There'd been a bad scene earlier, that much I remembered, but the details were vague and that was just fine by me. Amnesia is one of the great gifts of alcohol, and I'm not one to refuse it. I groped under the bed for the bottle I kept stashed there, but when I picked it up it felt light in my hand. There were only a couple of swigs left and I took them both, then I shut my eyes and waited for the whiskey to kindle me. My stomach was empty so it didn't take long. I might have gone back to sleep, but I had to piss too bad. I fumbled for the lantern on the bedside table and lit it. Pappy's bed was empty. There was a pitcher of water sitting on the table, along with a basin, a neatly folded towel and some cornbread wrapped in a napkin. Laura must have left them there for me.

Laura. It came back to me then, in a rush of images: Her hair falling down around my face. Her breasts filling my hands. The dusky sweet scent of her. My brother's wife.

I went outside. It was full dark, but the lights were on in the house. I stood at the edge of the porch and added my own stream to the downpour, wondering what time it was. A flash of lightning lit up the yard, and I saw that both the truck and the car were gone. We didn't expect Henry till tomorrow, but why wasn't Pappy back? Maybe the old goat had gotten stuck in the rain. Maybe he was sitting in the truck in a ditch at this very moment, cussing the weather and me both. The thought cheered me.

As I was zipping up my pants I saw a light moving near the old sawmill. At first I thought it was Pappy coming home, but no headlights approached the house. The light bobbed along the river, winking in and out like somebody was walking through the trees with a lantern, then it went out. Whoever it was must have gone inside the sawmill. Ronsel, probably, or a drifter seeking shelter from the storm. They were welcome to it. I wasn't about to go investigate, not in that downpour.

I went back inside and got myself cleaned up. I didn't want to face Laura and the girls stinking of sweat and vomit and whiskey. I was half-dressed when I remembered the fifth I had stashed out in the sawmill. As soon as I pictured it, I wanted it. Without that bottle, I'd be on my own with Laura, and then

with my father and Henry whenever they showed up. I knew
Ronsel wouldn't drink my whiskey without invitation, but a
drifter sure would, if he found it. The thought of some bum
sucking down my Jack overcame my aversion to getting wet.
I stuffed some cornbread in my mouth and put on my jacket
and my hat. At the last second I grabbed my .38 and stuck it
in my pocket.

I was wet through within seconds of leaving the porch. The
wind tore my hat from my head, and the mud tried to pull my
boots off with every step. It was so dark that if it hadn't been
for the occasional bursts of lightning, I wouldn't have been
able to see a thing. As it was I almost ran straight into a vehicle
parked off to one side of the sawmill. The hood was warm.
When the lightning came again I recognized Henry's truck.
And there was another car parked beside it. *What the hell?*

I went around back of the building. Strips of light showed
between the planks, and I put my eye up to one of the gaps.
At first all I saw was white. Then it moved and I realized I was
looking at the back of somebody's head, and that he was wearing a white hood. He wasn't the only one. There were maybe
eight of them standing in a loose circle.

"How many times did you fuck her?" I heard a voice say.

One of the figures shifted, and I saw Ronsel kneeling in the
center of them. His hands and feet were tied behind his back,
and there was a noose around his neck. The rope was slung
over a beam in the ceiling. The man holding the other end gave
it a vicious yank. Ronsel gagged, and his head came up.

"Answer him, nigger!" said my father.

RONSEL

I STARTED TO RUN but then I heard the sound of a shot-gun round being chambered. I froze and held my hands up. A high tight voice said, "If I was you, boy, I'd stay right where I was." It sounded like Doc Turpin, the sonofabitch who'd messed up my daddy's leg. He'd talked through his nose like that, that day at Tricklebank's. And Daddy had told me he used to be in the Klan.

"Get him in the car." That voice I recognized straight-away—it was Old Man McAllan. I wondered if Henry McAllan was there too underneath one of them hoods. Somebody came up behind me and threw a burlap sack over my head. I flailed out and he punched me in the kidneys, then somebody else grabbed my arms and tied them behind my back. They drug me to the car and threw me in. One of them got in on either side of me, then we started moving.

The wet sack on my head smelled like coffee, I reckoned they got it at Tricklebank's. They must've met up there before they set out to find me. That gave me a little hope. If Mrs. Tricklebank had been there and heard them talking she

would've called Sheriff Tacker as soon as they left. He wasn't
no great friend to Negroes but surely he wouldn't stand by and
let one of us be lynched. Surely he wouldn't.

"Listen," I said, "I'll leave town."

"Shut up, nigger," said the man I thought was Turpin.

"I'll leave tonight, and I won't ever—"

"He said, shut up," snarled the man on my other side.

Something hard slammed into my ribs and all the breath
went out of me. The pain was fierce, felt like some of my ribs
were cracked. I kept quiet after that and so did they. Somebody
lit a cigarette. I'd never been much of a smoker but when my
nose caught the smell of it I wanted one bad. Funny how the
body keeps right on wanting what it wants even when it thinks
it's about to die.

The car made a turn and the ride got rough, I figured we'd
gone off the road. A couple minutes later we stopped. They
jerked me out of the car and marched me a ways into a building. The rain on the roof sounded like a thousand people clapping, cheering them on. I was shoved to my knees and I felt a
rope go around my neck. They tightened it, not quite enough
to choke me but one more hard tug and it would. It was hot
under the sack and hard to breathe. Sweat and coffee stung my
eyes and the burlap was itching my face. How long did it take
to choke to death? If I was lucky my neck would break and I'd
go quick, but if it didn't . . . I felt panic take ahold of me and
I fought it down, slowing my breathing like they'd taught us
in survival training. I would keep calm and wait for a chance
to escape. And if I couldn't, if they meant to kill me, I'd show

these fuckers how a man died. I was an NCO of the 761st Tank Battalion, a Black Panther. I wouldn't let them turn me into a scared nigger.

One of them jerked the sack off my head. At first all I seen was legs but then they stepped back some and I realized where I was: the old sawmill, where I'd spent so many nights drinking whiskey with Jamie McAllan. Seven or eight men stood in a circle around me. Most of them were just wearing white pillowcases but two of them had on real Klan robes with pointed hoods and round badges on the chest. The badges had square black crosses on them with red dots in the middle like drops of blood. I looked up to where the rope was slung over a beam, then followed it down to the hands of one of the men in robes. He was tall, maybe six foot five, and built like a bear. Had to be Orris Stokes, he was the biggest fellow in town. I'd helped his pregnant wife carry her groceries home from Tricklebank's one time.

"Do you know why you're here, nigger?" he said.

"No sir, Mr. Stokes."

He handed the rope to one of the others, then reached out with one of his huge arms and backhanded me. My head snapped back and I felt one of my teeth come loose.

"You say that name again or any other name and we'll make you even sorrier than you're already gonna be, hear?"

"Yes, sir."

The other man in Klan robes stepped forward. It was Doc Turpin, I was sure of it now. I could see his paunch pushing his robe out and his little beer-colored eyes glinting through the holes in his hood. It was plain he and Stokes were in charge.

"Bring forth the evidence," Turpin said.

One of the others held something out to him. Soon as I seen that old yellow hand I knew what had to be in it. Turpin took the letter and the photograph from Old Man McAllan and held them up in front of my face. Resl and Franz smiled out at me. I wished I could climb into that picture with them, into that other world.

"Did you rut with this woman?" Turpin asked.

I didn't answer, even though he had the letter right there in his hand. There were worse things they could do to me than hang me.

"We know you did it, nigger," said McAllan. "We just want to hear you say it."

Another one jerked on the rope and the noose dug into my windpipe. "Go on, say it!" he ordered. His voice was deep and raspy from chain-smoking. No doubt who that was: Dex Deweese, the owner of the town diner.

"Yes," I said.

"Yes, what?" said Turpin.

"Yes, I . . . was with her."

"You defiled a white woman. Say it."

I shook my head. Stokes hit me again, this time with his fist, knocking the tooth he'd loosened earlier out of its socket. I spat it out onto the floor.

"I defiled a white woman."

"How many times did you fuck her?" said Turpin.

I shook my head again. Truth was, I *had* fucked Resl at first. I'd taken what she offered thinking of nothing but my own pleasure, knowing I'd soon be moving on to another post.

When had it gotten to be more than that? I closed my eyes, trying to remember, trying to smell her scent. But all I could smell was my own sweat and their hate. The animal stench of it filled the room.

Deweese gave the rope a hard yank and I gagged.

"Answer him, nigger!" said old man McAllan.

"I don't know," I choked out.

Turpin waved the photo in the air. "Enough times to get her with this—I won't call it a child—this . . . abomination! A foul pollution of the white race!" The men shifted and muttered. Turpin was working them up good. "And what's the penalty for abomination?"

"Death!" shouted Stokes.

"I say we geld him," one of them said.

The fear that took ahold of me then was like nothing I ever felt in my whole life. My guts were churning and it was all I could do not to shit myself.

Turpin said, "And if a woman approach any beast and lie down with it, thou shalt kill the woman and the beast. They shall surely be put to death, and their blood shall be upon them."

"String him up," said Old Man McAllan.

Right then the door banged open and we all turned toward it. Jamie McAllan stood there dripping water all over the floor. He had a pistol in his hand and it was pointed at Deweese.

"Let go of the rope," Jamie said.

JAMIE

"LET IT GO," I said.

One of the others moved, a shotgun in his hands, rising. I pointed the pistol at him. "Drop it!" I said.

He hesitated. For a few seconds everybody froze. Then my father spoke up. "He's bluffing," said Pappy, "and he's half-drunk besides. Point the gun at the nigger. Go on, he won't shoot you. My son don't have the balls to kill a man up close." He stepped in front of the man with the shotgun, blocking my aim. I found myself staring down the sight of the pistol into my father's pale eyes, framed in white cotton. "Do you, son?" he said.

Behind him I could see the barrel of the shotgun, now pointed at Ronsel's head. Pappy took a step toward me, then another. There was a roaring in my ears, and the hand holding the pistol was shaking. I put my other hand under the butt to steady it.

"Stop right there," I said.

He took another step toward me. "You gonna betray your own blood over a nigger?"

"Don't come any closer. I'm warning you."

"Kill me, and the jig still dies."

Hate rose up in me—for him, for myself. I'd lost, and we both knew it. I only had one play left to make. "If you kill him, you better kill me too," I said. "Because if Ronsel dies, I'm going straight to the sheriff. I swear I'll do it."

"What are you gonna tell him, boy?" said the fat one in Klan robes. "You can't identify nary one of us, except for your father."

Without taking my eyes off Pappy, I said, "You know, Doc, white's not your color. Makes you look a little hefty. Now Dex here can wear it because he's so skinny, and Orris, well, he's gonna look big no matter what he has on. But if I were you, Doc, I'd stick to brown and black."

"Shit," said Deweese.

"Shut up," said Stokes. "He can't prove nothing."

"And I don't want to," I said. "I'm leaving here in a few days. Just let Ronsel go, and he'll leave town and I'll leave town and neither one of us will ever say a word about this to anybody. Isn't that right, Ronsel?"

He nodded frantically.

"Let go of the rope, Dex," I said. "Come on now, just let it go."

It might have worked. Ronsel Jackson and I might have walked out of there, if my father hadn't laughed. I'd always hated his laugh. Harsh and pitiless as the cawing of a crow, it broke the spell I'd been trying to weave. Stokes and one of the others rushed me. I could have shot one of them, but I hesitated. They barreled into me and we crashed to the floor. Stokes punched me in the face. My arms were wrenched behind me, and somebody kicked me in the stomach. At some point I lost the gun.

"Nigger lover!" Turpin shouted. "Judas!"

The punches and kicks were coming from all sides now. I could hear Pappy yelling, "Stop it! That's enough!"

Finally a boot connected with the back of my head, and that was all. *Goodnight, Pappy. Goodnight, Ronsel. Goodnight.*

HAP

"PLEASE JESUS," I SAID, "shepherd Your son Ronsel, keep him from harm and light his way home to us." I was praying loud on account of the storm, hollering at the Lord like He couldn't a heard me elseways. So when we heard that knocking we all just about jumped out of our skins, all of us cept for Florence. It was like she'd been waiting for it to come. She didn't even open her eyes, just kept right on praying. But when I got up to answer the door she grabbed ahold of my leg and held onto it so tight I couldn't move.

"Don't answer it," she said.

I could feel her shivering against me, quaking like a spent mule. I'd never seen my wife brung so low and afraid, not in all the years we'd been married. It hurt my heart to see that. Lilly May let into crying and the twins was hugging themselves, rocking back and forth on their knees.

"Come on now," I said. "Ain't the time for weakness now. We got to be strong."

The knocking come again, harder this time, and Florence let go of me. Ruel and Marlon gave each other a look like twins do when they talking without words, then they helped their mother to her feet and stood on either side of her. Drew themselves up tall, like men, and put their arms around her and Lilly May.

I went and opened the door. There was a fellow standing on the porch, I couldn't tell who it was at first on account of his head was bent, but then he looked up and I seen it was Sheriff Tacker and I thought, *He's dead. My boy is dead.*

"I've got bad news, Hap," the sheriff said. "It's about Ronsel." He looked behind me to where Florence and the children were standing. "You better step outside with me," he said.

"No," Florence said. "Whatever you got to say, you say it to all of us."

The sheriff shifted on his feet and looked down at the hat in his hands. "Seems your son ran afoul of an angry bunch of men tonight. He's alive, but he's hurt bad. They were pretty riled."

"Where is he?" I said.

"How bad?" Florence said.

He answered me and not her. "My deputy's taken him to the doctor in Belzoni. I'll drive you there now if you want."

Florence came over and stood beside me. She took ahold of my hand and gripped it hard. "How bad?" she asked the sheriff again.

He fumbled in his pocket and pulled out a piece of paper. "We found this laying on the ground next to him." Sheriff Tacker handed it to me. It was a letter and it had blood all over it, at first I thought it was just spilled on there but then I turned it sideways and seen the word and the numbers written in it, Ezekiel 7:4, written in blood by somebody's finger.

"What does it say?" Florence asked me.

But I couldn't answer her, fear had closed up my throat like a noose.

"Apparently your son was having relations with a white woman," the sheriff said.

"What? What white woman?" Florence said.

"Some German gal. That letter's from her, telling him he's the father of her son."

"It ain't true," Florence said. "Ronsel wouldn't do that."

I didn't want to believe it either but it was right there on the paper, I could read it through the blood. *You have a son*, it said. *Franz Ronsel.*

"Says there's a photograph with it but we didn't find it," the sheriff said.

"What did they do to him?" Florence said. I couldn't feel my hand, she was squeezing it so hard.

"They could've hanged him," the sheriff said. "He's lucky to be alive."

"You tell me what they done," Florence said.

And mine eye shall not spare thee, neither will I have pity: but I will recompense thy ways upon thee, and thine abominations shall be in the midst of thee: and ye shall know that I am the Lord. Ezekiel 7:4.

"They cut out his tongue," the sheriff said.

FLORENCE

MY SON'S TONGUE.

"Dear God," Hap said. "Dear God, how can this be true?"

They cut out his tongue.

"They could've hanged him," the sheriff said again.

They.

"Who did it?" I said.

"We don't know. They were gone by the time we got there," he said. He was lying though, a five-year-old could a told that.

"Where?" I said.

"The old sawmill."

I knowed right then who was behind this business. "How'd you know to go looking for him there in the first place?" I said.

"We got a tip there might be trouble," the sheriff said.

"Who from?"

"That ain't important. What matters is, your boy's alive and he's on his way to the doctor. If you want to get to him, we need to leave now."

"Why'd you send him all the way to Belzoni? Why not take him to Doc Turpin in town?"

The sheriff's eyes slid away from mine, and I knowed something else too. "He was one of em, wasn't he?" I said. "Who else was there besides him and Ole Man McAllan?"

The sheriff's face hardened up and his eyes got squinty. "Now you listen to me," he said. "I understand you're mighty upset, but you got no call to be pointing fingers at Doc Turpin or anybody else. If I was you, I'd be more careful what I said."

"Or what? You gone cut my tongue out?"

His Adam's apple gave a jerk. I stared him down. He was a scrawny little fellow, no more meat on him than a starving quail. I could a snapped his neck in about two seconds.

"You're lucky we followed up on that tip," he said. "Lucky we found him before he bled to death." His face was like a child's, I could see everything in it. His fear of us. His anger at my son for laying hand to a white woman. His disgust at what they done to Ronsel, and his sympathy for the devils who done it. The little bit of shame he felt for covering up for em. His impatience to be done with nigger business and get home to his wife and his supper.

"Yessuh, sheriff," I said, "we're one lucky family."

He put on his hat. "I'm leaving now. You want me to take you to Belzoni or not?"

Hap nodded and said, "Yessuh. My wife'll come with you."

"No, Hap," I said. "You go. I'll stay here with the children."

"You sure?" he asked, surprised. "Ronsel will be wanting his mother."

"It's better if you go."

My husband gave me a stern sharp look and said, "You keep that door locked, now." Meaning, *You just stay put and don't do nothing foolish.*

And I looked right back at him and said, "Don't you worry bout us, you just take care of Ronsel." Meaning, *And I'll take care of what else needs taking care of.*

I would use Hap's skinning knife. It wasn't the biggest knife we owned but it had the thinnest blade. I reckoned it would go in the easiest.

LAURA

I WOKE TO CURSING and pounding: Pappy's voice, punctuated by his fists hitting the front door. "Wake up, goddamnit! Let me in!"

I'd fallen asleep on the couch. The room was pitch dark; the lantern must have burned out. I'd barred the door earlier, something I seldom did anymore, but after Florence left I'd felt unaccountably afraid. The night had seemed full of terrible possibility waiting to coalesce, to shape itself into monstrous form and come for me. As if a flimsy wooden door and an old two-by-four could have kept it out.

"Just a minute, I'm coming," I said.

Either the old man didn't hear me or he was enjoying himself too much to stop, because the racket continued while I got the lantern lit and went to the door.

"About time," he snapped, when I opened it. "I've been standing out here for five minutes." He pushed past me, tracking mud all over the floor, and looked around the room. "Jamie hasn't come home yet?"

"No, unless he's asleep in the lean-to."

"I checked already. He ain't there." Pappy's voice had an edge to it I'd never heard before. He removed his dripping hat, hung it on a peg then went back to the doorway and peered out into the night. "Maybe he missed the place in the dark," he said. "He was on foot, and you didn't leave a light on."

As they were meant to do, his words let loose a storm of guilt in me. Then their meaning penetrated. "How do you know he was on foot? Did you see him?"

"He ain't got a car, that's how I know," said Pappy. "So if he left here, he had to been walking."

The old man's back was to me, but I didn't have to see his yellow teeth to know he was lying through them. "You asked me if he'd come home *yet*," I said. "If you haven't seen him, how'd you know he left in the first place?"

He reached into his shirt pocket and pulled out a pack of cigarettes. He shook one out, then crumpled the pack in his fist and threw it out onto the porch. "Shit!" he said. "They're soaking wet."

I went to him and gripped his shoulder, turning him toward me. It was the first time I'd touched him on purpose since my wedding day, when I'd given him a dutiful, and obviously unwelcome, kiss on the cheek.

"What's wrong? Has something happened to him?"

He jerked his shoulder out of my hand. "Let me alone, woman. I'm sure he's fine." But he didn't sound sure, he sounded guilty and oddly defiant at the same time, like a wicked boy who's done some longed-for forbidden thing: hit his sister, or drowned a cat. A dark suspicion bloomed in me.

"Has this got something to do with Ronsel Jackson being missing?" I said, watching his face.

"Who says he's missing?"

"His mother. She came by here looking for him around seven."

He shrugged. "Niggers go missing all the time."

"If you've harmed that boy, or Jamie—"

The old man's features contorted, and his eyes lit with hate. "You'll what? Tell me what you'll do." His spittle flecked my face. "You think you can threaten me, gal? You better think again. I've seen the way you sniff after Jamie like a sow in rut. Henry may be too thick to notice but I ain't, and I ain't afraid to tell him either."

I could feel my face reddening, but I brazened it out. "My husband would never believe that."

He cocked his head to one side, calculating. "Well maybe he will and maybe he won't, but I bet it sure will stick in his craw. Henry ain't got much of an imagination but with a thing like that you don't need one. A thing like that, a man will always wonder about. There'll always be a little bit of doubt."

"You're despicable."

"I'm wet," he said. "Fetch me a towel."

He sauntered to the kitchen table, planted himself in one of the chairs and waited. For a moment I just stood there, paralyzed by the emotions tearing through me—shame, anger, fear, all battling for dominance. Then my limbs seemed to move of their own accord: walking to the linen cupboard, taking out a clean towel, walking back to him. He snatched it from my hand. "Now fix me something to eat. I'm hungry."

As mechanically as a windup toy, I went to the stove, took

cornbread from the oven and spooned chili onto a plate. Thinking of Henry, and how he would feel if Pappy carried out his threat and said something to him. I set the plate down in front of the old man and started to leave the room.

"If you hear Jamie come in," he said, around a mouth full of cornbread, "you come wake me up. And if Henry or anybody else asks you where I was tonight, you tell em I was right here at home with you, hear?"

I pictured those pale hateful eyes closed, the mouth shut, the skin waxen. Pictured it melting away until there was nothing but smooth white bone, crumbling slowly into dust. "Yes, Pappy," I said.

He gave me a malicious smile, knowing he'd won. Still, I thought, there were plenty of ways for an old man to die on a farm. You never knew when tragedy might strike out of the blue.

I LAY ON MY BED with my eyes open, waiting for Pappy to finish eating and turn in. When I heard the front door open and close, I got up and checked on the children. They were sleeping, with an untroubled abandon I envied. I set about cleaning up the mess the old man had left, grateful for work to keep my hands busy while I waited for Jamie and whatever else would come that night. But imposing order on the house did nothing to ease the turmoil in my mind. *A sow in rut.* Had I really been so transparent? Was that how Jamie thought of me? *A thing like that, a man will always wonder about.* I couldn't bear the thought of causing Henry such pain, even if it meant lying for Pappy. But if he'd harmed Jamie . . .

Suddenly remembering what the old man had said about Jamie being lost in the dark, I took one of the lanterns out to the front porch with the intention of leaving it there as a beacon. It was then that I saw the light in the barn. Jamie—it had to be.

I didn't even stop to change into my boots or put on my coat. I simply walked into the storm, my one thought to reach him. The night was wild: lashing rain, furious gusts of wind that whipped my hair and my clothes. The barn door was shut, and it took all my strength to get it open. Jamie was curled on the dirt floor of the barn, sobbing. The sounds that came from him were so anguished they were nearly inhuman. They mingled with the plaintive lowing of our cow, who was moving restlessly in her stall.

I ran and knelt beside him. He'd been beaten. There was a cut above his eyebrow, and one cheek was red and swollen. I pulled his head into my lap and when I did, felt a large lump on the back of it. Hot rage surged through me. Pappy had done this to him, I had no doubt of it.

"I'll go fetch some water and a clean cloth," I said.

"No," he said, wrapping his arms around my waist. "Don't leave me." He clung to me, shuddering. I murmured soothing nonsense to him and dabbed at the cut on his forehead with my sleeve. When his sobbing quieted I asked him what had happened, but he just shook his head and squeezed his eyes shut. I lay down behind him and curled my body around his, stroking his hair, listening to the droning patter of the rain on the roof. Time passed, ten minutes or twenty. One of the mules whickered, and I felt rather than heard movement, a displacement of air. I opened my eyes. Saw Florence standing in the open doorway of the barn. Her dress was soaked through, and her legs were muddy to the knee. Her face was a blasted ruin. The hairs on my arms rose up and I shivered, knowing something terrible must have happened to Ronsel. Then I saw the knife in her hand. *Ronsel is dead,* I thought, with absolute certainty, *and she means to kill us for it.* I was strangely unafraid. What I felt most keenly was pity—for Florence and her son, and for Henry and the girls, who would find our bodies in the barn and grieve and wonder. There was no way I could stop her; I didn't even think to try. I closed my eyes, pressing myself against Jamie's back, waiting for what would come. I felt a stirring of air, heard a whisper of bare feet on dirt. When I opened my eyes she was gone. The whole incident had taken perhaps fifteen seconds.

For a long while I just lay there, feeling my heart trip and gradually slow down until it kept pace with Jamie's again. A boom of thunder sounded, and I thought of the children. They'd be frightened if they woke and I wasn't there. Then I thought of Pappy, sleeping alone in the lean-to. And I knew where Florence had been headed.

I sat up. Jamie made a whimpering sound and drew his knees up to his chest. Before I left the barn I got a horse blanket and covered him with it. Then I knelt beside him and kissed him on the forehead.

"Sweet Jamie," I whispered.

He slept, oblivious, his breath whistling softly with each exhalation.

I DREAMED OF HONEY, golden and viscous. I floated in it like an embryo. It filled my eyes, nose and ears, shutting out the world. It was so pleasant, to do nothing but float in all that sweetness.

"Mama, wake up!" The voices were piercing, insistent. I tried to ignore them—I didn't want to leave the honeyed place—but they kept tugging at me, pulling me out. "Mama, please! Wake up!"

I opened my eyes to find Amanda Leigh and Bella hovering over me. Their mouths and chins were smeared in honey speckled with cornbread crumbs, and their hands on me were sticky. I looked at the clock on the bedside table; it was after nine. They must have gotten hungry and helped themselves to breakfast.

"Pappy won't wake up," said Amanda Leigh, "and he's not in his eyes anymore."

"What?"

"He's in his bed but he isn't in his eyes."

"We can't find Uncle Jamie," said Bella.

Uncle Jamie. I pictured him above me, mouth open, head thrown back in pleasure. Pictured him as I'd left him last night, curled in a ball on the floor of the barn.

I got up and put on my robe and slippers, then led the girls

out to the lean-to. The rain had stopped, but it was a tempo-
rary respite; the clouds were dark gray for as far as I could see.
The door creaked loudly when I pushed it open. I knew what I
would find inside, but even so I wasn't prepared for the feeling
of elation that shot through me when I saw Pappy's body lying
stiff on the cot, vacant of malice and of life.

"Is he dead?" asked Amanda Leigh.

"Yes, darling," I said.

"Then how come his eyes are open?"

Her mouth was pursed, and there was a familiar vertical
furrow between her eyebrows, a miniature version of the one
that creased Henry's face when he was perplexed. I kissed her
there, then said, "They must have been open when he died.
We'll shut them for him."

I pushed down on his eyelids with the very tips of my fingers, trying not to touch the eyeballs, but the lids wouldn't
budge—the old man was contrary even in death. I rubbed my
fingers against my robe, wanting to rid them of the feel of that
cold, hard flesh.

"Does he not want you to shut them?" Bella whispered.

"No, honey. His body is just too stiff right now. It's a natural
part of dying. We'll be able to shut them tomorrow."

There was no blood and no knife wound, but Jamie's pillow was on the floor. She must have decided to suffocate him
instead. I was glad; a wound would have raised unwelcome
questions. I bent down to pick up the pillow and put it back on
the bed. There was a piece of white fabric on the floor beneath
it—a pillowcase, I saw when I picked it up. It wasn't one of

ours; the cotton was dingy and coarsely woven. Then I turned it over and saw the eyeholes cut in the fabric, and bile rose in the back of my throat. I balled the hideous thing up quickly and stuffed it in the pocket of my robe. I would burn it in the stove later.

"What is it, Mama?"

"Just an old dirty pillowcase."

It was impossible not to picture the scene: the taunting men in their white hoods, the sweating and terrified brown face in their midst. I wondered how many others there had been, and where they'd done it; whether they'd hanged him or killed him some other way. Jamie must have found out about it—that was why he'd been so distraught last night. I wondered if he'd seen what happened. If he'd watched his father murder that poor boy.

"Is Pappy in heaven now?" asked Bella.

The old man's face was expressionless, and his untenanted eyes gave away nothing of what he'd felt in his last moments. I hoped he'd seen Florence coming for him and been afraid; that he'd begged and struggled and known the agony of help-lessness, as Ronsel must have. I hoped she'd taken pleasure in killing him, and that it would give her some kind of grim peace to know she'd avenged her son.

"He's in God's hands," I said.

"Should we say a prayer for him?" asked Amanda Leigh.

"Yes, I suppose we should. Come here, both of you. Don't be scared."

They came and knelt on either side of me. Mud from the

dirty floor oozed through the thin cotton of my nightgown. I felt a fat plop of water hit my head, then another; the roof was leaking. The girls waited for me to begin, their small, soft bodies pressing into mine from either side. I closed my eyes, but no words came. I would not pray for Pappy's soul; that would be the worst sort of hypocrisy. I could have prayed for Florence, that God would understand and forgive her a mother's vengeance, but not in front of the children. And so I was silent. I had no words to give them, or Him.

A shadow fell across us, and I turned and saw Jamie in the doorway. The light was behind him so I couldn't see his expression. Bella got up and ran to him, hugging him around the knees. "Pappy's dead, Uncle Jamie!" she cried.

"It's true," I said. "I'm sorry."

He picked Bella up and moved to stand at the foot of the bed. He was still in his dirty clothes from the night before, but he'd combed his hair and washed his battered face. There was bitterness in his eyes as he gazed down at his father's body, and sorrow. I'd expected the one but not the other. It tore at my heart.

"It looks like he went peacefully, in his sleep," I lied.

"That's how I'd like to go," Jamie said in a small voice. "In my sleep."

He looked down at me then, a look of such tender desolation that I could hardly bear to meet it. I saw a brother's guilt in that look, but none of the shame or contempt I'd feared to find. Just love and pain and something else I recognized finally as gratitude, for what I'd given him. Gone was the gallant and fearless aviator, the laughing cocksure hero of my imaginings. But even as I mourned his loss, I knew that that Jamie wouldn't have needed my comfort, or lain with me.

That Jamie had never really existed.

The realization stunned me, though it shouldn't have. He'd given me all the clues I needed to see the weakness at the core of him, and the darkness. I'd ignored them, preferring to believe the fiction. Jamie had created that fiction, acting the part almost to perfection, but I'd been the one who swallowed it whole. I was to blame, for having fallen in love with a figment.

I loved him still, but there was no longing to it, no heat. Already the memory of our lovemaking was beginning to seem distant, as though it had happened to someone else. I felt strangely empty, without all that carnal furor.

I think he saw it in my eyes. His own dropped to the floor. He set Bella down and knelt beside me, bending his head. Waiting for me to begin. For the second time, I was at a loss. What honest prayer could I, an adulteress kneeling with my lover beside the body of my hated, murdered father-in-law, possibly offer Him? And then I knew, and I clasped Jamie's hand in mine and started to sing:

> Praise God, from Whom all blessings flow;
> Praise Him, all creatures here below;
> Praise Him above, ye heavenly host:
> Praise Father, Son, and Holy Ghost. Amen.

My voice was strong and clear as I sang the familiar words of thanksgiving. The girls joined in at once—the Doxology was the first hymn I'd ever taught them—and then Jamie did as well. His voice was raw, and it splintered on the *amen*. I found myself thinking that Henry wouldn't have waited for me to begin. He would have led us in prayer unhesitatingly, and his voice wouldn't have cracked.

JAMIE

THE BIBLE IS FULL of thou-shalt-nots. Thou shalt not kill, that's one. Thou shalt not bear false witness against thy neighbor, that's two. Thou shalt not commit adultery, thou shalt not uncover the nakedness of thy brother's wife—three and four. Notice how none of them have any loopholes. There are no dependent clauses you can hang your sins on, like: Thou shalt not uncover the nakedness of thy brother's wife, *unless* thou art wandering in the blackest hell, lost to yourself and to every memory of light and goodness, and uncovering her nakedness is the only way back to yourself. No, the Bible's absolute when it comes to most things. It's why I don't believe in God.

Sometimes it's necessary to do wrong. Sometimes it's the only way to make things right. Any God who doesn't understand that can go fuck Himself.

Thou shalt not take the name of the Lord thy God in vain—that's five.

THE DAY AFTER the lynching passed with the slow heaviness of a dream. I hurt everywhere, and I had the mother of all hangovers. I couldn't stop thinking of Ronsel, of the knife flashing, the blood spurting, the clotted howling that went on and on.

I took refuge in work. There was plenty of it: the storm had wrecked the chicken coop, peeled half the roof off the cotton house and sent the pigs into a murderous frenzy. Henry hadn't returned from Greenville yet, but we expected him back any time. I'd gone earlier to check the bridge and found it just barely passable. From the ominous look of the clouds, it wouldn't stay that way for long. In weather like this Henry would know to hurry home.

I was in the barn milking when Laura came and found me. Venus hadn't been milked since the previous morning, and her udders were full to bursting. She'd already punished me for it twice by swatting me in the face with her cocklebur-infested tail. Still, it was good to sit with my cheek against her warm hide, listening to the snare-drum sound of milk hitting the pail, letting the rhythm empty my head.

"Jamie," Laura said. I looked up and saw her standing just outside the stall. "Henry will be back soon. We need to talk before he gets here."

With some reluctance I left the shelter of the stall and went to her. She had on lipstick, I noticed, but apart from that she was totally without artifice, probably the only woman I'd ever known who was. That would change now, because of me. I had turned her into a liar.

"How are the girls?" I asked her.

"Fine. They're both asleep. All this has worn them out."

"I expect it has. Death is unsettling. Especially the first time you see it."

"They wanted to know if you and Henry and I would die someday, and I said we would, a long time from now. Then they asked if they would die. I think it was the first time it ever occurred to them."

"What did you tell them?"

"The truth. I don't think Bella believed me, though."

"Good," I said. "Let her have her immortality while she can."

Laura hesitated, then said, "I need to ask you about something." She pulled a crumpled piece of white cloth from her pocket. Even before I saw the eyeholes I knew what it was. "I found this on the floor of the lean-to. I imagine it belonged to Pappy." When I didn't answer, she said, "You've seen it before, haven't you?"

I nodded, the memories exploding like grenades in my head.

"Tell me what happened, Jamie."

I told her. How I'd seen the light near the sawmill and gone over there. How I'd discovered Ronsel with a rope around his neck in a room full of hooded men, my father among them. How I'd broken in on them and tried to get Ronsel out of there. How I'd failed. "I didn't even fire my gun," I said.

"Listen to me," Laura said. "What happened to that boy isn't your fault. You tried to save him, which is more than most people would have done. I'm sure Ronsel knew that. I'm sure he appreciated it."

"Yeah, I bet he's just overflowing with gratitude towards me. He probably can't wait to thank me."

"He's alive?"

"Yes."

"Thank God," she said, her eyes closing in relief.

"At least, he was when I left," I said. And then I told her the first lie: how I'd come to with Sheriff Tacker bending over me, and the others gone, and learned they'd cut out Ronsel's tongue. Laura's hand flew to her own mouth. Mine, I remembered, had done the same.

"Tom Rossi drove him to the doctor," I said. "He'd lost a lot of blood." It had been everywhere: drenching his shirt, pooling on the floor, spattering Turpin's white robes.

"Why?" she asked. "Why did they do it?"

I reached in my pocket and pulled out the photo and handed it to her. She looked at it, then back at me. "Who are they?"

"That's Ronsel's German lover, and the child she had by him. There was a letter with it, I don't know what happened to it."

"How did they get hold of this?"

"I don't know," I said. Lie number two. "I guess Ronsel must have dropped it somewhere."

"And one of them found it."

"Yes."

"Who else was there, besides Pappy?"

"I didn't recognize any of the others," I said.

Lie number three, this one for her own safety. I'm sure she saw through it, but she didn't call me on it. She just gazed at me thoughtfully. I had the feeling I was being weighed, and found wanting. It gave me an unfamiliar pang. I'd cheerfully disappointed dozens of women. Why, with Laura, did it feel so bad?

"What will you tell Henry?" she asked.

"I don't know. He's going to be upset enough as it is, without having to know that our father was part of a lynch mob."

"Did Tom or Sheriff Tacker actually see Pappy at the sawmill?"

"I don't think so. But even if they did, this is the Delta. The last thing the sheriff wants to do is identify any of them."

"What about Ronsel?"

"He won't talk. They made sure of that."

"He could write it down."

I shook my head. "What do you suppose would happen to him if he did? What would happen to his family?"

Laura's eyes widened. "Are we in danger?"

"No," I said. "Not as long as I leave here."

She walked to the barn door and looked out at the brown fields and the bleak crouching sky, hugging herself with her arms. "How I hate this place," she said softly.

I remembered the strength of those arms around me, and the surprising sureness with which her hand had gripped me and guided me into her. I wondered if she was that fierce and sure with my brother. If she cried out his name like she'd cried out mine.

"I can't see any reason to tell Henry your father was involved," she said finally. "It would only hurt him needlessly, to know the truth."

"All right. If you think so."

She turned and looked at me, holding my gaze for long seconds. "We won't ever speak of it," she said.

WHEN HENRY GOT home he was already in a welter because of the storm. Laura and I met him at the car, but he barely gave us a glance as he brushed by us to kneel in the fields and examine one of the flattened rows of newly planted cotton. It had started to rain again, and we were all getting soaked.

"If this keeps up all the seed will be washed away, and we'll have to replant," he said. "The almanac predicted light rain in April, damnit. What time did it start here?"

"Around five o'clock yesterday," said Laura. "It poured all night long."

Her voice sounded strained. Henry looked from her to me and frowned. "What happened to your face?"

I'd forgotten all about my face. I tried to think up a story to explain it, but my mind was blank.

"Venus kicked him," Laura blurted out. "Last night, when he was milking. The storm agitated her. All the animals. One of the pigs is dead. The others trampled it."

Henry looked from her back to me. "What in the hell's the matter with the two of you?"

She waited for me to tell him, but I shook my head. I couldn't speak. "Honey," she said, "your father is gone. He died last night in his sleep."

She went and stood next to him but didn't touch him. He wasn't ready to be touched yet. *How well she knows him,* I thought. *How well they suit each other.* He bent his head and stared at his muddy boots. Eldest child, now the head of our family. I saw the weight of that settle on him.

"Is he . . . still in his bed?" Henry was asking me. I nodded. "I guess I'd better go and see him," he said.

Together the three of us walked to the lean-to. Henry went in first. Laura and I followed, coming to stand on either side of him. He pulled the sheet down. Pappy's eyes, vacant and bulging, stared up at us. Henry reached out to close them, but Laura took his hand and gently pulled it back.

"No, honey," she said. "We already tried. He's still too stiff."

Henry let out a long breath. I put an arm around him and so did Laura. When our hands accidentally touched behind his back, she shifted hers away.

I hadn't expected Henry to cry, and he didn't. His face was impassive as he looked down at our father's dead body. He turned to me. "Are you all right?" he asked.

I felt a flare of resentment. Did he never get tired of being the strong one, of being stoic and honorable and dependable? I saw in that moment that I'd always resented him, even as I'd looked up to him, and that I'd bedded his wife in part to punish him for being all the things I wasn't.

"I'm fine," I said.

Henry nodded and squeezed my shoulder, then looked back down at Pappy. "I wonder what he saw, at the end."

"It was a dark night," I told him. "No moon or stars. I doubt he saw much of anything."

Lie number four.

"Nigger lover!" Turpin shouted. "Judas!"

Finally a boot connected with the back of my head, and that

was all—for five minutes or so. When I came to, somebody was none too gently slapping my cheek. I was lying on my side with the other cheek against the dirt. The room was a blur of legs and white robes.

"Wake up," said my father, giving me a hard shake. A half dozen overlapping hooded heads swam over me. I tried to push him away from me. That's when I realized my hands were tied behind my back. He pulled me to a sitting position and propped me against the wall. The sudden motion made the room spin, and I felt myself starting to topple over. Pappy yanked me back up again by my jacket collar. "Sit up and act like a man," he hissed in my ear. "You make one more wrong move, and these boys are liable to kill you."

When the room resettled itself I saw Ronsel, still alive, his head straining upward in an effort to keep the noose from choking him.

"What are we gonna do with him?" said Deweese, waving in my direction.

"No need to do anything," said Pappy. "He won't talk, he told you so already. Ain't that right, son?"

My father was scared, I realized. He was scared as hell, and he was trying to protect me. I think it was right then that I really began to feel afraid myself. My heart started to pound and I felt sweat breaking out all over me, but I made my voice stay calm and confident. For me and Ronsel to walk out of here alive, I would need to give the performance of my life.

"That's right," I said. "Just let him go, and as far as I'm concerned this never happened."

The hulking figure of Orris Stokes loomed over me.

"You ain't in a position to make demands, nigger lover. If I was you, I'd worry less about what happens to him and more about your own skin."

"Jamie won't go to the law," said Pappy. "Not when we tell him what the nigger did."

"What did he do?" I asked.

"He fucked a white woman and got a child on her," Pappy said.

"Bullshit. Ronsel wouldn't do any such thing."

"Is that a fact," said Turpin. "You think you know him, huh? Well, what do you say to this?"

He thrust a photo in front of my eyes, of a thin, pretty blonde holding a mulatto baby. It definitely hadn't been taken in Mississippi. The ground was covered with snow, and there was an alpine-style house in the background.

"Who is she?" I said.

"Some German gal," said Turpin.

"And what makes you think Ronsel's the father?"

He waved a piece of paper in the air. "Says so right here in this letter. She even named it after him."

My feelings must have shown in my face. "See?" Pappy said. "I told you boys he'd be with us on this."

I looked over at Ronsel. He blinked once, slowly, in affirmation. There was no shame in his eyes. If anything, they seemed to challenge me, to say, *What kind of man are you? Guess we're about to find out.* I looked at the photo again, remembering how shocked I'd been when I first saw Negro GIs with white girls in the pubs and dance halls of Europe. Eventually I'd gotten used to it. Soldiers will be soldiers, I'd told myself, and the girls were obviously willing. But I'd never been easy with it, and I still wasn't. And if *I* wasn't, I could only imagine what that photograph stirred up in these white-sheeted men. That, and Ronsel's quiet pride in himself, which must have infuriated them. I knew their kind: locked in the imagined glory of the past, scared of losing what they thought was theirs. They would make an answer. I understood that, and them, all too well. But I couldn't let them kill Ronsel. And if I didn't come up with something quick, they would.

"What do you fellows care about some Kraut whore?" I said.

That earned me a hard kick in the thigh from Orris's boot.

"Just tell em you won't talk," urged Pappy. I could hear the desperation in his voice, and if I could hear it, so could they. That was dangerous. Nothing goads a pack like the scent of fear.

"You're not taking my meaning," I said. "These fräuleins, they're not like our women. They're cold-hearted cunts who'll smile to your face then stab you in the back the first chance they get. They got an awful lot of our boys killed over there. So if Ronsel exacted a little vengeance on one of them and left her with a reminder of it, I call it justice."

There was silence. I began to have a little hope.

"You're good, boy," said Turpin. "Too bad you're full of shit."

"Listen, I'm not saying we should give him a medal for it. I'm just saying it doesn't seem right, killing a decorated soldier over an enemy whore."

Another silence.

"The nigger's still got to be punished," Pappy said.

"And kept from doing it again," said Stokes. "You know how these bucks are once they get a taste for white women. What's to stop him from going after one here?"

"*We're* gonna stop him," said Turpin. "Right here and right now."

He opened a leather case on the floor and pulled out a scalpel. Somebody whistled. Excitement crackled through the room. Ronsel and I started talking at the same time:

"Please, suh. I'm begging you, please don't—"

"You don't need that, he's learned his les—"

Doc Turpin's voice cut across ours like a whip. "If either of them says one more word, shoot the nigger."

I shut up, and so did Ronsel.

"This nigger profaned a white woman," Turpin said. "He fouled her body with his eyes and his hands and his tongue and his seed, and for that he's got to pay. What'll it be, boys?"

They all spoke at once: "Geld him." "Blind him." "Cut it all off!"

I caught a whiff of urine and saw a stain spreading across the front of Ronsel's pants. The smell of piss and sweat and musk was overwhelming. I swallowed hard to keep myself from throwing up.

Then my father said, "I say we let my son decide."

"Why should we do that?" Turpin demanded.

"Yeah," said Stokes, "why should he get to do it?"

"If he decides, he's part of it," said Pappy.

"No," I said. "I won't do it."

My father bent down to me, his eyes narrowed to slits. He put his mouth up to my ear. "You know where I found that letter?" he said. "In the cab of our truck, on the floor of the passenger seat. Only one way it could've got there, and that's if you let him ride with you again. This is *your* doing. You think about that."

I shook my head hard, not wanting to believe it, knowing it had to be true. Pappy pulled away and raised his voice so the others could hear. "You had to stick your nose in. Busting in here like Gary Cooper, waving that gun around and making threats. Threatening me, your own father, over a nigger! Well, you're in it now, son. You don't want him killed, fine. You decide his punishment."

"I said I won't do it."

"You will," said Turpin. "Or I will. And I don't think your boy here will like my choice." He made a crude stabbing gesture toward his crotch. There were hoots and chuckles from the others. Ronsel was shuddering, his muscles straining against the ropes that bound him. His eyes implored me.

"What's it gonna be?" said Turpin. "His eyes, his tongue, his hands or his balls? Choose, nigger lover."

When I didn't answer Deweese swung the shotgun around, pointing it at me. My father stepped away from me, leaving me alone in the shotgun's field. Deweese cocked it. "Choose," he said.

Here it was, the oblivion I'd been chasing for so long. All I had to do was stay silent, and I would have it—an end to pain and fear and emptiness. Here it was, if I just had the guts to reach out and grab hold of it.

"Choose, goddamnit," said my father.

I chose.

LAURA

I WENT TO SEE Florence the day after we found Pappy dead. I wanted to find out how Ronsel was. I also needed to have a private talk with her. I couldn't have her working for me anymore. I didn't think she'd want to in any case, but I had to be sure of it, and of her silence.

I told Jamie where I was going and asked him to watch the children for me. As I was about to walk out the door, he pulled something from his pocket and handed it to me: the photograph of Ronsel's German lover and their child. My arms broke out into gooseflesh; I didn't want to touch it. I tried to hand it back to him.

"No," he said. "You give that to Florence, for Ronsel. Ask her to tell him . . ." He shook his head, at a loss. His mouth was tight with self-loathing.

I gave his hand a gentle squeeze. "I'm sure he knows," I said.

I intended to drive, but both the car and the truck were mired too deeply in mud, so I took my umbrella and set out on foot. The rain had slackened a little since yesterday, but it was still coming down steadily. As I walked past the barn, Henry saw me and came to the open door. "Where are you going?" he asked.

"To Florence's. She didn't show up for work yesterday or today."

Henry still didn't know about what had happened to Ronsel. Hap hadn't come and told him, and we'd been cut off from town since last night. Jamie and I had said nothing, of course. We weren't supposed to know about it yet.

Henry frowned. "You shouldn't be out in this mess. I'll go over there later and see about it. You go on back to the house."

I thought quickly. "I need to ask her some questions. About how to prepare the body."

"All right. But take care you don't fall. The road's slippery."

His concern for me brought a lump to my throat. "I'll be careful," I said.

Lilly May answered my knock. Her eyes were red-rimmed and swollen. I asked to speak to her mother.

"I'll see," she said.

She closed the door in my face. I felt a clutch of fear. What if Ronsel hadn't survived his wounds? For his family's sake, and for Jamie's, I prayed that he had. I waited on the porch for perhaps five minutes, though it felt like much longer. Finally the door opened and Florence came out. Her face was drawn, her eyes sunken. I feared the worst, but then there came a long, guttural moan from inside the house. It was a horrible sound, but it meant he was alive. They must have brought him back home yesterday afternoon, I thought, before the river flooded the bridge.

"How is he?" I asked.

Florence didn't answer, just gave me a cold, knowing stare. I stared back at her, adulteress to murderess. Reminding her that I knew things too.

"We leaving here soon as the river goes down," she said curtly. "Hap'll be by later today to tell your husband."

Relief flooded me, overwhelming the small bit of shame that accompanied it. I would not have to see her, even from a distance; would not be reminded daily of how my family had destroyed hers. "Where will you go?" I asked.

She shrugged and looked out over the drowned fields. "Away from here."

There was only one thing I could offer her. "The old man is dead," I said. "He died night before last, in his sleep." I emphasized the last part, but if she was reassured her face didn't show it. If anything, she looked even more bitter. "God will know what to do with him," I said.

She shook her head. "God don't give a damn."

As if to prove her words, Ronsel moaned again. Florence closed her eyes. I don't know what was more terrible: listening to that sound, or watching Florence listen to it. It might as well have been her own tongue being torn from her body. I shuddered, imagining how I would feel if that sound were coming out of Amanda Leigh or Bella. I thought of Vera Atwood. Of my own mother, still grieving after all these years for Teddy's lost twin.

"I have something for him, from Jamie," I said. I took out the photograph and handed it to her. "It was taken in Germany. The child is —"

"I know who he is." She brushed her fingers lightly across the surface of the picture, touching the face of the grandson she would never see. Then she shoved it in her pocket and looked at me. "I need to get back to him," she said.

"I'm sorry," I said. Two words, pitifully inadequate to carry the weight of all that had happened, but I said them anyway.

Ain't your fault. Three words, a gift of absolution I didn't deserve. I would have given anything to hear Florence say them, but she didn't. All she said was goodbye.

JAMIE

THE FIVE OF US staggered through the mud to the grave. It was still raining lightly but the wind had picked up, coming in violent gusts that seemed to blow us in every direction but the one we needed to go. Henry and I carried the coffin and the ropes. Laura walked behind with the children, Bella in her arms and Amanda Leigh hanging onto her skirt.

When we got to the hole we set the coffin down and worked the ropes underneath it, one on each end. Henry moved to the other side of the hole and I threw him the two rope-ends. But when we tried to lift it, the ropes slipped to the center and the coffin teetered, then tumbled to the ground. The wood groaned, and there was a loud crack from inside the box—Pappy's skull, hitting the wood. One of the boards on the side had pried loose. I bent and pushed the nails back in with my thumb.

"This isn't gonna work," I said. "Not with just the two of us."

"It'll have to work," Henry said.

"Maybe if we stood at either end and ran the ropes lengthwise."

"No," he said. "The coffin's too narrow. If it falls again it could break open."

I shrugged—*so what?*

"No," he said again in a low voice, with a glance at the children.

Laura pointed at the road. "Look. Here come the Jacksons."

We watched their wagon approach. Hap and Florence sat up front, and the two younger boys walked behind. The wagon was piled high with furniture. As it got closer I saw they'd strung up a makeshift tarp in back. I knew Ronsel was under there, suffering.

When they came abreast of us Henry waved them down.

"Don't," Laura said. "Just let them go."

He shot her an indignant look. "It's not my fault, what happened to that boy. I warned him. I warned both of them. And now Hap's leaving me in the middle of planting season when he knows damn well it's too late for me to find another tenant. The least he can do is give us a quick hand here."

I opened my mouth to agree with Laura, but she gave a slight shake of her head and I swallowed the words.

"Hap!" Henry shouted over the wind. "Can you help us out here?"

Hap whoa'd the mule, and he, Florence and the two boys turned and looked at us. Even from thirty yards away, I could feel the force of their hate.

"We could use some extra hands!" Henry shouted.

I expected them to refuse—I sure as hell would have. But then Hap handed the reins to Florence and started to get down.

She grabbed hold of his arm and said something to him, and he shook his head and said something back.

"What are they dithering about?" Henry said impatiently.

Hap and Florence were really going at it now. Their voices weren't quite loud enough for me to make out what they were saying, but I could guess well enough.

"*No, Hap. Don't you do it.*"

"*It's the Lord's doing we passed by here just now, and I ain't gone argue with Him. Now come on and let's see it done.*"

"*I ain't helping that devil get nowhere.*"

"*You ain't helping him, he's already burning in hell. You helping God to do His work.*"

I saw Florence spit over the side of the wagon.

"*That's for your God. He ain't getting nothing more from me. He done taken enough already.*"

"*All right then. I won't be long.*"

Hap climbed down. He turned toward the two boys, and Florence spoke again. Her meaning was plain enough: "*And don't you ask the twins to do it neither.*"

Hap trudged to the grave alone, head bent, eyes on the ground. When he reached us, Henry said, "Thank you for stopping, Hap. We were hoping you and one of your boys could help us get the coffin in."

"I'll help you," Hap said, "but they ain't coming."

Henry frowned and his forehead knitted up.

"It's all right," Laura said quickly. "I can do it."

She set Bella down next to Amanda Leigh and took up one of the rope ends. Henry, Hap and I took the other three. Together we maneuvered the coffin over the hole and lowered it down. When it touched bottom we managed to wiggle one of the ropes out from under it, but the other one caught and wouldn't come loose. Henry cursed under his breath and let the ends fall down into the hole. He looked at Laura.

"Did you bring a Bible?" he asked.

"No," she said, "I didn't think of it."

I saw Hap look up at the sky, head cocked like he was listening to something. Then he bowed it and said, "I've got one right here, Mist McAllan." He pulled a small, tattered Bible from his shirt pocket. "I can send him on if you want. Reckon that's why I'm here." I searched his face for irony or spite, but I saw neither.

"No, Hap," Henry said. "Thank you, but no."

"Done this plenty of times for my own people," Hap said.

"He wouldn't want it," Henry said.

"I say we let him do it," I said.

"He wouldn't want it," Henry repeated.

"*I* want it," I said. We glared at each other.

Laura broke the stalemate. "Yes, Henry," she said, "if Hap is willing to do it I think we should let him. He is a man of God."

"All right, Hap," Henry said after a moment. "Go on then."

Hap leafed through the Bible. He opened his mouth to begin, then something flickered in his eyes, and he turned to an earlier page. I was expecting, "The Lord is my shepherd"; I think we all were. What we got was something else entirely.

"Call now, if there be any that will answer thee; and to

which of the saints wilt thou turn?" Hap's voice was strong and ringing. I saw Laura's head lift in surprise. She told me later the passage was from Job—hardly the thing to comfort the bereaved at a burial.

"Man that is born of a woman is of few days, and full of trouble," Hap went on. "He cometh forth like a flower, and is cut down: he fleeth also as a shadow, and continueth not. And dost thou open thine eyes upon such a one, and bringest me into judgment with thee? Who can bring a clean thing out of an unclean? Not one."

Henry was frowning. I think he would have put a stop to the reading if the clouds hadn't erupted just then, loosing their contents and drenching us all. While Hap shouted about death and iniquity, Henry and I grabbed the shovels and began filling the hole back up.

So it was that our father was laid to rest in a slave's grave, in a hurried, graceless ceremony presided over by an accusatory colored preacher, while the woman who meant to kill him looked on, stiff-backed and full of impotent rage that somebody else had beaten her to it.

If Pappy had woken up when I came in with the lantern, Florence might have gotten her chance. But he didn't. He slept on peacefully, his face relaxed, his breathing deep and steady, the way a man sleeps after a long and satisfying day's work. I stood there watching him for some time, dripping water and blood onto the floor, feeling the fury build inside me. I heard his voice saying, *You'd think I had three daughters and not two.* And, *My son don't have the balls to kill a man up close.*

And, *"The nigger's still got to be punished."* I don't remember
picking up the pillow on my bed, just looking down and seeing
it in my hands.

"Wake up," I said.

He jerked awake and squinted up at me. "What are you doing there?" he said.

"I wanted to look you in the eye," I said. "I wanted you to
know it was by my hand."

His eyes widened and his mouth opened. "You—" he said.

"Shut up," I said, bringing the pillow down over his face and
pressing hard. He thrashed and clawed at my hands, his long
nails digging into the skin of my wrist. I cursed and let go for
a second, long enough for him to turn his head and gasp in a
last breathful of air. I pressed the pillow back down, smashing
it against his face. His struggles grew weaker. His hands loosened and let go of mine. I waited another couple of minutes
before I lifted the pillow off his face. Then I straightened the
covers and closed his mouth. I left his eyes open.

I took the lantern and went to the barn. Laura found me
there half an hour later, and Florence found us both not long
after that. Laura thought I was asleep by then, but I wasn't. I
saw Florence come in with the knife, saw her rage and knew
what she meant to do. I wished there was some way to tell her
it was already done, that he didn't die a peaceful death. I put
my guilt in my eyes, hoping she would see it.

What we can't speak, we say in silence.

HENRY

THIS IS THE LOINS of the land. This lush expanse between two rivers, formed fifteen thousand years ago when the glaciers melted, swelling the Mississippi and its tributaries until they overflowed, drowning half the continent. When the waters receded, settling back into their ancient channels, they brought a rich gift of alluvium stolen from the lands they'd covered. Brought it here, to the Delta, and cast it over the river valleys, layer upon sweet black layer.

I buried my father in that soil, the soil he hated to touch. Buried him apart from my mother, who'll lie by herself forever in the Greenville cemetery. She might have forgiven me for that, but I knew better than to think Pappy would. I didn't mourn his death, not like I'd mourned hers. He wouldn't have wanted my grief in any case, but he ought to have had somebody's. That was the thought in my mind as I shoveled the earth on top of his coffin: that not one of us was really grieving for him.

A few days later I lost Jamie too. He was hell-bent on going to California, even though I'd made it plain I could use his help for a few more weeks now that the Jacksons were gone. That was a terrible business at the sawmill, but nobody could say I didn't warn the boy. I wondered what he'd done, to make those men punish him like that. Had to been something pretty bad. I think Jamie knew, but when I asked him about it he just shrugged and said, "It's Mississippi. There doesn't have to be a reason."

In spite of everything that had happened, I would miss him, and I knew Laura would too. I figured she'd take his leaving hard, thought she'd probably end up mad at me over it. But when we finally talked about it—in bed, after the light was out—all she said was, "He needs to leave this place."

"And you?" The question just slipped out, but as soon as I said it I felt my mouth go dry. What if she said she wanted to leave too, to take the children and go back to her people in Memphis? I never thought I'd come to fear such a thing, not with Laura, but she'd changed since we moved to the farm, and not in the ways I'd expected she would.

"What I need," she began.

All of a sudden I didn't want to hear her answer. "We'll get a house in town after the harvest," I blurted out. "And if you can't wait that long I'll borrow the money from the bank. I know it's been hard for you here, and I'm sorry. It'll be better once we're living in town. You'll see."

"Oh, Henry," she said.

What the hell did that mean? It was pitch dark and I couldn't see her face. I reached for her, my heartbeat loud in my ears. If she turned me away—

But she didn't. She rolled toward me, settling her head in the hollow of my shoulder. "What I need, I have right here," she said.

I put my arms around her and held on tight.

LAURA

JAMIE LEFT US three days after the burial. He was bound for Los Angeles, though he wasn't sure what he would do when he got there. "Maybe I'll go to Hollywood and get a screen test," he said with a laugh. "Give Errol Flynn a run for his money. What do you think?"

The bruises on his face were starting to fade, but he still looked haggard. I worried about him being all alone out there, with no one to look after him. But then I thought, *He won't be alone for long.* Jamie would find someone to love him, some pretty girl to cook his favorite foods and iron his shirts and wait for him to come home to her each day. He would pluck her like a daisy from the side of the road.

"I think Mr. Flynn's in real trouble," I said.

The front door opened, and Henry joined us on the porch. "We need to head out if you're going to make your train," he said.

"I'm ready," said Jamie.

Henry gestured at the fields in front of us. "You wait and see, brother. You're going to miss all this."

"All this" was a sea of churned earth stretching from the house to the river, bereft of crops and the furrows they'd been planted in. A newly hatched mosquito landed on Henry's outstretched arm, and he swatted at it irritably. I hid a smile, but Jamie's expression was serious as he answered. "I'm sure I will."

He bent and kissed the girls goodbye. Bella cried and clung to him. He gently pried her arms from around his neck and handed her to me. "I left you something," he said to me. "A present."

"What?"

"It's not here yet, but it will be soon. You'll know it when you see it."

"We'd better be off," said Henry.

Jamie gave me a swift, awkward hug. "Goodbye. Thank you for everything."

I nodded, not trusting myself to speak. Hoping he would comprehend all that was contained in that small movement of my head.

"I'll be back by suppertime," said Henry. He kissed me, and then Jamie was gone, down the road to Greenville, and to California.

In the days that followed, the girls and I looked everywhere for Jamie's present. Under the beds, in the cupboards, out in the barn. How could he have left me something if it hadn't yet arrived? And then, a few weeks after he'd gone, I found it. I was weeding the little vegetable patch Jamie had helped me put in when I spied a clump of small tender plants at the edge. There were several dozen of them, too evenly spaced to be weeds. I knew what they were even before I broke off a sprig and smelled it.

All summer long I slept with Henry on sheets scented with lavender.

AND NOW HERE we are at the ending of the story—my ending, anyway. It's early December, and I'm packing for an extended stay in Memphis. Henry and I agreed I should go home for the birth. The baby's due in six weeks, and at my age it's too risky to stay here in Tchula, two hours from the nearest hospital.

We moved here in October, just after the harvest. Our house isn't as nice as the one we lost to the Stokeses in Marietta, and there's no fig tree in the backyard, but we do have electricity, running water, and an indoor toilet, for which I'm profoundly grateful. Our days here have settled into a pleasant routine. We get up at dawn. I make breakfast for us all, and Henry's lunch to take with him to the farm. After he leaves I get the girls dressed and we walk Amanda Leigh the eight blocks to school. By the time Bella and I return home our colored maid Viola is here. She only comes half days; there's not enough work to warrant having her full-time. I spend the morning reading to Bella or running errands. At three we go and fetch Amanda Leigh, and then I cook our supper. We eat half an hour after sunset, when Henry gets home. Then I knit or sew while we listen to the radio.

Our life here is a world away from Mudbound, though it's only ten miles on the map. Sometimes it's hard for me to believe in that other life and that other self—the one capable of rage and lust, of recklessness and selfishness and betrayal. But then I'll feel the baby kicking, and I'll be forcibly reminded of that other Laura's existence. Jamie's baby, I have no doubt of it; I felt the tiny flare of its awakening that night, a few hours after we were together. I won't ever tell him the child's his, though he might wonder. It's a small bit of dignity I can give back to Henry, that he doesn't know I've taken from him. I give him whatever I can these days, and not just out of guilt or duty. That's what it is to love someone: to give whatever you can while taking what you must.

Jamie married in September. We weren't invited to the wedding; he let us know after the fact, in one of his breezy letters. And then, a week later, we got an almost identical letter telling us the news again, as if he hadn't remembered writing us the first time. Henry and I both knew what it had to mean, but we didn't say the words out loud. I pray his new wife will help him stop drinking, but I also know, as she doesn't, how much he has to forget.

I won't be allowed to forget. The baby will see to that. It will be a boy, who will grow into a man, whom I'll love as fiercely as Florence loves Ronsel. And while I'll always regret that I got my son at such terrible cost to hers, I won't regret that I got him. My love for him won't let me.

I'll end with that. With love.

RONSEL

IT'S DAYTIME, OR IT'S NIGHT. I'm in a tank wearing a helmet, in the backseat of a moving car with a burlap sack over my head, in the bed of a wagon with a wet rag on my forehead. I'm surrounded by enemies. The stench of their hate is choking me. I'm choking, I'm begging please sir please, I'm pissing myself, I'm drowning in my own blood. I'm hollering at Sam to fire goddamnit, can't you see they're all around us, but he doesn't hear me. I shove him aside and take his position behind the bow gun but when I press the trigger nothing happens, the gun won't fire. I have a terrible thirst. *Water*, I say, *please give me some water*, but Lilly May can't hear me either, my lips are moving but nothing is coming out, nothing.

Should my story end there, in the back of that mule-drawn wagon? Silenced, delirious with pain and laudanum, defeated? Nobody would like that ending, least of all me. But to make the story come out differently I'd have to overcome so much: birth and education and oppression, fear and deformity and shame, any one of which is enough to defeat a man.

It would take an extraordinary man to beat all that, with

an extraordinary family behind him. First he'd have to wean
himself off laudanum and self-pity. His mama would help him
with that, but then he'd have to make himself write his buddies and his former COs and tell them what had been done
to him. He'd write it down and tear it up, write it down and
tear it up until one day he got up enough courage to send it.
And when the answers came back he'd have to read them and
accept the help that was offered, the letters that would be written on his behalf to Fisk University and the Tuskegee Institute
and Morehouse College. And when Morehouse offered him a
full scholarship he'd have to swallow his pride and take it, not
knowing whether they wanted him or just felt sorry for him.
He'd have to leave his family behind in Greenwood and travel
the four hundred miles to Atlanta alone, with a little card in
his shirt pocket that said MUTE. He'd have to study hard to
learn all the things he should have been taught but wasn't
before he could even begin to learn the things he wanted to.
He'd have to listen to his classmates talk about ideas and politics and women, things you can't fit on a little portable slate.
Have to get used to being alone, because he made the others
uncomfortable, because he reminded them of what could still
happen to any one of them if they said the wrong thing to the
wrong white man. After he graduated, he'd have to find a pro-
fession where his handicap didn't matter and an employer who
would take a chance on him, at a black newspaper maybe, or a
black labor organization. He'd have to prove himself and fight
off despair, have to give up drinking three or four times before
he finally kicked it.

Such a man, if he managed to accomplish all that, might one day find a strong and loving woman to marry him and give him children. Might help his sister and brothers make something of themselves. Might march behind Dr. King down the streets of Atlanta with his head held high. Might even find something like happiness.

That's the ending we want, you and me both. I'll grant you it's unlikely, but it is possible. If he worked and prayed hard enough. If he was stubborn as well as lucky. If he really had a shine.

ACKNOWLEDGMENTS

If James Cañón hadn't been in my very first workshop at Columbia. If we hadn't loved each other's writing, and each other. If he hadn't read and critiqued every draft of this book, plus countless early drafts of individual chapters, during the years it took me to write it. If he hadn't encouraged and goaded me, talked me off the ledge a dozen times, made me laugh at myself, inspired me by his example: *Mudbound* would have been a very different book, and I would be writing these acknowledgments from a nice, padded cell somewhere. Thank you, love, for all that you've given me. I could not have had a wiser counselor or a truer friend.

I am also grateful to the following people, organizations and sources:

Jenn Epstein, my dear friend and designated "bad cop," who was always willing to drop everything and read, and whose tough, incisive critiques were invaluable in shaping the narrative.

Binnie Kirshenbaum and Victoria Redel, whose guidance and enthusiasm got me rolling; Maureen Howard, friend and mentor, who told me I mustn't be afraid of my book; and the many other members of the Columbia Writing Division faculty who encouraged me.

Chris Parris-Lamb, my extraordinary agent and champion, for seeing what others didn't; Sarah Burnes and the whole Gernert Company team, for embracing *Mudbound* so enthusiastically; and Kathy Pories at Algonquin, for believing in the book and being such a thoughtful and sensitive shepherd of it.

Barbara Kingsolver, for her tremendous faith in me and in *Mudbound;* her help in turning the story into a coherent, compelling narrative; her passionate support of literature of social change; and the generous and much-needed award.

The Virginia Center for the Creative Arts, the La Napoule Foundation, Fundación Valparaiso and the Stanwood Foundation for Starving Artists, for the gifts of time to write and exquisitely beautiful settings in which to do so; and the Columbia University Writing Division and the American Association of University Women, for their financial assistance.

Julie Currie, for the price of mules in 1946 and other elusive facts; Petra Spielhagen and Dan Renehan, for their assistance with Resl's broken English; and Sam Hoskins, for lessons in orthopedics.

Theodore Rosengarten's *All God's Dangers: The Life of Nate Shaw;* Stephen Ambrose's *The Wild Blue;* Byron Lane's *Byron's War: I Never Will Be Young Again;* Lou Potter's *Liberators* (and the accompanying PBS series); and Joe Wilson's *The 761st "Black Panther" Tank Battalion in World War II,* for helping me put believable flesh on the bones of my sharecroppers, bomber pilot and tankers.

Denise Benou Stires, Michael Caporusso, Pam Cunningham, Gary di Mauro, Charlotte Dixon, Mark Erwin, Marie Fisher, Doug Irving, Robert Lewis, Leslie McCall, Elizabeth Molsen, Katy Rees and Rick Rudik, for their unwavering friendship and belief in me, which sustained me more than any of them will ever know; and Kathryn Windley, for all that and then some.

And finally, my family: Anita Jordan and Michael Fuller; Jan and Jaque Jordan; my brothers, Jared and Erik; and Gay and John Stanek. No author was ever better loved or supported.

MUDBOUND

An Interview with Hillary Jordan

A Reading and Discussion Guide

AN INTERVIEW
WITH HILLARY JORDAN

What inspired you to write *Mudbound*?

My grandparents had a farm in Lake Village, Arkansas, just after World War II, and I grew up hearing stories about it. It was a primitive place, an unpainted shotgun shack with no electricity, running water, or telephone. They named it Mudbound because whenever it rained, the roads would flood and they'd be stranded for days.

Though they only lived there for a year, my mother, aunt, and grandmother spoke of the farm often, laughing and shaking their heads by turns, depending on whether the story in question was funny or horrifying. Often they were both, as Southern stories tend to be. I loved listening to them, even the ones I'd heard dozens of times before. They were a peephole into a strange and marvelous world, a world full of contradictions, of terrible beauty. The stories revealed things about my family, especially about my grandmother, who was the heroine of most of them for the simple reason that when calamity struck, my grandfather was inevitably elsewhere.

To my mother and aunt, the year they spent at Mudbound was a grand adventure; and indeed, that was how all their stories portrayed it. It was not until much later that I realized what an ordeal that year must have been for my grandmother— a city-bred woman with two young children—and that, in fact, these were stories of survival.

I began the novel (without knowing I was doing any such thing) in grad school. I had an assignment to write a few pages in the voice of a family member, and I decided to write about the farm from my grandmother's point of view. But what came out was not a merry adventure story but something darker and more complex. What came out was, "When I think of the farm, I think of mud."

So, your grandmother's voice was the one that came to you first as you started writing this?

Yes, hers was the first, and only, voice for some while. My teacher liked what I wrote and encouraged me to continue, and I tried to write a short story. My grandmother became Laura, a fictional character much more fiery and rebellious than she ever was, and the story got longer and longer. At 50 pages I realized I was writing a novel, and that's when I decided to introduce the other voices. Jamie came next, then Henry, then Florence, then Hap. Ronsel wasn't even a character until I had about 150 pages! And of course, when he entered the story, he changed its course dramatically.

But you never let Pappy speak.

Nine drafts ago, Pappy actually narrated his own funeral (the two scenes at the beginning and end of the book). And people—namely, my editor and Barbara Kingsolver, who read several drafts of *Mudbound* and gave me invaluable criticism—just hated hearing from him first, or in fact, at all. Eventually I was persuaded to silence him. The more I thought about those two passages, the more fitting it seemed that Jamie should narrate them.

Still, even without having his own section, it's clear that Pappy really struck a chord with readers. Why do you think that is?

Yes, people really do seem to hate him! Which is as it should be—he's pretty detestable. He embodies not just the ugliness of the Jim Crow era but the absolute worst possibilities in ourselves.

What was the hardest part of writing *Mudbound*?

Getting those voices right—the African American dialect especially. I had a number of well-meaning friends say things to me like, "even Faulkner didn't write about black people in the first person." But ultimately I decided I had to let my black characters address the ugliness of that time and place themselves, in their own voices.

Your book takes on racism on many levels—the most obvious forms, but also the more insidious kinds, like the sharecropping system, for example.

In researching this book, I was astounded by what I learned about the perniciousness of the sharecropping system. Owning your own mule meant the difference between share tenancy, in which you got to keep half your crop, and sharecropping, in which you got to keep only a quarter. A quarter of a cotton crop wasn't nearly enough for a family to live on, so people went further and further into debt with their landlords. And they were so incredibly vulnerable—to misfortune, to illness, to bad weather conditions. Being a sharecropper wasn't that far removed from being a slave.

The climactic scene with Ronsel is absolutely wrenching to read. I imagine it was equally wrenching to write.

Yes, it was. I'd been unsure for months what was going to happen in that scene. And when it finally came to me, all the hairs on my arms stood up, and I called my best friend James Cañón (who is also an author and was my primary reader during the seven years it took me to write *Mudbound*), and I said, "I know what's going to happen to Ronsel," and I told him. And there was this long silence and then he said, "Wow."

I dreaded writing the scene, and I put it off for a long time. When I finally made myself do it, I cried a lot. I was reading it out loud as I went—which for me is an essential part of writing dialogue—and having to speak those horrific things made them that much more real and terrible.

What books would you recommend to those who want to know even more about the period?

All God's Dangers: The Life of Nate Shaw, by Theodore Rosengarten. This is a true first-person account of a black Alabama cotton farmer who started out as a sharecropper and ended up owning his own land, with many adventures along the way. Nate was an indelible character, smart (though illiterate) and funny and wise about people. He was eighty years old when he told his life story to Theodore Rosengarten, a journalist from New York. And what a fascinating life it was.

James Cobb's *The Most Southern Place on Earth.*

Pete Daniel's excellent books *Breaking the Land* and *Deep'n as It Come: The 1927 Mississippi River Flood* and *Standing at the Crossroads: Southern Life in the Twentieth Century.*

A PBS series of documentaries about black history from *The American Experience.*

Clifton L. Taulbert's *When We Were Colored.*

And of course, the works of James Baldwin, William Faulkner, Flannery O'Connor, Eudora Welty, and Richard Wright, among others.

Have you begun working on another novel?

Yes, and it's absolutely nothing like *Mudbound*! After seven years of working on it, I was extremely ready to leave the Deep South, the past, and the first person. My second novel, *Red,* is set in a dystopian America roughly thirty years in the future. It begins in Crawford, Texas, and ends—well, who knows?

A READING AND DISCUSSION GUIDE

1. The setting of the Mississippi Delta is intrinsic to *Mudbound*. Discuss the ways in which the land functions as a character in the novel and how each of the other characters relates to it.

2. *Mudbound* is a chorus, told in six different voices. How do the changes in perspective affect your understanding of the story? Are all six voices equally sympathetic? Reliable? Pappy is the only main character who has no narrative voice. Why do you think the author chose not to let him speak?

3. Who gets to speak and who is silent or silenced is a central theme, the silencing of Ronsel being the most literal and brutal example. Discuss the ways in which this theme plays out for the other characters. For instance, how does Laura's silence about her unhappiness on the farm affect her and her marriage? What are the consequences of Jamie's inability to speak to his family about the horrors he experienced in the war? How does speaking or not speaking confer power or take it away?

4. The story is narrated by two farmers, two wives and mothers, and two soldiers. Compare and contrast the ways in which these parallel characters, black and white, view and experience the world.

5. What is the significance of the title? In what ways are each of the characters bound—by the land, by circumstance, by tradition, by the law, by their own limitations? How much of this binding is inescapable and how much is self-imposed? Which characters are most successful in freeing themselves from what binds them?

6. All the characters are products of their time and place, and instances of racism in the book run from Pappy's outright bigotry to Laura's more subtle prejudice. Would Laura have thought of herself as racist, and if not, why not? How do the racial views of Laura, Jamie, Henry, and Pappy affect your sympathy for them?

7. The novel deals with many thorny issues: racism, sexual politics, infidelity, war. The characters weigh in on these issues, but what about the author? Does she have a discernable perspective, and if so, how does she convey it?

8. We know very early in the book that something terrible is going to befall Ronsel. How does this sense of inevitability affect the story? Jamie makes Ronsel responsible for his own

fate, saying, "Maybe that's cowardly of me, making Ronsel's the trigger finger." Is it just cowardice, or is there some truth to what Jamie says? Where would you place the turning point for Ronsel? Who else is complicit in what happens to him, and why?

9. In reflecting on some of the more difficult moral choices made by the characters—Laura's decision to sleep with Jamie, Ronsel's decision to abandon Resl and return to America, Jamie's choice during the lynching scene, Florence's and Jamie's separate decisions to murder Pappy—what would you have done in those same situations? Is it even possible to know? Are there some moral positions that are absolute, or should we take into account things like time and place when making judgments?

10. Why do you think the author chose to have Ronsel address you, the reader, directly at the end of the book? Do you believe he overcomes the formidable obstacles facing him and finds "something like happiness"? If so, why doesn't the author just say so explicitly? Would a less ambiguous ending have been more or less satisfying?

Hillary Jordan grew up in Texas and Oklahoma. She received her BA in English and political science from Wellesley College and spent fifteen years working as an advertising copywriter before starting to write fiction. She got her MFA in creative writing from Columbia University. Her first novel, *Mudbound,* won the 2006 *Bellwether Prize for Fiction*, awarded biennially to a debut novel that addresses issues of social justice, and was the New Atlantic Independent Booksellers Association Fiction Book of the Year for 2008. Jordan's short fiction has appeared in numerous literary journals, including *StoryQuarterly* and the *Carolina Quarterly*. She lives in Tivoli, New York.

Other Algonquin Readers Round Table Novels

Water for Elephants, a novel by Sara Gruen

As a young man, Jacob Jankowski is tossed by fate onto a rickety train, home to the Benzini Brothers Most Spectacular Show on Earth. Amid a world of freaks, grifters, and misfits, Jacob becomes involved with Marlena, the beautiful young equestrian star; her husband, a charismatic but twisted animal trainer; and Rosie, an untrainable elephant who is the great gray hope for this third-rate show. Now in his nineties, Jacob at long last reveals the story of their unlikely yet powerful bonds, ones that nearly shatter them all.

"[An] arresting new novel . . . With a showman's expert timing, [Gruen] saves a terrific revelation for the final pages, transforming a glimpse of Americana into an enchanting escapist fairy tale." *—The New York Times Book Review*

"Gritty, sensual and charged with dark secrets involving love, murder and a majestic, mute heroine." *—Parade*

AN ALGONQUIN READERS ROUND TABLE EDITION WITH READING GROUP GUIDE
AND OTHER SPECIAL FEATURES • FICTION • ISBN-13: 978-1-56512-560-5

An Arsonist's Guide to Writers' Homes in New England,
a novel by Brock Clarke

The past catches up to Sam Pulsifer, the hapless hero of this incendiary novel, when after spending ten years in prison for accidentally burning down Emily Dickinson's house, the homes of other famous New England writers go up in smoke. To prove his innocence, he sets out to uncover the identity of this literary-minded arsonist.

"Funny, profound . . . A seductive book with a payoff on every page." *—People*

"Wildly, unpredicatably funny . . . As cheerfully oddball as its title."
—The New York Times

AN ALGONQUIN READERS ROUND TABLE EDITION WITH READING GROUP GUIDE
AND OTHER SPECIAL FEATURES • FICTION • ISBN-13: 978-1-56512-614-5

Saving the World, a novel by Julia Alvarez

While Alma Huebner is researching a new novel, she discovers the true story of Isabel Sendales y Gómez, who embarked on a courageous sea voyage to rescue the New World from smallpox. The author of *How the García Girls Lost Their Accents* and *In the Time of the Butterflies,* Alvarez captures the worlds of two women living two centuries apart but with surprisingly parallel fates.

"Fresh and unusual, and thought-provokingly sensitive." *—The Boston Globe*

"Engrossing, expertly paced." *—People*

AN ALGONQUIN READERS ROUND TABLE EDITION WITH READING GROUP GUIDE
AND OTHER SPECIAL FEATURES • FICTION • ISBN-13: 978-1-56512-558-2

Breakfast with Buddha, a novel by Roland Merullo

When his sister tricks him into taking her guru, a crimson-robed monk, on a trip to their childhood home, Otto Ringling, a confirmed skeptic, is not amused. Six days on the road with an enigmatic holy man who answers every question with a riddle is not what he'd planned. But along the way, Otto is given the remarkable opportunity to see his world—and more important, his life—through someone else's eyes.

"Enlightenment meets *On the Road* in this witty, insightful novel."
—*The Boston Sunday Globe*

"A laugh-out-loud novel that's both comical and wise . . . balancing irreverence with insight." —*The Louisville Courier-Journal*

AN ALGONQUIN READERS ROUND TABLE EDITION WITH READING GROUP GUIDE AND OTHER SPECIAL FEATURES • FICTION • ISBN 13: 978-1-56512-616-9

The Ghost at the Table, a novel by Suzanne Berne

When Frances arranges to host Thanksgiving at her idyllic New England farmhouse, she envisions a happy family reunion, one that will include her sister, Cynthia. But tension mounts between them as each struggles with a different version of the mysterious circumstances surrounding their mother's death twenty-five years earlier.

"Wholly engaging, the perfect spark for launching a rich conversation around your own table." —*The Washington Post Book World*

"A crash course in sibling rivalry." —*O: The Oprah Magazine*

AN ALGONQUIN READERS ROUND TABLE EDITION WITH READING GROUP GUIDE AND OTHER SPECIAL FEATURES • FICTION • ISBN-13: 978-1-56512-579-7

Coal Black Horse, a novel by Robert Olmstead

When Robey Childs's mother has a premonition about her husband, who is away fighting in the Civil War, she sends her only son to find him and bring him home. At fourteen, Robey thinks he's off on a great adventure. But it takes the gift of a powerful and noble coal black horse to show him how to undertake the most important journey of his life.

"A remarkable creation." —*Chicago Tribune*

"Exciting . . . A grueling adventure." —*The New York Times Book Review*

AN ALGONQUIN READERS ROUND TABLE EDITION WITH READING GROUP GUIDE AND OTHER SPECIAL FEATURES • FICTION • ISBN-13: 978-1-56512-601-5